Mango,
Mambo,
and Murder

Mango, Mambo, and Murder

A CARIBBEAN KITCHEN MYSTERY

Raquel V. Reyes

CROOKED LANE

NEW YORK

PUBLISHER'S NOTE: The recipes contained in this book are to be followed exactly as written. The publisher is not responsible for your specific health or allergy needs that may require medical supervision. The publisher is not responsible for any adverse reaction to the recipes contained in this book.

Published in the United States by Crooked Lane Books, an imprint of The Quick Brown Fox & Company LLC.

Crooked Lane Books and its logo are trademarks of The Quick Brown Fox & Company LLC.

Library of Congress Catalog-in-Publication data available upon request.

ISBN (hardcover): 978-1-64385-784-8
ISBN (trade paperback): 978-1-63910-100-9
ISBN (ePub): 978-1-64385-785-5

Cover illustration by Jo Burleson

Printed in the United States.

www.crookedlanebooks.com

Crooked Lane Books
34 West 27th St., 10th Floor
New York, NY 10001

First Edition: October 2021
Trade Paperback Edition: September 2022

10 9 8 7 6 5 4 3 2 1

For Elena, who taught me how
to cook frijoles negros.

Chapter One

"¡Basta, Alma! I told you I'm not doing the show." I accentuated each word with the knife I held in my hand before I stabbed the packing tape and sliced open box number five of forty-eight.

"You are perfect for it. And come on, Miriam, what else are you doing?"

I narrowed my eyes and glared at my best friend, Alma. "¿Qué es esto?" I waved my hand like a hostess showing someone to their table. "Is this house going to unpack itself?"

"Porfa, this is not going to take all week. The cooking spot is next Friday. Today is Tuesday. You have a week and a half. It's a short cooking demo on a morning show." Alma shook her pinched hand like a stereotypical Italian grandmother. Except, of course, she wasn't Italian, and neither was I. We're Cuban American. Both cultures talked with their hands. Or, in my case, with whatever was in my hands at the moment.

I crumpled the *New York Post* page that wrapped a chipped green dinner plate. Before placing it on the stack that was building in the cupboard of my new Florida home, I shook the plate like a tambourine, "But I don't cook!"

"You do cook. Your cooking is excellent." Alma, dressed in a sleeveless white dress, stepped away from the mound of newsprint

1

about to tumble off the quartz countertop. This was the most expensive kitchen I'd ever had the luck to possess. The biggest too.

"I am not a celebrity chef. I am an academic. Find me a job at a university."

"Do you want to work-work? Or work-parent? I thought you said you were taking a little time off to be a full-time mom."

"Roberto wants me to stay home for a year. At least until Manny is ready for school."

"That makes the UnMundo morning show super for you. You need to do it. La Tacita is perfect for you. One morning a week, and you get a paycheck." Alma raised her shoulders to her ears and flicked her palms out in a "voilà."

"But I'm not a chef. I'm a food anthropologist." I felt heat building in my chest.

"Casi igual." Alma dismissed my protest and checked her phone, which had just beeped a notification. "The Women's Club luncheon is in forty-five minutes. Hurry up and get ready, already."

"I told you, I. Don't. Want. To. Go. I know it's important for you and your real estate business, but come on, Alma. ¿Qué carajo am I going to do while you're talking bayfront views and terrazzo floors with ladies that lunch?"

"Get dressed. Your mother-in-law will be here any moment to babysit."

"You conspired with my mother-in-law? That's a cardinal sin!"

"Amiga, you gave me no choice. This town works on connections. If you want Manny to get into the best school, then you need to make nice with the women that run this town. Lo siento, but that's the way it is."

"Manny is going to go to St. Brigid's." I chucked the empty box in the corner with the others. A cardboard fort was in my son's near future.

"All the more reason to go to this lunch. The president of The Patricians will be there. It's not like it was when we were little and going to St. Joe's. Any tithing family was guaranteed spots for their children. Now, it's who you know and how much money you give to the booster club." Alma looked at me. We'd been friends since kindergarten. She always made fun of my faces. "If a fly crosses your face, it will freeze like that. Wrinkled and puckered is not a good look on you."

I threw a wad of used packing tape in Alma's direction. She swatted it away like Serena Williams returning a volley. The ding-dong-dwong of the doorbell had barely finished when my mother-in-law appeared in my unfurnished living room. My mouth was faster than my good sense. "Did I leave the door unlocked?" My tone didn't help either.

"Well, hello to you too." Marjory Smith, my husband's mother, posed at the edge of the unpacking chaos like an egret about to peck a lizard from a shrub, and that lizard was me. A petite woman with a frosted blonde bob, she wore bright red pedal pushers, a lightweight pink sweater set, and black flats with a metal monogram on the toe. From my little time in Coral Shores, a 1950s time-warped village within the city of Miami, it appeared to be the standard-issue uniform of women over the age of fifty-five. The shoes came in all colors, but the brand was always the same.

I kicked myself for having stepped into it again and hurried to give my mother-in-law a hug. "I'm sorry for being rude. Hello and welcome." The hug was about as warm as an icicle on a Vermont cabin in February. Marjory barely tolerated me. Giving her a grandchild was my one and only credit. By contrast, the embrace Marjory gave to Alma was like butter on bread fresh from the oven.

"So, good to see you again, Mrs. Smith," Alma cooed.

"Call me, Marjory, darling. Over the years, you've earned enough commission off me and my friends to put us on a first-name basis."

They both laughed hollowly.

"Yes." Alma squeezed Marjory's upper arm. "Thank you for the Fleming referral. Their house is gorgeous, and I may already have a buyer for it."

3

"Oh, that's good news, dear." Marjory jangled a set of keys hooked in her hand, making a show of them before slipping them into her pocket. "Miriam, please tell me you're not wearing that to the country club."

I stuttered like a beater car cranking on an empty tank of gas. "I–I –I . . ."

"She was headed to her bedroom just as you walked in." Alma put her arm around me like I was a lost child. "You were asking me for my opinion, right? The bold print dress or the light blue suit. What do you think, Marjory?"

"Understated is always in good taste."

"Sage advice. I agree. The suit it is. Come along, Miriam, we need to be there in thirty minutes." Alma pushed me down the unlit hall.

"How did she get a key to my house?"

"I don't know." Alma shrugged and avoided my suspicious stare. "Hurry up." She went to the closet and pulled out my one summer-weight suit. It had a short jacket that fell just below my waist. I'd worn it to defend my dissertation because it made me look a little like Alexandria Ocasio-Cortez. I had needed all the confidence I could beg, borrow, or steal. One of the professors on my committee was a not-so-closeted misogynist that lumped all Spanish speakers into one heritage, Mexican.

"You gave her a set?" I stripped out of my shorts and NYU T-shirt. "Please tell me you didn't give her a key to my house!"

"I didn't give her a key, but that's not to say that she didn't get a set at the closing."

"Caridad, por favor, save me from that bruja."

"Witch or bitch, she did buy you a house."

"She bought her son and grandson a house. A bribe to get Robert down here. I was happy in New York. I was in line for a professorship." I heard the whining in my voice. "I didn't want to move three blocks away from my mother-in-law." I fake-sobbed, and Alma ignored me completely. She didn't give me even half an ounce of sympathy.

"Ponte las pilas. We should have been there already." Alma twisted the rod on the temporary window blinds. "Your backyard demands a pool. I have a guy. Best pool contractor in all of Dade County."

I sat on the side of our full-size bed and buckled the straps on my heels. "We don't have that kind of money."

"You don't have it now, but you will soon. My guy has an eight-month waitlist, and permits take forever. Trust me, Miriam, you need to get on it."

"Later. Maybe when Manuelito is older. Besides, swimming pools are dangerous with little kids in the house.'

"Kids? No me digas— You're pregnant?" Alma looked away from the window and gaped at me.

"No." I stood and went to the bathroom to apply eyeliner and lipstick. "But Robert's been dropping hints about Manuelito needing a little sister."

"I'll go ahead and make the appointment with my pool guy."

"No. For reals, we can't afford it."

"Let Marjory give you the pool as a baby shower present."

"Like I want to owe her more. No! The down payment and cosigning are bastante."

"Fine. But you know, Roberto is going to be making the big bucks."

"I can't believe he took the job. It is so opposite of everything— whatever. I can't think about it. We're here. We have a roof over our heads. It is all going to work out. Right?!"

"Yes." Alma said it like, "Duh!"

"How do I look? Can I fool these old ladies into thinking I'm upper crust and not a Cubanita from blue-collar Hialeah?"

"Dr. Miriam Quiñones-Smith, you have nothing to be insecure about."

Chapter Two

On the carpeted dais of the country club's Flamingo room stood a skeletal septuagenarian in a mauve skirt suit. With her bony legs and knock knees, she certainly favored the iconic Florida bird. She warbled an off-key aria that made me think of the waterfowl shaking a shrimp down its long neck. Alma turned to me and whispered, "I told you these lunches were entertaining." Alma was used to the tawny enclave of Coral Shores. It was her chosen hurting grounds. I was too stunned to enjoy the farce. When the high D crescendo finally came, my eyes watered. The rose and carnation centerpiece wasn't stirring up an allergy; my ears were in pain. The banquet room burst into applause. I dabbed the tears from my eyes and joined the ovation.

"Gracias a Dios, that's over," I said from behind a plastered grin. Alma laughed, but not loud enough to draw attention to our mockery. "I can't believe you dragged me to this circus. You know I can't stand clowns!"

"Shh. They'll hear you." Alma sat and arranged her napkin in her lap. A small army of bow-tied servers swooped toward us with plates. "Oh, look, lunch is served. I can't wait for you to try this chicken salad, Miriam. It's the club's specialty."

As if I hadn't guessed from her sarcastic tone, the salad was a travesty. It had more mayonnaise than meat. And the celery was mushy when it should have been crunchy-crisp. My taste buds rioted after the first bite, and I set my fork down. I buttered a piece of stale, hard bread and looked around the table. The lady to my right, the only other attendee under sixty besides Alma and me, was not eating her lunch either.

"Not hungry?" I asked.

"No." She pushed the salad away from her.

"Hello, I'm Miriam." I offered her a handshake.

"Nice to meet you." She clamped my hand weakly, then let go. "Excuse me." The woman pinched her temples.

"Headache?"

She nodded and pointed to the back of the room. "Ladies' room. Be right back."

I watched her walk away, a little unsteady on her feet. She stopped to talk to a tanned woman with short black hair, wearing tinted eyeglasses. The lady gave her something, an aspirin, I hoped.

"Miriam, meet Olive Morgan. She's a member of St. Brigid's Patricians," Alma said.

I smiled at the older woman next to Alma. She had light gray hair, and her pink lipstick was badly applied.

"Excuse me, I need to visit the ladies' room," Alma said as she got up to leave the table.

"Alma tells me you have a little boy?" The woman's head bobbed with a touch of palsy.

"Yes, he's four," I said.

"They are little rascals at that age. My daughter, Daisy, teaches the four-to-six group on Sundays. I haven't seen you at church yet." A blob of chicken salad launched from her fork. The poor woman shook like she was over ninety. Maybe she was. Only a ninety-year-old would use the word "rascals." I immediately pictured Manny in suspenders and a newsboy cap.

"No, we haven't made it yet. I'm still unpacking from the move." Thinking about the warning Alma had given me, I added. "But we will soon. I promise."

7

"Goody-good-good. I'll tell my Daisy to be expecting you," Olive said. Her pink lips were now white with mayonnaise.

The young lady with the headache returned, with Alma only a few steps behind her.

"Did you find an aspirin?" I asked.

"Yes, thank you," she said with a sniffle. She used her napkin to daintily blow her nose before pouring a black packet of powder into her water glass. The powder turned the water a faint shade of pink before it dissolved completely. She drank the mixture in its entirety.

Alma went clockwise and introduced me to the other ladies at the table. When she got around to the lady with the headache, it dawned on me she hadn't told me her name.

"Are you okay? Is your headache worse?" I asked, preempting Alma's introduction. The woman looked sweaty and bluish. Before I could grab her, she collapsed face-first into her lunch. The splat her forehead made when it landed in the mound of chicken salad was almost as loud as the club members' gasps.

"Call nine-one-one," the lady with a skunk stripe of white roots at the adjunct table yelled, "Sunny's fainted!"

"I'm sure she's on another one of her crazy diets. Sit her up, and I'll force a Coca-Cola down her," said a stylishly dressed woman from the table in the farthest corner of the room. I watched as she walked with confidence and grace toward our table. She didn't fit the mold of the Women's Club membership I'd seen thus far. Her face was youthful, but her hair was unabashedly steel gray. She had it coiffed in an asymmetrical swing bob. She wore black wide-legged pants with a boho knit sweater over a white V-neck shirt. It was effortless, sophisticated-casual, and reeked of wealth. The four bands of multicarat eternity rings on her finger also pegged her for one of the founding village families.

I asked Alma who the lady was, and she told me. "Stormy Weatherman, Sunny Weatherman's mother."

"Sunny is the lady in the chicken salad?"

8

"One and the same," Alma replied and then switched to Spanish to tell me the relevant gossip of the tableau.

After the initial gasp of horror at the faux pas of planting one's face into one's lunch, the ladies who lunched did not seem too troubled by the event. And what Alma told me in the few seconds before Stormy reached her daughter's side explained why. Sunny was addicted to diets and exercise fads. She was often seen running around Coral Shores in the midday sun with her concaved midriff showing. Her dietary and athletic regiment also caused her to faint—a lot.

Fire Rescue marched through the heavy twelve-foot oak doors, carrying their medical equipment, just as Stormy made it to Sunny. Because of the conjunction of Florida, golf, and middle-aged men that drank more beer than water, Fire Rescue always had a truck parked in the country club parking lot in case of heatstroke and lightning strike. Or so Alma told me.

"Don't worry. I'm sure she'll rouse in a moment," Stormy called out to the rescue team. She patted her daughter's back, and then she shook her by the shoulders. Her shaking became more animated, and Sunny's head lolled from side to side in the chicken salad, making a squishing sound like bare feet in mud. "Did you bring the defibrillator?" she asked the blue and red uniformed team. "It looks like she might have gone and done herself in this time." Stormy spoke in a calm and matter-of-fact tone as she moved away from the body to make room for the EMTs.

Alma, our tablemates, and I had already moved several feet from the scene of the trauma. Stormy's demeanor alarmed me. If it were my child lying lifeless, I would be in hysterics. I whispered as much to Alma, in Spanish. I made the sign of the cross to keep Manuelito safe.

"Well, you have to understand Stormy and Sunny's history," Alma said. "The girl has been nothing but trouble and angst since age thirteen. She's been in and out of rehab, been to every ashram in India, California, and New York. Miriam, esa niña es una vergüenza."

9

I sucked my lower lip and made an "uh" sound in recognition of the sad situation. It was a shame when a family member had gone astray despite the family's best help and love.

The whole room watched as Sunny's limp body was laid on the sled-shaped carrying board the team had placed on the banquet hall's paisley carpet. Nobody bothered to wipe the chicken salad from her face. She looked like a spa patron with a lumpy oatmeal masque. Suddenly, the action around the passed-out woman shifted. It changed from the basic first response of taking a pulse to the "this is serious" opening of plastic-encased medical equipment. One of the team members called "Clear." The round paddles of the defibrillator were placed on Sunny's still chest. The machine wound up and popped its charge. Nothing. The crew hit her with another bolt of electricity. It must have gotten the expected results because the rescuers lifted the board she was strapped onto and carried her to a waiting stretcher in the country club's main hallway.

The Women's Club, or at least those of us that didn't need walkers, followed the stretcher. We watched as the ambulance pulled out of the parking lot with its sirens wailing. Stormy waited for the valet with the same measured pace and unruffled manner I'd seen in her earlier. It made my heart ache that a mother had seen her child put into an ambulance so often that it no longer caused a panic. She got in her silver Cadillac coupe and drove after the emergency vehicle. Alma locked arms with me. So as not to step on the heels of the crowd of shuffling matrons, we did the bridal walk. Step. Pause. Step. Pause. "No te preocupes. I am sure she will be fine," Alma reassured me, but I wasn't so sure.

By the time we were back in the meeting room, the chairs had been straightened, and Sunny's mangled salad had been removed. The waiters busied themselves with clearing the main course. Coffee and dessert were quickly served, and the gavel summoned the group to order. I played at eating my pastry but had lost all appetite for anything other than a sip of water. The business part of the club meeting went by with slurps of coffee and scrapes of forks on china. I pushed my cheesecake around the plate while the president, a waspy lady in a brown sheath dress with a knotted string of pearls, gave the rallying cry for the club's annual fundraiser. The theme for the year was the Caribbean. The cause was to feed the children stricken by the hurricanes that had hit the islands of Puerto Rico, St. Maarten, and Dominica.

Alma elbowed me and whispered, "You should be on the steering committee for the event. You'd add some sabor y sazón to it."

I shook my head, a controlled but adamant, "No way. ¡Estás loca!"

"I'm going to nominate you. You're perfect for the job, with your degree in Caribbean food," Alma said. She raised her hand to gain the floor. I quickly spilled my glass of water into her dessert plate, causing her to forget her insane plan in lieu of saving her silk suit.

In the car, Alma asked, "What were you thinking? You nearly ruined my best suit."

"What was *I* thinking? What were *you* thinking? I've been here less than two weeks, everything is still in boxes, I have to find Manny a preschool, and I don't know anyone other than you and my in-laws. Plus, those ladies are sooooo—"

"Lost in a time warp? I know it's a little 1950s, but that is exactly why they need new blood like you and me," Alma interjected. Her enthusiasm for her adopted town was admirable. She and I were Cuban American and raised ten miles away in the Latino stronghold of Hialeah, Florida. Coral Shores might be in the same Miami-Dade County, but it was culturally a world away—no, a *galaxy* away.

"No, what I was going to say was "white"!"

"Miriam Quiñones Smith, you married a *white* man from this very town."

"I know. I know. But we were in New York and in college, and the city makes everyone more appealing."

Pulling into the driveway of my new home, she came to an abrupt stop. With great concern, Alma looked me in the eye. "Are you and Roberto having problems?"

"No, I don't think so, not really. It's just been stressful. He's busy with work. When he does have free time, he goes golfing with some old friend I've never heard of and—well, I never knew he even played golf! And then my suegra is driving me crazy. She insists on calling Manny by his middle name, Douglas. I hate that name! I only agreed to use his grandfather's name as an appeasement to Robert. And I want a job, but Robert keeps telling me to hold off on my search until next fall, when Manny is in kindergarten. That's a long way away." I began to sob.

"Cógelo suave. You just got here. Give yourself a break. Get settled in." Alma unbuckled her seat belt and reached across the armrest to hug me.

A knock on the passenger-side window startled us into peeping like chickens caught by a swooping hawk. I mouthed to Alma, "See what I mean?"

Alma lowered the window with the push of a button. The once silent yakking of the petite ash-blonde, blue-eyed monster, a.k.a. my mother-in-law, a.k.a. Marjory Smith, became audible.

"Douglas is down for his nap. Thank goodness. I love the dear, but boy, does he have a set of lungs. Miriam, you have to work on teaching him to use his inside voice. How was the lunch? What did I miss?" She bombarded us with queries. I was afraid she was going to climb into the car via the window. She pulled on the door handle several times. Each time it fell with a soft clang. Alma unlocked it after the third attempt. I hurriedly got out of the car, thanking Alma for the outing. I excused myself with a made-up need for the bathroom. Marjory circled to Alma's window. As I slipped through the front door, I looked back over my shoulder and saw Alma's selling skills take control of the interrogation. She had my mother-in-law silenced as she reported the highlights of the luncheon. Alma was smiling and gesturing and giggling with the light air of a spokesmodel.

When I emerged from straightening the smudges of eyeliner my sobbing had caused, my mother-in-law was gathering her things to leave. I was thankful I wouldn't have to entertain her for the afternoon. I knew Manny was the reason for her quick departure. She'd insisted on babysitting so I could go to the Women's Club despite the fact that she really wasn't a toddler lover. Marjory liked children when they were well behaved, which four-year-olds rarely were. But before she escaped, she gave me a tirade about Stormy's lack of control over Sunny. Her tone was disapproving and condemning of Stormy. Obviously, the women had a history. I was slightly curious, but not enough so to ask my mother-in-law to stay.

Chapter Three

Gracias a Dios, Manny was still a good napper. After I changed into yoga pants and a T-shirt, I took advantage of his two-hour recharge to unpack my office. The first box I opened had our diplomas—two for me and two for Robert. I removed the Bubble Wrap on my University of Chicago undergraduate degree. The gothic calligraphy was hard to decipher, but I knew it by heart. It read "Miriam Quiñones, Bachelor of Arts, Magna Cum Laude."

"Miriam, you went a little crazy with the packaging," I said to myself. Talking to yourself was a sign of intelligence. At least that's what internet memes assured me. I'd gone overboard with the cushioning. Three layers. "You wrap the plates in newspaper, but these pieces of paper you wrap in a football field of plastic. Pri-or-ities," I chastised myself.

I put Robert's undergraduate diploma from the University of Miami against the wall, along with our his and hers master's degrees from NYU. That's where Robert and I had met. It was at an interdepartmental workshop. He was a dashing, slightly older (by six years) adjunct professor, and I was a teacher's assistant. Cliché? Perhaps, but we had so much in common. We were both from South Florida, and we both dreamed of a life of academic study.

I planned to write a book, based on my dissertation, about the Caribbean kitchen and its importance in retaining cultural identity

14

in times of diaspora. With his degrees in environmental engineering, Robert was going to lead a research team and solve the global greenhouse gas problem. We would publish and rise in the ranks to become tenured professors. We'd be sought-after guest lecturers. It was a match made in heaven in the life-goals area and a little mango con arroz in the cultural heritage area, but we were going to make it work.

We got married and moved into a tiny apartment. The streets smelled of rice, beans, and platanos. Our mostly Puerto Rican and Dominican neighborhood was great. At first, Robert was a strictly hamburgers and pizza guy, but I quickly converted him into a foodie. He'd call me from the train platform and ask what was for dinner. *"Babe, you know your dinners are the thing that gets me through the Brooklyn commute."* Then he'd do a bad Princess Leia imitation: *"Help me, Obi-Wan Kenobi. You're my only hope."* If we got tired of comida criolla, then we'd walk a few blocks to Chinatown or Little Italy.

Our lives were perfect, I thought as I tucked a stray hair behind my ear.

I rolled the yards of plastic into a baton and wielded it like a light saber. I'd find a way to recycle it.

We were so in love.

We'd thought love and good cooking could conquer all of life's inconveniences and unpleasantness. The walk to the F was nothing when we had love. The crazies on the train were tolerable when Carlota had invited us to dine on her pastelón.

Manny was born a year later. We'd spend whole evenings staring into our newborn baby's sweet face. But the babymoon ended for Robert about the time Manny began to walk. He complained about all the things a baby needs.

"Why do we need a bouncy chair and a playpen?"

"Eighty-eight dollars for a cloth diaper service? Why can't you wash them yourself?"

Our apartment was too cramped. His adjunct gig was too low paying. Robert's list of grievances grew and grew. He put out feelers and applied for full professor positions at small colleges. I didn't want to move to the middle of Iowa or Montana. I wanted to stay in the city with its vibrant ethnic communities that fed my work and passions. My PhD wasn't complete. I put my foot down. We weren't going to move until after I'd finished my degree.

Ay Dios, do I remember that fight! Mr. Ortiz almost poked a hole through the floor, banging on his ceiling with his broom.

About a year and a half later, Robert got an offer from Florida International University in South Miami. That's when I got on board. Miami would be an excellent place to continue working on my book. It was my hometown, the place where I was born. It'd be exciting to go back and see how the city had changed over the decade I'd been away. I told myself I could explore the Kreyòl community of Little Haiti, maybe document the dwindling Puerto Rican community of Wynwood and, of course, the Cuban stronghold of Calle Ocho.

Miriam, keep your promise to yourself.

I ripped open another box. The top layer had two matching blue picture frames. I placed them carefully on a high shelf. The rest of the box held textbooks and reference books. After I'd filled the lowest level of the bookshelf-lined wall, I let my eyes wander to all the space yet to be filled.

This office was bigger than our old apartment's bedroom, bathroom, and kitchen combined.

My emotions were running to the sad and not the happy.

"All this space for Manny to grow should make me happy. What's wrong with you, mujer? Ungrateful," I said aloud.

I reached for the matching blue picture frames on the top shelf. One was of my family and the other of Robert's.

"Here I am back in Miami with a grandchild for you to spoil, and you aren't even here," I yelled at the photograph. "Mami y Papi, why did you move to Punta Cana? Why?"

I, of course, knew the answer, but it didn't make me feel any better. They'd been offered an amazing opportunity to manage a four-apartment vacation rental in the Dominican Republic. It wasn't the dream of returning to Cuba after the fall of Fidel, but it was pretty close to it.

"Miriam, get a hold of yourself!" I dabbed a tear from my eye.

I never thought I'd be alone ten miles from my childhood house. In my left hand, I held a photo that made me mournful. And in my right hand, I had a photo that made me angry, Robert's family. I'd liked them well enough when they were a thousand miles away, but now that they were literally within jogging distance, I hated them. It was Robert's father's fault our academic dreams were squashed. His business connections had gotten Robert a job with the Department of Environmental Resources and Management.

"I know, I know. But it pays triple what the university offered. How can we say no? Come on, babe. We'll have a house with a yard for Manny."

This house was too big. I stomped off to the kitchen to do what I did best— find food that healed hurts.

I sat at the kitchen bar with my plate of guava paste and queso de campo and looked at my empty living room. I had to buy furniture. A lot of furniture. But what style? Did I have a style?

Our move had been sudden, and I hadn't been physically in on the housing selection. The housing market in Coral Shores was hot. Robert begged me to move to his hometown, a village within greater Miami, instead of the more metropolitan heart of Miami. He'd convinced me that the schools were better and that his parents would help with Manny when I found work. His parents had sweetened the deal by loaning us fifty thousand for a down payment if we moved to the village. I'd agreed with the condition that we used my friend Alma to find the house. Alma had done her best to include me in the house search. She'd sent me tons of pictures and e-mails with listings. The houses all looked so grand. In the end, it came down to price. We could not afford a waterfront property or even one with a pool. Four hundred ninety thousand had bought us a three-bedroom, two-bath house with a big backyard.

I looked out the double French doors. *Stop feeling sorry for yourself.* I daydreamed about what that yard could look like in a few years. I'd build an outdoor kitchen for entertaining, put in a swing set for Manny, and when he got a little older, a treehouse in the northwest corner of the green pasture. My mood lifted. It might turn out okay. My parents could visit for a few weeks in the summers, and maybe I could reconnect with some of my high school friends if they still lived nearby.

The doorbell sounded.

Ay, Dios—*please don't let it be Marjory.* I prayed it wasn't my mother-in-law returning with some new, well-meaning advice for me or to take me shopping for rich-people furniture like brown leather and chintz. *Okay, well, at least I know what I don't want.*

Peering through the narrow rectangular window, I saw a police officer dressed in shorts and wearing a bike helmet.

"Hello, may I help you?" I asked, standing in the open doorway.

"Mrs. Miriam Smith?"

"Yes, that's me. Miriam Quiñones-Smith. How can I help you?"

The officer looked at me with a goofy grin.

"Are you married to Bobby Smith?"

"Yes."

I was not sure where this was leading, but I hoped it wasn't bad news. Robert had developed all kinds of new and unknown-to-me habits since returning to his hometown. The golfing was time-consuming, but his new lead foot was dangerous. Driving in South Florida was fatal.

"Bobby's my cousin. You're just as pretty as he said you were. Gorgeous, really. You look just like Sofia Vergara but with jet-black hair." His goofy grin grew wider.

I noticed the officer's name embroidered on his tan polo-style shirt: Gordon Smith. I didn't think he'd been sent to give me bad news the way he was fawning like a lovestruck teen. Was he part of Marjory's army? Had he been given orders to instruct me on the proper way to lead my life in the village?

18

"Well, Cousin Gordon, why don't you come in? My little boy is napping, and I need to listen for him. He should be getting up any moment now." I waved him in.

"Dougie?" he asked.

I cringed. Would no one in this family use my son's first name? I acted like he was mistaken about the name. "You mean Manny. Manuel, actually. Douglas is his middle name. Robert and I never use it." Changing the subject, I asked, "Do you need to secure your bike?"

"Oh no. Coral Shores is a very safe neighborhood."

"Then this a social call?"

Officer Gordon Smith's face changed. He straightened his shoulders and took out a notepad.

"I'm afraid I have some bad news. Sunny Weatherman died."

It took me a second to recognize the name. It was the lady from the Women's Club luncheon.

"Oh my goodness. How? She couldn't have been more than thirty. What was it?" I was stunned. Everyone at the luncheon had acted so blasé about her loss of consciousness that I hadn't been overly worried about it. We had been told the medical team had it under control.

"I can't say. This is just procedure. We just need to rule out any extenuating circumstances."

"Foul play?"

He ignored my question and proceeded to ask his own. "You were seated next to Miss Weatherman? Did she take any pills? What did she eat?"

I thought back to a few hours ago. I'd been introduced to everyone at the table, but mostly I'd chatted with Alma. Sunny had been polite but quiet. "I don't think she ate anything."

"Typical," he said to himself and jotted down a note in his book.

"Let's see. We were served iced tea and then tomato soup with croutons. I don't think she had any of the soup because the server asked if something was wrong with it when she cleared the plates.

Then we were served the main course, chicken salad on a bed of lettuce. She fainted soon after that, and I don't think she had any of it. I'd only had a few bites myself."

"Do you remember her drinking anything?

"Hmm. She asked for a glass of water with no ice. She mixed something into it. I thought it was Crystal Light or one of those zero-calorie flavor enhancers."

"Drops or powder?"

"I'm pretty sure it was powder. I don't remember exactly. I was talking to my friend when I noticed her stirring it into her water."

"Alma Diaz?"

"Yes. Do you know her?"

"Who doesn't know Alma? She sponsors the Coral Shores Crabs," he said with admiration, then noticed my confused look. "They're a Little Cleats soccer league. Her name is on the back of every shirt. She's always at the refreshment tent, helping the boosters sell sodas. Everyone knows Alma. If she's not the listing agent, then she's the buyer's agent for just about every house sold in the village."

"I knew she sold houses, but I had no idea she was such a sports fan." Her fandom was obviously another part of her wild success. Antiquated women's groups and little league—Alma wasn't letting any chance of exposure slip by her.

The door to Manny's room opened, and I heard his bare feet on the wooden floors. They quickened from a sleepy walk to a pounding run by the time he traveled the long hallway to where we were standing in the living room. He wrapped his arms around my knees and laughed.

"There's my happy príncipe," I called him by the royal endearment and lifted him to my hip. He was no longer a baby, and I felt it in my back. I would have to stop carrying him or else get a personal trainer. Another thing to add to my extensive list of settling-in must-dos: self-care. He gave me a big kiss and then looked at Officer Gordon Smith. He pointed to the officer's police badge patch and chanted, 'Po-le-z, Po-le-z, Po-le-z."

"Yes, Dougie," he said.

I gave the man a stern look.

"Yes, Manny," he corrected himself. "I am a police officer, and I'm your cousin."

Manny's wide eyes signaled he didn't understand. I translated. "Primo. Este señor es un primo de tu papá y policía también." In order for Manny to grow up bilingual, I spoke to him almost exclusively in Spanish. His father was supposed to be the English teacher in the house, but he hadn't been around much these last few months, between traveling to interviews and then the move. Manny only had a few English words. That, much to my mother-in-law's delight, would change as soon as he got into school.

"Pre-mo-see-ah," Manny began to sing, combining words the way little ones do.

"Si, Manny. Primo policía. Vete a jugar," I said and set him down. He ran over to a box I'd decorated with stickers and knocked its contents out. Plastic building blocks and blinking learning toys spilled onto the rubber A-B-C mat I had on the floor to define his play space.

"I can see you need to get back to unpacking," Officer Smith said. His face beamed with happiness as he watched Manny play with an alligator xylophone.

"Sorry I couldn't be of any more help. What did she die of? Do they think it was salmonella or botulism? Did any of the rest of the women fall ill?" I knew that foodborne illness affected the young and old the quickest. Though Sunny wasn't either of those two. She was only a few years younger than me, from what I could tell. I didn't feel queasy, and I'd drunk the water and tea, and eaten at least some of the soup and salad. But her low body weight and crazy diets might have compromised her immune system and heart.

"I can't reveal the exact cause," he began.

I interrupted him with a warm smile and a touch to his exposed bicep, "Come on, I'm family. I won't tell."

He blushed a little. "I guess you're right, and it will be in the gossip mill soon enough anyway. Sunny died of a heart attack, but a tox screen has been ordered because of her age and her history with drugs."

I escorted Officer Smith to the door, but not before giving Manny a round of applause for his musical oeuvre. Manny giggled and struck the rainbow keys again with the mallet.

Robert's cousin got on his bike and pedaled down the tree-lined street. I wondered which house was his next stop and what had killed Sunny. Could it have been something in the drink she mixed?

Chapter Four

By four thirty, the sun was low enough to walk to the park without melting from the heat. Coral Shores had a large park in the center of the village. It was near one of the three main thoroughfares that divided the village into zones. There was the waterfront zone, the corridor, and then the westside. The waterfront and the westside were both trapezoid shaped, with the corridor sandwiched between them. I knew this because my mother-in-law had given me a fold-out map of the village, with our house labeled "Bobby's" and her house labeled "Mother's." In red marker, she'd drawn the correct walking path to take to get between them. I understood she was excited to have her son back, but I suspected she was the reason he'd left in the first place. "Controlling" would be one of the words I'd use if I were doing a field observation of her. Nonetheless, the map had been useful. I'd used it to find a path to the park that avoided her street altogether.

Manny loved his new park. He knew as soon as I got out his tricycle that we were going for a trip. His tricycle was the kind with a long handle in the back for the adult to push when little legs got tired. He could pedal pretty far by himself now, but I'd done most of the pushing when we'd been in New York. It was probably time to get him a two-wheel bike or at least remove the handle from his trike, but I couldn't bring myself to do it. A big-boy bike would mean he wasn't little anymore.

Despite being near a busy four-lane street, Manny's new park was very safe. It was protected by a line of trees and a double gate. The latches on the gates were at adult height, so little ones could not get out on their own. Manny jumped off his trike as soon as we were inside the first gate. Unlocking the second gate, I parked the cycle by the fence. I turned around to see Manny digging in the sandpit with a group of newfound friends. I wished it were as easy for adults to make friends as it was for small children.

I contented myself with observing the park for its sociological significance. The servant–master divide was evident. In scrubs of many hues and designs were the nannies. They were seated on the benches in the middle of the park. The benches allowed them to watch their charges and socialize at the same time. In designer yoga pants and coordinating tops, the stay-at-home moms were underneath the orange canvas canopy that protected the picnic tables. They were laying out a feast of organic, non-GMO snacks that they'd unpack from their stainless steel coolers in the back of their Escalades. I wished I'd brought *In the Time of the Butterflies*, the novel I was rereading. A book usually gave one a socially acceptable reason to be antisocial. I felt more comfortable with the nanny group. I heard several Spanish accents in their chatter—Cuban, Dominican, and Puerto Rican, to name a few of them—but I knew I should force myself to meet my new neighbors. After offering Manny a juice box that he refused, I walked over to the mom's klatch.

"Did you hear that Sunny Weatherman died?" asked the well-toned woman in the capri-length purple pants.

"Was it a sweat lodge accident? I heard how they deprive you of water while you're in there so that you'll have spiritual visions," offered the stout mom with her hair in a high ponytail.

"No, I heard it was a night of Red Bull and vodkas that killed her," said the one in the huge Donna Karan sunglasses.

"She died at the country club. I was there. Anyway, she supposedly stopped drinking last year," said a tall lady.

I didn't recognize her as one of the Women's Club members, but then again, I hadn't been introduced to everyone there, thank goodness. The tall lady was close to my age, maybe five years older or maybe just forty. Her hands showed some thinning of the skin, but her face was plump in all the right places. I wondered if it was natural or expensive products that gave her her youthful glow.

"Hi, I'm Miriam Quiñones-Smith. I just moved here a few weeks ago," I said, offering a wave to the group. "Sorry to interrupt your chat. I just wanted to get out of the sun. Mind if I sit at this picnic table?" I pointed to the food-laden table next to the one where they were seated.

"Miriam Smith? You're Marjory's daughter-in-law, aren't you?" asked the purple-pants one. When I'd nodded an affirmative, she introduced herself as Elliot Truman. Being Marjory Smith's in-law had some weight with the group, as they quickly moved their lattes and made a space for me at their table. Elliot then introduced the rest of her group. The stout one was Amanda Payne. The one in the sunglasses quickly extended her hand for a chummy handshake. She was called Pepper Hallstead. And the Women's Club member's name was Juliet Pimpkin. Everyone was warm and inviting except for Juliet, who wasn't cold exactly. She was not exactly rude either. I couldn't name it, but it felt like when a little dog follows a big dog, marking the exact spot the big one had just peed on.

Elliot tittered and grabbed the edge of the table.

"Are you light-headed again?" Pepper asked. "You should have that checked out."

"I'm fine. It's probably just low blood sugar. I lost my lunch again. I think I'll go off dairy for a while and see if that helps." Elliot moved to a patch of sun and sat on the ground lotus style.

Pepper watched her with concern, then turned to talk to me. "So, how are you settling in?"

"Slowly. I still have plenty of boxes to unpack," I answered

"You bought the house on Manatee?" Amanda asked.

I nodded. "I'm afraid we don't have enough furniture to fill it. Apartments in New York are so small we barely had more than a sofa and an ottoman. And it did double duty as blanket storage and a desk." Everyone laughed with me at the ridiculousness of making do in small spaces, everyone except Juliet. She had her head turned, watching the children on the swing set. "Are those yours?" I asked her, pointing to an older boy pushing a younger one. Her shoulders jerked up like a hornet had just dive-bombed her.

"Mine? No. I don't have any." Juliet's distaste for offspring was evident.

Pepper answered the question my puzzled face was asking. "We have yoga together at the wellness center. When we're done, we get the kids from the daycare room and head to the park for a gossip session. We force Juliet to come with us, even though she doesn't have any rug rats."

"Juliet is Coral Shores's Andy Cohen. She throws late-night parties and always has the latest dish." Amanda giggled. "Like today at the club. She knows about everything before the grapevine does."

"Do you mean the poor girl that died?" I asked. "I was seated right next to her. It was awful. So sad. She was so young."

"Thirty," Juliet stated. Her tone was like a knife as she twisted her long legs out from beneath the picnic table.

"Oh my," said Pepper, "you were at her table. Was that your first time at the country club? Did Marjory drag you to it? She's past president, you know."

"Actually, my friend Alma Diaz invited me."

"You know Alma? What a small world," said Amanda. "She sold me my house."

"Mine too," voiced Pepper.

Elliot pointed her finger to her chest and nodded her head in a me-too gesture. Juliet had three-quarters of her back to the group and was staring into the trees. Was she annoyed that I'd stolen her limelight?

I smiled. "Alma and I went to high school together. She's the only one from that time that I've kept up with. I've been away from Miami so long I don't think I have any friends left here."

"Well, now you have us!" Pepper said as she patted my forearm. Again, everyone except Juliet chimed in agreement.

"We'll save you from the Women's Club," Amanda said, giving Juliet a silly face. "I don't know why Juliet goes to those boring things."

Hearing the spotlight turning back to her, Juliet turned to the group again. "Well, as I have told you all before, the Women's Club hosts most of the galas and golf tournaments. They practically write the Coral Shores social calendar. The club ladies have put in years of service to this village, and I believe they deserve some help from the younger generations," Juliet said with smug satisfaction.

"That's very noble of you," I said, hoping my compliment would erase whatever interloper fears she had of me. "Alma wants me to join. And my mother-in-law would be thrilled, but I've never been much interested in social clubs. Plus, I have Manny to occupy my time at the moment." I pointed and waved to my son. He'd moved from the sandpit to the jungle gym. He and a curly-headed girl were playing with a wall of mix-and-match cylinders. Each of the three cylinders had a person on it, divided into head, shirt, and pants. When the girl turned the head cylinder to the policeman's head, Manny shouted, "Pre-mo-see-ah!" The girl giggled and joined in with his mash-up word cry. They marched in circles, chanting it.

Pepper motioned that the little girl was her daughter. We smiled at each other as we delighted in their silly play.

"I can see you have your hands full. Too bad. We could use some new blood at the club. You're about thirty-nine. Same age as Bobby, right? I see it in your—" Juliet pointed to the sides of her mouth. "You'd still be twenty-five years younger than most of our members."

I am not vain about my age, but being called six years older than I actually am stung. And I don't have wrinkles around my mouth—they're laugh lines from smiling. "Robert's six years older than me," I corrected her. "Alma and I are the same age, just a few months apart."

"Well, then you two would be the youngest after me," Juliet said, batting her eyes like a baby lamb.

"Sunny's the youngest, isn't she?" asked Elliot.

"Sunny's dead. Remember?" Juliet said.

My shock at Juliet's callous tone was overrun by Manny and his playmates barreling into the appropriate parental laps. The curly-headed girl went to Pepper. A boy with grass-stained knees went to Amanda, and the oldest boy of the group went to Elliot. Elliot patted the boy on the back and directed him to the Handi Wipes. I helped my son clean his sandy hands as well. The mothers busied themselves with serving snacks to the group, and they kindly didn't leave Manny out of the feast. When I looked up, I noticed Juliet had slipped away. The double gates clanged shut. She clicked the alarm on her Mercedes and got in without a goodbye glance at her friends. I didn't know what to make of these yoga moms, but I certainly had formed my opinion of Juliet.

Chapter Five

Walking home from the park, I thought about my new town. It was architecturally handsome with its mixture of Colonial Revival and mid-century modern houses. The lawns were impeccably cared for, and every street was lined with trees and fancy lampposts. It was a pretty town. But were the people that lived there nice?

"Pájaro, mira Mami," Manny squealed. He was enjoying his new landscape. I looked where he'd pointed and saw a cardinal. It was not as bright or big as the ones up north, but the blue jay that flew at the red bird was mega-sized. Manny jumped up and down on his bike seat. The wildlife was putting on a pre-dusk show. I stopped at the lane of oak trees that arched over the street, so Manny could watch. The trees touched in the middle of the road, making a superhighway above our heads. While my son watched the squirrels racing from limb to limb, I thought about who would be my "mom friends." Manny had gotten along well with the yoga moms' kids. But other than our children, would we moms have anything in common?

Of the group, Pepper was the one I liked most. She seemed genuine. Her little girl was Manny's age, and they had played well together. I didn't have an opinion about Amanda or Elliot yet. But I knew I wanted to stay away from Juliet. There was something in Juliet's body language that set off a "bing" for me. All four had been gossipy about the death. It was not the nicest thing to do, but it was the normal thing to do. Chisme goes with cafecito like bread and butter. I even had a T-shirt that said as much. Pepper, Amanda, and Elliot had expressed normal curiosity about the death. Juliet, on the other hand, had spoken with authority and satisfaction. When she'd said 'Sunny's dead. Remember?,' I'd gotten chills. Juliet was mean. And she was obsessed with being the youngest. Her insult about my age was rude. My "wrinkles" were from a life of giggles and smiles, something she apparently hadn't experienced. Her face was like an airbrushed billboard, not a blemish or mark on its static surface.

"Basta, Miriam," I said. I needed to stop analyzing the park meeting and focus on what was right in front of me, my new house. I should worry about making it a home before I worried about making new friends. Alma was all the friend I needed for the moment.

"¿Qué pasa, Mami?" Manny looked at me with great concern.

"Nada, mi príncipe, nada." I comforted him. I needed to stop talking to myself out loud, or my son would think I was crazy. That was bound to come sooner or later. But I didn't want to propel him into the my-mom-is-so-embarrassing years just yet.

Entering through the garage's side door, I parked Manny's bike next to the washer and dryer. Robert kept his car in the driveway. We hadn't bought me a car yet because of finances. I could get by without one as long as the weather stayed nice. Almost everything I needed (the grocery store, the library, and the park) was within walking distance. A bike might be in my future, but for the present, the garage was without vehicles. It was reserved for laundry and storage. Empty wire shelves lined the side walls. They'd be filled soon enough with holiday decorations and other things we hadn't had room for in our tiny apartment.

Thinking about all the things we couldn't do in our New York rental, I got excited about our future. Robert loved Cuban food, and I loved to cook it. But in New York, I hadn't had time or space. Here I had a big refrigerator to store meats and tons of cabinets for pots and pans. I could finally get a big olla de presión for making frijoles negros. There was plenty of counter space for fruit to ripen. My mind was reeling at all the meals I would make. Just thinking about a kitchen filled with conversation and the aroma of tomatoes, garlic, onion, and culantro from the sofrito, bubbling on the stove, made me happy. I didn't have the family and friends to fill the kitchen with chatter yet. But I did have Robert, and he'd be home within an hour. I could make him his favorite meal in that time. I was pretty sure I had everything I needed to make chicken fricassee.

Quickly, I made Manny a fort of boxes and left him to his own imaginative play. The open concept of the house let me keep an eye on him from the kitchen. On the counter, I propped up my iPad and set Pandora to my Afro-Cuban station. Soon, the congas of Mongo Santamaria were drumming. I hadn't bought fresh fruits and vegetables, but I had purchased frozen and canned. From the freezer, I took a bag of tostones. Once they defrosted, I would fry the sliced plantains to a golden crisp. From the cupboard, I took a twelve-ounce jar of sofrito, along with the spices I used to boost the flavor from store-bought to homemade.

Every Latin kitchen had a rice cooker. Ours was the small three-cup variety, which was plenty for tonight's meal. I measured out the water and rice and pressed the start lever. The two skillets I owned were heating on the stove's large eyes. The one with an inch and a half of oil was on the back burner, to lessen Manny's chance of getting a pop of oil on him if he came to check out what I was cooking. The other pan was on the front eye, and into it I poured a drizzle of olive oil. I crushed three cloves of garlic and threw them in. As soon as they hit the sizzling oil, the room filled with deliciousness. Removing the plastic wrap from the chicken, I dusted them with flour, then gently lowered the thighs and legs into the hot skillet. The only thing I was missing were the olives. Robert wouldn't miss them since he always just pushed them aside. But they did add a certain layer of flavor to the dish.

"Mmm, rico, tengo hambre," Manny said. His dark brown head of hair could be seen toddling toward the kitchen.

"Quédate en la sala hasta que la cena esté lista." I told him dinner wasn't ready and to stay in the living room. The fact that my son had smelled my cooking and proclaimed it delicious made me proud. I hoped Robert had the same reaction. I wanted to do something nice for him. Of late, we hadn't really connected. We were kind of living opposite lives. He was learning a new job, meeting new people, and coming home tired, not wanting to talk much. I was alone all day with a child or my mother-in-law, so I was desperate for real adult conversation by nightfall.

While the chicken cooked, I set the counter for dinner. Since we hadn't had a dining room table in New York, I'd invested in nice placemats and napkins to transform our coffee table into an eating surface. Pulling them from the counter drawer, I set our three places with yellow mats and orange napkins. The next drawer over held the eating utensils. Robert and I got knives, forks, spoons while Manny's place got his special kid-sized utensils. From the barely filled cabinet, I took out two wine glasses. They were dirty with newsprint smudges, so I washed them. Robert had received several bottles of wine as welcome-home gifts. I selected a Malbec from the wine rack next to the refrigerator. It was the only thing in the house that was full. Every day that first week in Coral Shores, it seemed like I'd open the front door to find a gift bag on the step. The Malbec's dry finish would work well with the rich olive oil in the chicken fricassee.

The oil was hot, and the tostones defrosted. Preparing a plate of paper towels to soak up the excess oil, I set to frying the green bananas. After they were all cooked golden, I sprinkled salt over the lot of them. I broke one of the round chips in half and ate it. There was nothing better than a hot tostone fresh from the fryer unless it was a hot tostone dipped in mojo. Sadly, I didn't have any of the lime and garlic marinade. The next trip to the grocery store would remedy that crime.

The rice cooker clicked off. Checking the pollo, I turned the heat off and covered it to stay warm while we waited for Robert. A salsa was playing on the station. I picked Manny up and danced between the cardboard boxes with him. He giggled like he was being tickled. As the song ended, the phone rang.

"Hola," I answered.

"Hi, honey," Robert said, "Dad asked me to meet him for a drink at the club, so I'm running a few minutes late. I'll try to be home within thirty minutes. Okay?"

"Okay, mi amor." I tried to hide my disappointment and must have done a good job of it, as he rang off with an "I love you."

We always tried to eat dinner as a family, but I wasn't going to make my hungry prince wait for his father. He was already at my side, tugging at my shirt to feed him. I spooned a small helping of rice in a bowl, placed the meat I'd cut from the bone over it, and stuck a plantain on the edge like an edible garnish. Manny followed my directions and washed his hands in the guest bathroom.

"Mira, Mami. Limpia." He showed me his clean but dripping wet hands.

"Muy bien." I went to lift him into the tall chair.

"No. Yo puedo." He refused my help and climbed into the tall chair at the counter by himself.

He gobbled up his dinner while bopping his head to the drums and beats of the Cuban music pulsing from the small speaker. *Maybe he'll become a percussionist,* I thought to myself.

"A bañarte mi príncipe," I said to him once he'd drunk his milk. It was early for Manny's bath, but bathing him before Robert got home would give the adults a little more time to linger over dinner. He skipped to his room, where we selected his pajamas. He chose a blue set that had spaceships and stars on it. The bathtub was full of plastic sharks from the previous night's ocean explorer bath. Once the water was up to his waist, I turned it off and let him play while I lathered his neck and toes. After he was dried and dressed, we returned to the living room to wait. It had been at least forty minutes, if not an hour, since Robert and I had spoken. I checked my phone for the time and noticed a missed text message: *I'll be home late. I ran into an old friend.*

My hope sank. Robert and I were not going to have a romantic dinner tonight. I texted him back: *Too bad. I made your favorite.*

He replied, *Save me some! I love your chicken. Sorry, babe.* A second after that text, I got another one, *Wait until you meet Juliet. She's tons of fun. I bet she'll be your new best friend.*

My eyes bugged out of my head. Juliet was the old friend he'd run into. I grabbed the bottle of Malbec I'd left to breathe and poured myself a large glass. Robert didn't know me at all if he thought I would like Juliet. Robert was choosing a shallow, mean girl over a homecooked meal with his wife. Robert had no idea what a mad Cuban looked like, but he was going to find out.

Chapter Six

The doorbell sounded, and my head knocked. Who was pestering me at eight AM? I peeled myself off the floor of Manny's room, where I'd fallen asleep last night waiting for Robert to come home. My make-do cot of blanket and pillow hadn't softened the floor ni un poco, and I was feeling it in my back and my hips. I was also feeling the bottle of wine I'd drunk. Manny stirred when I got up, but didn't awaken. Moving as fast as I could to stop the offending ringing, I looked out the window to see Alma on my doorstep.

"What are you doing here?" I asked.

"Buenos días to you, too, sunshine." Alma gave me a hug and a kiss, then pushed past me. "Get your workout clothes on. We're going to a shake-your-booty class."

"What? I can't. I've got Manny. He hasn't even had breakfast," I said, using him as my excuse instead of admitting to my raging headache.

"Pack a banana and a yogurt. The fitness center has a daycare. He'll love it."

Alma gave me a pat on the rump and ushered me to my room. There was no arguing with my best friend. She always had a plan and a strategy. I found a pink and orange outfit that was passable, betting that the fitness center wasn't a T-shirt and shorts type of place. I dug through the box in the closet for my sneakers, then went to brush my teeth. While I was pulling a comb through my hair, Manny pattered in.

"Mi príncipe." I leaned down to get my morning kiss.

"Mami!" Manny kissed me with a wet smack and a tight hug around my neck. He used his step-up to get to the toilet, where he pulled his Superman underwear down and did his business. "¡Hombre!" he said triumphantly. Robert had taught him to pee "like a man" and so every time Manny peed standing up, he'd yell the Spanish word for man. I smiled despite myself. Then the thought of my husband's disregard for his wife and child made my head throb.

I'd heard him come in last night but hadn't bothered to get up. It had been late, and my mad voice would have woken Manny. Robert had poked his head in Manny's room. He even went so far as to kiss his sleeping son on his head, but Robert hadn't tried to wake me to come to bed in our room. I let out a snort that sounded like a bull's. Then I looked in the mirror and caught my angry face. *Manny doesn't deserve an angry mother,* I told myself. Changing my attitude quickly, I helped Manny brush his teeth. I told him he was going to a playroom, and he got excited about a new adventure with new toys.

Alma helped get Manny dressed while I packed his breakfast. I threw a baggie of oatmeal "Os" into the insulated lunch sack. In the refrigerator, I found a squeeze yogurt. My missed romantic reconnect stared me in the eyes. I'd put the whole rice cooker in the fridge, along with the covered skillet of chicken. It didn't look like Robert had even touched it. There wasn't a dirty dish in the sink either. Maybe I'd imagined his coming home last night. Maybe he'd spent the night with Juliet.

What was I thinking? Robert wouldn't do that. He wasn't a cheating husband. I slapped myself on the cheeks. "Get a grip, Miriam," I said aloud.

Manny laughed. I turned from the open cold storage and saw him pointing at me like I was a silly cartoon. I made a funny face and played it up. Behind Manny and out of his sight, Alma held up the empty bottle I'd left on the counter. She gave me a "now it all makes sense" look.

"I'll explain later," I told her. I added a few bottles of water to our meal-on-the-go bag and zipped it closed.

"You're going to love Mambo-cise," Alma chided. "Maybe you should take an Advil before we get there. The music will be loud."

"What?"

"For your hangover," she whispered, shielding her mouth from Manny.

"He can't read lips, loca." I rolled my eyes. "Mambo-*what*?"

"Mambo-cise. It's like Zumba and Jazzercise had a child."

This time the question was written on my face.

"The instructor got a cease and desist order from Zumba. So, he changed the name of his class and added a few mambos, but it's basically aerobic dancing to Latin beats."

Manny transitioned into the playroom at the fitness center with nary a kiss goodbye. The girls that staffed the room were college aged. Their youth didn't frighten me, though, as they showed great professionalism. I was asked to sign an agreement-of-use form, fill out a contact sheet confirming my village residency, review the health guidelines (no fevers or diarrhea), and return within an hour and a half or be charged twenty dollars.

Alma pulled me out of the playroom. "So, what's with the weekday drinking?" she asked in a whisper. The hallway was empty, but the various exercise rooms were humming with activity, and people could walk out of them at any moment.

"I made dinner for Robert, and he didn't make it home to eat it. The bottle was already open, so I had a glass and then another and then, well—"

"Another," she said, finishing my sentence. Alma tsk-tsked and wagged her finger at me, then shook her head in disbelief. "That doesn't sound like him."

"I know. He's like a different person since coming back here."

A sweaty senior came out the door papered with Jazzercise flyers. Alma and I quit talking and smiled. The lady waved at Alma affectionately before hurrying to the bathroom.

"Mrs. Thelma Morgan. I did both sides of her deal. I sold her five-bedroom waterfront house when she wanted to downsize last year and got her into a two-bedroom on Manta Ray Road. Sweet woman. Anyway, what do you think is going on with Robert?"

"I don't know. But I do know he gave up his favorite meal for drinks at the club with an old friend."

She heard my sarcastic tone and asked, "You don't think he's having an affair, do you?"

"I don't know what to think!" I was on the verge of tears. "I just can't believe it. He's acting like a man without a family. We've been here two weeks, and I've seen him all of ten hours total. He's always playing golf or stopping at the club for drinks. It's not like the Robert I married."

"Do you know who the friend was?" Alma asked.

"Juliet Pim-something. I met her at the park yesterday, believe it or not. She doesn't seem like a nice person."

Alma's face was frozen in a mask of shock.

"What?" I asked her.

"Juliet is something of a flirt. But don't worry. I'm sure it was innocent. I'll ask around and see what's what."

The classes let out as we reached the Mambo-cise room at the end of the long putty-colored corridor. The hallway rapidly filled with tired, sweaty participants. The noise level rose with moans and groans about how hard the workouts had been. It was mostly women coming out of the Jazzercise room, but I saw a few older men as well. At the opposite end of the hall, a door opened, releasing a younger set of health nuts. They were more equally mixed in gender, and they all carried yoga mats. Someone inside the room called out, "Namaste." It was the yoga lady from the park, Elliot. "I hope you liked today's meditation. Remember to stay in the present. Savor each moment," she said, and waved to the class from the doorway. Elliot stood on her tiptoes to see above the meandering patrons. When she was sure it was me, the newbie from the park, she smiled and flapped her arm in a big hello. I returned the greeting before stepping into the Mambo-cise studio.

The instructor, intent on the playlist, had his back toward us. He'd stop on a song for a few seconds and do a little hip shake or cha-cha-cha step, then move to a different track. Alma ran over and goosed him. He turned around, and a high voltage stream of Spanish ensued between them. Alma introduced me to the instructor, Jorge. His high cheekbones were aided by a bronzer, and his lashes were so thick and long I thought they might be fake. In the brief conversation we had before Jorge called the class to order, he bragged that he was a drag queen by night and a fitness trainer by day, which explained the lashes and mascara residue from his night job. Our chitchat was all in Spanish, and it made me feel at home. Even though I slipped in and out of English with fluidity and fluency, I preferred the Spanish idiom for shooting the breeze. Jorge promised to show me a selfie of him as Cha-Cha Minnelli from his drag show on Miami Beach after the class was over.

"Te vas a volver loca, when you see me in my Cabaret traje," he said, then clapped his hands to call us all into line.

The studio was full. We made four lines of five and faced the mir-rored wall. Jorge led us through a series of stretches, then showed us the basic steps for my benefit. "As you can see, we have a new student today, Alma's friend Miriam." Jorge pointed at me, and the whole class turned to look. "She's Cuban, so I'm sure she'll pick up the steps easily. Miriam, just follow along. There are six basic steps I use in this class: salsa, rumba, cumbia, samba, merengue, and bachata," Jorge said. He performed each step and then showed how he might com-bine them. Before I'd caught on to the combination, he hit the "Play" button. Forty-five minutes later, I was exhausted but happy. The music was vibrant, and the dancing was fun. I'd had such a good time that my mind had gotten off the worry train it had been on. My headache was gone too.

"Good workout, chicas," Jorge cheered. "Now, down on the floor for a cooldown and final stretch."

The cooldown song was a romantic ballad. Jorge had us bending side to side like swaying tree branches. While flexing and pointing our toes to stretch our burning calf muscles, Elliot came into the room. She bent and whispered to Jorge. He nodded an affirmative to her and then said, "Elliot, the center's meditation teacher, has something to share with you."

"Thank you, Jorge," Elliot said, pronouncing it "George," the Anglo version of his name. "Some of you have already heard this announcement. Hi Paige"—she waved to the lady in the pink breast cancer shirt—"since you take meditation or yoga stretch with me. Anyway, I am so excited to be telling you about a seminar that is happening right here in Coral Shores. Doctor Mario Fuentes will be speaking tomorrow, Thursday night. He is a preeminent MD who combines Western medicine with ancient herbal practices from the West Indies. His antiaging creams are used by celebrities. The talk is free. So, I encourage you to bring a friend and come learn about this noninvasive face-lift product."

"Thank you, Elliot," Jorge said. He gave her a "bye-bye" wave that made me think of that *Saturday Night Live* sketch with the airline stewards. Polite but impatient.

When the studio cleared, Jorge kept his promise and showed me his drag selfies. "That can't be you! Wow," I said. "Your makeup is on fleek."

"Ay, chica, gracias, but we don't say that anymore." Jorge shook his head tightly. "No, no, no, no, no. That is so 2018."

"She's had her head in a book for the past five years. Forgive her," Alma interjected.

"Ooh, what have you been reading? I love books." Jorge clapped prayer hands. "Believe it or not, I read a lot of YA—young adult. The rainbow is brighter there, if you know what I mean."

Alma looked at my puzzled face. "More gay. He means more gay. No, mi amor, Miriam has been studying to be a doctor."

"Wow. What kind of medicine?" Jorge began packing his things.

"No, not MD. PhD," I corrected.

"Oh, so a doctor in name but not in practice como ese loco Doctor Fuentes." Jorge flicked the flyer Elliot had left at us. "Please tell me you are not going to it."

"No," I said.

At the same time, Alma said, "Yes."

"Alma, no me digas que tú usas esa basura." Jorge had disgust written all over his face.

"It's networking. And yes, you are going." Alma hooked arms with me.

"Promise me you won't buy any of his youth cream. I tried it, and my skin turned red and began peeling like a chemical mask. It was horrible. I almost had to cancel a performance. It was that bad." Jorge put his towel around his neck.

"Thanks for the warning," I said. "And thanks for the class. It was more fun than I expected. It was more like dancing than exercise. I loved it."

"Gracias." Jorge gave me an air kiss. "I have a "buy two months, get one free" package ahora mismo. The deal ends tomorrow, so register at the desk on your way out. Ciao, bellas." He exited dancing.

"Alma, I'm not going to that talk."

"Yes, you are. You have to keep me company. I hate those things. And you owe me anyway."

"Owe you? For what?"

"You'll see."

Chapter Seven

When we returned from the fitness center, there was a bouquet on the front step of my house. My house—I wasn't used to saying that. I had a house, an actual freestanding house with front and back yards.

"Flores," Manny said.

"Si, rosas," I said.

The roses were bright orange, my favorite. I read the card and passed it to Alma for her to read.

Dearest Miriam,
I'm sorry I missed dinner. Please forgive me.
Love, Your Roberto

"Ay, que sweet," Alma said, holding the vase so I could unlock the front door. "See? I told you it would all be okay."

"Actually, I think you were the one that mentioned an A-F-F-A-I-R before I'd even thought of it."

Manny squeezed between us and ran to his cardboard fort.

"Forget about him for right now. We need to change. We have an appointment at UnMundo."

"What?"

"You heard me."

"I never said I'd do that. No."

"Yes!"

"I have nothing to wear."

"I know, that's why I brought you an outfit from my closet. It's in the car. I'll get it."

After I'd washed my face and freshened myself with some coconut and jasmine body spray, I found Alma laying out several outfit choices on my bed.

"I was planning on wearing this one." She pointed to a black sheath dress with a colorful scarf looped over the hanger. "But if you like it, you can wear it."

"No, that is definitely more you."

"True. So, I was thinking this for you." She touched the pant leg of a blue palazzo jumpsuit. "It's fashionable, but not trendy. Comfortable, but not casual. Or you could wear this one." Alma fiddled with a striped handkerchief-hem dress.

"I don't know."

"Try them both." Alma looked at her watch. "But hurry—we don't have a lot of time."

"Doesn't this feel like high school?" I laughed as I slipped into the jumpsuit. "You lending me clothes."

"You still don't have much fashion sense."

"I resent that. I've gotten better with age." Looking in the mirror, I tilted my head from side to side. I stood on my toes. The jumpsuit was too long. I'd catch the hem with my heel. I took it off and tried on the dress.

"Better." Alma nodded enthusiastically. She'd changed into her outfit and was headed to the bathroom to apply her makeup.

"Why are you doing this? Don't you have houses to sell?"

"Yes, and I also have a friend that needs a life beyond being Robert's stay-at-home wife."

She had a good point. It had only been a few weeks, and I already didn't feel like myself. I was never what one would call the life of the party. That was Alma, for sure. But I was fun. I loved being social. I loved having interesting conversations. I loved trying new things. But lately, I was uninspired and moody.

"What about Manny? Won't it be weird to bring a child to an interview?"

"An interview? I said appointment, not interview. So, you've changed your mind?"

"I haven't changed my mind, but I have, maybe, opened it."

"¡Éxito!" Alma grinned at her success. "UnMundo is Latino. Children are not a problem. They probably have a daycare onsite."

"The fewer times I have to call Marjory, the better. And that reminds me. I need to change the locks."

The drive to the Hialeah studio took about thirty minutes. In which time Manny fell asleep and didn't want to wake once we'd parked. He was so grumpy that he didn't want to walk and begged to be carried.

"You'll wrinkle your dress," Alma said. She squatted and got eye level with my son. "Manuel, si tú te portas bien, yo te prometo un helado después de este viaje."

"Did you just bribe my child?" I asked her in shock.

"¿Chocolate?" Manny rubbed his eyes with his fists and stood up straight.

"Chocolate, vainilla, fresa, mamey, coco," Alma said. "Whatever you want."

Manny grabbed my hand and began walking. "Vamos, Mami, vamos."

"You will make the best or the worst mother. I don't know which."

"Neither. I'm already the best tía," Alma said. She led us to double doors with the UnMundo logo etched into the glass. "And that's all I want. No kids for me. I plan to be rich and retired by forty-five."

"You say that now, but you might change your mind if the right guy came along. ¿No?"

"Hola," she said to the receptionist at the front desk. "Soy Alma Diaz. Ella es Miriam Quiñones. Tenemos una cita con Ileana Ruiz."

"Si. Unos minutitos, por favor," the receptionist said. She relayed the message into her headset and smiled. She was young, twenty-something, with long hair and nails. Her clothing was tight and bright. She took a white hinged-lid jar from the shelf behind her and walked around the counter to Manny. She opened the canister and offered him its contents. He looked at me for permission, and I nodded that it was okay. His little hand went into the jar and came out with a Chupa Chups lollipop. As I helped him unwrap it, that very specific not-real-cherries smell formed a scent cloud between us. It took me back to my childhood and my tíos' tiny three-seat café. I'd worked summers there up until my father and his brother had an argument that splintered the family in two. No one ever told me what the argument was about, but I was forbidden to talk to my cousin, Yolanda. It was Yoli's and my job to staff the café window for one hour after the breakfast rush so that Tía could have a break. Yoli would make the coffee, and I would serve the pastelitos from the shelved plexiglass box with the hot lamp to keep the pastries warm. Tía would always give us a Chupa Chups with our pay for the day. Even though we were fourteen and not kids anymore, I had looked forward to the candy more than the money. I missed Yoli and Tía Elba and even grumpy Tío José. With Papi y Mami not living here anymore, I needed family.

"I should call her."

"Call who?" Alma asked.

"Did I say that out loud?"

Alma gave me her same-old-crazy-Miriam look.

"Yoli, my cousin. She and I worked at my tíos' ventanita for a few summers."

"I didn't know that. Where?"

"Actually, not too far from here. They had a three-stool lunch counter with a walk-up window that served breakfast and lunch from seven AM until three PM. In the afternoon, they prepared the cantinas."

"So, that's where you get your love of food from."

"Maybe some of it. Tía Elba made the most delicious sopa de pollo with a disc of corn cob and carrots and garlic and—"

"Damas y caballero," the receptionist winked at Manny, "por favor follow me. Do you want your son to play in our daycare while you met with Señora Ruiz?"

Alma mouthed, "I told you so." We followed the young woman down a hall that was lined with promotional posters for the network's shows. After a right turn and another hall, we were at the company's daycare center. In the Disney-decorated room, there were five older women, abuelitas. Two of them were in rocking chairs, quieting babies; two were playing dress-up with a group of three- and four-year-olds; and the fifth was cleaning a snack table. The one cleaning noticed us and came to the door. When she opened it, the floral smell of Fabulosa from the rag in her hand hit my nose. Americans had Pine-Sol and Latins had purple Fabulosa. It was the smell of clean and home and goodness.

"¿Y quién es este niño tan guapo?" the woman asked. She patted Manny's head. The receptionist explained that we had a meeting and that Manny would only be there for an hour. I filled out a simple form with my name and cell number. I checked the appropriate boxes about allergies, fever, etcetera, then kissed Manny goodbye.

"No te preocupes, él está en buenas manos," said the daycare woman.

I wasn't worried about him being in good hands. I was worried about how I would get him out of there when we were ready to leave.

Chapter Eight

Ileana Ruiz was shorter than she looked on TV. On-screen, she looked like a six-foot-tall Rubenesque goddess. In her office, she was a five-foot six-inch Puerto Rican-Colombian businesswoman with light brown hair and average good looks. She was still celebrity-level intimidating, but slightly less so in her low heels. She and Alma exchanged kisses. Oohs and aahs were made about this and that before I was introduced. Alma embellished my credentials to the point of ridiculousness. I felt my cheeks heat with embarrassment. Ileana offered us drinks. Alma refused, but I asked for a glass of water. My throat was already tightening with fear. Before we sat, she instructed the receptionist to bring me cold water and her a cup of hot water.

"Okay, so let's get down to business," Ileana said. "Alma tells me you're a food expert. What does that mean? I hope it means you can cook because I need someone who can cook. You don't have to be a chef, but you must be able to cook delicious food." She tapped her nails on her desk like she was playing scales on a piano.

"I'm a food anthropologist."

"You dig up old food?" Ileana asked.

"No, I . . . I . . . ." I'd never had it put that way before, and I wasn't going to insult her by explaining that archeology and anthropology were two very different fields of study. I gulped air and tried again. "I study how food, culture, and history intersect." Ileana looked like an animal caught in headlights. Alma kicked me with the side of her shoe and lifted her eyebrows. *Third time's a charm*, I told myself and tried again. "For example, guarapo. The sugar cane drink we all love supposedly came to Cuba from the Canary Islands via Africa and Spain's colonization, of course." I was digging a deeper hole with every word out of my mouth. A reprieve came when the receptionist entered with our drinks. She placed a promotional stainless steel travel cup in my hands.

"A gift from us to you." She smiled. I felt like she probably said that sentence multiple times a day. The tumbler was nice, even if it had the network's logo on it. I thanked her and took a long sip of cold water.

Ileana opened a drawer from which she removed a box of tea. The package was bright green with black lettering: "Dr. Mario Fuentes, Te de Juventud." I pointed to the box and silently queried Alma: *Isn't that the doctor that's giving the talk at the fitness center?*

"It tastes horrible, but it works. También tengo his diet tea and his digestion tea." The morning show star removed more boxes from her desk drawer.

"May I look at them?" I asked.

"Claro. This one is the best tasting. It's like instant lemonade."

She handed me the diet drink box. On the side panel, in a white oval, there was an image of the doctor along with his origin story.

Dr. Mario Fuentes, born in Matanza, Cuba, learned herbal medicine from Lucumi elders. He has traveled the Caribbean, studying with the best traditional herbalists of Jamaica, the Dominican Republic, Haiti, Puerto Rico, and the Bahamas. He spent a year in the Brazilian Amazon, living with and learning from the Kuripako tribe, all to bring the ancient wisdom of health to modern times.

I read the ingredients list: garcinia cambogia, green tea extract, ginger, lemon, and monk fruit for sweetness. I handed the box back.

"Well, it must work because you look amazing. Like a twenty-five-year-old," Alma said. She knew how to schmooze and compliment. Ileana was definitely in the over-forty category. She looked great, but her twenties had clearly come and gone.

"Well, it is true what they say about the camera adding five pounds. This tea is a career saver." Ileana tapped the diet drink box with her index finger. "Now, where were we? Ah yes, Alma says you're writing a cookbook?"

I fumbled for words. Alma kicked me under the table again. I was going to have a bruise on my ankle before we got out of the office. Simplicity. When I talked to laypeople about anthropology, I reminded myself I had to leave out the academic language: *Don't say "ethnographic" or "diaspora" or "foodways." KISS—keep it simple, stupid.*

"Yes, I am. It is about the Caribbean kitchen."

"Perfect. Can you give me an example of the recipes?" Ileana tilted her head and crossed her hands. She looked like a cat waiting by a mouse hole.

"I have several tropical fruit smoothie and batido recipes. Tamarindo, mamey, mango, and my son's favorite, fruta bomba. My version has condensed milk, lime, and mint. I give a brief history of how canned milk came to be a staple in island homes. In nineteen—"

Kick.

"Excelente. That's what you'll make on this Friday's show."

"This Friday?" I asked. Ay, mi madre, my stomach did a somersault, a backflip, and a round-off.

"Is that a problem? The host you're replacing is due to give birth any day, and I don't want her water to break on air. That would be"— Ileana twisted her mouth and wrinkled her nose—"very unsanitary."

"No. No, problem. I'm available this Friday."

"Good. La pobrecita, her ankles are so swollen they looked like softballs, and her brain has gone to marshmallow. Last week, she told the audience to use a cup of salt in a flan recipe!"

"Pobrecita," Alma and I said in unison.

"Cocina Caribeña is normally a five-to-seven-minute spot, but until we see how you do and if the viewers like you, I think we will start you at three minutes. Be here at six AM for makeup and wardrobe. Please give my production assistant, Delvis"—Ileana passed me a business card—"a list of ingredients and cooking utensils you will need by tomorrow at noon." She stood and pressed a button on her desktop phone; it buzzed and someone opened the office door. We were being dismissed. "Don't forget your mug."

"What just happened there?" I whispered to Alma as we followed a few steps behind Ileana's administrative assistant.

"You got the job."

"I thought this wasn't an interview."

"Whoever said that?"

"You said that!"

"No. No, I don't recall that."

"Alma, I could . . ." I gripped the air like I was wringing her neck.

"Mami! No quiero ir." Manny was on the edge of whining. Just as I'd predicted, extracting him from such a fantasy land of toys would be difficult.

"Remember, we're going to get ice cream," Alma said in a singsong way.

"Spanish. Tell him in Spanish." It was my turn to kick her.

"Recuerda que vamos para helado."

Manny dropped the Simba and Timon action figures and dashed into Alma's arms. He knew who buttered his bread. The assistant led us back to the lobby, where she gave me a Friday-only parking pass.

"Bienvenidos to the UnMundo family," the assistant said. "See you soon."

Chapter Nine

In the car, Manny listed all the flavors of ice cream that he knew and some, like cookie-jelly-bubblegum, that he made up. We were on our way to the Latin American Café for lunch when I saw my tíos' little café. It was still there. *Did they still own it? Could they be there now?*

"Alma, turn around," I said. I twisted and fought with the seat belt to look over my shoulder.

"What's wrong? Did you leave your phone at the studio?"

"No, I'd like to eat at Tres Palmas. It's back there in that shopping strip."

"Okay, but why? I don't think I've ever heard of it."

"Yes, you have. You just don't remember. I called it Tres Sillas, not Palmas. It's—or was, I don't know—my tíos' three-stool café. I worked there the summer before high school."

Horns tooted as Alma made an illegal U-turn. We parked a few doors down from the café in front of a botanica with a six-foot-tall St. Lazarus statue. Walking by it, Manny petted the plaster dogs licking the saint's wounds.

"Guau guao. Mami, quiero una guau guao," Manny begged.

"No, mi amor. No perros ahora," I told him. No dogs now or ever. I was glad Manny dropped the subject. His short attention span was nabbed by the pool toys in the dollar store window. I didn't want to tell my darling child his father would never go for it. Robert was not a dog person.

When we got to the restaurant door, I froze.

"What's wrong? Is it full?" Alma asked.

"No, it's not full." I looked through the glass door. "There are empty tables. Oh my god, it's bigger."

"So, open the door. I'm hungry."

"I can't. I'm afraid."

"Afraid. ¿Por qué?"

"Because I haven't seen my tíos or cousin in, like, ten years. Not since the argument."

"Move." Alma placed her hand on the door bar and pulled. "Holding onto a grudge is like holding onto an anchor and jumping into the sea. Come on."

It looked like the café had tripled in size. The tiny counter was still there, but there was now a row of booths and four freestanding tables. Maybe my tío had sold it, and the new owners had expanded. I looked around for Tía Elba and Tío José but didn't see them. Tía would be behind the counter and Tío in the closet-sized kitchen if they were still the owners. My shoulders relaxed. I was relieved but at the same time disappointed. I missed family, but I didn't necessarily want to open a can of worms.

"I don't know what I was thinking?"

"Are you talking to me or to yourself?" Alma asked.

"Both."

We sat in the middle booth. A server in a red apron filled the plastic water glasses already on the table. She returned quickly with a basket of bread. Most Cuban restaurants in Miami toasted the left-over fresh bread, from the day before, with butter, to serve the next day. Some places added garlic powder in varying amounts. Both versions were delicious and an excellent way to use the cracker crust Cuban baguette that went stale after a day. I removed a wet wipe from my purse and cleaned Manny's hands before giving him a disc of toast. The waitress recited the specials: ropa vieja and pescado frito. Alma ordered pollo a la plancha from the menu. I chose the ropa vieja and asked for an extra plate so I could share it with Manny.

"So, are you excited?" Alma asked. When I didn't reply with gushing enthusiasm, claps, and squeals, she took my hand and squeezed it. "I'm excited for you. This is exactly what you need to kick your depression in the butt."

"I'm not depressed. A little worried and lonely, maybe."

"Okay, so not depressed right now, but it was coming. I know you. When you don't have a project, you get too into your head. You're like Sigmund Freud."

"Excuse me, que, qué ?" I chuckled. Alma always made the wildest comparisons.

"You overanalyze." She leaned back and pretended to hold a pipe. In a bad German accent, she said, "You say you dream about cigars . . . hmm. I say you are really dreaming about—"

"Okay, stop before you hurt yourself and corrupt my son."

"But seriously, this cooking show is going to be great for you. You're going to be a star."

"Before you go putting my star on Calle Ocho's Walk of Fame, let me get through the first show. Oh my god, I can't believe I'm going to be on TV in two days."

"I know! It's going to be *espectacular*." She exaggerated the Spanish word à la Walter Mercado.

Our food arrived. Alma's malanga had steam dancing above it. The olive oil and garlic marinade made the boiled root vegetable fragrant and glistening. I resisted stealing a taste. I spooned some white rice onto Manny's empty plate and then transferred some of the shredded beef over it. Manny and I both loved the classic comfort food, ropa vieja. Except for the green bell peppers—my son, who was a good eater, did not like the green ones. The red ones were okay, but not the green. I picked them out of his portion before setting the plate in front of him. He wiggled onto his knees to be at a better height and took the spoon from the wax-paper utensil packet. He was growing up so quickly. My little baby wouldn't need my help much longer. I watched him eat a few bites before taking my first bite.

"Delicious. It tastes just like Tía Elba's. She always used a lot of thyme and vino seco, just like this one." I looked toward the espresso machine. No Tía. Instead, there was a twenty-something-year-old in a tank top, with a bandana holding her corkscrew coils off her face.

Returning my gaze to my friend, I asked, "What is that?" I couldn't believe what I was witnessing. "Tell me you're not taking that stuff."

Alma tore the corner off a packet of Dr. Fuentes's diet drink and poured the powder into her water. "I thought it was worth a try. A client gave me a few packets the other day, and they've been in the bottom of my bag ever since." Alma stirred the cloudy mixture into a water tornado. "Today, when Ileana said that it tasted like lemonade, that's when I remembered I had a sample. Do you want the other one?"

"Are you calling me gorda?'

"Miriam, that's not what I meant. You're not fat."

"I know, and neither are you."

"Thank you." Alma drank the lemonade and puckered. "Eeww, it's like a super-sweet SweeTart. But if it does what it promises— makes me drop five pounds in five days—I can deal with it."

"Miracle diets have the word 'die' in them. They will kill you."

"I'm not Sunny Weatherman. I don't want to be a Skinny Minnie. I just want to look great for the regional awards photos next week when I win top sales."

"Another one? Felicidades. You are running out of shelf space, chica. What is this—like the twentieth one?"

"Seven, but who's counting." Alma cut a piece of her grilled chicken and popped it in her mouth.

"Sunny, that was the lady who collapsed at the luncheon, right?"

"Si, pobrecita. Really sad what she put her mother through."

"What do you mean?" I nibbled a tostone and gave Manny one of the twice-fried plantains too, along with a Fisher-Price Little People giraffe I had with me for be-patient-a-little-longer situations like this one. "Drugs? Cancer? Mental illness?"

"It started when she was twelve from what I've been told. Depression, anxiety, starving herself, coke. She went to rehab a few times for that. There was a rumor that she charged $300,000 on Stormy's credit cards over a weekend, binge shopping."

The waitress interrupted us to ask if we were going to want coffee. We told her yes, two espressos and a warm milk for my son.

"Three *hundred* thousand? On what? How? That is a lot of money. That's a house."

"Pfft. Easy to do in the Design District. Gucci, Prada, Versace. You haven't been there in a while. It's changed."

"The Design District? Not since high school, for that big diocese event at Archbishop Curley Norte Dame. You were with me, right? A bunch of us snuck off campus to go find pizza, and all we found were bathroom fixtures and drapery stores for interior designers."

"Yeah, it was the basketball playoff, and you abandoned me."

"Whhaaat? No way. I would never abandon you."

"Ay si, you did. The one and only time St. Joe's made the finals. I was captain of the cheerleading squad. We'd practiced our half-time routine for months, and you missed it. It was to Gwen Stefani's "Hollaback Girl." The clean version. I was so mad at you. Come to think of it, I'm still mad at you?" Alma crossed her arms and pouted.

"Ay, stop fooling." I threw my used napkin at her.

"¡Mami! No tires," Manny interjected.

"That's right, Mommy—no throwing." Alma smirked.

I loved my bestie. It was like we'd picked up where we'd left off fifteen years ago. Sure, she'd visited me a few times in college, and of course I'd see her over Christmas break when I came home to Miami. She'd been the maid of honor at my wedding, and she flew up to New York for Manny's baptism, but none of that was as intense as high school. We'd been inseparable. Her mother called us Ibeyi, the twins, because we were always together. A warm joy filled my chest. It was all going to be okay. I wasn't starting new in a place where I didn't know anyone. I was back home with my best friend. "Oye, I'm glad I'm back."

"I'm glad you're back too," Alma said.

"Thanks for today. I needed the push. The idea of being on camera is scary as h-e-l-l, but kinda cool at the same time."

The waitress came with our coffees. She placed the cups and saucers in the middle of the table and slipped the check under them. I snagged the handwritten bill. "My treat."

Alma was about to protest.

"No, I've got it." I smacked her hand away. "You've been my rock and savior this week. My treat."

I tested the temperature of Manny's milk and poured a few drops of my coffee into it. The steamed milk turned from white to light beige. Americans would think I was crazy for giving coffee to a toddler, but it was a cultural thing. Every Cuban family did it, and it's only a few drops. I took a sip from the doll-sized coffee mug. The cup had a Cuban flag and a rooster on it, the same design as the one's my tíos had used. I was being nostalgic. These couldn't be the same ones. They were unscratched, new. I reminded myself that they were sold everywhere—Navarro drug stores, Sedano's and Presidente grocery stores. Half the homes in Hialeah had a set. The other half had the ones with the pink roses on them.

"Helado. Helado. Helado." Manny's angelic temperament was about to expire. He wanted his promised treat.

"Finish your coffee," I said to Alma. "I'll go pay so we can get out of here quicker." I took my wallet and the bill to the cash register. The woman in the tank top rang up our meal. Her Spanish had a Dominican accent. She was cute and had a bright smile, a winning combination for a barista. Someone waited their turn outside at the ventanita. One of her regulars, from the way she joked with them. I handed her

56

my debit card. She swiped the stripe, and nothing happened. She swiped it again. It was an older model credit card machine. She tried a third time.

"Un momento," she said. She went to the kitchen. I heard annoyed mumbles. A person, the owner I guessed, followed her back to the register.

"Yoli? Yolanda? Is that really you? Ay, mi madre, it is you!" I knew my face must look like that kid's from the *Home Alone* movie. Big round eyes, an oval mouth, and utter disbelief.

"Miriam? No way!"

My cousin, Yolanda, came around the counter and launched herself at me. Her hug was intense. I had to take a step backward so as not to tumble from her momentum.

"Oh my god, I haven't seen you in forever!" Yoli said.

"I know. I can't believe your parents still own this place. I thought Tío José would be retired and playing dominos all day."

"He is. It's mine now. I own it."

"No me digas. Wow. That is super."

"Gracias, gracias." Yoli looked me up and down like she was trying to memorize me in case it was another eighteen years until our next reunion. "Chica, wow, I have missed you so much!" She gave me another hug.

"So, how's your mom? Your ropa vieja tastes just like Tía's."

"It should. She made it." Yoli laughed. "She can't stay away. She's here in the mornings, helping me prep."

"¿Quién es este, mi amor? Aren't you going to introduce me?" the barista asked with her arms on the counter, leaning toward us.

Yoli caressed the woman's upper arm. "Miriam, this is my fiancée, Beatriz. Bette, this is my cousin, the one that I wasn't allowed to talk to."

Yolanda and I both frowned. So, she'd gotten the same don't-talk-to-them orders as I had. I grabbed my cousin's hand and squeezed it tightly. "I'm sorry. I could have been braver. I'm sorry I didn't talk to

you in high school and then I went away for college. I could have—
I'm sorry."

"It wasn't your fault. Or mine. Mami told me the whole story."

"You'll have to tell me the details. ¿Qué pasó? What was the fight
about?" I asked. My dad had refused to explain. It was like a cleaver
to a chicken's neck. One moment we were a whole family, and the
next, we were missing a vital part. I sensed my son and Alma beside
me and introduced them to Yoli and Bette. My cousin and her girlfriend gushed about his good looks.

"Mami, carro." Manny wanted to get to the car. My family
reunion would have to be postponed for another day. Yoli wouldn't let
me pay for lunch. I thanked her and congratulated her on the restaurant and her engagement. We exchanged phone numbers and promised to catch up electronically. In the car, en route to Carvel for
Manny's ice cream, Miriam asked me if I'd known my cousin was
gay. I hadn't.

"Could that have been what the family fight was about?" Alma
asked.

"No, I don't think so. Papi is conservative, but not like that." I
adjusted my sunglasses and brushed a clump of hair from my forehead. "God, I hope not." Could that have been what it was? If so, that
was stupid. The anger and hurt I'd felt as a teenager surfaced. I
thought back to that time. "No. I don't think so. A gay couple lived
in 3C, and I don't remember Papi having a problem with them. He
was in and out of their apartment plenty of times to fix plumbing and
things. I would've heard something if he was homophobic." I'd ask
Yoli when we talked next. She was the only family I had in Miami,
and I wasn't going to lose her because of my dad, not again.

Chapter Ten

"Look at the time. I took your whole day. Please tell me you didn't lose a sale because of me. I'd hate myself."

"Cálmate. My assistant has been updating me by text. Most of my showings are after five anyway. Don't worry. This was important to me. *You* are important to me."

"Where would I be without you?" I gave Alma a kiss on the cheek and a hug across the car console.

"You'd be renting a condo with no view, mildew, and a funny smell coming from the trash chute. Do you need help with him?" Alma motioned to the back seat.

"No, I've got it, but I'll leave his booster in your car if that's okay. I can get it later."

With key in hand, I lifted my sleeping son from his car seat and hurried into the house before he woke. I kicked off my shoes and padded to his room, where I laid him down on his blanket. He curled onto his side, still sound asleep. My fingers were crossed that he'd nap for an hour or more, which would give me time to practice what I was going to do on air. *On air!* I was going to be on live TV in less than forty-eight hours. The ropa vieja revolted in my stomach as reality hit. I gently closed the door to Manny's bedroom and headed to the kitchen.

"Where did that come from?" I stopped mid-stride, dumbstruck.

A white sofa had magically appeared in my living room. In my rush to get Manny to bed, I'd missed seeing it. It was slightly camouflaged, being white against white walls. Had Robert ordered furniture without consulting me? Doubtful since he'd hardly helped with packing or unpacking. He'd lived in the house for weeks before Manny and I arrived, and all he'd had to show for it was a toothbrush and a coffeemaker. I texted him for an answer, and he called me in reply. We hadn't spoken since yesterday afternoon. I didn't want to talk to him over the phone or have a fight about his standing me up last night. It was a conversation best had face-to-face, but I answered the call anyway.

"Hey, babe. Did you get my flowers?"

"Yes. Thank you. They were lovely." I sounded like that Nicole Kidman movie with the animatronic wives. *The Stepford Wives.* Boy, had it creeped me out. Tomas, my boyfriend in junior year, had taken me to see it on a date and joked that the woman in the film were perfect wives because a wife was supposed to be pretty and do everything her husband asked. I broke up with him a week later. Now was I turning into one?

"I'm sorry. Time got away from me. I love your chicken fricassee, babe. I'm sorry."

"You love my chicken, but do you—" I stopped myself from saying the rest: *love me?* "That's not why I texted. I wanted to ask if you had a sofa delivered while I was out."

"No, babe. It was probably Mom. You know how sweet she is. She always wants to help."

Robert was delusional, but most mama's boys were like that. He couldn't see anything ulterior or malicious in Marjory's actions.

"That reminds me. Mom asked us to family dinner tonight."

"Family dinner? Who else is coming? Do we have to go? I wanted it to be just you, me, and Manny tonight. I have some news to tell you."

"Me too. So, seven PM at Mom's. Listen, I've got to go, babe. I've got another call. Love you. Bye." My husband disconnected before I could reply. Normally, I'd have replied with besos y cariño, but just then I wanted to shout, "You can make it home on time for your mother's bland cooking, but not your wife's savory dinner?"

Let it go, Miriam. Let. It. Go. I closed my eyes, took a deep breath, and waved the negativity away. Who gives a white sofa to someone with a child? Tengo una suegra loca. Well, not completely away.

I cleared the kitchen counter, got a notepad, and began assembling the things I'd need for Friday's show. Cutting board, knife, blender, measuring cups, measuring spoons, can opener. My ingredients were simple. A whole ripe papaya, mint, a lime, and a can of condensed milk. "Do I need to add water and ice to the list?" I probably did, so I jotted that down too. I knew I didn't have any of the ingredients on hand, but I could practice what I would say and pantomime the rest. Manny and I would go to the grocery after his nap. It wasn't a far walk from the house. Nothing like the distances I'd walked in New York.

I stacked a box onto the stool and propped my phone on it, using two mugs to steady it. Then I set the stove timer for three minutes and I hit "Record."

"Hello, I have a delicious, nutritious, easy recipe for you. First slice a ripe papaya, remove the seeds, and chop it into chunks." I pretended to do it. "Next, put some ice cubes in the blender, add two cups of fruit or about half of the papaya. Zest a lime." Oh. I needed to add a zester to my list of supplies. "Cut the lime and squeeze half of it into the mixture. Next, four tablespoons of condensed milk and a splash of water. Julienne five mint leaves and throw them in. Now blend." I mimed turning on the blender and holding the top. I then poured my imaginary smoothie into an imaginary glass. *Duh.* I added glasses to the list. "Mmm, rico." I took a sip, smiled, and stopped the recording. Looking at the timer, I saw I'd barely used two minutes of my time. This was going to be impossible without the real ingredients.

"Well, let's see how bad I am." I played the video. My smile was extra cheesy. "Ay, ay, ay, Miriam, vas a cortar un dedo haciéndolo así."

My eyes had never looked at what my hands were doing. If I did it like that for real, I'd cut off a finger or two. Plus, it looked weird as hell. Robotic. Maybe I was becoming a Stepford wife after all. *Delete!*

What had I gotten myself into? It was going to be a disaster. But there was no backing out. *You're not a quitter, Miriam. Figure it out.* Maybe I could practice it on set before the show began. *That's not a bad idea. Where's that number for Ileana's assistant?* I found the card and dialed Delvis. She answered immediately and bombarded me with questions and information. What size dress did I wear? Was the recipe mine? Did I need cue cards? Did I need the stove to work? Don't wear makeup. Be at the studio at five AM sharp. Filming began at six. What ingredients did I need? She talked fast and used a lot of jargon. What was a DOP? I wrote the acronym down to google later. I gave her my list and explained how I'd be demonstrating the recipe. When I asked her if I'd have time to practice before filming, she told me I'd get a walkthrough, but not a full practice. She hung up without pleasantries.

"I think I'm in over my head," I said aloud.

"¿Parque, Mami?" Manny was up from his nap.

I hated to disappoint him, but there wouldn't be any park trip today. I'd have to make our grocery shopping entertaining. Panic tingled my skin. How was I going to get to the studio on Friday? And what was I going to do with Manny? There was no way I was going to ask my mother-in-law to babysit. And Alma had already done more than enough for me. Did UnMundo's daycare open early? I texted Delvis my question and was shocked by the answer. The child center was open twenty-four hours a day. One obstacle down, one to go. Maybe I could borrow a car? I'd figure it out. I had no other option.

A cruiser pulled into the driveway as Manny and I exited the garage with his trike.

"Pre-mo-see-ah." Manny pointed to the man getting out of the police car. He was correct. It was his father's cousin, the police officer.

"Hello, Officer Smith." I called to him.

"Good afternoon, Miriam. Call me Gordon. I'm sorry to bother you and Dougie—um, I mean Manny, but the detective here needs to ask you a few questions if that's alright."

A man in a suit stepped from the passenger's side of the car. "I'm Detective Frank Pullman. Do you mind if I ask you some questions about Sunny Weatherman?"

"Sure. I don't know what I can tell you. I didn't know her."

"Yes, but you were sitting next to her when she died. Do you mind if we do this inside?"

Detective Pullman walked toward the front door. It was an order, not a suggestion. I left Manny's trike and my insulated shopping bag in our walkway and opened the front door. Manny, fascinated with Robert's cousin, didn't bemoan our interrupted adventure. It appeared that Gordon was equally enchanted. Or perhaps Officer Gordon Smith had kids and was an involved dad. It was a sweet scene—the two of them, one big and one little on the A-B-C playmat building a tower. I wished Robert were more like his cousin Gordon.

"Mrs. Smith," Detective Pullman said.

"Quiñones-Smith. Miriam Quiñones-Smith." I sat on one corner of the sofa. I guessed it was advantageous and good timing that I had a sofa to sit on.

Detective Pullman sat opposite me on the other end. He opened his notebook, just like on the British police shows Robert used to watch before the baby came. "Can you tell me exactly what happened yesterday at the Women's Club lunch?"

It felt like I was in one of those old-timey detective films. Pullman didn't have the hat and overcoat, but he did have that world-weary air about him. Fatigued, hopeless, but on the case, nevertheless. He looked like a Black Humphrey Bogart, long face, good chin.

"Well, lunch was served, she fainted into her plate, fire rescue came quickly, they shocked her with the paddles, and then took her away in their ambulance." My hands talked as I chronicled the action.

Pullman closed his eyes and sighed softly. "Did you see Sunny Weatherman eat or drink anything?"

"No. The chicken salad had just been served, and I'm pretty sure she didn't eat any of the bread that was on the table."

"In Officer Smith's report, it said you saw her mix something into her drink? Is that correct? Can you elaborate on that for me?"

I thought about it. What had I seen? "Sunny mixed a drink powder into her water. I think it was a diet aid. My friend Alma Diaz used one just like it today at lunch."

"Alma Diaz? She was at the same table as you and Ms. Weatherman. Right?"

Oh crap. I hoped I wasn't making trouble for Alma. "Yes. She's a respected Realtor."

"I have her on my list of people to question. Can you tell me more about the drink?"

"There's not much to tell. I think she took it out of her purse. I saw her mix it. Then she drank it."

"And what is your relationship to Ms. Weatherman?"

"I don't have one. I didn't know anyone at the luncheon besides my friend Alma. I've only been in town for a few weeks."

"But your family lives in Coral Shores, is that correct?"

"My husband's family."

"I see. Alright, thank you for your time. Here's my card if you remember seeing anything else. Anything. Someone she might have talked to before lunch. Or someone giving her a pill? Prescription or OTC." The detective signaled to Gordon that they were leaving.

Prescription or over-the-counter? *They don't think this was natural. They think she was killed.* A chill ran up my spine.

Gordon high-fived Manny, and my son followed him to the door. "We'll see you all tonight at family dinner."

"Right. Family dinner." I replied. There was my answer to who would be at Marjory's family dinner. I guessed I was meeting the entire clan. "Caridad, save me."

64

Chapter Eleven

Robert, Manny, and I arrived at Marjory's ten minutes past seven. We'd walked the three blocks hand in hand, a chain of cut-out dolls. Tall-little-tall. Robert didn't mention standing me up, and I had other things on my mind. Thirty-six hours and counting until I was on TV. I wanted to tell him my exciting news, but Manny, hungry for his dad's attention, was a chatterbox. "Papi, what this?" Manny showed him the grenade-shaped seedpod from a mahogany tree. "Papi, what that?" He pointed to an orchid in bloom. "Gato. Gato. Gato," he chanted at a tuxedo cat darting under the cars in Marjory's driveway as we approached her four-column colonial.

"Promise me we can get out of here early," I said. "I feel like I haven't seen you all week."

"We'll leave immediately after dinner." Robert put his hand on the back of my head and drew me to him for a kiss. "I promise."

It was a nice kiss. I wanted it to linger a little longer, but the front door opened. Andrew, the middle brother, had a highball in his hand. "Come on in, baby brother. Mom's driving us crazy."

"What about?" Robert asked as he stepped past him and into the foyer.

"The regular—anxious for her favorite son to arrive. Hello, Miriam. You look as lovely as ever. I still don't know why you married this twerp." Andrew kissed my cheek. "Dougie!" Andrew messed Manny's hair. "Your cousins are in the den, watching a movie. Go find them."

"Oh, your girls are here?" Andrew's two daughters, Reagan, age six, and Savanah, age seven, were usually with their mother. He and his wife had a bizarre arrangement. They were basically separated but living under the same roof. I'd met Sally and their daughters only once, at Thanksgiving dinner two years ago. She seemed nice, but I felt she was there under duress.

Andrew laughed. "Mother demanded the whole family be here."

"Great." My tone lacked enthusiasm, but no one seemed to notice. "Where are the girls?" Andrew pointed at the hallway to his right. "I'll take Manny and introduce him to his cousins. He probably doesn't remember them. He was just two the last time they saw each other."

Andrew shrugged. He put his arm around Robert and tinkled the ice in his glass. "Come on, baby brother, I need a refill."

The girls were watching *Mira, Royal Detective*, a Disney Jr. show. I occasionally let Manny watch the Spanish language version, *Mira, La Detective del Reino*, on Disney Latino. He joined them on the floor and instantly fell under the spell of the colorful animation. A twinge of fear squeezed my heart. English-language kid shows were ubiquitous. I didn't want him to lose his Spanish.

"Las abuelitas del daycare will be good for him," I reassured myself.

"And good for you."

I startled at the voice that came from behind the door. Sally, the girl's mother, sat in a wingback leather chair in the corner of the room, out of my view.

"I'm hiding," she said.

"From who?"

"From everyone, but mostly Marjory," she whispered.

"Oh . . ." Not knowing Sally well enough, I didn't want to stick my foot in my mouth by saying something mean. She was an outsider to the Smiths, like me, but that didn't automatically put us on the same team.

"I've used all my get-out-of-jail-free cards." Sally approached me and gave me a hug. "If I were you, I would've stayed in New York. Ha-um-ha." Her laugh was sardonic. "Girls, be sweet to your little cousin. Remember, he's new here. Savanah?"

"Yes, ma'am." Savanah moved to the other side of Manny and patted his back. She said something to make him giggle.

"They'll be fine," Sally said. "Us, on the other hand, I'm not so sure." We exited the den and headed toward the back of the house. "Shields up."

The Smith family men were gathered in the lounge. William Sr., my father-in-law, was conversing with Andrew. Cousin Gordon, out of uniform, was at the bar making a drink with Robert. The French doors that led to the garden were open. I saw Robert's eldest brother, Bill, sometimes called Junior, smoking on the veranda. He was with a blonde woman whose back was toward us. His latest girlfriend? Junior was twice divorced.

"There's my gorgeous wife," Robert said to Gordon.

"Nice to see you again, Miriam. Where's Manny? I brought him a little gift," Gordon said.

"Oh, how sweet. He's watching TV with Reagan and Savanah," I replied.

"Okay, well, I'll save it until after dinner. I think he's going to love it. It's a police car! The sirens work and everything." Gordon was beside himself with glee.

Robert slapped his cousin on the back. "Ladies, something to drink? Sally, you're a vodka tonic, right?"

"Not tonight, Bobby. White wine is fine," Sally said.

"Babe? White wine?" Robert uncorked a bottle of pinot grigio that was in a champagne bucket. He poured two glasses and gave Sally hers. Handing me mine, he leaned in and kissed me on the neck just below my ear. "I love you," he whispered. I got goose bumps. My

Roberto was back. He was acting more like the husband I'd had in New York and less like the new one that golfed, missed dinner, and ignored his wife.

The four of us took our drinks and sat. Gordon and Sally shared the loveseat. Robert sat in an armchair, and I perched on the matching ottoman. Sally asked how we were coming along with the unpacking. I was about to answer when Bill and his date stepped in from the porch.

"What is she doing here?" I asked, my mouth being faster than my brain, again.

Sally whipped her head to see who'd caused my outburst. "So, you've already met our Juliet? I'm sorry."

Robert jumped from his seat to refill Juliet's glass and knocked my elbow with his knee, causing my wine to splash. My warming feelings toward him went cold. What was she doing here? She wasn't family. And what was going on with my husband?

"Dinner is almost ready," Marjory called from the large passthrough opening that linked the kitchen with the lounge. She had on an apron embroidered with an orchid and "Coral Shores Women's Club" in cursive below it. "Sally. Miriam. Help me serve."

Sally and I looked at each other, then we each scanned the room. Under her breath, Sally said, "Time warp 1952. Women in the kitchen."

I was liking Sally more and more.

Even though Marjory's yellow oak kitchen was large, I felt claustrophobic. The air was warm and filled with scents. The Formica island was at capacity with tinfoiled dishes. My mother-in-law unwrapped them with antagonism. She took no pleasure in cooking. It was a duty to her, not an act of love. I recognized most of the recipes from her Thanksgiving menu. A green bean casserole made with cream of mushroom soup, potatoes au gratin from a box (I saw the Betty Crocker proof on the counter.), and a broccoli-cheese bake. There was also a cold three-bean salad and a basket of rolls. Marjory gave us each

68

a set of potholders and told us to put the food on the table. When I came back for more instruction, she was filling a water pitcher. She gave it to Sally with a precise directive to fill the goblets three-fourths full.

"Miriam, get a teacup from the china cabinet," Marjory said.

"Just one?"

"I said one."

I placed an ivy-patterned cup and saucer on the counter.

"Sally, please get everyone to the table," she barked. "Thank you."

I heard bodies moving and chairs sliding.

"Here," Marjory said, transferring hot water from the kettle to a small white teapot. "Take this to Juliet."

I didn't appreciate being treated like a servant. It didn't go unnoted that Sally got a "please and thank you," and I didn't.

I swallowed my pride and put on a smile. "Are there tea bags to go with this?"

"Juliet has her own. She drinks a special tea from that swarthy doctor. Doctor Fuentiz or some such. He's one of yours."

"Excuse me?" I asked. My fake smile was gone.

"Cuban, like your people." She took a spiral-cut ham from the oven and marched into the dining room with it.

No te agites. It's not worth getting upset about. Juliet's teacup rattled in my hand. I set it on the island before I chipped it or threw it across the room. I couldn't let Marjory get under my skin. She was a control freak who hated that she hadn't been able to pick the woman her favorite son had married. Her passive-aggressive behavior was about her, not me.

"Get the children," Marjory commanded on her return to the kitchen. "I have a plate of chicken fingers in the microwave for them."

The kids were well mannered and came with me to the dining room with little resistance. Manny held Reagan's hand. The six-year-old was a fair-skinned strawberry blonde with a freckled and sun-kissed nose. Savanah, the older girl, a brunette, looked more like her father. Manny seemed to like his cousins, and they him. I sat the trio at the children's table. Besides the chicken tenders, each plate had applesauce, baby carrots, and potato chips. I wasn't a fan of kid food, but one meal wasn't going to ruin his taste buds. I began to cut Manny's chicken but stopped when he reminded me he wasn't a baby anymore. He was past the toddler choking stage. I put on a brave face and asked Savanah to help him if he needed it.

"I'm okay, Mami," he said.

"Estás bien. Bueno," I translated. Twenty minutes of English-language cartoons, and he'd already forgotten his Spanish. I sighed.

I kissed the top of his head and turned to find my seat. The eight-person table was full. Senior and Marjory were at the ends of the table. On one side, there were Junior, Juliet, and Robert, and opposite them were Sally, Gordon, and Andrew. There was no place for me.

"Miriam, take my chair. I'll sit at the kid's table," Gordon said.

"No, it's fine. It's probably better I stay with Manny anyway," I replied.

"I'll arrest you if you don't take my place." Officer Gordon Smith got a round of laughter from the others at the table.

I thanked him and slipped in between Sally and Andrew. Juliet was directly across from me. Her eyes and hands were on my husband. And not in an old-friends-who-played-sports- together kind of way. I wanted to kick Robert under the table. What was up with him? What was up with her? His *wife* was in the room.

The meal was bland and boring. There was sports talk and law firm talk. Sally kept me entertained with under-her-breath comments. Senior asked if I'd applied to teach at the University of Miami. I reported that I'd looked, but there weren't any openings. He mentioned that he knew the president of Grove College, the private institute on the edge of Coral Shores that had once been a pineapple farm. He said he'd put in a good word for me. That was kind of him, but I'd already checked. Grove College's offerings weren't wide. Unless I learned to coach basketball, I doubt they'd have a position to fit my degree.

Clink. Clink. Clink. Marjory tapped her knife on her water goblet. "Before dessert, I think we should hear Robert's big news."

"Mom," Robert said.

"Let me, Bobby," Juliet said, pushing her chair back to stand. "I'm happy to announce, finally"—she grinned in Robert's direction—"that Bobby is joining Daddy's company! He will be heading our land acquisitions and development team."

The applause and cheers that erupted from the family added to my disorientation. Robert was quitting his government job. The job that was a compromise to his save-the-environment dream, but still on the right side of good ecological practices. He was leaving it for private enterprise. My head spun.

"Dessert is my Robert's favorite, pineapple upside-down cake," Marjory proclaimed. She conscripted Sally to clear the plates. The children were given ice-cream sandwiches. Marjory made a big deal of cutting a large piece of cake for her son. I wanted to scream that pineapple upside-down cake wasn't his favorite. His favorite dessert was my flan de calabaza. But instead, I pushed the sticky cake around my plate and counted the seconds until we could leave.

As soon as the last bite was eaten and Senior ordained it time for brandy, I pulled Robert aside. "It's late. You promised we'd leave after dinner."

"We will, babe. Just one drink with Dad," Robert said, kissing my cheek.

"You promised," I said to his back as he walked away from me.

I gathered Manny and had him say goodbye to his cousins. I found Sally and gave her my phone number. "Maybe we can get the kids together soon." Then, I thanked my mother-in-law for dinner and announced I had to leave as it was close to Manny's bedtime. Robert told me to wait a few minutes, but I politely refused and started for the door. Gordon came after us, holding a colorful gift bag.

"Don't forget this," Gordon said. "Can he open it now?"

"Sure, of course." My fight-or-flight instincts were teetering. If I stayed in the Smith house one moment more, I might tip over to fight mode. "But let's do it outside."

On the sidewalk, under the glow of the ornate streetlamp, Manny opened Gordon's gift. His eyes became moons and his mouth an oval. He held the ten-inch plastic police car in silent awe.

"If you press this button"—Gordon pushed a red dot on the roof of the car—"it makes sounds."

"Gracias, Pre-mo-see-ah." Manny hugged cousin Gordon's leg.

"I'm glad you like it, little buddy." He shifted his gaze from Manny to me. "Miriam, let me drive you two home."

"Thanks, but we'll be fine. It's only three blocks. And I thought you said Coral Shores was safe."

"It is, but I'm not happy with the way Aunt Marjory treated you tonight. She should have set a place for you at the table. She has more chairs. I've seen twelve, hell, sixteen people at Christmas diner. Let me make it up to you. I'll put on the flashing lights. Manny will love it."

"Alright, but no sirens. Okay?"

"Okay." Gordon rubbed his hands together. He was a big kid with a big toy. With Manny in my lap, Gordon drove slowly. The blue and white lights' strobe made it feel like we were in a parade of some sort.

Manny repeated, "Police. Police."

"I think you have a new recruit," I said.

Gordon laughed. "Listen. I'm sorry about Aunt Marjory. She gets a little . . ."

"Bossy?"

"Yeah. I was going to say a little one-track mind, but that too. She didn't mean any harm."

"Mm-hmm."

"Bobby is her baby. She's been dying for him to come back home. And him working for Pimpkin Development is her dream come true."

"Why? What's so special about the Pimpkin company? He already had a job, a good job with the county."

From Dolphin Street, Gordon turned onto Reef Drive and passed my street, Manatee. Our conversation had me too curious to point out his error.

"The Pimpkins, Smiths, and Weathermans are founding families."

"Weatherman. That's the name of the lady that died."

"Yeah, Sunny Weatherman. The Weathermans and Pimpkins were business partners. WPD. They developed Greynold Greens, Oleta Mall, and Surf Isle Condos. A bunch of big projects. Then something happened. Tom, Sunny's grandfather, and Paul, Juliet's dad, dissolved the company, or the Pimpkins bought him out or something like that. The named changed. It was all very quiet and quick. After that, the two families hardly spoke to each other. The Smiths were caught in the middle."

"Do you know why?"

"It might've had something to do with the law firm. I think each side wanted Smith and Smith to represent them, and Senior—he wasn't a judge then—said no. I get the feeling that Aunt Marjory wasn't happy about his neutrality, being that she's Paul's cousin and all."

"Wait, Marjory is related to Juliet? So, Juliet and Robert are cousins?"

"Sort of. But not close cousins, third cousins. I mean, we did tease them about being kissing cousins when they dated in high school."

"Didn't you say the families weren't talking to each other?"

"When Juliet and Robert started dating, that's when the ice melted between the families."

"What about the Weathermans? Are they forgiven too?"

"Oh no, the Weathermans and the Pimpkins can't be in the same room together. Juliet hates the Weathermans," Gordon said.

So, I hadn't misread Juliet's callous tone at the park. She really loathed Sunny. Had Juliet had anything to do with Sunny's death? Did she hate her enough to kill her? She couldn't have. She had been nowhere near our table.

"Here you are, home sweet home." Gordon cut the engine. He exited the car and opened the door for us. "Did you like riding in my police car, Manny?'

"¡Si! Gracias, Pree-mo-see-ah." My son high-fived Gordon. Next time I needed childcare, Gordon would be top of my list. He and Manny had bonded.

"Thank you for the ride home, Gordon."

"My pleasure, Miriam. I'm sorry if Aunt Marjory made you feel unwelcome. Please, don't let her get to you. She's just that way, but she doesn't mean it."

Gordon stayed until Manny and I were inside the house. He turned off the flashers and drove away.

"She doesn't mean it. She's just that way." I mulled over Gordon's words. "I'm pretty sure she does mean it." Family dinner would've been very different if it had been at my parents' house. And the food would've tasted better too. I wished my parents hadn't moved to Punta Cana. The time was nine thirty PM. I could call them. I hurried Manny to bed and skipped his story time. He refused to let go of Cousin Gordon's gift and cuddled the car like a teddy bear. I snapped a picture of him and sent it to my mom. Two seconds later, my phone rang.

"Que hermoso. ¿Como esta ese nieto mío?" Mami asked about her grandson.

"Ay, Mami . . ."

"¿Qué pasa, mi'ja?" My mother knew something had me troubled.

Tears pooled in my eyes, and a raging river of words flowed from my mouth. I told it all, and she listened. Sometimes, a girl just needs her mom, even if that girl is a grown woman.

Chapter Twelve

Robert was in the kitchen with Manny. Last night's emotional download to my mother had been better than a sleeping pill. I woke up a little late but rested and refreshed.

"I made coffee. American but extra bold," Robert said, pouring me a mug. "I'm sorry about last night."

I looked him in the eyes. "You've been saying sorry a lot lately."

"I know. I'll be better. This new job—"

"Yeah, and about that new job. Why didn't you tell me you were leaving the county? Your mother knew about it before me!"

"Babe . . ." Robert tried to put his arms around me, but I fended them off. "Babe. I was going to tell. Really, I was, but things—and timing—I'm sorry. Please forgive me."

"Roberto, what is going on? Why'd you take the job? With a developer? A private developer that builds malls and condos and—and—and probably on ecologically sensitive land!" My hands flapped. I'm sure I looked like I was having a seizure.

"Babe, that's why I took the job. It's where I can do the most good. Pimpkin has been approved to build beyond the Urban Development Boundary. Practically in the Everglades. It's crazy. There's been so much loss of habitat already. I want to minimize the harm, you know?"

That was the husband I married—my Roberto. I put my hands on his face, drew him to me, and planted a big kiss on his lips.

"Beso. Beso." Manny clapped. Children sensed things. Our son was happy his parents were back to normal.

"So, I'm forgiven?" Robert wrapped me in a hug.

"Forgiven-ish."

"Hey, didn't you say you had some news?"

"It's nothing," I replied.

"Don't do that. I know you made a sacrifice moving to Miami."

"This isn't Miami." I shook my finger like a metronome.

"I know. Coral Shores isn't Miami." Robert mimicked my Cuban accent when he said Miami. "But, it's going to be great for our little family in the long run. So, tell me your news."

"I'm going to be on TV tomorrow." I weighed how much more to tell him. "I'm doing a favor for Alma. It's only a two-minute spot."

"Whoa. TV. Wow. What station?"

"The morning show on the Latin station. They needed someone to talk about tropical fruit. It's a cooking segment. The woman that normally does it is out for a few—"

"Babe, that's so cool," he interjected, not letting me finish my sentence. It was probably better that he didn't know the job was for a few months. "I'm going to tell my mom to record it." Robert unlocked his phone's screen.

Suddenly, I felt protective of the opportunity that had fallen in my lap. UnMundo was my world, and I wanted to keep it unspoiled. I didn't want anyone in his family to know about it. "No, don't." I took the phone from him. "Please don't say anything. What if I bomb? I might make a fool of myself."

"You are going to be the best substitute cooking host star ever." Robert smiled at me.

"Not if I don't practice. I need to go to the grocery store. I need papayas and limes—"

"Take the car. Go to the store while I get dressed for work. Babe, go." He pushed me out of the kitchen. "Manny will help me shave. Right, little man?"

76

Over my shoulder, I saw Robert tickle his son and pick him up like a log. It reminded me of Saturday mornings in New York. Robert and Manny would go to the Dominican bakery and buy a bizcocho de pasa, a raisin pound cake, for breakfast. Then later we'd all go to Tompkin Square Park or stroll in Chinatown.

Instead of going to the Coral Shores Publix, I drove a few miles west to shop at the Latin supermarket. Thirty minutes later, I stuffed the trunk of Robert's Prius to capacity. "Miriam, te exageraste," I said to myself. I'd overdone it. I'd gotten all the ingredients I'd need to practice my smoothie times three. And I'd purchased a yerba buena plant, a seven-quart caldero, tons of spices, fresh bread, a twenty-pound bag of rice plus a ten-cup rice cooker, and a decorative tinajón. The yerba buena, a Cuban variety of mint, and the pint-size terracotta tinajón were destined for the kitchen windowsill. The heavy aluminum stock pot was perfect for the arroz con pollo I planned to make for dinner. Everything else was—I don't know, therapy?

At home, Robert helped me unload the groceries. He grunted and hammed carrying the huge bag of rice in jest. The bags spilled vegetables and canned goods onto the counters. I placed the one with the chicken and other meats directly into the fridge.

"I'm sensing a feast in our future," he said.

"Will it get you home in time for dinner?"

"Ouch." He mocked being hit in the chest. "I promise to be home at five thirty on the dot."

"Good. Te amo."

"I love you too."

We kissed goodbye, and I waved as he drove away. Then I put away the shopping and took a moment to be grateful. "This is amazing. I can't believe this kitchen is mine. Look at all this space." I stuffed the plastic bags under the sink for use later and then cleaned the counters.

"Time to practice."

Manny played while I ran through my bit. I made three blenders full of smoothies. I had the cutting and measuring well rehearsed.

What I was saying, on the other hand, changed from one practice to the next. My script was all over the place.

"I'm going to freeze on TV. This is going to be terrible."

I filled Manny's sippy cup, the one with the silicone straw, with papaya milkshake and took a break. While he slurped, I thought about what I should say. Papaya, called fruta bomba in Cuba, is native to the tropics. I could go the historic route and mention the 1526 journal entry by the Spanish explorer Oviedo or the tale about natives curing Christopher Columbus's crew of digestion problems. This was going to be harder than I thought. I could give a lecture on the fruit's recent commercial cultivation, it's nutrition, and the folkloric medicinal uses. But condense that into a minute? No way.

"Aaaaaayyyy."

"¿Qué pasó, Mami?" Manny asked.

I looked at his cherub face. "Nada, mi amor. Nada." There was nothing wrong other than I was in over my head. Graduate school had not prepared me for television. I was not Anthony Bourdain. He mixed storytelling and food. His show was an adventure the viewer wanted to go on. Bourdain made it a shared experience.

"That's it," I shouted. I needed to share more. Make it personal. And I had the perfect story.

Manny stopped playing and stared at me. I told him his mother was a little crazy today. He accepted my diagnosis and renewed playing with Cousin Gordon's police car gift.

My phone rang. It was Alma. "Hola."

"Hola, chica. I'm in the neighborhood. Can I stop by?"

"Of course."

"Good, because I'm in your driveway."

I opened the front door for her. Alma, in a turquoise skirt with a coral shirt, barreled into my house.

"¿Un sofa? When did you get that? Not really your taste." She pointed at the lonely white couch as she sped through the living room.

"Yesterday. Marjory, I think." I trotted after my friend. "Do you want some smoothie? I have bastante. I've been practicing my recipe all morning."

"Sure."

I poured a large glass of the peachy slurry. "Tell me what you think."

"Delicious. The mint makes it." She drained half the glass.

"Okay. So what's bothering you? Something is not right."

"Did you tell the detective that I gave Sunny diet powder?" Her glass landed hard on the counter.

"What? No. No, I said you had a drink powder and that maybe that's what Sunny put in her drink. Not that it was yours or that you gave it to her—just that it looked alike. ¿Qué pasó?"

"A detective came to my office yesterday and questioned me for thirty minutes."

"He questioned me too. It's routine. I'm sure he's talking to everyone that was at the lunch. He asked you normal stuff, right?"

"He asked me if Sunny had any enemies. The answer was no. Sunny had problems, but not personality problems. She was sweet. He asked me about Stormy too. And the club members."

"That sounds like normal stuff."

"Normal, except he kept asking me about the drink powder. What color was it? What did the packet look like? What did it taste like? He was super annoying. Finally, to get rid of him, I gave him the other one that was in my purse. I was never going to use it anyway. Ayer, after I drank that one at lunch, I was jittery the rest of the day."

"Good. I mean *not* good that you didn't feel well. But good because you don't need to lose weight. You're perfect."

"Gracias, chica. This was delicious," she said, finishing her smoothie. "You are going to be espectacular, tomorrow."

"I hope so. Light a candle for me and say a prayer." I laughed.

"Oh, do you want your car seat back?" She fished her keys from her bag.

"Actually, I need a favor. Can I borrow your car tomorrow? I need to be at the studio super early in the morning."

"Claro. You know what's mine is yours. You can take the car home tonight after the seminar and then return it after your show. I don't have any appointments until after lunch tomorrow."

"The tea doctor? No me digas que you're still going to that. You just told me the drink made you sick."

"I'm not going to listen and buy. I'm going to network. And you are going with me."

"Oh shoot. I made a big deal about Roberto being home in time for dinner. I'm making arroz con pollo. You'll have to go without me. I wouldn't be ready in time. Sorry, not sorry."

"Miriam, you are going with me—too bad, so sad. Eat fast. The seminar is at seven. See you then. Adios," Alma said, blowing kisses to Manny and me. "The couch isn't bad. It needs a few accent pillows. I'll mention it to Marjory."

"Don't you dare, Alma." I raised my fist in a mock threat.

"Estoy bromeando. Just kidding." She beeped her car alarm off and waved goodbye.

Chapter Thirteen

"That looks too good to eat, babe." Robert stood behind me with his arms around my waist as I put the finishing touches on the arroz con pollo.

The red pimento strips and the green olives were laid in a compass rose. Against the deep yellow of the rice, it was beautiful. The new pot was huge. There was enough chicken and rice to feed a family triple our size. We'd be eating leftovers for a few days. I placed a folded kitchen towel on the counter and moved the heavy two-handled pot to it. I'd already set three places with plates and utensils. Robert held the stool steady as Manny climbed to his seat.

"Wait, I want a picture. I know this isn't our first meal in the house, but something about it feels special." I snapped a shot of my boys with the pot in the foreground. I took an aerial of my gorgeous dish. It looked as good as any of the Caribbean food accounts I followed on Instagram. Then I got on the other side of Manny and passed my phone to Roberto. His long arm held the camera at the right distance to get all of us in the picture. "Bella." The photos really were gorgeous. We were a handsome family. I sent the pictures to my parents before I forgot. "Okay, let's eat."

"This is delicious. You are such a good cook. How'd I get so lucky? Beautiful, smart, and a whiz in the kitchen."

I knew Robert was being especially complimentary to make up for standing me up the other night. "I appreciate the flattery, but you know you're not in the doghouse anymore."

"Guau guao," Manny said, rice falling from his mouth. The police car toy hadn't replaced his obsession with dogs. Any time he saw or heard a dog, he'd say guau guao, the Spanish version of bow-wow. I feared he was in for a childhood of heartache. I didn't know if Robert would ever change his mind about having a dog.

"Dog."

"Perro."

At least Robert and I were on the same page when it came to Manny using the proper words for things. We smiled at each other. It was nice to have him home. Parenting was a lot less lonely with him there.

"Babe, this meal deserves a real table. Why don't we go furniture shopping this weekend?"

"You aren't going golfing?" Painful memories from the last few weeks seized me, and the warming feeling of family togetherness faded.

"Sunday, but not Saturday. Saturday, I'm all yours. I know I've left the unpacking to you, and that's not fair." He wrapped his hand over mine and squeezed. "We need a dining room table and some chairs to go with that sofa. Do you like the sofa? If not, we'll buy a different one."

"Can we afford all that?" I scooped another serving of arroz onto his plate.

"Don't worry about it. Pimpkin pays well." He looked at me in earnest and I melted. That look of confidence and compassion, paired with his noble dream to save the environment, is what had made my knees buckle on our first date. Roberto was chiseled-jaw gorgeous, but his character is what I had fallen for.

"Mi amor, are you sure you haven't sold your soul?"

Ding-Dong-Dwong.

"Shoot." I checked the time. "It's Alma. I forgot to tell you. She's making me go to this talk at the fitness center." I dabbed my mouth with a napkin.

"No problem, babe," Robert said. "Manny and I can handle it. Have fun with your friend. You deserve a night out."

"I'd prefer a night in with you." I pouted and went to open the door.

I made a small plate for Alma. She ate and chatted with Robert while I freshened up. When I returned to the kitchen, my best friend and my husband were clearing dinner from the counter.

"Miriam, your arroz con pollo might be better than my abuela's. Super yummy!" Alma stole an olive from the pot before putting the lid on it.

I held the refrigerator door for her. "Take some home. Hay bastante. I'll make you a to-go," I offered.

"Later, after the talk. Let's go."

As Alma rushed me out the door, I reminded Robert to brush Manny's teeth. The drive to the fitness center was quick. Exercise classes were still going on, so the facility was buzzing with activity. We parked at the far end of the lot in the only empty space. Walking through the car park, Alma was greeted warmly by folks coming and going.

"See what I was saying? Networking. See and be seen."

"You've always loved the spotlight," I said.

"Speaking of spotlights, are you ready for your television debut tomorrow?"

"As ready as I can be. I wrote a script and memorized it. I pray I don't panic and forget it."

"Chica, if you can defend a dissertation without notes, this will be as easy as cake.

"I think the saying is 'easy as pie.'"

"Whatever,—you knew what I meant." Alma swatted me on the upper arm. "Let's find a seat on the end."

We sat in the fourth of six rows. I counted the chairs, eight in each. The forty-eight seats filled quickly, and staff brought in another two rows of chairs. Dr. Fuentes, in a white lab coat, had his back turned to the audience. He had two assistants, also in lab coats but light green. The trio had their heads together. One of the assistants broke from the huddle and began passing out pamphlets. I studied mine. It had the same origin story as the box I'd seen in Ileana Ruiz's office. The list of products was more varied than I'd anticipated. He had the diet and youth teas, but he also had ones for calm, digestion, circulation, mood, menstrual cramps, and menopause.

"You should buy that one and drink it tomorrow before the show," Alma said, pointing to the calming tea.

I read the list of ingredients. Liden flower and other natural herbs. "Pfft, what a rip-off. He's basically selling tilo for twenty-five dollars a box." Tilo was a cure-all tea that sold at any Latin grocery or pharmacy for a few bucks. Most Spanish-speaking households in South Florida had a box. It was good for nerves, sleeplessness, and supposedly blood pressure.

Juliet Pimpkin sauntered to the front and looked around the packed house with indignation. She narrowed her eyes, put on a menacing smile, and tapped the shoulder of the woman two rows ahead of me. The woman surrendered her seat without a fight. Juliet snapped her fingers to get Dr. Fuentes's attention. When he didn't jump at her beck and call, she cleared her throat and snapped again. The doctor complied. At Juliet's side, he bent to hear her, and I eavesdropped.

"You should say a few words about Sunny," Juliet said.

"No. I don't think that is a good idea," replied Dr. Fuentes, ready to leave her.

She pulled his tie, forcing him to bend again. "She was one of your best clients."

"No." The doctor jerked his tie from her grip, smoothed it, and buttoned his lab coat.

I elbowed Alma as he walked away. She was exchanging small talk with an older lady in a colorful caftan. "¿Qué?" Alma asked, annoyed.

"They're talking about Sunny," I whispered.

"Tell me later." Alma used her lips to point to the front of the room. The presentation was about to begin.

"Good evening, ladies. I'm Elliot Truman, and I'm excited to introduce you to an amazing man." Presenter Elliot looked completely different from yoga instructor Elliot. No longer in a headband, her brunette curls were loose and shiny. She wore a navy maxi dress that made her blue eyes pop and sparkle. "He uses ancient wisdom and the power of plants to stop the march of time," she continued. "His non-invasive remedy for wrinkles is truly the fountain of youth. Please welcome Dr. Mario Fuentes."

Elliot gave the podium to him and sat in a spot that was saved for her. It looked like the women to either side of her were the moms from the park, Pepper and Amanda.

"Thank you, Elliot." Dr. Fuentes was short, with light brown skin and wavy black hair. He had a thick mustache that covered most of his top lip, and his bottom teeth were crowded. "It is my honor to be here. I first discovered the power of herbs when I lived with the Kuripako in the rainforest of Brazil. The women in the tribe had skin like babies. No wrinkles. It was a miracle. I asked them to teach me their secret. Today, I share that secret with you."

The packed room burst into applause. Who would have guessed that the elite of Coral Shores would crowd into a gymnasium to hear a "swarthy" doctor? I looked around. Besides the doctor and his assistants, Alma and I were the only people with a warmer tint to our skin. Fuentes continued to talk as one of his assistants dimmed the lights. The other controlled the pace of the PowerPoint slides. The audience oohed and ahhed at every before and after picture. He signaled for the lights and asked Elliot to give her testimonial. She told her story fast and danced from foot to foot like she had to go to the bathroom.

When she finished, she moved to the side, crossed her wrists over her chest, and braced herself against the wall.

"Qué raro," I said. Alma wrinkled her nose, and I pointed to Elliot with my chin. "Weird that she has no problem teaching yoga, but here she gets stage fright."

"Public speaking is people's number-one fear." Alma made an it-happens face.

During Amanda's testimonial, I watched Elliot as she took several deep breaths to calm herself. She clapped for Amanda when she mentioned her Miami stand-up paddling race win. Amanda credited Fuentes's Energy Tea for her first-place stamina. Pepper went next. I liked her. She seemed genuinely nice, and Manny had played well with her daughter. She talked about Fuentes's Mother's Milk Tea saving her sanity when she had trouble breastfeeding. We heard two more stories. Each lady praised Dr. Fuentes for his miracle teas that had changed her life.

"This is like a cult," I whispered to Alma. I feared the group might link their arms and start swaying next. I looked around the room again. In the back, near the door, I spotted Frank Pullman. He hadn't been there a moment ago. He stuck out for two reasons. He was a man, and he was Black. "Is that the detective who spoke to you?"

Alma turned to look. "Si, that's him."

"I wonder what he's doing here?"

She was about to share her thoughts with me when we got aggressively shushed by the lady behind us. Alma's chest moved with a stifled giggle as she gave me a caught-by-the-teacher look.

"Ladies, thank you for sharing your stories." Dr. Fuentes gave a measured clap. He reclaimed the spotlight and the mic. "And thank you to Señora Elliot for inviting me and organizing tonight's seminar." He paused for Elliot to take a bow. The audience twisted in their seats and looked for her, but she wasn't in the room. "I have a gift for each of you, a free sample of my Calming Tea. Please, come to the front and get your gift. If you have questions, my assistants can answer them. We take checks, cash, and credit cards. Tonight, we have a special: buy three, get one free."

The audience charged to the display tables, and a checkout line formed rapidly.

"I should say hello to a few people. Can you go get our samples?" Alma asked.

"Seriously?"

"Sí. Gratis is gratis."

She had a point. Free is free, and something to soothe my nerves tomorrow might not be a bad idea. I got in line. People were taking the four-for-three deal, and the assistants in the green coats were busy. I scanned the room. Detective Pullman was still by the door, but his I'm-just-observing mood had morphed into an I'm-a-dog-on-the-hunt vibe. His eyes were fixed on the doctor. Fuentes was talking to Juliet Pimpkin.

"That woman is everywhere," I said.

"Who?" the lady in front of me asked. When she turned toward me, I recognized her as the mother of the dead lady.

"Oops, I didn't mean to say that out loud."

Stormy Weatherman laughed and introduced herself. She was chicly dressed. If I hadn't been a witness to her daughter's death, I'd have never guessed in a million years that she was in mourning.

"I'm so sorry for your loss."

"Thank you, dear. We all knew it was coming sooner than later." Stormy sighed. "This gentleman certainly didn't help with her longevity."

"Excuse me, what do you mean?"

"Sunny was his patient." She wrapped a long, beaded necklace around her finger as she talked. "I don't know if it was him or her, but she stopped eating and only drank tea. Youth tea, calming tea, energizing—he even made her a special blend that was supposed to curb her drug cravings. I'm not saying he killed her, but a tea to stimulate her appetite would have been helpful." She sighed again and dropped the beads from her finger.

"So, if you don't mind me asking, why are you here? You aren't angry with him?"

"Oh no, dear, she did it to herself. It's been years in the making." With a wave of her hand, Stormy pushed away the mere idea of anger. "I'm here for his youth tea. It really does work."

"Aaaaaaaa!" Someone screamed from the hallway. "Call nine-one-one!"

Chapter Fourteen

Several attendees went to investigate the scream, and I followed them. With all the commotion, it was hard to see what had happened. There were gasps of shock and worry, but no one said who was in trouble.

"Excuse me. Police. Let me through," Detective Pullman said.

A cluster of people parted for him, and I caught a glimpse of a navy dress on the floor. I wedged my way further to the front. It was Elliot. She was on the floor, with a spilled thermos beside her. Detective Pullman put his fingers on her neck, then he put his ear to her mouth.

"¿Qué pasó?" Alma had found her way to me. She put her hands on my shoulders and got on her tiptoes.

"It's Elliot Truman. She passed out or something."

"Ay, ay, ay. Is she okay?"

"I don't know. The detective checked her pulse and looks worried."

"Maybe she's pregnant, again, la pobrecita."

"What do you mean?"

"She can't stay pregnant. She's had un montón de miscarriages, and each time she had fainting spells like this."

I wondered how many was a lot. One miscarriage was one too many, but still, it might explain why she was unconscious on the floor. Maybe what I'd thought was stage fright was actually something else.

A squad of EMTs arrived. Detective Pullman said something to one of them, then corralled the onlookers into the assembly room.

"Ladies, please return to your seats. I know everyone is concerned, but let's give them space to do their job." Pullman stood at the door. "Please do not leave this room. I will update you as to her condition in just a moment." The detective closed the door.

Murmurs and speculation filled the room. Fuentes, still in the front of the room conversing with Juliet, grew increasingly agitated. He looked back and forth from the audience to the few customers making purchases. He left Juliet and walked to the microphone. He cleared his throat. "I'm sure Señora Elliot is going to be fine. Don't forget our buy three get one free offer." He went to the display table. "For the low price of seventy-five dollars, you get four boxes of tea, any combination." Fuentes demonstrated the options.

The door opened, and Detective Pullman asked, "Who came with Ms. Truman this evening?" Amanda and Pepper raised their hands. "May I have a word with you?" He motioned for them to exit the room.

Behind Detective Pullman, I could see the EMTs leaving the building. They did not have a stretcher. Did that mean Elliot was okay?

"Excuse me, Detective," I said. "Is she alright?"

"I'll be back to answer that question." He let Amanda and Pepper exit to the hall, then closed the door. We were sequestered again.

One of the two women wailed.

"That doesn't sound good." I looked at Alma.

"You're right. Eso no suena bien."

About five minutes later, the detective opened the door. In the background, I could see Amanda and Pepper in tears, hugging each other. Something was not right.

"I am sorry to inform you that Ms. Truman is dead."

There was a collective gasp of disbelief.

"Her next of kin has been notified and will be here shortly. Please do not leave the room. We will need to ask each of you a few questions." He shut the door.

"Questions? Is this a crime scene?" someone yelled.

"She was killed?" a high-pitched voice asked.

"I'm calling the chief of police," said a lady in a paisley caftan.

"I'm calling the mayor!" a strong and loud voice proclaimed.

"Murder in Coral Shores?" several people murmured.

Dismay and fear echoed through the room.

Alma and I made the sign of the cross. I said a prayer for Elliot's soul and her family. I'd never experienced a single death, much less a suspicious one, in all the time I'd lived in "dangerous" New York. Here I was in little Coral Shores, and I'd been in the same room with two. What was going on? Was it something in the water?

I called Robert to let him know I'd be a little late getting home but didn't tell him why. While we waited to be questioned, Alma answered emails on her phone. The room was solemn. Most people had their heads in their phones or were talking to one another quietly. I watched the doctor's staff dismantle their display and pack it up. Fuentes paced and mumbled to himself, occasionally looking in Juliet's direction. Juliet had her legs crossed and seemed to be unbothered by the evening's turn of events.

"Isn't Elliot one of Juliet's friends?" I asked Alma.

"Juliet doesn't really have friends." Alma turned off her phone and looked at me. "She has a social circle. You are either in her circle or out of her circle."

"So, Elliot was in her circle, right?"

Alma nodded.

"So, why isn't she more upset? I mean, look at her. She looks like she is at a picnic or at the mall. Not one tear."

Alma grinned. "Botox."

"Really?"

She shrugged. "Probably. Anyway, crying would cause wrinkles. And wrinkles are Juliet's enemy."

"I like her less and less, and I don't even know her. How can Roberto be friends with her? Was she ever a nice person?"

"From what I've heard, she was pretty and popular in high school. And sometimes that makes people a 'B' word that rhymes with 'witch.' Not in my case, of course. I was both, and I stayed nice." Alma gave me a cheeky smile.

"Did I tell you she was at the Smith family dinner last night?"

Before I could tell her the story, a police officer came in and began taking everyone's name and phone number. Another officer took people, singly and in pairs, out of the room. After about an hour, Alma and I were called. We were led to a bank of chairs in the lobby, where Detective Pullman was waiting.

"Thank you for your patience. This shouldn't take long."

I heard him talking, but his words didn't register. My eyes and mind were on the crime scene techs. One of them was putting Elliot's thermos into an evidence bag. The liquid from the thermos was collected on swabs and placed in tubes. There was a blanket over Elliot's body, but the hem of her blue maxi dress could still be seen.

"Ms. Quiñones, could you please answer the question?"

"Huh?"

"Ms. Quiñones, did you speak with Ms. Truman this evening?"

I blinked and brought my attention to the detective. "No. I didn't speak to her, but I did notice that she didn't look well."

"Really? When was that?"

I proceeded to tell the detective about what I thought was Elliot having a case of public speaking anxiety. Alma concurred with my description.

He asked a few more questions, then let us go. It was past ten PM when I dropped Alma at her house. I thanked her for letting me borrow the car. She told me I was going to be great tomorrow. In less than seven hours, I needed to be at the studio. In less than ten hours, I'd be on TV. My stomach did somersaults. Dr. Fuentes's calming tea was sounding more and more like a good idea. But then again, maybe not. Dead calm was too calm. Two people had just died, and both were tea drinkers. No thanks. I'd stick to café.

Chapter Fifteen

I buckled my sleeping son into his car seat at four forty-five AM. Thank goodness there wasn't any traffic at that hour, because I was fifteen minutes behind schedule. It was a Latin cable network, but I suspected they didn't run on Latin time. I laughed to myself, remembering my quince. I'd made my mother put six PM on the invitations so that everyone would be there at the correct time, seven PM. It worked for the most part. All the Cubans and Latins were "on time" to the banquet hall. My two American friends arrived early at five forty-five, and my Haitian friend, Marie, split the difference.

"I should find out if Marie still lives in Miami" I said out loud, then checked the rearview mirror. My talking hadn't roused Manny.

At the UnMundo gate, I put my "Friday Only" parking pass on the dash and found a space near the door. The front desk attendant saw me struggling to carry my forty-pound, PJ-clad child, and opened the doors for me. She helped me get him to the daycare center and showed me the way to the studio. I asked a man with a tool belt for Delvis, the production assistant, and he pointed to a short twenty-something-year-old with blue hair and tattoos.

"Hola, soy Miriam Quiñones. Estoy aquí para la Cocina Caribeña," I explained.

"Good," she answered in English. "You need makeup and wardrobe. Where's your script? I need it for the teleprompter. Have you ever used a teleprompter?"

"Um . . . um . . . I'm new to this. I've never been on camera."

Delvis tilted her head back and huffed. "Yeah. I forgot. Okay, let's do a walkthrough."

Stepping over cables and weaving around production crew, I tried to keep pace with Delvis. She led me to a dark set that lit up as soon as she gave orders into her headset. The Cocina Caribeña kitchen counter was white. It had a sink and glass stovetop with a prep area between them. The backdrop was white, with a sunburst of orange and lime dots above the segment's title in green letters, with palm trees like parentheses.

"Stand on the X," Delvis said. She moved me to stand over the neon pink tape on the floor. "Look at this camera. Someone will be here giving you a countdown like this." She spread her hand and went from five fingers to one. "If they make this sign, that means you need to hurry up. You are out of time." She turned her hands around each other like a spinning wheel. "If they make this sign, then you finished too early and need to fill in time." Using both hands, she stretched the air. "Your ingredients are under the counter."

I opened the refrigerated drawer and saw a papaya whole and chunked. There were two limes and a container of mint leaves. "What about the ice and condensed milk?"

Delvis bent and retrieved several items from a bottom shelf. "Arrange the space the way you want it. I'll be back in two minutes." She left, talking into her headset.

There was a second drawer, which I opened. Inside, I saw a bowl of ice and several packages of frozen fruit puree. The blender on the counter was green, as were all the utensil handles. I placed a knife and a spoon on the cutting board. Reviewing my list, I realized there were still a few things missing. I needed serving glasses and a zester, which I found after a quick search.

"Okay, time for wardrobe and makeup." Delvis materialized by my side.

"I haven't gotten to practice." I fanned my index card notes at her.

"So, you do have a script? I'll take those." She plucked them out of my hands and took off. I trotted after her. She left me in the wardrobe department, where I was given a scoop-neck T-shirt embroidered with the segment's logo. A small microphone was wired under my shirt and taped to my chest. Since no one would see me from the waist down, I was told that my jeans were fine but that next time, I should wear white pants or shorts in case Ileana called me over to the couch. A wardrobe assistant shuttled me to the makeup room, where my hair was styled with product. There was a monitor mounted to the wall. *La Tacita* was live.

"You're sweating. Stop sweating." The woman doing my makeup clipped a fan to the chair arm. Face powder flew into my nostrils, and I sneezed. "No sneezing." She handed me a Kleenex.

For the next half hour, I watched and listened to the show, trying not to sweat or sneeze. It was interesting to see Ileana in action. Her on-air personality was bubbly. She joked with the meteorologist and the traffic reporter. When the show switched to the news anchor giving updates, someone would rush on stage and touch up her makeup. The entertainment reporter was almost like a cohost who sat on the sofa with Ileana for his bit. The two gossiped about a starlet caught by paparazzi sunbathing topless on her reggaeton boyfriend's boat that past weekend in Vieques. When they broke for commercials, Ileana teased the viewers with what was still to come.

"No se vaya. Cuando regresemos del break, tendremos al doctor especialista en pérdida de peso, Dr. Mario Fuentes y el segmento Cocina Caribeña."

"I love him. Have you tried his tea? I lost fifteen pounds in two weeks." The makeup artist removed the protective tissue from my neck and T-shirt. She showed me to another chair and wished me luck.

Ileana's announcement that I was up soon made my heart flutter at hummingbird speed. I was going to be on live TV in a few minutes. Wiping my sweaty palms on my jeans, I asked where I could stow my purse. The person pointed to a row of lockers, and I found the one labeled with the show's name. Before putting my bag in the locker, I checked my phone. On vibrate and in my purse, I'd missed Alma's barrage of motivational messages and well wishes. I took a selfie giving a thumbs-up, and sent it to her. It was fake bravado.

"Miriam, time to get on set," Delvis said. She waved me out of the room, and I followed her. She put me on the pink X and left me.

My kitchen set was dead. The crew, cameras, and action were thirty feet away on the main stage. I watched Ileana interview Dr. Fuentes. I couldn't hear well, but I could see that the conversation was lively. A parade of women in bikinis walked on the stage. One by one, they stood in front of a green screen.

"Hey, are you ready? You have about one minute." Delvis was back by my side.

"Why are those women in front of that green screen?"

"The graphics operator will drop in a before picture. Get your ingredients ready. Don't forget to plug our sponsor, Arboleda de Osain."

"Sponsor? What am I supposed to do? No one told me about that."

"Shh!" A sound tech quieted me before he checked my microphone's battery pack and turned it on. The kitchen set perked to life. Someone was behind the camera. A tall guy held a long stick with a furry mike dangling from it. Several others milled around with tablets and headsets.

"Miriam, remember to watch for the countdown. Look here." Delvis pointed to a monitor. "This is your prompter. I typed your cards into it."

I covered my chest mic with my hand, and a guy with headphones gave me an angry look. "Can I have my index cards back?" I whispered at Delvis.

"No. No cards on set. Trust me. They're all on the prompter. You are going to be fine. Just read the prompter."

There was no time to argue with her. The headphone guy, still angry, motioned for me to uncover the mic. The teleprompter screen turned on, and a woman squatted beneath it with her hand up for the countdown. I heard a muffled version of the segment's theme music, and suddenly I was live.

"Buenos días. Soy Miriam Quiñones y hoy yo voy a enseñarte a cómo hacer un batido fresco, saludable, y delicioso." I'd practiced that line so many times that I didn't have a problem reading it from the screen. It was all the words after it that got me tongue-tied. The next minutes were a herky-jerky blur that felt painstakingly slow and race-car fast all at the same time.

Delvis hadn't told me I was supposed to hold up the packet of pureed fruit and thank the sponsor, but she'd put it into the teleprompter. "If you can't find fresh fruit, then use frozen fresh fruit from Arboleda de Osain." I fumbled getting the packet and stumbled over the sponsor's name. Then I had trouble opening the can of condensed milk and spilled a third of it on the counter. I almost zested my thumb instead of the lime in my hand because my eyes were glued to the teleprompter. My poignant Anthony Bourdain–type story about picking papayas with my abuelos in Cuba the summer I was seven was probably lost since I told it while the blender whirled. Finally, the teleprompter went blank, the theme music played, and the woman under it said, "And you're out." I'm sure the last image the viewers saw was me frozen on stage with a dripping glass of pastel orange smoothie.

The sound guy unplugged my mic from its battery pack and told me to return the unit to wardrobe. The crew moved back to the main set, but Delvis stayed. She took the glass from my hand and patted me on the back. "Not bad for your first time. Hang around until the show finishes. Ileana will want to talk to you." Delvis left me on set and went to her next task.

My feet were lead, and my legs were jelly as I convinced myself that Leana was probably going to fire me. To stop my emotional breakdown, I went to see my son and was surprised to find him awake and eating breakfast: Mickey Mouse Eggos.

"¡Mami!" Manny shouted.

I knelt beside the low table. "Hola, mi príncipe."

"Bigote." He laughed and put his syrup-sticky fingers on my mouth.

I'd walked the halls of UnMundo with a milk mustache. I just kept embarrassing myself. Using Manny's napkin, I cleaned my face and tried to laugh it off. One of the abuelitas, Rosario, offered me un cafecito. She told me she'd seen me on the show and liked my story. How had she heard me over the blender and the playroom noise? I looked at the triptych of televisions above the hallway windows. One had the network's program schedule, one had the names of the children in care, and the middle screen played the channel with closed caption. Maybe I hadn't goofed my television debut entirely.

I drank my coffee and vacantly stared out the windows. Mario Fuentes and his entourage of bathing suit models entered the hallway. He was stopped by a woman with a staff ID. She was gushing over him like he was a movie star. The doctor gobbled it up. He called to one of the women in his group, and moments later, a box of tea appeared in his hands.

"¿Si me permites?" Rosario asked.

I didn't know what she was asking permission to do, but I nodded an "of course." She waddled to the window, tapped, waved, and made prayer hands. The doctor met her at the daycare door. Hands were held, kisses were given, and I swore I saw him anoint her forehead like he was the pope. Rosario encouraged him to step further into the center while she went to look for something. He was a few feet from me. He looked unnatural. There were dark hollows under his cheekbones, and his lips were very red. I realized he still had on his makeup.

"Uh, do I look like that?" I said.

"¿Perdón?" Dr. Fuentes asked.

I needed to learn to keep my inner thoughts silent. "Sorry, I wasn't talking to you."

"You look familiar," he said, not looking at my face, but at my diamond wedding ring. "Are you a private client?"

"No. But I was at your event last night in Coral Shores. The one where a woman di—" I looked at Manny and chose a different word. "Collapsed." My son took his paper plate and cup to the trash can. He left the boring adults and went to play.

"Ahh, yes. Very sad." The doctor searched the room for Rosario.

"Elliot Truman. She introduced you. She's a longtime client of yours. What were you treating her for?" I remembered what Alma said about Elliot's miscarriages and took a chance. "Infertility?"

"Huh? Um . . . I didn't know her." The doctor twitched and rubbed his nose. Psychology 101 had been one of my required undergrad courses. In week one, we learned that people touched their faces when they lied. Dr. Fuentes was lying, and I wanted to know why. He avoided further interrogation thanks to Rosario and two other workers who wanted a picture. She handed me the phone, and I took several shots for them. The ladies asked for individual photos with him, but he said he was late for an appointment. He couldn't get out of the room quick enough.

I returned Rosario's phone to her, and she asked if I wanted to see the other photos. When she opened the cupboard, I noticed that the interior doors were papered with pictures. It seemed every notable persona that passed the daycare center's windows had to pay the abuelita toll. I recognized Gloria Estefan, Shakira, the mayor of Miami, a few famous baseball players, and the Florida International University football team's mascot, Roary the panther. The grandmothers didn't let anyone slip by them. Rosario closed the trophy gallery and attended to the parents dropping off their children. It was eight thirty AM. UnMundo's office staff was arriving, and *La Tacita* was almost over.

In the wardrobe room, I changed and docked my microphone. The wardrobe mistress reminded me to wear white pants next week. If there was a next week. I bet Ileana wanted to see me after the show so she could fire me. The makeup department was empty except for an older man asleep in a barbershop chair. His hair was in a skullcap, and an orange wig was on the vanity. He was the comedian from the late-night show. His impersonations of the world leaders were hilarious and vicious. I gave him a wide berth and got my purse from the locker. There were a ton of messages from Alma, Robert, Cousin Yoli, and my mom.

"Oh no! I forgot to tell Mami. I'm in so much trouble." I clicked on her name and read. Her message bubble filled the screen. She chastised me for not telling her. Then she told me I looked pretty. Then she asked if I'd abandoned teaching, and if so, why had I bothered going to school all those years? Then there was a crying emoji and a heart for the story I told about my summers in Cuba. "Soy una idiota." Of course, my mom was bound to see the show in the Dominican Republic. The UnMundo network aired throughout Latin America and the Spanish-speaking Caribbean.

I breezed over the other messages. Yoli cursed me like only a close cousin can and demanded I come to the diner. Robert said he was proud of me. Alma laughed at my milk mustache and let me know she'd recorded my segment.

The final message was unrelated to my television debut. It was an invitation from Pepper Hallstead, the park mom, for a playdate at her house that afternoon. She was good friends with Elliot. If Elliot had been pregnant or going through fertility treatments, a good friend would know. I wondered if that was the underlying cause of her death because two suspicious deaths within a week, both with connections to Dr. Fuentes, smelled fishy. Women barely in their thirties didn't usually drop dead.

I texted Pepper that Manny and I would see her that afternoon.

Chapter Sixteen

Pepper Hallstead's house, on Tarpon and Bay, was a two-story modern mammoth.

"It looks like a giant H," I said. The span between the two towers was bridged by a glass walkway.

"Huh, I never noticed that, but you're right." Alma idled the car in front of the Biscayne Bay boardwalk. "I sold it to them."

"Of course, you did. It's waterfront and probably over a million dollars."

"Two point seven five million."

"Wow! That's cuckoo."

"It's Salim Besson's first American project. I could sell it for almost double that now."

"Who's he?"

"A French-Arab architect. Very in demand. Unique pools and cloistered gardens are his signature." Alma popped the trunk with her key fob so I could get Manny's tricycle from it.

"Really? It looks so plain from the outside."

"It's like an oasis behind there." She pointed to a row of traveler's palms that filled the ground between the two towers like peacock tails. "Take pictures. I'd love to see what she's done to it."

"I'll try." The rubber handle of the bike raked the hatchback window and sounded like a squeegee. "Thanks for the ride." I closed Alma's trunk and got Manny from the back seat.

"Don't forget Mambo-cise tomorrow at eight," Alma said as she drove off.

"Okay, hasta mañana." I waved goodbye to her. Manny sat on his push-bike and we crossed the street to Pepper's house.

Pepper and her daughter Sophia greeted us. While the kids played under the watchful eye of Pepper's live-in helper, I got the grand tour. The first floor was stylish with a muted color scheme and metal accents. Upstairs the colors in the four bedrooms were bolder. The master had the bay view.

"We can see the sunrise from bed," Pepper said.

"What an amazing way to wake up. I bet it's beautiful." I looked out the window at the boardwalk. A teenage couple kissing at the rail startled when a dachshund sniffed their ankles.

"But wait until you see the pool. That's the real reason we bought the house." In the hall, Pepper opened the door to the sky bridge that linked the towers. "Come on."

"It's glass?! Is it safe?"

"Of course it's safe, silly." Pepper took a step onto the see-through walkway. "I was scared my first time, too. And I completely freaked out the first time Sophia ran across it without me. But trust me, what's on the other side is amazing."

"What's underneath it is pretty amazing," I said, referring to the garden below my feet. I could see rain forest sized elephant ear plants and ferns.

"Yeah, but don't look down. That will make it scarier."

I inched my way across the bridge and sighed with relief when my feet touched concrete. "Wow! I don't think I've ever seen a rooftop pool in a house."

"I know. It blew me away, too. Sometimes I still can't believe that a farm girl from Guthrie, Oklahoma, gets to live here." Pepper twirled with her arms spread. I swear I heard, "The hills are alive with the sound of music."

"Oklahoma? Is your husband from there as well?" A breeze swept in through the long rectangular opening in the wall.

"No. Mike's from here. We met at a conference in Tulsa. That's a story! I only tell it after a couple of glasses of pinot grigio." She cupped her hand over her mouth. "It's a little 'R' rated." She fanned herself. "Come on. I'll show you the garden."

We walked down a spiral staircase. I was happy I didn't have to cross the glass bridge again. The garden felt like the property of a five-star hotel. A waterfall cascaded fifteen feet from a slit in the wall that was the pool's edge. There were teak lounge chairs and a long table with huge pillar candles for alfresco dining. The wall opposite the fountain was a living wall of plants. The Pothos vines hung like spiral tresses from Gaia or Pachamama. Toward the back, there was a play-set shaded by canvas sails.

"That's better than the tot lot," I said, pointing to the play structure. "If I had that in my backyard, I'd never go to the park."

"I know it's a little much. But Mike says, 'Only the best for my Sophia.' I like the park better. Kids need to meet other kids. Know what I mean? And so do the moms. I never would have met Elliot and Amanda or you if it wasn't for the park."

A sadness passed over Pepper, and I knew she was thinking about Elliot. It had been less than twenty-four hours since the death of her friend. I bet it didn't feel real yet. Death never does until the funeral. "I'm sorry about your friend. I only met her a few times, but she seemed like a good person."

"She was the best. I wouldn't have survived my first year in Coral Shores if it hadn't been for her. Everyone was so mean. Worse than middle school cliques. I didn't fit in. It was terrible. Someone had a bale of hay delivered to my door with a note that said—Hayseed, go home!"

"Who would do a thing like that? That's awful."

"When it happened, I thought it might be Juliet Pimpkin. I swear I heard her call me Mrs. Hayseed one time." Pepper sighed deeply. "Hayseed, Hallstead. I mean, sure, maybe I misheard. But, whatever, water under the bridge. We're all friends now. Hey, I'm going to get the kids and some drinks for us. Okay?"

A glass door slid open, and two streaks of giggling kid energy ran straight to the playground. I moved closer to them and sat on the love-seat that faced the seesaw. Pepper set a potbelly pitcher on the low table. Her helper put a tray with glasses and snacks for the kids next to it.

"I should have introduced you to Gabriela earlier. She's godsent." Pepper gave the young woman a side hug. "She's at Grove studying early childhood education. She's teaching Sophia Spanish. I love her like a little sister."

"Gabriela, un placer. Soy Miriam," I said.

The woman returned my smile, and we chatted in Spanish for a few seconds. From her accent, I guessed correctly that she was from Peru. Grove College had a homestay program for non-American students, and that's how she'd met the Hallsteads. The mother's helper job helped her pay for her studies.

"Gabriela, I can take it from here. It's the weekend. Go do something fun. The pool's yours if you want to invite a few friends over," Pepper said.

"Are you sure you don't want me to watch Sophia tonight? It's no problem, I don't mind."

"Go. Get out of here!" Pepper encouraged her to leave.

"Okay. I have some studying to catch up on. So, if you need me . . ."

"I know, I know. You'll be in your room."

Gabriela took some juice boxes and snacks to the kids then went into the house.

"She's very serious about her studies. She's going to be an amazing kindergarten teacher—such a sweet girl. I'm going to miss her. She graduates this year." Pepper burst into tears.

"Ay Dios, what's wrong?" I gave her a napkin from the tray.

"All the nice people are leaving me. Elliot. I can't believe she's gone. And they're saying it's suspicious. Does suspicious mean murder? Who would want to hurt Elliot?"

Pepper was near hysterics. I poured her a drink from the pitcher, put it in her hand, and stroked her back. She drank the whole glass and shakily refilled it.

"Where are my manners? I'm a terrible hostess." She poured me a glass of the fizzy apple juice colored liquid and took several ragged breaths. "I invite you to my house, and then I cry all over you. I'm sorry for dumping on you."

"You have nothing to apologize for. My goodness, you just lost a friend." I took a sip from my glass. To my surprise, it was sweet—and alcoholic. "Mmm. What's in this? I see peaches," I held the glass to the sun. Chunks of fruit had settled at the bottom.

"Peaches, Granny Smith apples, white grapes, pinot grigio, and you'll never guess what else. I call my concoction Saint-Tropez Sangria." Pepper dabbed her red eyes. The tears had stopped, but they were still close to the surface.

"Let me try." I tasted it, letting the liquid rest on my tongue for a few seconds. "Apple juice?"

Pepper shook her head. "Not juice, but apple flavored."

I put my nose close to the surface of the drink and was anointed with effervescence. "Sprite? And apple schnapps?"

"So close. You're better than my book club. None of the book club girls guessed Sprite."

"I give up. What's the apple flavor?"

"You have to promise not to tell anyone. Girl Scouts promise?" Pepper held up three fingers.

I wasn't allowed to join the Girl Scouts because of the Young Pioneers in Cuba. My mom believed clubs were fronts for indoctrination. I don't think she thought the Girl Scouts were communist, but their sash reminded her of the red pañoleta. I made the hand sign and promised anyway. "I promise not to tell."

"It's Boone's Farm Apple Blossom!" Pepper laughed at the top of her lungs. "These snobs have been drinking $3 Boone's Farm all this time. Put a fancy name on it, and you can sell a cow patty as a brownie." She finished her drink and poured a third. "More? It's five o'clock somewhere."

"No, thanks. It's a little early for me, and I skipped lunch."

"You aren't doing the Fuentes Fast, are you?"

"The tea doctor?"

"Yeah. Everyone in the book club is doing it. And most of the Friends of the Library girls. Elliot's not, but she'd been on his teas for over a year." Tears welled in her eyes. "Ellll-iii-ooooot."

I sat with Pepper and listened to her reminisce about her friendship with Elliot. After a while, the reminiscing turned to venting. The cheap wine sangria loosened her lips. It also brought out the Oklahoma farm girl. Juliet had been born with a silver spoon, and Pepper wanted to shove it where the sun don't shine. And the Garden Club ladies were cackling hens that gossiped more than the old biddies at church. She spilled the tea like a TMZ reporter and in very colorful language.

"Coral Shores is a pit of vifffffurs," Pepper slurred.

"Oh, look at the time. I need to get home. Let me find Gabriela for you."

"Don't bother her. I'm fine."

No way was I leaving a tipsy mom with a young child. I located Gabriela, made my excuses, and left. On the walk home, Manny narrated. He identified every moving creature, furry, feathered, and six legged. His zoological survey scrubbed my brain of the sordid tales Pepper had told me. Affairs. Backstabbing. Embezzling. Mafia connections. What kind of town had I moved to?

"Carros. Mira Mami, carros." Manny rocked in his push-bike. Our packed driveway had him excited. There were three cars in it. Our Prius, a red car, and "Mira Mami, policía."

I guessed the police car belonged to Cousin Gordon. It had a bike on the bike rack. The red car, a Tesla model S, had a paper license plate. Had Robert brought someone home for dinner?

"Dinner!" I had let the time get away from me. It was almost six. What was I going to make? Something easy and quick. "Picadillo."

"Yum. Cuban Sloppy Joes."

Robert's voice came from behind me, and I jumped. "Where'd you come from?"

"Saw you out the window." He kissed my neck, giving me a tickle. "Did you see my surprise?"

"I mean, I wish you'd give me a little notice, but of course, your guests can stay for dinner. I always make more than the three of us can eat."

Robert had Manny on his back. His short legs barely reached around Robert's waist. He stooped so that his son wouldn't fall. "Not Gordon. The car."

"The red car. Whose is it?" I closed the side door and followed my boys to the front of the house.

"It's mine. I mean ours." Robert shifted Manny to his hip and slid him down his leg. He took a key fob from his pocket and used it to open the door of the Tesla. Manny scrambled into the front seat.

"You bought a car? A very expensive—new—car?" My fists were on my hips, and my mouth was gaping.

"Yeah, babe. The Prius is all yours." He tossed me the keys to the Prius. I caught them and crossed my arms over my chest. "You need a car. Miami is a car city. You can't borrow Alma's car every week to get to your TV show."

"But a Tesla. How much did this cost? How can we afford it?" I tried to remember how much one cost. Robert was a fan of the luxury electric car. He constantly rattled off energy factoids about them.

"I'm not going to lie to you. It was upward of eighty thousand."

"Eighty . . . thousand."

"Babe, it's good for the environment," Robert said. He was in the driver's seat, playing race car with his son.

"So, what do you think of it? Pretty car." Gordon was suddenly a few feet away. "Pretty fast too. I caught Bobby going fifty in a thirty-five zone. I told him I'd let him off with a warning if he invited me for dinner. Hope that's okay, Miriam." Dressed in his uniform shorts and polo, he looked like a teenager, not a man with authority.

I rotated to Gordon and smiled. "Of course. You are always welcome here." Then I leaned in and hissed at my husband, "We will talk about this later."

Chapter Seventeen

"Can you believe him?" I slammed Alma's car door.
"You need two cars. And the Tesla is good for the enviro—"

"Don't you dare say the environment." I held up a finger to her. "I love the environment just as much as him, but eighty-seven thousand dollars! That's more than my parents make in a year. Where is he getting all this money? Is he borrowing it from Senior and Marjory? I hope not. My head is going to explode. I just can't. I just don't—I mean—and then we're going furniture shopping today. Where is the money coming from?"

"Chica, take a chill pill." There was a drizzle of rain, and Alma put on the windshield wipers. "This is Miami. And more importantly, this is Coral Shores. Status is everything. Robert's a Smith, and he's working for Pimpkin Development. He has to look the part." She put the car into park. We were outside the fitness center. "And de verdad, so do you. So, let's talk furniture. No Ikea. You hear me?"

"Claro que no. I was thinking El Dorado. Maybe something in red velvet." I stuck my tongue out at her.

"I thought you were serious for a second. Do you remember the lips loveseat?"

We both cackled as we dashed through the rain, remembering the tacky sofa that the furniture store had advertised when we were in high school. We'd all thought it was the coolest. One of our class-mates bragged she was getting it for her quince. I think we all hated her for a few weeks.

We reached the shelter of the center and shook the rain off us. In the lobby, someone had framed an image of Elliot in a tree pose from her yoga class flyer and placed it on a table. A memorial of flowers, hurricane candles, and Buddha beads encircled it.

"So young. Do they know the cause yet?" A middle-aged woman in black leggings and an oversized shirt gazed at Elliot's picture.

The similarly dressed woman with her put a potted orchid on the table. "No. She just collapsed."

"She was the healthiest and least stressed person I've ever met. How can that happen?"

"Maybe she had an aneurysm. My brother-in-law had one. He was cycling one minute and dead the next. No signs. Perfectly healthy." The orchid lady tsked, and the pair walked off.

"Robert's cousin let something slip last night," I said in a low volume. "It wasn't natural causes."

"Really? Did he say what it was?" Alma asked. She gripped my upper arm and pulled me closer. I shook my head.

"Excuse me, coming through," said someone with their face obscured by an armful of Whole Foods bags. The person dropped their wet umbrella on the floor and put the paper bags on the memorial table.

I lunged as the orchid fell on its side, sympathy cards cascaded to the ground, and a candle toppled, splattering hot wax. "Watch what you're doing. Be careful." I righted the plant and retrieved the cards.

"Uh, who put this nonsense here?" scoffed the bag lady. It was Juliet Pimpkin. She fixed her bangs and adjusted her sunglasses.

"What's in the bags?" Alma asked.

"Not that it's any of your business, but I'm treating the staff to breakfast. Bagels, fruit salad, yogurt, juice, the usual." She kicked her umbrella under the table and lifted the grocery bags to her hips, bumping the table with her thigh in the process. Elliot's picture fell onto a bouquet of tea roses. "Oops." Juliet strode across the lobby to the fitness center's administration office.

"I swear that looked like she did that on purpose. Am I right?" I looked to Alma for validation.

"Blame it on the rain."

"Really?" I looked harshly at my friend. "That was rude. Elliot was her friend."

"Don't let her get under your skin." Alma moved toward the Mambo-cise room, and I followed her. "And don't make her an enemy. Be Swiss."

"Like chocolate?" I asked. It was an inside joke from our geography class days.

"Ha ha. Like neutral." In middle school, Alma had Switzerland confused with Sweden and Austria mixed up with Australia. I drew pictures on her map as a mnemonic device to help her study and pass the test. Switzerland was a chocolate bar. Australia was a kangaroo. Sweden was a red fish, like the candy. Austria's image was a bearded man with a cigar that looked more Castro than Freud. But, since the island's shape and location were seared into our psyches since birth, neither one of us was going to mistake Austria for Cuba.

"Is the Saturday morning class different from the Thursday one?" I asked as we walked into the almost-full room. The bamboo screen and riser in front of the mirrored wall were new.

"Not usually." Alma tossed her workout bag into the corner, and we took the last spaces in the back row.

"What's that smell? Is something burning?" There was a haze like the smoke from incenses, but it didn't smell like Nag Champa. The smell was woodsy with pine and lemon notes.

The lights dimmed, and Andes flute music started. Heads turned. Shoulders shrugged. It was a what-the-hell-is-going-on? moment. Jorge, in a sequined and feathered cape, emerged from behind the screen.

"Is this his drag show? Is he supposed to be Walter Mercado?" I asked Alma. Her eyes widened, and her mouth opened in dismay.

"Elliot Truman has moved from the earth to the heavens. To help her spirit leave, I am purifying this space with palo santo and asking the goddess of wind to help. Please join me in a mediation chant." Jorge whooshed his cape out from under him and sat cross-legged on the riser. The class followed his lead. He put a hand drum in his lap and beat a syncopated rhythm. "You may not understand the words, but try to repeat them."

"Ajalaiye, Ajalorun," he sang in Yoruba.

"¿Qué es esto un bembe con un babalao?" Alma's question was incredulous.

Jorge was calling on Oya, the orisha of wind, change, and the keeper of the graveyard keys. What was he thinking? He was tempting fate. The belief systems of the African diaspora, Santería, Ifa, Candomble, and Vodou, were ancient and sacred. I knew the seven major orishas even though I was raised Catholic. Practitioners did not make a public show of their worship. Jorge was breaking all kinds of religious rules by drumming and singing with the uninitiated.

"Peligroso," I replied. Dangerous. Very dangerous. "This doesn't feel right. I'll be back when he starts the exercise part." Alma nodded. She understood.

In the hallway, I took a breath of unscented air and leaned against the wall to wait. The door to the administration office was in my view, and staff were coming and going. Juliet's breakfast bonanza was a hit. All the folks leaving the buffet carried food and had smiles. Was Juliet being kind, or were there strings attached to her organic feast? Other than my mother-in-law, no one had a nice word to say about Juliet, and actually most had warnings.

"Hello, Ms. Quiñones."

"Uh, hello, Detective." Detective Pullman following up at a crime scene wasn't what surprised me. It was the sweatbands, Adidas, and weight belt. "You work out here?"

113

"I just joined. And you?" He indicated the administration office he'd walked out of the moment before.

"Me too. I guess. This is only my second time at Mambo-cise."

"Jorge Trujillo's class?"

Frank Pullman's tone was all business. I felt like he was interrogating me.

"Yes, and I need to get back in there." I used my thumb to point and took a step toward the class. The drumming had stopped, and the dance music had begun.

"Alright. By any chance, is Ms. Diaz with you?"

"Yeeess?"

"Okay, thank you. I'll see you soon."

I hoped not. Detectives and dentists gave me the same anxious feeling.

A few moves into the first song, and I was drenched in sweat. The class kept up the high energy moves for six songs. During the cooldown, Jorge lit another stick of wood. The melding of body order and palo santo created a funky smell. I was happy when the stretching and resting ended.

"Good job, ladies." Jorge clapped, then pressed his hands into prayer and bowed. "Namaste." More than half the class returned his greeting. "The divine in me sees the divine in you. Don't forget to buy your class package. I've extended the 'buy two, get three' another week."

"Well, that was interesting," said the lady in the green and pink geometric print leggings to her friend. "All the mumbo jumbo in the beginning."

"I know. Very witch doctor," the friend said with equal parts excitement and ridicule. "I hear he's taking over Elliot's classes." The friends left the room, mopping sweat from their upper body.

"Don't you have to be certified to teach yoga?" I asked Alma, but she was no longer by my side. She was busy showing someone a picture of a house.

"It's not on the MLS, and I already have an offer. But between you and me, I expect it to fall through, so I'm taking backups. Call me after you talk to your husband. I can show it to you this afternoon." The woman Alma was pitching took the bait, hook, line, and sinker. She was already on the phone to her husband. Alma gave her a thumbs-up and made the "call-me" sign.

"You never stop working," I said as we exited the fitness center.

"Nope." She grinned. "What did you think of the class today?"

"The Zumba part—"

"Mambo-cise." Alma wagged her finger at me and unlocked her car.

"Whatever. The dance part was great, but Jorge's drumming and singing was strange. ¿Verdad? Is he a santero? Because only a santero should be performing ritual stuff like that."

"He's into everything—tarot, angels, crystals, horoscopes . . . todo."

"You know those aren't the same thing."

"He's just being theatrical." She honked her horn and waved at the couple on the sidewalk. The men blew kisses. "I sold them the duplex on Lobster. Investment property."

"Is Jorge also into yoga?"

"Probably. Why?"

"I overheard someone say he's going to be teaching Elliot's classes." I unbuckled my seat belt.

"I guess he finally got what he wanted." She idled the car.

"What do you mean?"

"He and Elliot had a mega-fight about a year ago. Elliot's Yoga Rocks class bumped his Broadway Boogie class off the schedule. Both classes were popular, but because Elliot lived in Coral Shores, she got the time slot. That's how the village government works. Coral Shores residents get first dibs. Jorge was so mad. He didn't talk to her for months."

"Mad enough to kill her?"

"Estás loca. You've watched too many murder mysteries. He didn't kill Elliot. No one killed her. You wait and see: she was probably pregnant or doing IVF or algo así, and it made her overstress her system or something."

"Maybe. But he seemed different today, and like they say— revenge is a dish best served cold." I opened the car door.

"You're crazy." Alma rolled her eyes. "Goodbye, Jessica Fletcher."

"Ha ha." I put my fist on my hip and gave her a look. She'd loved to call me that in high school. Her Friday nights were spent at Westland Mall or with some guy at the movies, and mine were spent on my couch, watching *Murder She Wrote* reruns with my mom. Mami would make us a special snack, sometimes salty mariquitas other times sweet merenguitos. Sometimes, I'd have to translate a word or two she didn't understand. My mom loved the town more than the story. She said it was like a vacation to Maine menos el nieve y vuelo.

Alma might not see it, but I did. Coral Shores and Cabot Cove had a lot in common, namely, mysterious deaths.

Chapter Eighteen

"Get the one you want, babe." Robert massaged my shoulders. We were at our third furniture store. "If you like the blue one, get the blue one."

"Turquoise." I ran my hand over the waxed surface. "Are you sure it's not too casual? I can hear your mother saying something about it. And Alma too." With its wash of white and turquoise paint, the nine-foot table had a beachy driftwood meets distressed farmhouse feel to it. The dining room set had a bench, three side chairs, and two armchairs. A sideboard and china cabinet with matching X lattice motif completed the look. Manny vroom-vroomed his police car the length of the bench. I was sure that he liked it.

"Babe, you're the cook in the family. Get the table you like. Who cares what my mother says? If you love it, get it." Robert straddled the bench and made a roadblock. Manny drove the cruiser over his father's leg.

"You're right. I really do love it. It's big. We can finally have those dinner parties we could never have in our New York apartment. I can make paella. Can you imagine a big dish of saffron rice sitting in the middle with clams and mussels?"

"With a cream cheese flan next to it." Robert raised his eyebrows.

I looked at the price for the entire set. "Okay, wow. Maybe they have a payment plan."

Robert reached his long arm across the table and held the information card up to view. "Don't worry." He scanned the showroom for a salesperson and motioned for them to come over. "How soon can we have this delivered?"

The man tapped on his tablet. "The warehouse has it in stock. So, depending on where you live, we could have it delivered tomorrow. What's your zip code?"

Robert gave him our address.

"That address is already in our system. Have we delivered something to you recently?" The man showed us the screen. "A white sofa? Are you Mrs. Marjory Smith?"

"No, that's my mother-in-law. Speaking of which, is there any chance we can return the sofa? It's not really our style."

Steve, the salesperson, assured us an exchange could be arranged. He guided us through the multilevel store and showed us several contemporary options. We decided on a dark grey sectional sofa with clean lines. The sample room was decorated with orange and blue accents. Robert and I liked the whole look, down to the rug, coffee table, and lamps. I was speechless when Robert told Steve we'd take it all and passed him a platinum American Express card.

"Roberto, how are we affording this?" I flapped my hand at the store we'd just left and at his new Tesla.

"I've got it handled. Don't worry." He held Manny's toy as he got into the back seat.

"I am worried. We just spent over eight thousand dollars on top of your Tesla and the house. How are we affording this?"

Robert sat behind the wheel. The premium electric car's smart key fob started the engine without pressing a button. He put it into reverse and backed out.

"Babe, I can't really tell you the details. But I promise—"

"Details? Just answer me this— Is the money coming from your parents?"

"You have to trust me."

Robert took his eyes off the road for a second and glanced at me. He put his hand on my thigh and lovingly squeezed it. I wasn't soothed or convinced. He'd never lied to me before, or at least I thought he hadn't. But since moving to Coral Shores, he'd changed. My husband was keeping secrets and telling me things after the fact. He was saying out late with women—one particular woman: Juliet.

I removed his hand from my body. "Then trust me and tell me what's going on." My voice rose an octave.

"I can't. Not yet."

"Robert!" I seethed.

"Mami. No. No seas bravo con Papi," Manny interjected.

"Listen to him. Don't be mad at Daddy." Robert winked and accelerated as soon as the light turned green.

Internally, I let out a string of curses in Spanish and clamped my jaw so hard I thought I heard my teeth crack. We rarely fought. And when we did, we made a concerted effort not to do it in front of Manny. Hearing a parent yell in anger can be scary. I felt bad for letting my temper get the better of me, but not for being mad. A good marriage is built on transparency and trust. Neither of which mine had at the moment. What was going on with Robert? Did the money have something to do with Juliet and his new job? Did he take me furniture shopping out of guilt?

"Are you having an a-f-f-a-i-r?" I asked in a low and calm voice.

"Babe!" Robert whipped his head to face me. "You don't really think that, do you?" He put his eyes back on the road. "Baaabbee. Come on—me? Your Roberto?"

My phone rang. I wasn't going to answer it, but I saw it was Delvis from UnMundo. Ileana's notes on my performance had been meager. She'd said she would review it over the weekend and let me know what she wanted for the next episode. I'd done okay, but just okay. There was room for improvement.

"Hello."

"Miriam, Ileana wants you in the studio Monday," Delvis said. "We're going to prerecord your segment. She wants it five minutes long. A real dish—you know, a meal, not a drink. Got it?" Background noise obscured her next words. It sounded like she was at a patio party.

"What?"

"The story. She liked the story part. So, do more of that. Get me a list of what you need by Sunday noon. Okay?"

"Okay. Got it. Thanks." I ended the call. My conversation with Robert wasn't over, only interrupted. "Back to what we were talking about. Are you having—"

The phone rang again. This time it was Alma. I hesitated accepting the call. Robert and I weren't finished.

"Alma, can I call you back?"

"The police are here! They have a warrant!"

"A warrant? For what? What's going on?"

"I don't know, but it's not good." Her voice quivered. "There are people in blue gloves taking evidence bags out of my house. This is going to wreck my reputation. It's going to kill my business."

"Calm down." I covered the microphone. "Take me to Alma's," I said to Robert. Then, back to Alma again: "Start from the beginning. Tell me everything."

There wasn't much to tell. Officer Smith found Alma at an open house for prospective buyers. He told her she needed to follow him to her house that instant. She left her assistant in charge of the advertised event. When they arrived at Alma's, Detective Pullman was on the front step with a warrant. A team of officers searched her kitchen, her purses, and her home office.

"Your cousin is involved," I said to Robert.

We'd turned the corner and were approaching Alma's house. Neighbors were being nosy. There was a group of about ten onlookers. A man with a standard poodle with a large red bow in its coifed mane was filming. He was probably livestreaming it to the Around Town neighborhood site. My best friend was going to be the gossip of the day.

"It's not his fault. He's only doing his job," Robert said.

"Did you know about this in advance?"

"No!"

I jumped out of the car as it rolled to a stop. Alma was being escorted from her house. She wasn't in handcuffs, but it appeared she was in custody. I ran to Alma, and a female officer put her hand out to stop me.

"Sorry, ma'am. Please, no physical contact with Ms. Diaz," the female officer said.

"¿Alma, que está pasando?" I asked.

"They're arresting me," Alma replied.

"Why? On what grounds?"

"They found something."

"What?"

"I don't know."

"That's enough, Ms. Diaz. No more talking." The officer put her hand on my friend's head and guided her into the caged portion of the police cruiser. Detective Pullman got in the passenger's side.

"Llámame a un abogado," Alma ordered.

"Okay, but who? I don't know any lawyers."

"Call your brother-in-law!" The cruiser door slammed shut. The officer got behind the wheel and turned on the lights.

I watched the flashing lights fade into the horizon and couldn't believe what I'd witnessed. My friend Alma Diaz was not a criminal. There was no way she was involved in a crime.

"Get a hold of yourself, Miriam." In times of stress, I talked to myself. "There's been a mistake. You have to get to the bottom of it." I looked for Robert's cousin. He owed me an explanation.

"Gordon, what is going on? Why has my friend been arrested?" I had both fists on my hips.

"Miriam, I'm sorry, but I can't disclose the details."

"Then answer yes or no."

Gordon thought about it for a second, then nodded. "Okay. I can do that."

"Is this about Elliot?"

"No."

"Is this about Sunny?"

"Yes."

"Was Sunny murdered?"

Gordon danced from foot to foot. I rephrased the question.

"Is Alma's arrest about Sunny's death?"

"Yes."

"Do you have evidence that links Alma to Sunny?"

"Yes."

"What evidence?"

Gordon locked his lips with a make-believe key.

"Argh." I stomped my foot. "Where are they taking her?"

"I can tell you that. They are taking her to the county jail. Coral Shores doesn't have an overnight holding cell."

"Overnight! Why are they keeping her overnight? She's an upstanding citizen. There's been a mistake. Don't they release people like her on their own recognizance or something?' My hands and arms expressed my astonishment at the situation.

"The judge might give her bail at her probable cause hearing. But that won't be until tomorrow."

"What does that mean?' I made pigtails with my hair to give my hands something to do. Because what I wanted to do with them would probably get me arrested too. I wanted to beat my fists on Gordon's chest.

"Ms. Diaz will be at the downtown Miami jail until she can make bail, *if* bail is granted." Gordon made a pained it's-beyond-my-control look.

"Hey, babe. So, what happened?" Robert asked. He was on the sidewalk, holding our son's hand. Manny gripped his toy police car and broke loose for his father. He sprinted to Gordon.

"Alma is going to j-a-i-l."

"Jail?"

"Shh." I pointed to Manny. "Yes, j-a-i-l. We need to call your brother. Alma needs a lawyer."

Chapter Nineteen

The thought that my best friend had a hard bench for a bed kept me tossing and turning the whole night. I was jealous of how well Robert had slept. Like always, he was in dreamland the moment his head hit the pillow. And as soon as the alarm sounded in the morning, he was bright-eyed and cheery.

"Babe, I'm going to take Manny to Dunkin with me." Robert kissed me on my temple. "We'll be back in a few. Have a long shower and relax. Andrew's a great lawyer. He'll get Alma off."

I rubbed my eyes and turned to lie on my back. "She's not guilty."

"I meant to say *out*, not *off*. He'll get her out." Robert kissed me on the lips. "Cinnamon or chocolate?" He tugged on my blanket-covered toes as he moved away from me.

"Whichever. I don't care."

I couldn't think about food when my best friend was in jail. And coffee needed to be a priority after so few Zs. I dragged myself to the bathroom, thinking about what Alma would be getting for breakfast.

"Jailhouse food, pobrecita. Food. Oh no, I need a recipe. Delvis needs a list. What am I going to cook for the show?"

I turned the shower to hot and threw my "Anthropologists do it in the field" nightshirt into the clothes hamper. Under the rainfall showerhead, I reviewed yesterday's roller-coaster afternoon. We'd spent thousands of dollars I didn't know we had. I had confronted my husband about our suddenly flush finances, but he wouldn't tell me where he had gotten the money. Then Delvis had surprised me with her news. And immediately after that blip, Alma called. What had the police found? What possible connection was there between Sunny and Alma?

"I can't believe she is in jail." I put my head under the water and sobbed. Once I'd gotten the sorrow and fear out of my system, I turned the water to cold. "Wake up, chica. You have to help your friend."

Dressed in a pair of jean shorts and an embroidered Mexican huipil blouse, I went to the kitchen to caffeinate. While the espresso percolated, I put a mug of milk into the microwave. Anxiety warped my sense of time. The digital numbers were not counting down quickly enough. I wanted everything to be fixed, solved, handled right that second, and that was impossible. Nothing I could do in that moment would get Alma out of jail any quicker. She'd hopefully be out this afternoon. She wasn't guilty. There had been a mistake. Alma was a good person. She sponsored the village's little league, bought a table at the gala, volunteered with the Women's Club. That's where I needed to start. Someone at the Women's Club lunch must have seen something. But being new in town, who did I know that would talk to me? Pepper had drunkenly spilled some of the gossip. Officer Gordon. But he couldn't or wouldn't tell me anything. Sally?

"Sally!" I slammed the metal coffeepot down and splattered coffee on the counter. With a wet rag, I cleaned the spill. "Sally will know people."

I took my mug of café con leche into the room next to the kitchen. A soft stream of sunlight fell on the carpet from the large window in the study. The royal poinciana tree's orangey-red flowers, dotted the driveway. I heard a colony of parrots squawking. I tried to spot them in the sky but failed. Nature was a nice distraction, and I wished I could fly away from my troubles. But that wouldn't solve anything.

"Okay, Miriam, let's find that journal. And check one thing off the list."

Delvis said Ileana wanted me to demonstrate a real dish, a substantial meal. What came to my mind was the meat stew called sancocho. The recipe varied from place to place, but they all shared the same feel. Sancocho was a special occasion food. I'd done some preliminary field research, gathering stories and recipes for my book. I'd recorded them in a composition notebook that I needed to find. A Dominican woman had given me her version of the stew that she and her family made at Christmas time or whenever there was a birth in the family. It had seven types of meat in addition to corn and starch vegetables.

"I packed it with the Ortiz encyclopedia of herbs." I closed my eyes and visualized the book. "The cover is a photograph of bottles, and the spine has a yellow "Used" sticker on it."

I tilted my head, looked at the towers of book, and searched for the sticker.

"Ahh, there you are." The journal was sandwiched between the Ortiz book and Padma Lakshmi's herb and spice book. I sat on the window seat and flipped through my notes. On a stained page, I'd taped an index card with the handwritten recipe, which was mostly a list of ingredients: goat, chicken, hambone, flank steak, sausage, pork belly, ribs, calabaza, yucca, green plantains, corn on the cob. The list went on.

I noticed movement in my peripheral vision. Robert's red Tesla was pulling into the driveway. When Manny was freed from the car, he energetically pranced up the pathway and to the front door. Sugar high. How many doughnuts had he already eaten?

"¡Mami, Mami, Mami, Mami, Mami!"

"Aquí, mi amor," I called so he could follow my voice.

"¡Mami!" He made airplane arms and nose-dived to me. I got to my knees and met him in a hug. He gave me a wet smooch. His pure joy was the perfect remedy to my maudlin mood.

Robert, a few steps behind him, chuckled. "He's very excited."

"I can see! Did you save any for me, or did he eat them all?"

"We didn't go to Dunkin. I found a Haitian bakery in North Miami. I can't wait to show it to you. You'll love it, babe. They have codfish patties. I brought you some bread and a few pastries. Have you had coffee yet?"

While Robert made a pot of American coffee, I texted the list of ingredients to Delvis. She replied with a bulging eyes emoji and a thumbs-up. I'd practice the recipe while I waited for the furniture delivery. We had to call the store's warehouse at nine AM, give them our order number, and they'd tell us what stop on the day's delivery route we were. Fingers crossed they'd get to us early. I wanted those things checked off my list so I could see about my best friend.

"Do you think I can visit Alma at the j-a-i-l? Can I bring her a meal? I think her hearing isn't until the afternoon."

"I don't know, babe." Robert poured our mugs. He took a pastry from the brown paper bag and put it on a small plate. "Here, try this. I think the filling is coconut."

"You come from a family of lawyers. You're supposed to know these things, aren't you?"

"My father and brothers might, but I don't. I've never even been to the courthouse. Call Andrew and ask him. Sally would know too. She's in and out of the jail every day." Robert sat on the stool next to me.

"Really?" I took a bite of the dense sweet bread.

"Yeah, she's an advocate at some nonprofit law firm. Andrew hates it when the other side has her on their team."

"Really? I feel stupid that I didn't know that. I thought she was— well, actually, I've never thought much about it at all." There was so much to learn about Robert's family. We'd been distanced from them our entire married life. I really didn't know my in-laws at all.

"You should get to know her. I think you'd like her. She's definitely—" He brushed a crumb from my face but didn't finish his thought.

"Definitely, what?"

"Let's just say she doesn't take anyone's crap, including my mother's."

My jaw dropped. Robert admitting his mom was less than angelic? He put his fingers under my chin and closed my mouth.

"I know my mother can be pushy." He turned me to him and kissed my lips. "Don't let her get to you." He kissed me again. "Mmm, coconut."

I put my arms around his neck and threw my legs around his waist. My stool wobbled. Robert put his foot on the rung and steadied it. He stroked my hair, and we kissed. My tension evaporated with the heat of our passion. It felt like a Sunday morning in our little apartment in New York. Sundays were us time. No work or school allowed. No other commitments.

"Roberto, te amo."

"I love you too, babe. But I've gotta go." He broke our hug. "Tee time in an hour." He rubbed his lips dry. "I want to get in a few putts before we hit the greens. I don't want to embarrass myself in front of my new boss."

"Mad" was a good word for how I felt. "Peeved" was too. Robert had left me cold. He'd turned the heat on, then switched to AC in a millisecond. Golf with his new boss over romance with his wife. I called him names in my head and found my purse. There were things I had to do too. I also had a new boss.

"Vamos, Manny. Tenemos que cazar una cabra."

"Mee-mee," he bleated.

Thank goodness for my son. My mood changed instantly. His goat imitation was irresistible. On our way to the store, he performed all the farmyard sounds. I knew the Coral Shores Publix might have the pork sausage I needed, but not the goat meat. So, we went to the Caribbean butcher in North Miami. The store catered mostly to the small Jamaican population and large Haitian population in the area. The no-frills grocery, at the end of a mostly empty strip mall, was a popular place. On the wall that faced the street, there were pictures of the kinds of meats sold. Under each animal was its name in Haitian Kreyòl—goat: kabrit, chicken: poul, guinea fowl: pintade, duck: kanna, cow: bèf, fish: pwason, and pig: kochon. The mural, signed by the sign artist Serge Toussaint, was a Caribbean tradition. Vibrant street art filled the islands. It was one of the many things I loved about island life.

In the checkout line, Manny made friends with a girl about his age. She wore a frilly, bright pink dress that looked spectacular against her dark skin. Her two braids were clamped at the ends by plastic bunny barrettes. The girl's mother was also dressed well. Iglesia. It was Sunday. They were dressed for church. I needed to get back in the habit of going. Especially if we wanted Manny to attend Catholic school.

As we left the store, Manny whined that he wanted to stay and play with his new friend, Nadege. Kids never needed an excuse to engage with one another, like grown-ups did. I wanted to pick Sally's brain but felt weird about calling her since I hardly knew her. Manny and her daughters had gotten along well, and Sally had said we should get them together soon. I'd use a playdate as my excuse. Before starting the car, I called the warehouse about the furniture delivery time and was given an eleven AM to one PM window. Perfect. That gave me time to practice the stew and then eat it for lunch. I texted Sally an invitation to my house and promised her and the girls lunch. She texted back:

Great timing because I've been meaning to tell you something about your friend.

I replied with three question marks: *???*

I'll tell you in person, she texted back.

Chapter Twenty

"What's the stew called again?" Sally asked. She was dressed casually in a color-block jumper.

"San-co-cho," I said as I cut the longaniza sausage into bite-size pieces. The other meats and hambone were already in the stew pot along with the garlic, oregano, and cilantro. Next, I chopped the yucca, malanga, and calabaza.

"What kind of pumpkin is that? I've seen it in the store but have no idea how to cook it." She pointed to the rind of the dark green and light yellow–striped hard squash.

"In the Dominican Republic and Colombia, it's called auyama. In Cuba and Puerto Rico, it's calabaza. It's similar to a butternut squash. It grows all over the West Indies. Auyama is the Taino name for it." I dropped handfuls of root vegetables into the stew and covered the pot with the heavy lid. "Now we wait one hour." I cleaned my hands with the kitchen towel my mother had sent as a housewarming gift. The thin material had the cartoonish image of a big-eyed boy and girl. The boy wore a flag cap and the girl a flag dress.

"I'm so glad you invited me over today. I've wanted to get to know you better."

"Me too."

A thud came from Manny's room. Instinctually, we both tensed, set down our drinks, and headed toward the potential destruction.

"Well, no one is crying. So probably no one is hurt," Sally said.

"True." I led her to Manny's room. We stood in the doorway and looked into the room. On the floor were all of Manny's stuffed animals, his pillow, and the cushions from the loveseat. The loveseat had been our living room couch in New York. Reagan, on the bed, was about to jump onto the soft pile.

"What do you think you're doing, young lady?" Sally asked her daughter. "Are you an acrobat?" The little girl shook her head no. "Are you a trapeze artist?" The little girl shook her head and giggled. "Are you a flying squirrel?"

All three children burst into giggles and howled, "Nooooo!"

"I didn't think so. No jumping inside the house. Is that understood?" Sally said in an I-mean-it voice. She then looked at her eldest. "You know better. So do better. Got it?"

"Yes, ma'am," Savanah replied.

"Manny, tú sabes que no bricamos ni corremos en la casa," I said.

"Yo sé, Mami," Manny said.

He did know the house rules but was having too much fun to obey them. A smile passed between us. Sally and I accepted the fact that we would be repeating those words again soon.

"Thanks again for coming over on such short notice," I said as we moved to the living room. "This is the first time we've lived close to family. I'm so happy Manny will get to grow up with his cousins."

"I agree. Cousins are your first friends." Sally sat on the white sofa, her back angled to the picture window. A trio of women power-walked by. I'd seen them before, exercise buddies.

"Speaking of friends, you said you had something to tell me about Alma."

"Oh yeah. You'd better take a seat." She patted the cushion. "This might not be good news. How well do you know your friend?"

"We've been best friends since grade school. She was my maid of honor. She's Manny's godmother. I've known her forever."

"Was she a party girl in high school?"

"Alma? No! I mean, she was always a social butterfly, but, like"—
I made air quotes—'party girl,' no way."

"But you left Miami for college. You've been gone a while, right?"
Sally pursed her lips.

"Yeeeess, I guess so, but what does that have to do with
anything."

"People change." She looked me dead in the eye.

"What are you saying?"

Sally leaned in. "Cocaine."

She said it in a hushed voice that seemed to pull all the oxygen
out of the room. I sucked in air but couldn't breathe. Alma did not do
drugs. And cocaine? Not her. Not Alma. Not my best friend. I stuttered to get a thought out. "Huh?"

"That's the rumor."

"What rumor?" I asked.

Before Sally could tell me, there was the grind of brakes and the
baritone rumble of a large truck motor. Both of us looked to the window. The furniture delivery had arrived. Two men climbed down
from the high cab. One went to the back of the truck, and the one
with the clipboard and green ball cap came up my front path. The
doorbell rang when my hand was on the knob. I opened the door and
greeted the man.

"Mrs. Smith?"

I was about to correct him but realized it was fruitless. "Yes.
You've got the right house."

"It says here we are supposed to pick up a white couch?" The man
used his pen to point to the typed block of instructions on his
itinerary.

I pointed to where Sally was seated. The kids ran out of the hallway and stopped at the edge of the living room. They looked like a
pack of curious raccoons. Their hair was mussed, and they chittered
to one another.

Sally got up. "I've got this," she said to me. "Come on, wild ones. Let's get out of the way." With her arms extended, she corralled the kids. "Who wants to hear a story?" I heard all three answer enthusiastically as they retreated to Manny's room.

The delivery men tilted the sofa on its end, moved it to the opposite wall, and returned to the truck. I heard the cargo gate roll up and a pneumatic lift clank onto the asphalt. A table wrapped in plastic was carried into my house. Ball-cap guy asked where the dining room set was to go, and I pointed to the space next to the kitchen. In no time, the chairs and bench joined the table. The men moved the white sofa to the lawn and began marching the living room furniture into the house. I busied myself, freeing the chairs from their protective packing. The corner of the dining room that had been filled with boxes a few days ago was now filled with yards of industrial Saran wrap.

"Miriam?"

A chill went up my spine. That was not the voice I wanted to hear in my house. I slowly turned around.

"What is the sofa I gave you doing on the curb? You don't like it?" Marjory asked.

"Um."

"Quite a surprise to be coming back from church and see my gift thrown to the gutter for the Salvation Army."

"No! Um—"

"Well, out with it," she said.

"Excuse me, lady. Do you mind moving out of the way?" asked the delivery guy carrying an end table.

Marjory huffed but did as she was asked. "Well, what is going on here?"

"I—we—Robert—" I said.

Over Marjory's shoulder, I saw Sally and Reagan peeking from the hall. The little girl had glee in her eyes. She opened her mouth to call to her grandmother, but Sally covered it before a peep was made.

My sister-in-law shook her head at me, put a "shh" finger over her mouth, then backtracked with her daughter and vanished.

"Robert didn't think the style matched the furniture he wanted. He's arranged for it to be exchanged."

Marjory smoothed her pastel yellow dress. From her finger, she swung her key ring like a hypnotist's pocket watch. "Humph."

"It was a lovely gesture. Thank you. Un—" I stopped myself from saying "unwanted" and instead said "unexpected."

Marjory took in the new furnishings and harrumphed again. "Where is Robert?"

"He's playing golf." I balled a five-foot streamer of plastic and dug my fingernails into it.

"Oh yes, that's right. At the club, with Juliet and her father." Marjory smiled a cat-that-ate-the-canary grin.

I used the plastic in my hand as a stress ball. Robert hadn't mentioned Juliet would be part of his golf date. Lies of omission are still lies.

"I really like that girl. She's an upstanding citizen. You'd be wise to get into her circle and away from that Realtor friend of yours." Marjory moved toward the door. "Genes. You can't escape criminal genes."

"Excuse me?" I felt my brow furrow. Laser beams were probably shooting from my eyes. What was she implying about Alma?

"Mariel. Alma told me. Her parents were part of the boatlift. Castro opened the prison gates and dumped all his criminals on our shores." She stepped aside for the delivery guys carrying the rug.

"What . . .?" I began but heard Sally clear her throat. I glanced to the hallway. She was shaking her head in an exaggerated "no, don't do it" gesture. Sally stayed out of Marjory's sight and pushed Manny into the living room. I took the cue and changed my words. "What are you doing leaving without seeing your grandson?" I guided Manny toward the door. "Mi príncipe, da saludos a tu abuela."

"Grandma," Manny said. He hugged her legs, and she patted his head.

"Hello, Douglas. Have you been practicing your English?"

"Yes, Grandma." Manny smiled with pride.

"That's a good boy. If you want to succeed in life, you must speak English." Marjory pinched his cheek. "English is what we speak in America."

I regretted using my son as a way to avoid conflict with my mother-in-law. And her condescending tone was a microaggression aimed at me.

"Manny, no le hagas caso." I smiled at my mother-in-law while telling my son to ignore her. "It's Robert's job to teach him English. If he were home more often, then maybe his son would be proficient in both languages, not just his mother's tongue. Studies have shown that bilingual children are better at problem-solving. They have more career opportunities. Oh, and it helps prevent Alzheimer's. All good things."

"Yes, yes." Marjory moved her hand like she was brushing crumbs onto the floor.

"One of the reasons"—I used the sweetest voice I could muster, picturing myself as an anime character with a cloud of flowers and twinkling stars around my head and a knife behind my back, sweet but deadly; that was going to be my new tactic—"other than our getting to be closer to you, that we were happy to come back to Miami is that it is such a culturally diverse city. I mean, our county government prints all official material in three languages. How great is that? I hope Manny picks up Haitian Kreyòl as well."

"I have places to be. Goodbye, Douglas." She blew a kiss at Manny and turned her back to me. "Goodbye, Miriam," she said, and primly walked away.

"Hey, lady." The ball-cap man held a floor lamp by the neck. "Where do you want this?"

I absentmindedly pointed somewhere to my right.

"Okay. We're done. Sign this." He tapped his pen on the metal clipboard.

"You're done?" I twirled around the suddenly full room. The furniture was placed willy-nilly. "Aren't you going to arrange it for me? I can't move that sofa by myself."

"Sorry, lady. I've got ten more stops to make today." He pushed the paper at me.

I signed it and closed the door after him. When the door clicked shut, Sally poked her head out from the hall.

"Is it safe? Is she gone?"

"Yes, and so is the muscle." I sighed. "I guess I'll have to wait for Robert to come home to get this set up."

Manny used the rolled rug as a balance beam. Reagan and Savanah got in line to take their turns at it.

"Pishposh. Girl power has got this." Sally flexed a bicep.

"I didn't invite you to my house to put you to work. Don't worry. I can wait for Robert."

The kids, tired of the balance beam, began throwing a ball of plastic wrap around the room.

"Hush. I'm happy to help." Sally grabbed the ball and shooed the kids back to their room. "Some of us in the family are decent people. Sorry about Marjory. She is such a pill. What was that crap about Mariel?" Using her knee, she pushed the ottoman to the wall.

"You heard that?" I put the end table next to the footrest.

"Yeah. My eavesdropper skills are CIA level." Sally took one end of the long sectional, and I the other. "Being one step ahead of Marjory is how I survived all those premarriage dating years. She was not my biggest fan. I wasn't good enough for her Andrew." We lined the sofa up with the other pieces of furniture awaiting placement. "She even tried to buy me off."

"No way!" I mopped my forehead with the hem of my shirt.

"Not with money. I might have taken that."

"Huh?"

"I'm joking. No, she tried to ship me off to Tallahassee with a job offer from the governor. They're old friends."

"Do you regret not taking it, now that you're separated?"

"Andrew and I aren't separated." Sally chuckled. "I love that big lug."

"But . . ."

"I mean, we were for a hot minute. I was so fed up with Marjory and her meddling in our lives that I threatened to leave." Sally took the scissors from me and cut the paper wrapping from her side of the rug. "And then it was like, all of a sudden, I had a free pass to ignore Marjory. No more Women's Club. No more church guild. It was so liberating. So we've kept up the façade, and our marriage is peaceful again."

"Wow. Too bad I can't use that trick." I motioned that we should turn the rug clockwise.

"Sorry," Sally said. "Limit one per family."

Sally and I laughed. It was nice to know I wasn't alone in my feelings about Marjory. We arranged the living room so that the sectional was against the long wall, and the armchairs faced the window. The end table went between the chairs. The ottoman that made a section of the sofa into a chaise I put on the window side of the couch. In the middle of it all, there was the marble and metal coffee table.

"It looks good." Sally crossed her arms and nodded approvingly. "You could use an entryway table here." She pointed to the wall between the front and office doors.

"I agree. I think there was a long table, like a behind-the-sofa-type table, that matched all of this. We didn't think there would be enough room for it. But yeah, now I wish we'd gotten it. I'll have to wait a bit. This is already more than I've ever spent on furniture in my life."

"Don't wait. Order it now. You deserve it, and you need it."

I didn't know if I agreed with Sally's logic. I liked to pay for things, not put them on credit. In my house, growing up, when you opened a can of Café Bustelo, you never knew if it was going to be coffee or coins. My parents used the yellow and red cans like savings deposit accounts. There was one for my quince and one for Christmas, another for car repair. Their save-and-plan mentality had rubbed off on me.

The kitchen timer sounded.

"Lunch. I'm so glad we get to eat at a real table." The scented steam hit my face as I stirred. I laid the spoon on a rest shaped like a parrot. "Do you mind setting the table?"

"Sure, where are the placemats?" Sally asked.

I opened the drawer under the counter and pulled out the placemats Alma had given me. The furniture delivery hubbub had interrupted our conversation. Sally had dropped a bomb on me about Alma. Cocaine. No way. Alma did not do recreational drugs.

"Before we call the kids to lunch," I said as I gave Sally the stiff placemats, "um . . . you were telling me about a rumor?"

"Oh yeah. So, the rumor going around is that Alma is a drug dealer."

"What!" The stack of bowls clinked when I set them down hard. "That's crazy!"

"Yeah, supposedly the real estate thing is just a front. That's why I asked how well you know her."

"Alma is the hardest-working person I know, besides my parents." I unstacked the bowls. "She eats, sleeps, breathes selling houses. Drug dealer? Her agency name and photo are all over town sponsoring this and that. Where is this rumor coming from? Is it just because she's Cuban? That whole Scarface stereotype burns me up." I ladled the stew into the bowls and made sure that the kids' servings had more vegetables than meat.

"I don't know about that, but there is some basis for it." Sally twisted her mouth.

"Tell me." I pointed a soup ladle at her.

"Okay, so, about five years ago, when she first started selling houses in the area, she rented that big house on the bay to Sunny Weatherman. For a party. I guess that's a thing that happens. Expensive properties like that get rented out for events and parties. Anyway . . ." Sally folded the napkins and put a spoon on each one. "The party got out of hand. There was a DJ and a ton of crashers. The neighbors called the cops, and they shut the party down. When everyone cleared out, the police found cocaine all over the place."

"That doesn't prove anything! The coke probably belonged to Sunny and her friends. She's been in and out of rehab, right?" I looked for the polished wood bowl I'd gotten in Port au Prince and found it in the cabinet.

"Yes, but when Sunny was taken away in the ambulance, blitzed out of her mind, she kept repeating Alma's name. That was her answer to every question. Whose house is this? Alma. Who's in charge? Alma. Who gave you the drugs? Alma. Or so I've been told."

"That's crazy. Alma is not a drug dealer. And where is the proof? If drugs were involved, I'm sure there would've been an investigation, right?" I cut a baton of bread and put it in the wood bowl.

"I don't know what the cops did about it. It was probably swept under the rug." Sally took a small piece of bread and nibbled on it as she transferred the bowl from the counter to the table.

"Alma would have said something to me if she was in trouble. I think someone has their story wrong." I poured three glasses of juice for the kids.

"Money talks. The Weathermans have a lot of money, and . . ." Sally set the glasses at the bench seat.

"And what?"

"And you know, . . . your friend Alma seems to have made a lot of quick money."

"She works *hard*." I threw my arms into the air. "Who is saying these things?"

"We're hungry," said a chorus of little voices.

The kids put a stop to my learning who had started the rumor. We seated them at the bench and took a photograph of the cousins. It was nice to have an eating space to host family and friends. The stew was delicious, and the kids devoured it, but I couldn't truly enjoy it. I was thinking about Alma and the hypocrisy in Coral Shores. If they really thought Alma was a drug dealer, why would they let her sponsor their children's athletic team?

Wait—had I just implied that there might be some truth to the rumor? Could Alma be dealing drugs? She had been spending more time shuttling me around town than selling houses.

No.

No.

No?

Chapter
Twenty-One

A s I washed the dishes from the leftovers Manny and I had eaten for dinner, I anxiously checked my phone for a reply from my best friend. Alma's hearing yesterday afternoon had not gone well. Because of the seriousness of the crime, Andrew could not convince the judge to release Alma on her own recognizance or that she should be granted bail. But he was able to get her released to house arrest. As of late yesterday afternoon, a Coral Shores officer was stationed at her home twenty-four hours a day. I'd wanted to welcome her home and bring her a bowl of sancocho, but the judge ordered no visitors other than her lawyer. I'd texted her a dozen times, but she hadn't answered. Sunday afternoon had been a mix of research and practice for my cooking segment, paired with catastrophizing every time my mind strayed from food.

On top of which, Robert had come home sunburned and reeking of cigar smoke. His golf game had evolved into an afternoon in the club's humidor lounge, followed by an early steak dinner. His breath had smelled of bourbon. When I confronted him about driving buzzed, he swore he had gotten a ride home but wouldn't tell me from whom. He accused me of being suspicious, which caused a terse argument that I walked away from. Okay, truth be told, I stomped away. We'd slept with our backs to each other.

Is my marriage falling apart? I turned off the faucet and dried my hands. There was too much going on with Alma and my new job to add another layer of worry. "Don't jump to conclusions, Miriam." I took my phone from the windowsill, and stared at the black screen, willing it to give me a message from my friend. "Come on, Alma, wake up. Let me know you're okay."

"Talking to yourself again?" Robert asked.

I startled and turned to face him. Dressed for work, he looked like a *GQ* cover. His red nose and cheekbones had faded to the lightest pink. I hated how easy it was for his good looks to weaken my anger.

"About last night, I'm sorry. It was a long day, and I just wanted to get a shower. I didn't want to fight." Robert wrapped me in his arms.

The basil and sage notes of his cologne were memory heavy. They took me back to the night we'd met at the interdepartmental mixer. I'd been smitten with him then as much as now.

"Forgive me for being—what's that word you use?"

"Un come mierda," I replied.

"Yeah, that's the one. I'm sorry." He tightened his hug.

Honk. Honk.

"My ride is here." He kissed me on the forehead. "I've got to go."

"What about breakfast?"

"I'll grab something on the way. Don't worry." He jogged toward the door, then stopped to look around him. "The furniture looks great." He pointed to the empty wall by the front door. "But I think we need a table here."

"Yes, I know," I said as he exited. I heard a muffled "Love you. See you later."

"Love you too." I went to the window to wave and saw Robert get into the passenger side of his red Tesla. Whoever had dropped him off last night must have kept the keys so they could return in the morning. I sat on the ottoman to be able to see into the car as it drove past. The driver was a blonde with sunglasses.

"Juliet!"

What kind of fool was I? Even if my husband wasn't having an affair with his boss's daughter, who also happened to be his high school girlfriend, something was going on that Robert was being very careful to avoid telling me.

"Juliet, you are my nemesis." My nemesis list might not be as long as Roxane Gay's, but it was definitely written in permanent ink. "Argh!" I saw my gnarling teeth in the reflection of the window just as the morning exercise ladies passed by and glanced toward my house. They quickly looked away, and I swore they sped up their pace. "Great."

Manny and I left the house at eight thirty AM and got to the studio a few minutes before nine. When I dropped Manny off at the daycare center, Rosario offered me a cafecito, which I gladly accepted. She also shared, as is the Cuban custom, the latest studio chisme. Coffee and gossip go together like guava y queso or bread and butter. According to the gossip mill, a married cameraman was having an affair with a lady in Human Resources.

"Pobrecita," Rosario said about the clueless wife, who worked in the wardrobe department.

My heart exploded into a million shards of glass. Someone in Coral Shores could be sipping a Starbucks and saying the same thing about me. I left the daycare center before tears filled my eyes. At the wardrobe department, I exchanged my blouse for the show logo T-shirt, then hurried to the makeup room.

The late-night comedy guy was asleep in the same chair as when I'd seen him Friday. This time he wore a going-to-the-nightclub dress and a woman's wig. He looked like a bad version of Jorge's artful drag. A strand of hair rose and fell with each snore. I wondered how it didn't tickle his nose and wake him.

"Why are you here?" the makeup lady asked. "Today isn't your day."

"No, is that a problem? I can do my own makeup if it's a problem." I picked up a powder brush the size of a carnation.

"Dame eso." She snatched the brush from me. "You do not know what you are doing. Stage makeup is not the same as street makeup. If I let you do it, you will look like Casper or a yellow balloon. No, no, no." She pushed me into the chair, stuffed tissue around my collar, and dabbed my face with a foundation sponge. I felt like I was at the school nurse's, getting ointment put on a scraped knee. The makeup artist emitted the same pity and annoyance vibe.

Before she got to the lipstick application, Delvis found me. On our way to the kitchen set, she explained that Ileana had given her *Cocina Caribeña* as a solo project. It would be Delvis's first unsupervised production for the show, and she was excited. She also had big plans for it.

"But I don't want to jinx my plans by talking about them," Delvis said. "Get your ingredients organized, and I'll be back in a second."

As I inventoried the meats and veggies, I heard chatter coming from the set of *La Tacita* as it shut down for the day. Ileana's high heels click-clacked on the polished cement floor. Different voices called orders in Spanish. Then the bright stage lights were cut, and it became a ghost town. Delvis returned with the same film crew we'd had on Friday.

"Are you ready, Miriam?" Delvis asked.

"I think so. Don't you want to put my note cards into the teleprompter?" I gathered the index cards that I had spread on the counter and offered them to her.

"No. We're going to try something different today. I want you to talk to the camera like it's a friend. Imagine I'm at your house, and you're showing me how to cook. Make it casual."

"What about time? I practiced doing it in five minutes."

"Don't worry about the time. I have four days to edit it in post. I want you to talk to the camera. Tell your story. Let the audience fall in love with you. Show us what makes you special."

"Special? I'm not special. I'm not even a chef." My hands were all of a sudden super clammy.

"Our viewers aren't chefs either." Delvis came on set and stood next to me. She leaned back and put her elbows on the counter. "Remember the story you told us last time? About your grandparents and how they'd give you papaya for your tummy aches?" She propelled herself from her rest to pat me on the shoulder. "That's what we want more of. Tell the viewers a story."

The sound person checked my mic levels, the camera turned on, and Delvis yelled, "Action!" I froze. I stared unblinking into the lens.

"Cut!" Delvis called. "Miriam. I know I've thrown you a curveball, but you can do this. Come on, shake it off. Talk to the camera like it's your best friend."

I wished it *were* my best friend. If Alma were with me, she'd tell me that I was amazing and smart. She'd remind me that I'd slayed my dissertation committee. Something came over me then, and I knew what I needed to do to get in the cooking mood.

"Delvis, is there any chance I can play a little music to get me into the mood? It's a Dominican recipe, so maybe a merengue or bachata?"

Delvis whispered to the production assistant with a laptop on a rolling pedestal, and within seconds Romero Santos was streaming from the overhead speakers. I turned away from the crew, closed my eyes, and danced. When I spun to face the camera, Delvis nodded an order, the music faded out, and I began talking. About fifteen minutes later, I finished my story about Doña Adela and her special baby baptism stew.

"Cut. That's was amazing! You are a natural!" Delvis clapped as she walked toward me.

"But I haven't plated it yet. It's not done. The stew has to cook about an hour."

"Don't worry. Cecilia will do that. I promise it will look delicious." Cecilia was the woman with the laptop. Delvis talked to her, and Cecilia nodded like a bobblehead doll. "Miriam, you can go."

"Okay, but don't let it boil. That will make the meat tough. It should simmer," I said as I stepped off the lit stage.

"Simmer. Okay, don't worry. Lucy will watch it."

"And make sure there is a wheel of corn and a piece of plátano in each bowl."

"No te preocupes, yo sé lo que estoy haciendo. Soy dominicana," Cecilia said.

"¿Ay de verdad? ¿De qué parte?" I asked. Not that I had an encyclopedic knowledge of the island, but I had visited it several times.

"Juanillo, cerca de Punta Cana." Cecilia stirred the stew. She put her nose close to it, closed her eyes, and smiled. "Sancocho reminds me of my tía. She'd make it for New Year's Day every year. She said you had to start the year eating like a rich man if you wanted to end the year rich. Loca." She laughed.

We chatted a few minutes about the Dominican Republic. I told her my parents were living in Punta Cana. Cecilia had been a DJ at the Hard Rock resort there before moving to Miami last year. That explained her having music at the ready when Delvis had asked for it. I left the set knowing my sancocho was in good hands and that it would be eaten by Cecilia and the crew. I hated for food to go to waste.

In the makeup room, as I removed the heavy blush and lipstick from my face with goopy cold cream, I watched Ileana on the monitor above the mirror. It was her weekly live interview show. According to my mother, Ileana's guests were mostly telenovela stars and tabloid celebrities. The show was self-promotion in the guise of a hard-hitting interview. Mami said people watched it because occasionally a star would do something outrageous and embarrassing. Like the time an actor known for his classy, romantic leading roles—think Mr. Darcy—threw up on stage after telling Ileana all about his quickie in the bathroom with one of his fans. He'd come straight to the show from a night of partying on South Beach. The fan, who'd posted their tryst on her Instagram story, got her fifteen minutes of fame the following week when *she* was the show's guest.

I didn't think anything salacious would happen that day, but I was glued to the screen. Her interviewee was Dr. Mario Fuentes. It seemed either I was being haunted by the man or else his star and bank account were on the rise. He was everywhere I turned. Reading the closed caption, I saw that Fuentes was giving a fuller version of his origin story.

"I took ayahuasca with the shaman of the tribe and had a vision. My body grew roots and branches, my hair transformed into leaves, I became the forest. It was then that I understood. The forest wanted me to spread its healing powers to all the people of the world. And that's how I discovered the herb that changed my life and will change yours."

Fuentes showed the camera a box of tea, and then he toasted Ileana. The pair clinked glasses. "Salud." And Ileana took a big drink of whatever was in it. She asked him something, but I didn't bother to read the conversation. I grabbed my purse from the locker and went to the wardrobe department to change shirts. My face was covered with my T-shirt when I heard someone scream.

"¡Ay Dios, Ileana!"

Quickly I put on my original shirt and stuck my head out from the changing room curtains. The wardrobe mistress had her hand over her mouth, watching the screen.

"¿Qué pasó?" I asked. I couldn't tell much from what I saw on the screen. There were several crew members on stage with their backs to the camera.

"Ileana fainted."

"What? Is she okay?"

"I don't know. She was talking one second, and then her eyes went white, and she slid off her chair like a piece of spaghetti. It was horrible."

I made the sign of the cross and prayed that Ileana wasn't going to go the way of Sunny and Elliot. Death, not health, sprouted from Dr. Fuentes. Why wasn't he in jail?

"He should be in jail, not Alma!"

"¿Qué?" asked the wardrobe lady.

"Nada. I was talking to myself."

The network broadcast a "We will be back in a moment" graphic, then played a public service announcement about recycling. I watched the live feed monitor and saw that the paramedics were on set. Ileana had on an oxygen mask but seemed to be alert and moving.

"Nos vemos la próxima semana," I said to the wardrobe mistress. She gave me a nonverbal goodbye. By the time I got to the daycare center, Ileana was sitting in a chair. The show hadn't resumed yet. There was an extended teaser for the network's talent show playing. Rosario and the other care staff had one eye on the show and the other eye on their charges. I found my son in the miniature kitchen area with two slightly younger kids. Manny had on an apron and an oven mitt.

"Mira, Mami. Soy tu. Soy cocinero," he said. He stirred a small neon pink pot and pretended to taste its contents. "Delicioso." After his friends were served their plates of imaginary food, Manny offered me a taste. I knelt and tried some. My guesses at what the delicious food could be failed. He proudly informed me it was "chocolate ice cream pudding flan with cookies." I laughed and gave Manny a five-minute departure warning.

Standing, I dusted the knees of my white pants and saw Detective Pullman in the hall. What was he doing here?

The receptionist that led him appeared to be giving him a tour. She motioned to the daycare viewing window as they walked. Pullman stopped mid-stride when he saw me. Anger boiled in me, and before I could stop myself, I was in the hall with my hands on my hips.

"What are you doing here?" I said.

"Hello, Ms. Quiñones," he replied coolly. "I could ask you the same thing. What are you doing here?"

"I work here."

"Interesting." He turned to leave. The receptionist resumed her guide role.

"Here to arrest another innocent person?"

Pullman stopped and looked at me. "Innocent like your friend?"

We glared at each other. It was a blinking contest, and I wasn't going to lose. Pullman shrugged. "Huh, for someone new in town, you seem to be in the middle of all the action. Maybe you were the one I should have arrested."

I heard the receptionist suck in a breath. Great, now I'd be the subject of office gossip. I felt the daycare staff's watching me. I relaxed my stance and approached the detective.

"My friend is innocent, and I'm going to prove it to you."

"Ms. Quiñones, I strongly advise you to let me do my job. Keep your nose out of it." Pullman and the receptionist walked away.

"Keep out of it? Keep out of it! Do his job." I pushed the daycare door opened. "Pfft. He needs to do his job better than he's doing because he has got the wrong person."

Rosario waddled up to me. "¿Quien era ese señor?"

"Policía," I answered.

She expressed curiosity but didn't ask anything more. My eyes followed hers to the live feed monitor. Detective Pullman was on set talking to Mario Fuentes. The static panoramic camera view made it hard to see the man's facial reactions, but his body language showed he was nervous.

What was he nervous about?

I had a lot of questions. Was Fuentes on Pullman's suspect list? I mean, his herbal concoctions were something all three women had in common. How had the detective gotten there so quickly? Hialeah was not his jurisdiction. Was Fuentes under surveillance?

And lastly, what evidence did Pullman have on Alma?

Okay, not lastly—I had one more important question.

Okay, two more questions.

What was wrong with my best friend? And why hadn't she called me yet?

Chapter
Twenty-Two

"¿Mami, dónde está el carro?" Manny asked.

"No sé mi amor." I was as perplexed as my son. Where was our car? It wasn't where we'd left it.

"Please tell me it hasn't been stolen!"

"¿Qué?"

"Nada, mi amor. No te preocupes." No need for him to worry when I was already at worry level red. I thought a gated and guarded lot would be safe. Had I forgotten to lock the car?

A security guard who was not doing a good job securing the premises sat in a golf cart parked by the fence. I tried to get his attention, but the reggaetón music coming from the Bluetooth speaker zip-tied to the dash was so loud he didn't notice Manny and me until we were an arm's length from him.

"Hola," I said.

The young man had clean edges to his close-cropped haircut and three notches in his eyebrow, a look that would require weekly visits to the barbershop. He turned off the Bad Bunny song about not harassing women when they danced and asked how he could help me.

"I can't find my car. I think it's been stolen."

"No way." He straightened his back, and the golf cart creaked and wobbled. "You probably forgot where you parked it. Get in. I'll drive you around the lot."

It was worth a try, but I was pretty sure I remembered where I'd parked that morning. With Manny standing between my legs, and my arms around his chest like a seat belt, the security guy drove us through the lanes of parked cars. My son was delighted by the adventure. I was not. Our car was not misplaced. It just wasn't there.

"Ohh," the security guy said. He stepped on the brakes, and we lunged forward as the cart stopped. "Is your car a Prius with New York plates?"

"Yes!"

"Yeah, lady. It was towed."

"Why?"

"The tow guy don't play around. No pass. Yo ass is grass. Oops," he said, apologizing for the crude word. He grinned at my young son. "Sorry."

"But I had a pass. I swear I put it on the dash. Please call the tow company. I need my car back." I made prayer hands, and my voice shot skyward. "Please."

"Lady, don't have a cow. Okay. I'll call."

The security guard talked to the tow company and arranged for the car to be returned. The cost to have it released was a hundred and one dollars. I moaned at the amount and went to wait in the lobby. The receptionist offered Manny a Chupa Chups. After I told her why we were waiting, she offered me one too. "Las penas con dulces son menos penas." I felt like Harry Potter eating chocolate after seeing a dementor. The banana-flavored lollipop sweetened the fifteen-minute wait and made me feel a little better about a bad situation. I left Manny in the care of the receptionist and dealt with the tow company. The driver informed me that my Friday-only parking pass did not give me Monday parking privileges. I rolled my eyes but didn't argue the technicality with him.

When I went to get Manny, I let the receptionist know I needed a new parking pass. She called for approval and a few moments later gave me a permanent sticker. It was during that lag that Detective

Pullman walked through the lobby with Dr. Fuentes, and the atmosphere turned dark. There was serious tension in the air. Neither man looked at his surroundings. They walked directly to the doors and left. Manny and I exited after them. As I got in my car, I watched Pullman and Fuentes get into their cars that were parked side by side in guest spots. Fuentes backed out first, then Pullman. The detective, close on his bumper, followed the doctor out of the lot.

"Where are they going?" If Fuentes was under arrest, he was getting better treatment than my friend Alma had. "Ohh, maybe it's a warrant!" Alma had been showing a house when they came for her. The police didn't wait for a person to finish work. Was Fuentes being escorted to his house or his office?

"Vamos Mami vamos. Tengo hambre."

"Sí, vamos." We were going, just not for food. I found a baggie of Maria cookies in the glove compartment and passed it to my son. The barely sweet cookies were probably stale, but they'd have to hold him for a bit because my curiosity was stronger than my maternal calling at that moment. I followed Detective Pullman, trying to stay a few cars behind him.

"¡Perros! Quiero ver los perros. Tengo hambre," Manny said. He pointed out the window. We were stopped at a light by my cousin's café. Manny wanted to pet San Lazaro's dogs and eat like we'd done last time after UnMundo daycare.

"Hoy, no, mi amor." I heard a tiny "uh" of disappointment from the back seat. Pullman turned left at the block after Yoli's. When I caught up to him, I saw he and Fuentes had parked in front of a strip of stores. I pulled into the parking lot and watched in my rearview mirror as the men entered the store next to the seamstress shop. I put the car in reverse and circled around so I could read the name of the store. Cruising by the foil-tinted windows, I read the three lines of green and black lettering on the door: "Dr. Mario Fuentes. Medicinas Naturales. Consultas con cita previa."

"Mami, tengo hambre."

"Okay, okay, okay." I couldn't ignore my son's hunger any longer.

Since I wasn't going to learn anything sitting in a car, watching an office I couldn't see into, I went to the closest eating establishment I could think of, Tres Sillas.

"Yoli," Beatriz called my cousin as soon as we walked in the door. She served an espresso to a waiting man and then left her station to give us hugs.

"¿Qué?" Yoli said. She emerged from the kitchen cleaning her hands on a towel. "Prima! Back so soon?"

"I was in the neighborhood." I kissed her hello.

"Tengo hambre!" Manny whined.

"¿Tienes hambre? Yo puedo ayudarte con eso." Yoli picked Manny up and plopped him on the counter. She opened the plexiglass box that kept the pastries warm and selected an empanada. Manny took a bite and said thank you with a crumb-filled smile and an "Mmm."

"What can I get for you, cuz?" Yoli asked.

"Nothing right now, but could I ask a super big favor?"

"Dale."

"Could you watch Manny for, like, thirty minutes while I run an errand?"

"Claro que sí. Of course," Yoli replied. "As long as you need. Do what you have to. I've missed four years of this little guy. We have to make up for all that time."

Yoli transferred Manny to the back counter. Beatriz tickled Manny and told him he was going to be her helper. She gave him an order pad and a pen. I left him and hurried back to Fuentes's office.

All the stores in the plaza were service-oriented businesses. I couldn't think of an excuse to be there if Pullman caught me. It wasn't like running into him at UnMundo. I'd belonged there. This strip mall was the opposite of the busy one where Yoli's café was. It was quiet, near dead. I didn't have a reason to be at the alterations shop or a tax place that also sent remittances to Cuba. Nor did I have a vacuum or sewing machine to repair. And I had no excuse to be at a closed evangelical church or an out-of-business portrait studio with a "For Rent" sign on it. With only a few cars parked in front of the plaza, mine would be obvious. And then I remembered my brief stint at my tíos' restaurant and the stinky job I sometimes had to do. Yoli and I would flip a coin. The loser had to take the trash to the dumpster. All these little plazas had dumpsters behind them and enough space for a garbage truck to have access. They also usually had a bathroom window that was left open. Maybe if I was lucky, I could hear what was happening inside the office.

I parked on the side of the building that was farthest from Fuentes's office and made my way past the church and the tax service.

"Yuck." I accidentally stepped on a squashed iguana that had flies swarming it. The South Florida sun was doing its best to bake it to a crisp. I scraped the goo off the sole of my shoe and kept moving. The next place had their door propped open with a box fan. As I carefully crept by it, I heard electric drill noises and Spanish-language talk radio. The next shop was the seamstress. By its door was a residential garbage bin with fabric tubes protruding from it.

"Hooray," I whispered. The Fuentes's bathroom window was as open as it could get. The metal frame of the crank window touched the security bars, and I could feel cooled air escaping. I wedged my ear as close to the opening as possible but only heard mumbles thanks to the repair shop's drone.

Fail! Sleuthing was harder than I'd anticipated. What would Jessica Fletcher do if she were in my position? I thought about the hours and hours of *Murder She Wrote* episodes that I'd watched with my mom. Angela Lansbury made it look so easy.

Suddenly, the mumbles got louder. I distinctly heard a "No!" followed by an "owlshowu."

I'll show you. Shoot! Someone was coming. Where could I hide? I looked at my lack of options and scurried behind the dumpster. The open lid touched the back wall of the property and gave me a covered two-foot-wide space. I squeezed into it, dirtying my white pants along the way.

The door banged open.

"See," Dr. Fuentes said. "Look at the boxes. I don't make it!"

Through the space made by the lid's hinge, I could see a little of Fuentes. He shook a cardboard box in Pullman's direction. "They come from China. See? Made in China."

"Dr. Fuentes, that doesn't mean the product wasn't tampered with or purposefully altered while in your possession."

"Impossible!" Fuentes threw the box into the full dumpster, causing a conga line of cucarachas to run my way. I bit my cheeks and tried not to scream, but I couldn't help squirming when one landed on my shoulder and then grazed my neck as it flew away.

"What was that?" Pullman asked. "I thought I heard something."

"Ratones."

Not rats, roaches! I wanted to say as I tried harder to be still in my tight hiding space. Pullman leaned his head into the dumpster.

Please, don't see me. Did he see me? He saw me. No. No, he didn't. Be still, Miriam. Please don't see me. Go, go, go. Okay, gone.

"Follow me. I'll prove it to you. I am not involved. I did not put any drugs in that woman's drink."

I dared to poke my head out of cover and saw Fuentes unlocking the door next to his office. He and the detective went inside the for-rent space. A few minutes later, they returned to the alley and went back to the doctor's place. I waited a couple of moments for the coast to clear and then went to see what was in there.

"Please don't be locked," I whispered as I tried the knob. "Thank you." I pulled open the door and stepped inside. It wasn't an empty photo studio. It was a storage unit for Mario's teas and natural products. Or, maybe, what was to become an expansion. Part of the drywall was cut away where a passage between the spaces would logically go. The drywall on Fuentes's office side was still in place. I could hear

Pullman and Fuentes talking, but it sounded like they were underwater.

I didn't know how much time I would get to snoop. So, I shot a quick 360-degree video to examine later. Boxes with Chinese lettering were stacked everywhere, and there was a cube-style display shelf in the front part of the store. In the middle of the floor, there was a table with jars and rolls of labels. I picked up the loose end of the roll and read the sticker: "Dr. Mario Fuentes Crema de Antiedad." I bet this was the cream that Jorge said burned his skin. I twisted the lid to examine what was inside the jar. It smelled like baby powder and roses.

I took one of the labeled jars, then looked in a few boxes. Nothing out of the ordinary jumped out at me. The boxes held his tea inventory. The tea was branded with his name, and the boxes were sealed in plastic film. I took a reusable gift bag from an open carton and filled it with samples of each type of tea plus a box of the powdered drink. Next, I turned my attention to the display shelves. Each cube showed a different product. A few were decorated with wooden sculptures, like a lotus flower and a Buddha head. There were no jars of loose herbs, scales, or scoopers like I'd expected. If Fuentes had an apothecary where he mixed custom teas, it must be in his office.

The muffled conversation next door became audible when Fuentes clearly shouted.

"Get out!"

I stood in the unfinished passageway and hoped the yelling would continue. And then the phone call I'd been hoping for came. Alma finally called, but at the worst possible time. Because if I could hear them, then they could hear me.

Oh no, oh no, oh no. I pressed "Decline," grabbed my bag of stolen teas, and zipped out the backdoor in time to squeeze behind the dumpster, where I sweated in a panic that I was going to be discovered and thrown in jail. And if I got arrested, then who would clear Alma's name?

I held my breath as Fuentes burst from his office with Pullman at his heels. He checked the storage room quickly, then locked the door. Pullman looked around the corner of the building but soon set his eyes on the dumpster.

Please, don't see me. Go away, go away, go away. Go, go, go!

The detective moseyed away at a snail's pace. When the door shut, I counted to sixty and then made a dash for my car. What had I been thinking? I had never been a risk-taker. I didn't even like Space Mountain. My heart pounded as I sat behind the wheel.

Calm down.

I looked at the bag of stolen merchandise in the passenger's seat. Super.

Add "thief" to your résumé, Miriam.

I cranked the engine to start the AC. Directing the vent to my chest, I closed my eyes for a second and told myself it was all going to be okay. Alma was innocent, and I was going to prove it by finding the actual guilty party. *Oh shoot, Alma.* I pressed "Call" and got her voicemail.

"Alma, please don't be mad. I'm sorry I didn't answer. Are you okay? Do you want something special to eat? I can make anything you want." I was rambling. "I know you're innocent. No te preocupes, I'm going to fix it. I know it's my fault. I shouldn't have told the detective you had that drink powder." *Oh no, that made it sound like Alma was guilty. What if the police listened to her voicemail?* "Don't worry, amiga. I'm going to clear your name. I know it wasn't you." The recording time lapsed. I threw my phone into the seat.

"Ay, Caridad, help me. Help me save my best friend."

Putting the car into gear, I took my foot off the brake and eased my way down the side of the building. I had a straight shot to the exit and stopped at the edge of the building to see if it was clear for me to speed out of there. I was about to accelerate when I had to slam on the brakes. Detective Pullman's car suddenly blocked my path. He got out of his car and came to my window. I opened it and smiled nervously.

"Good afternoon, Ms. Quiñones. Interesting that we keep bumping into each other. Twice in one day."

"Um, yes. What a coincidence?"

Frank Pullman smirked. He jutted his chin at the bag in the passenger's seat. "I didn't know you were one of the doctor's clients. I was just in there, and I didn't see you."

My heart rate spiked again. He'd heard me.

"Actually, I'm returning those to Dr. Fuentes. I'm worried they might be tainted. After Sunny and Elliot and now Ileana, I'm worried the teas might be dangerous."

"Uh-huh. Is there parking behind the building? You must be a very special client of his to have backdoor access."

He knows, he knows. I needed a lie to cover my tracks.

"Actually, I was going to ask for a refund but then thought maybe I should just throw them in the dumpster, but it was too full. Soooo, um."

"Be careful. I hear the dumpster has rats."

We stared at each other. No amount of AC was going to stop the buckets of sweat my nerves were producing.

"Thanks for the warning. I'll be very careful. Sorry, I've got to go pick up my son."

"No problem. I'll catch up with you later." Pullman withdrew from my window, patted the roof, and then swaggered to his car. He moved his vehicle out of my way, leaving me only a few inches of clearance.

I cut across traffic with the detective on my bumper. At the light, he turned right with me. When I put on my blinker to enter Yoli's, so did he.

Super. Great. Perfect. I bet I'm going to be arrested.

"Caridad, save me."

Chapter
Twenty-Three

Manny was right where I'd left him, sitting on the back counter. The only thing that had changed was his appearance. He had a folded bandanna on his head; the short sleeves of his T-shirt were rolled to expose his tiny little biceps, which were dappled with temporary tattoos; and there was a smear of guava paste on his chin that looked like a red goatee.

"Mami, me quiero quedar," Manny said.

Of course he wanted to stay. It was like a little kid's dream come true, a make-believe restaurant that was real. I shrugged, sat on a stool, and ordered a café con leche from my son. He repeated the order to Beatriz, and I melted from the cuteness. My momma-joy vibe fizzled in the tinkle of a bell. Detective Frank Pullman sauntered in and sat in the empty corner booth.

Really? Really!

The server gave him a menu, poured him a glass of water, and left a basket of bread. Was he going to hound me all day? There was no way I was going to be able to snoop around if I had a detective on my tail. I took my coffee and went to face the music.

"Glad you could join me. What's good here?" Pullman asked.

"Everything. They're all my aunt's recipes."

"Family restaurants are the best. My uncle has a soul food place in Overtown. Been there twenty-five years. Best oxtail stew you'll ever taste."

"I doubt it. My tía's is the best."

Detective Pullman chuckled, and it sounded to me like it was a sincere emotion, not sarcasm. What was going on? The mood had shifted. Was it a trap to let my guard down?

"What you like to order?" the server asked. Her English was accented, and I could tell she was Cuban. Her gold Caridad del Cobre medallion substantiated it.

"Rabo encendido con arroz y maduros," Pullman replied in perfect Spanish. "Let's see how your tía's stew compares to my tío's." He winked.

I ordered the chicken soup with a side of avocado salad. "Your Spanish is very good."

"Surprised?"

"A little."

"I'm a cop in Miami. It helps. Plus, my wife is Colombian."

"Ohh." I looked at his hand and noticed a thin gold wedding band for the first time. What else was there about him that I'd missed? "Do you have any children?"

"Two sons. One is a junior at New World. Dance. He's real good. Got his eyes set on Broadway. The other is at MIT doing an aerospace engineering degree. He's wanted to work for NASA ever since his fifth-grade class trip to The Kennedy Space Center." His cop attitude was gone. Frank Pullman glowed with the pride of a father. "So, now that you know something about me, it's my turn to ask a question." *And the cop-tude is back.* "What were you looking for in Fuentes's store?"

"I don't know what you mean; I wasn't in there," I answered way too quickly. What's that Shakespeare saying? *"The lady doth protest too much."*

"Uh-huh." Frank Pullman gave me a dead face. He wasn't buying my nonsense. "Let's try again. What were you allegedly doing in the good doctor's storage facility?"

I drummed my fingers on the table and weighed my options, of which there were none. The detective had me painted into a corner—a corner booth.

"If I was in there—and I'm not saying I was, okay?"

"Gotcha. Hypothetically. Go on."

"*If* I was in there, it was to find the evidence that will clear my friend. She's innocent."

"Hypothetically, you could also have been planting false evidence to steer the investigation away from your friend." Pullman tilted his head and raised his eyebrows.

"What? No! I would never!"

My protest was louder than I'd intended. The din of diner sounds went quiet for a second as all eyes turned to us. The hiss of the milk steamer was the only sound until, thankfully, Manny started singing one of his mashed-up-word ditties and the diner resumed its hum. Our waitress approached cautiously and delivered our lunch. "¿Todo bien?"

"Sí, todo bien," I replied and squeezed the lime wedge over my chicken soup.

After she'd served me water and cleared my used coffee cup, Pullman and I tried our food. He gave an "Mmm" and I countered with a "Delicioso." We were wrestlers in a cage fight, circling each other. The tension was killing me. I set down my spoon, took a drink, then wiped my mouth. I had to trust that we were on the same team: team justice and truth. He didn't want to put the wrong person in jail. I hoped.

"Alma is innocent. Whatever evidence you think you have on her, you don't. I've been thinking about it, and I think Dr. Fuentes is your guy. I think something in his tea is making people sick. Either on purpose or by accident. Sunny and Elliot were both longtime clients of his. And then today, Ileana got sick after she drank one of his potions right in front of him. Did you see that? She was on live TV. Wait—you were there like five seconds after the ambulance. How did you do that? Oh, were you watching? Probably. Whatever. Doesn't matter. The thing I can't figure out is why. Why would Dr. Fuentes want to hurt his patients? I mean that doesn't make any sense. Dead clients are not good for business. Unless he's a lunatic mass murderer like Jim Jones. Oh wow, maybe that's it. People do kind of fawn over him like he's a guru savior. That's it—he's a cult leader who wants to kill his followers with poisoned tea."

"Are you finished?" Pullman asked, but his face gave away what he was really thinking—¿Te falta un tornillo? My hypothesis was a little screwy, but I wasn't missing any of my screws. My head was on tight. Fuentes was the connection between all the incidents. He had to be the culprit. I just needed to prove it.

"It's a good theory," I said.

"Mario Fuentes is not a cult leader. He's not even a medical doctor. But you're right. He is in the middle of everything. And I can't figure out why either. Why does a man suddenly shift his business from working-class Hialeah to Richie Rich Coral Shores? That's not an easy jump. Those are two very different demographics." The detective sucked a piece of meat from a bone, then dropped it onto the plate. "And you, Ms. Veronica Mars, you are in both of them. I think you can help me."

I had whiplash from the 180-degree turn the conversation had taken. Detective Frank Pullman wanted my help. I wasn't about to join my BFF under house arrest.

"I'm confused. You want my help?"

"Uh-huh."

"Wait, who is Veronica Mars?"

"You've never heard of Veronica Mars? The show. The teenage girl with the camera—her dad's an ex-cop turned private investigator. Pfft. I'm old. You were probably in high school when it was on TV."

I shook my head and dipped a piece of bread into the last dreg of my soup. "At my house, we watched telenovelas and, for some weird reason, *Murder She Wrote* reruns."

"The old white lady that trips over dead bodies? Well, that explains a lot." Frank Pullman threw his head back and laughed. "Anyway, my point is, you are in a unique situation. You can bust the Coral Shores society bubble that I can't."

"I don't get it. You have a badge."

"Yeah, but you have the pedigree. Coral Shores society doesn't talk to Black men unless they're the help. Sundowner towns don't change their stripes that quickly."

"What's a sundowner town?" I'd never heard the term. "Like a retirement community?"

"American history class skips over that gem, don't it. Look it up."

Our server returned and offered coffee and postre. Frank ordered a café con leche and I ordered a cortadito, the version with less milk. We both passed on the dessert.

"As I was saying, since you seem to be in the right places at the right times, I want you to be my eyes and ears. Sunny Weatherman's memorial service is tomorrow. I want you to go. The society ladies are more likely to drop their guard around one of their own."

"Okay, but why a memorial and not a funeral? That seems weird."

"The ME hasn't released the body, despite Mrs. Weatherman's backchannel influence. Our medical examiner doesn't play politics."

"Is it normal to keep the body that long? It's been almost a week, right?"

"The ME has her reasons."

Pullman crossed his arms, ran his tongue over his teeth, and made a smacking sound. It was the end of that line of questioning. He wasn't going to share details with me, and that had me very curious. What reasons? Did they need to run more tests? From what Stormy and others had said, Sunny was pretty unhealthy.

"So, Ms. Quiñones-Smith, do we have a deal?"

"Huh?" My imagination was on fire, and it took me a second to clear the smoke. "Yes, the memorial. I'll be there, absolutely. Who's your main suspect? What should I ask them? Do you want me to wear a wire?"

"Slow your roll." He held his hand up for me to stop. "I don't want you asking questions. I want you *listening*. Listen and report back to me." He took a business card from his shirt pocket and snapped it down in front of me. "The same goes for when you are at UnMundo. Got it?"

Beatriz delivered our coffees and asked if Manny could have a milkshake. I told her that it would be fine but to make it a small one. Pullman and I sipped our sweet and highly caffeinated go-juice in silence. I'd been given my orders; there wasn't much else to say. At least I wasn't under arrest.

"Detective, since I'm doing something for you, can you do something for me?"

"I think I've already done you a favor. Hypothetically speaking." He raised his eyebrows.

I grimaced. I was pushing my luck. "I just want to see my friend, Alma. Can you give me permission to visit her?"

"Sorry. I can't override the judge. But . . ." Pullman drank some of his café con leche, moved the cup and saucer to the side, and then smoothed his tie. "Barney Fife will probably let you in during his shift."

"Barney Fife? Which one is he? What does he look like?"

"There I go showing my age again. Your husband's cousin, Officer Smith."

"His name's Gordon, not Barney." I chortled.

The detective paid for his lunch despite my insistence that it was my cousin's place, so therefore my treat. When he left, Yoli and Beatriz grilled me about my curious lunch date. I gave them the condensed version of the terrible events that I'd witnessed over the last week. Yoli urged me to go to the botanica a few doors down from them and get a hex-removing despojo. I'd never actually had one before, but I'd been with my mom when she'd had one of the herbal baths. Science-based or power of suggestion—either way, it had helped her feel better. When Manny stopped at the botanica to pet the San Lazaro dogs, I replayed Yoli's advice in my mind and decided Alma needed a despojo more than me. The dousing of herbs was best when administered freshly made by a santero who's spent years learning the Yoruba traditions that are passed from generation to generation. But since that wasn't an option for Alma, I bought her a bottled one along with a few saint candles. I treated myself to a book, an addition to my herbal encyclopedia collection: *Yerbas de Cuba*. Leafing through it, I could tell it was more medicinal than culinary, but if nothing else, it was a rare book with detailed botanical drawings that I'd likely not find again.

While Manny had a three PM power nap in the back seat, I thought about all that had transpired that day. I'd cooked a stew looking into a video camera, seen my boss collapse, had my car towed, followed a detective who then followed me, stolen a bag full of teas and creams, ate lunch with the man who I thought was the enemy, and been ordered to eavesdrop. If this was Monday, I feared what Tuesday would bring. Oh yeah: a memorial service.

Chapter
Twenty-Four

The *Around Town* website was the best and worst of insular community. After dinner, a sweet and spicy pineapple jerk chicken, I'd logged on to find out the time and location of Sunny's memorial. A lost cat post led me to a found set of keys that led me to the video of Alma's arrest that led to a deep dive into the Coral Shores gossip mill. The rumor circulating town was that Alma was a drug dealer. Sally had warned me, but it still hit me hard. My best friend would never touch an illegal drug. Her brother, older by ten years, had died of an overdose when we were in middle school. His death had affected her deeply. She'd talked about becoming a therapist so she could help people with addictions. I think she even did her senior year community service with a drug-prevention organization. Alma would not be selling, doing, or even touching cocaine.

"Pobrecita. She's probably a wreck." I sat up in bed.

Because I'd been down the rabbit hole until well past midnight, Robert had handled Manny's breakfast so that I could sleep an extra hour. His considerate gesture had been for naught because I was as tired as a new mother. My mind had churned all night, and Alma was my first thought as soon as I opened my eyes. I reached for the cup of American coffee Robert had brought me before he'd gone to work.

"Eww! Cold."

Mango, Mambo, and Murder

After checking on Manny, I made fresh Cuban coffee, poured myself a triple shot, and went to the study to caffeinate myself. Yesterday, I'd dumped my bags on the window seat. Moving the one from the botanica to the floor, the bottle of despojo rolled out. Was that the universe telling me Alma was doomed if I didn't get to her soon? I needed to see her before the memorial and hear her side of the story. What evidence did they have on her?

Manny, excited about his playdate with Sophia, was at the front door, waiting to leave before I'd finished applying my lipstick. I'd messaged Pepper last night about the memorial service, and she'd volunteered Gabriela as a babysitter. She'd told me to come by early and that Sophia couldn't stop talking about my son. I also got the feeling that Pepper wanted company. She'd even suggested that we ride together.

"¡Mami, vamos! Vroom. Vroom."

He ran his toy police car over the arm of the living room chair and then around the coffee table. I prayed that the giver of his new favorite toy was on duty, because my plan was to see Alma before going to Pepper's.

When we cruised by Alma's house, I let out a "¡Gracias!" that my prayers had been answered. Gordon, in his bike uniform, was standing in front of her door. Wanting to increase my odds of getting in to see my best friend, I decided to zip over to the Haitian bakery in North Miami. Gordon liked me, but he'd also refused to tell me information the other day. I planned to double-whammy him with Manny and a box of pastries. Who could say no to that?

"Buenos días," I said, holding two bakery boxes.

"Good morning, Miriam. Hey there, little man." He gave Manny a high five.

"I have something for you." I gave him the smaller of the two boxes. "Dous Makos, it's Haitian fudge. Have you ever tried it?"

"Nope, but I love fudge." He opened it and took a bite of the beige, pink, and brown striped delicacy. "Vanilla? Cinnamon?"

"Good, right?"

Officer Gordon popped the rest of the bar in his mouth and licked his fingers.

"I've got to get these fish patties into the fridge." I gestured at him with the twine tied box as I rang the doorbell with my free hand. "Keep an eye on Manny for me." *Come on, Alma, open the door before he realizes what I'm doing.* "He hasn't stopped playing with that car since you gave it to him." *Never ask for permission. Just act like you belong there.* "He really loves it." *Hurry, Alma, hurry before he stops me.* Gordon bent at the waist and spoke to my son. I heard the lock turn, pushed the door with my hip, and slipped into the house.

"Miriam? They let you in?"

"Shh!" I pulled her away from the door and into the kitchen in the back of the house. "I'm not supposed to be here."

My best friend looked awful. She was dressed in stained and baggy sweatpants. *I didn't even know she owned a pair.* Her normally salon-perfect hair was limp and oily. She had puffy eyes. And she smelled rank. I hugged her, holding my breath.

"You need a bath, amiga," I said.

"I know, but I can't motivate myself to take one. My life is ruined. Everything I've worked for is destroyed." Alma sobbed. "Have you seen what they're saying about me on *Around Town*? Drug dealer! *Drug dealer!*" She was hysterical.

"Shh." I motioned toward the front of the house. "Cálmate." I stroked her back. "I'm going to get to the bottom of this. But I need you to calm down and tell me everything. What evidence do they have? What does your lawyer say?"

I put the cod patties in the fridge and poured her a glass of water. "Here, drink this." When she stopped crying, she told me that cocaine had been found in Sunny's system.

"So? What does that have to do with you?" I asked.

"Nothing except that they got an anonymous tip that I was Sunny's drug dealer, and then they found cocaine in my purse."

"¿Que qué?" I put my hands on my head, bewildered. "Cocaine in your purse? Did she die from an overdose? Detective Pullman told me they hadn't finished with the body yet."

"I don't know the details or the science. I was so anxious when they read the charges in court that all I heard was drugs, drugs, drugs." Alma paced. "My career is ruined. Bye-bye, early retirement. Adios Rome, Paris, Madrid. Hello, minimum-wage job."

"Stop. You are talking like a guilty person. Are you? Is there something you need to tell me? Have you started . . .? I know your brother . . ." I regretted it as soon as the words left my mouth.

"What? You honestly think!"

"No! No, no. It just doesn't make sense. How did the drugs get in your purse?"

"I don't know! Andrew says the state's case is weak. He's going to challenge the forensics on the drink packet."

"What drink packet?"

"That stupid diet drink. There were traces of cocaine on the packet."

"Traces? That's not enough to arrest someone. Is it? What if the traces were on the packet before it came into your possession? Who gave them to you?"

"I don't remember!" Alma slammed her hands on the counter.

"Chica, think!" I stomped my foot several times.

"Mami, tengo que ser pee-pee," Manny called from the foyer.

His sneakers squeaked on the terrazzo floor, and I knew he was doing the bathroom dance.

"Think. Who?" I left Alma in the kitchen and went to take Manny to the bathroom.

"As soon as he's finished, you need to leave," said Officer Smith standing in the doorway. His eyes darted all around. "Ms. Diaz is not allowed visitors. I could get in trouble. I shouldn't have let you in."

"I understand." I opened the door to the guest bathroom in the hall. "I don't want to get you in trouble." Manny dashed in, and I followed to help him.

After we'd washed our hands, Manny latched onto Gordon again, and I begged a second to grab my purse that I'd left in the kitchen. Alma slumped over the counter, one side of her face on the cold granite, looking at me through disheveled hair that had fallen over her brow.

"Esto es un desastre," she said. "A complete and utter disaster. My career is over!"

I put my purse over my shoulder. "I'm going to fix it. Don't worry." I rubbed her back in circular strokes, then made to leave, but only got a few steps away before remembering I had something for her. I pulled the bottle of despojo and the saint candle from my bag. "Here." I placed them on the counter in front of her face. "You need these. Say a prayer. Light the candle. Wash away the negative energy and—the stink."

"Do I smell?"

"Sí, amiga. Apestas como un skunk, but I still love you." I blew her an air kiss, then walked away.

On the way to Pepper's, I mulled over the new information—an anonymous tip. Someone was setting up my best friend. But who?

Chapter
Twenty-Five

Pepper drove us to a church I'd never had the occasion to see. It was several blocks off the main shopping street, set in a residential neighborhood. The church looked like maybe it had once been a house. Whoever had designed it had clearly been a fan of Frank Lloyd Wright, because the building had that modern yet artisanal quality. A low coral rock wall edged the property. I followed Pepper through the wooden gate that was propped open with a large gray manatee statue. There was a locked donation box with a faded "Save the Manatees" sign taped to it in the creature's flippers. We stepped off the path and into the courtyard to let a group of Women's Club ladies go by. According to the metal placer staked in the ground, the front garden had native plants. A large and well-fed calico cat slept on a bench surrounded on three sides by shrubs with butterflies flitting around them. Mounted under the church's eaves there was a rainbow flag, a "Black Lives Matter" banner, and a blue planet earth flag.

"What denomination is this church?" I asked.

"Unitarian Universalist. They're kind of crunchy if you haven't guessed." Pepper pointed to a white pole with the words "May Peace Prevail on Earth" in four languages.

"Crunchy like granola like hippie?"

"Exactly."

"Huh. Coral Shores is full of surprises. Flower power and whirled peas. Who would have guessed that?"

"'Whirled peas'?" Pepper asked, her brow furrowed.

"World peace. Whirled peas. I saw it on a bumper sticker and thought it was funny."

"Oh, I get it. Punny."

We both grimaced at the bad joke. It was nice to have a moment of humor before what was surely going to be a somber event. The walkway through the courtyard was a steady march of people dressed in black, like ants to a picnic. And then there was Juliet in bright yellow.

"Goodness, that's a little insensitive, even for Juliet," Pepper said. "Come on. We'd better go in before all the seats are taken."

We were a little too late. The only two spaces available were in the middle of the middle, literally the fourth row of seven. The church did not have a cross or an altar, nor did it have traditional bench pews. Individual chairs were arranged in semicircular rows split by a central aisle. There were ten chairs in each section, a hundred and forty in all. Our seats were not best situated for observing the gathered. I'd have preferred to be in the back. Stormy Weatherman and those who I assumed were other family members sat in the front row. There was a handsome older man in the row opposite Stormy. Maybe Sunny's father? I think I'd heard her parents were no longer together.

In the second and third rows, I recognized a few faces from the Women's Club lunch. Then came our row, which was also my mother-in-law's, but thankfully she was across the aisle. When I waved at her, she blinked and then turned to talk to Juliet, seated beside her. I pivoted in my seat and scanned for any other faces I knew. Sally, my sister-in-law, was in attendance. She smiled at me, and I knew she was there out of social obligation. Directly behind me was a group of waifs that smelled of cigarettes. A man in an ill-fitting suit capped the end of their row. He had a round metal lapel pin, a square on its point in a circle, that I noticed matched the pins the waifs wore. The person I expected to see, Detective Pullman, was nowhere to be found.

On the raised stage, a man with a tie-dyed purple and blue tie began playing the grand piano. A projection screen to his right flickered with a slideshow of Sunny through the years. She'd been a cute and happy child, it seemed. There were several photos of her in fairy wings and crowns. Her teen years turned goth. Not only did she dress like a Tim Burton character, but she looked like a skeleton. That must have been when the dieting had started. The images that followed were from her traveling twenties: Coachella, Ibiza, South Beach's White Party, Art Basel, and a few that looked like they had been taken at a desert spa. After the last note of Let It Be, a woman in a rainbow clergy stole took the podium. Her elegy about compassion and forgiveness was brief but thoughtful. When she'd finished, the Reverend invited Stormy to speak.

"Thank you all for coming. Parents are not supposed to survive their children, and I've survived two," Stormy said.

"Two? Sunny had a sibling?" I whispered to Pepper, who shrugged that she didn't know either.

"Sunny was eleven when Raine took her life. Her death tore holes in all our hearts, but it had the greatest effect on Sunny. She turned from a bright and confident kid to a dark and confused adult, but in the last three years, thanks to the support of people like Sean Rosen and his group"—Stormy motioned to the man in the rumpled suit behind me—"the old Sunny was beginning to shine again. Thank you, Sean. I'd also like to thank Alma Diaz. Five years ago, she could have pressed charges against my daughter, something that would have ruined her life, but instead she encouraged her to go to rehab."

Alma was the reason Sunny had gone to rehab. Why hadn't my best friend mentioned this? Why had she kept it a secret?

Stormy gripped the sides of the oak podium. "And then she went a step further—she became a mentor and friend to my daughter, encouraging her to look to the future with hope. They had coffee every Wednesday morning. Sunny was starting real estate school next week. So"—she pointed to us—"I want all the nasty rumors about Alma Diaz to stop!"

The audience made a quick collective gasp. There were a few coughs, and several people cleared their throats. It was an uncomfortable moment, like being reprimanded in front of your classmates by the principal. I desperately looked for Detective Pullman and hoped he'd heard the mother of the deceased clear Alma's name, but again I didn't see him.

"I loved my daughter. I know people pitied her, some made fun of her struggles, and others took advantage of her kind nature. Those people"—Stormy took a beat and looked at someone near Juliet—"and they know who they are, I forgive, but I will not forget."

Stormy tilted her head back and closed her eyes for a second. She might have been holding in tears, but she didn't seem the crying type. Maybe it was rage she was tamping down. I looked at Pepper, who was wiping a tear from her cheek.

"I choose to remember my daughter, Sunny Viola Weatherman, as the joyful, sensitive child she was when she attended primary school here. Mrs. Lucy"—Stormy motioned to a woman with frizzy white hair, wearing a dark batik caftan—"thank you for creating Agape Montessori. Sunny was truly happy when she was here. With your permission, I'd like to donate a new playground, vegetable garden, and art room in Sunny's memory."

Mrs. Lucy put her hand over her heart and mouthed her thanks. The Reverend embraced Stormy and resumed command of the microphone. She announced an instrumental interlude followed by a vocalist singing Sunny's favorite childhood song. After which there would be an opportunity for people to share their happiest memories of Sunny. The pianist sat at the keys and flipped his sheet music to the right piece. According to the program, it was Carol King's "Child of Mine." Someone from the matching pin group knocked the back of my head as she stepped over a row mate to get out. She was taking a bathroom or a smoke break. Either way, it was a chance I didn't want to miss to talk to one of Sunny's friends. I followed her out of the church and into the courtyard.

"You too?" The woman brandished the cigarette between her fingers.

"No. I don't smoke," I said. "But don't let me stop you." She lit her cigarette with a skull-adorned Zippo and took a deep drag. "I just needed a break from the intensity in there. Right?"

The smoker thoughtfully blew her smoke away from me and shrugged.

"Did you know Sunny very well?" I asked.

"Yeah."

"I'm sorry for your loss. I'm Miriam, by the way." I extended my hand.

She clamped my fingertips in hers and replied, "Natalie."

"Did you go to school at the Montessori with Sunny?"

"Nah." The calico cat circled her Doc Martens. She squatted and scratched the cat's head.

"I noticed a bunch of you had the same pin on and thought maybe it was the school's logo or something."

"Huh?"

I tapped my chest in the spot where the square in a circle button was on her.

"Ha ha," she chuckled. "NA. That's how I know Sunny."

"Is that a club?"

"Narcotics Anonymous."

"Oh."

"Yeah, Sunny just got her three-year chip. It's weird. I mean, relapse happens. But Sunny—nah, not her. Doesn't make sense. She was, like, doing good."

"Oh, is that how she died?"

The woman stubbed her butt out on a terra cotta pot and put the filter into her box of Marlboro reds. "That's what somebody said." She made a "whatever" expression. "The Kermit song's about to end."

I trailed her, and we sat in our seats in time to hear the last bar of "Rainbow Connection." The vocalist urged us to join in on the "la-da-da-da-da-de-da-do" part. Mrs. Lucy was the first to speak. She shared how Sunny had mangled the words to the song until Mrs. Lucy had given her a solo in the children's choir, prompting her to practice until she learned it. Mrs. Lucy showed a candid shot of Sunny dancing in the school's flower garden while rehearsing the song. Three others spoke after her, another teacher, a childhood friend that had flown in from California, and Sean Rosen. His eulogy was the most interesting. He, like Natalie, mentioned Sunny's determination to stay clean and sober.

The Reverend then directed us to the fellowship hall, where a spread of baked goods, as well as coffee and iced tea, had been prepared. The campus of the church was bigger than it looked from street level. It was more than a converted house.

"Oh look, there's Amanda. Come on, let's join her," Pepper said. Amanda was talking to a pregnant woman who was fanning herself with the memorial program.

"I'll join you in a second. There's someone I need to speak to first."

The reality was, I wanted to study the gathered and eavesdrop. Stormy had set the record straight about Alma, but I knew that wasn't enough to free my friend. And unless Detective Pullman was hiding in plain sight, he hadn't been there to hear it. If Sunny had died from unnatural cases, someone there might know why and how. If it wasn't a drug overdose, then what had taken the life of a relatively healthy thirty-year-old?

"Decaf or regular?" The bald man behind the food table asked.

"Regular, please," I replied.

He handed me a plain white cup and saucer, almost full. I moved down the line and added cream and sugar. One drop of half and half turned the weak brew from brown to white. *Yuck, where could I get rid of it?* I put a Pepperidge Farm thumbprint cookie, the kind with jelly, on my plate and waited for the queue to move. The woman in front of me was having a tough time choosing. Her finger lingered over the chocolate chip, then the Milano, then the Chessmen, then the Pirouette.

"Shortbread is always a safe choice," I offered.

"I just love them all. It's so hard to pick just one. Isn't it?" The lady giggled.

"No one is stopping you from taking more than one."

She grinned at me like we'd found a hoard of gold and took one of each. I realized that she was the teacher that had spoken after Mrs. Lucy.

"I loved the poem you read. You kept it all these years. Sunny must have meant a lot to you," I said.

"I loved that little girl. I wished we could have kept her here." She took a bite of cookie. "Maybe things would have been different for her. She changed so radically that year. I don't know." She finished the cookie in two chomps, causing crumbs to fall from her mouth like a rockslide.

"You mean the year her sister died?" I faked a sip of my coffee and moved to the next food selection.

"No, no, no. Well, yes, that too." She stopped, studied the array of mini muffins on the tray, and chose both a carrot and a blueberry one. She placed them precariously on the saucer that she had on top of her cup. "But it was the bullying that warped her. It robbed her of her confidence. That's when she started dieting. Can you imagine? Eleven years old, worried about her body mass index. Children should be allowed to be children!" She clenched her fist and rattled it. "I wish our school went past fifth grade. Middle school is rough for most but especially for the sensitive souls."

We were at the end of the buffet. The woman was a talker, and although I was very curious about Sunny and her sister, Raine, I didn't think their childhood history held the key to unlocking the mystery of her death. I spied the Reverend and Sean Rosen talking near a corkboard that was decorated with a rainbow border. On my way to them, I got rid of my untouched coffee. The pair were still in conversation when I approached. Hoping to catch what they were saying, I feigned interest in the photographs on the corkboard.

"The members are very shaken up. If it's okay with the church, I'd like to double up on our meetings. At least for the next week. The death of a friend can be a trigger to start using again," Sean Rosen said.

"Of course, I'll move the social justice book club to another room and add your extra meetings to the calendar. Do you think she relapsed? Can that cause a heart attack?" The Reverend had lowered her voice.

"The pure stuff can. Especially with a damaged heart like hers"

"The anorexia."

"Yeah. That's partly why I don't believe it. She knew the next time she did coke—it could kill her. Of all of them, Sunny was not the one I thought I had to worry about."

So, Sunny had died of a cocaine-induced heart attack? It made sense that her mother might not want to make that public. There's a lot of stigma associated with drug addiction. But as brave as Stormy was in her speech today, that didn't fit. She seemed the type to be blunt and fearless.

I examined the photos on the wall with one ear perked to the conversation. The collage of images looked like your average church bulletin board. Well, except for the photos of the maypole ribbon dance, the flotilla of kayaks collecting plastic in the bay, an immigration rights march, and a Pride parade float. One of the people on the float looked familiar. Not the hair, but the face. Getting close to it, I saw that it was Jorge, the Mambo-cise instructor. I guessed he went to church here. Did he know Sunny? As I searched the crowd for him, Pepper caught my attention and signaled me to join her.

She introduced me to the pregnant woman who politely asked the standard get-to-know-you questions. What do you do? Do you have any children? When the small talk was done, I asked them if they'd seen Jorge. Neither had.

Scanning the room again, it dawned on me that my mother-in-law and Sunny weren't there. I'd made the effort to acknowledge her during the service, but I was sure that would not count as enough of an effort. Marjory would say that she'd been slighted because I hadn't spoken to her after the service. Did I care? A little. It was nicer to be on neutral terms rather than on the 'ungrateful woman that married my baby boy' list. What would Sally do? I hoped she was still there so I could get her advice.

"Excuse me, ladies," I said. "I see my sister-in-law. I'll be right back."

Sally slipped out of the room before I could get to her. I pursued her to the sanctuary and was about to call to her to slow down when a door opened, bringing me to a full stop. Detective Pullman, with his hand on the door, stood at the bottom of a stairwell.

"You," I said.

"Hello, Ms. Quiñones."

"Have you been here the whole time?"

"I told you I'd be here. Good to see you made it."

"Where were you? Did you hear what Stormy said about Alma?"

"The parents' room is very comfortable." He pointed up the stairs. "Soundproof for crying babies, rocking chairs, it overlooks the sanctuary. Real nice. My church could use something like that."

"Did you hear Stormy clear Alma?" I put my hand on my hip.

Detective Frank Pullman looked at me like I was a child asking Santa for the deluxe Barbie Dreamhouse, with the elevator, pool, and pink Jeep, that the family couldn't afford to put under the tree.

"Mrs. Weatherman is not in charge of the investigation."

"Well, what about Sunny's NA friends? They don't feel like she was back on cocaine."

"The criminal justice system requires evidence and facts. We do not operate on hopes and feelings." He closed the door to the stairs. "And who said anything about cocaine?"

"Well, that's how she died. Right? A cocaine heart attack?"

"That hasn't been made public."

"But that's what you believe, isn't it?"

"I can't say until the second autopsy confirms it."

"Oh, is that why this was a memorial and not a funeral?"

"Yes. An independent autopsy is being conducted." Pullman led me outside and off the main walkway. "Now it's my turn to ask questions. What do you know about Jorge Trujillo?"

"The Mambo-cise instructor?"

Pullman nodded. Why was he asking about Jorge? Was Jorge involved? It was so hard to read what the detective was thinking. His body language gave away nothing.

"I don't know anything about him," I said.

"But you attend his class, right?"

"Yeah."

"Well, keep going and let me know if you hear anything or see any changes in his personality. Okay?"

"Sure. Okay. I'll go tomorrow."

I knew Jorge was pleased to be taking over Elliot's classes, but what did that have to do with Sunny? I was about to ask Detective Pullman when I heard my name being called.

"Miriam. Oh, there you are. Are you ready to go? Gabriela has to be at Grove this afternoon for a test, and I need to get home," Pepper said.

I gave her a "just-one-second" finger and turned back to the detective to get my question answered. But he'd vanished.

Chapter
Twenty-Six

Elliot's table of flowers and candles in the fitness center's lobby had been disassembled. In its place, there was a framed photograph of her mounted on the wall. In the picture, taken during one of her classes, the heads and backs of students were in the foreground. And reflected in the mirror behind her were their distorted figures. Elliot sat in a lotus position, her eyes closed, her hands open on her knees. Her peaceful confidence and joy radiated in the captured moment. The loss to her yoga community would surely be felt for a long time. She had been a leader who'd had more to give. Passing by the spot in the hallway where she'd collapsed, I gave a silent prayer for a life cut short and wondered if her death could've been prevented.

It had taken a few minutes longer than I'd budgeted to get Manny checked into the childcare room. There was a fussy baby and a debate about whether it was teething or had a fever. So when I got to the studio, it was nearly full. Paige, the breast cancer survivor, made a spot next to her, and I thanked her for the kindness. She was wearing another pink ribbon shirt. Today's said "Save the Tatas. Get a Mammogram."

It was bien raro being at Mambo-cise class without Alma. Weirder still was that I was there not for exercise, but to scrutinize the teacher. How would I know if Jorge Trujillo's behavior had changed? I'd only met the man twice. The first time he'd showed me photos of his drag act, and the second time he'd practically been in costume. At least today there was no cape or incense. The class started with Lou Bega's fun and silly "Mambo No. 5." Followed by Joe Cuba's classic booga-loo "Bang Bang." I'd heard that song every Friday night coming from my New York City neighbor's apartment. It was his official start to the weekend anthem. The high energy set ended with a hip-shaking Sha-kira medley. I welcomed the cooldown segment and wished I'd remembered to bring a bottle of water. Alma would have.

"Great job, ladies," Jorge said, clapping. "I want to remind every-one that I have a new class." Jorge stopped clapping and pressed his hands together. He waited for everyone's attention, then spread his arms à la Evita's balcony scene. "Broadway Moves and Meditation." He twirled an arm above his head like he was throwing a lasso. "You will love it! It's in Elliot's old time slot. So, if you've already paid for her class, you can roll over to mine, no problem."

A lady with short hair raised her hand and asked, "Will it be like Elliot's, with gentle stretches and modifications for people like me that have a little extra padding?" The woman patted her rump and laughed in a self-deprecating way.

"Nannette, I've got you. Don't worry." Jorge pointed to the next person with their hand up.

"What type of yoga is it?" The only man in the class asked.

"Melton, it is not—" Jorge began but was interrupted by a volley of questions.

"Are you yoga certified?"

"Hatha?"

"Kundalini?"

"Ashtanga?"

"Is it the same as Elliot's?"

Jorge was getting frustrated. He tried to reply to each person, but the questions were popcorn kernels in accelerated popping. He clapped the crowd into control and made the close-your-mouths motion with both his hands.

"Ladies and Melton. The class. Is. Not. Yoga. It is movement and meditation. If you like yoga stretches and Broadway," Jorge made the word lyrical, "you will like my class. And actually, right before Elliot died, she told me she was taking a break from teaching, and I was the only person she'd trust with her students."

There were no "hmms" or "huhs" or "okays" from the group. Their questions were put to bed, and they seemed happy with his reply. I, on the other hand, was not. Had Elliot really been planning to quit teaching? Why? From the little I knew of her, she was on an upward swing, not a downward one.

I lingered, picking up my things until the room emptied. Jorge moved the sound system back to its shelf and was about to spray the room with Febreze air refresher.

"Gracias for the great class. Me encanta that song," I said, then sang and danced one of the intro lines. *"Cornbread, ham maws, and chitlins."*

Jorge put down the spray and replied with another of the song's fun lines. *"Oh, chuchi chuchi . . . Estás comiendo cuchifrito."*

He grabbed my hand and twirled me. We partner danced a few salsa steps until I broke from it and shouted another food line from the song: *"Lechon! Lechon!"*

Both of us laughed hard.

"Your playlists are always amazing. You could be a DJ on South Beach," I said.

"Mujer, that dream is dead." Jorge sighed. "I was set to do Miami Music Week. I was booked at E11EVEN. My name was on posters and everything. Pero then . . ." His voice trailed off and he pinched the bridge of his nose.

"¿Qué pasó?"

"No importa. It's in the past. I still love music and I still get people to dance. *'No hay que llorar,'* como dice Celia. *'La vida es un carnaval.'"*

I could tell Jorge was swallowing some big emotions. "I'm sorry. Whatever it was, I'm super glad you're a dance instructor now because my clubbing days are over and I would never have gotten to meet you."

"Gracias." His smile hid a sadness.

I tried to lighten the mood. "Leave it to a Puerto Rican to write a song with fried foods and pork in the lyrics," I said.

"I know, right?" he said, laughing. "That song always makes me hungry."

Now that I had Jorge relaxed again, I didn't know how to transition from food to Sunny and Elliot. Luckily, he did it for me.

"People should just eat the foods they want to and dance. Dance instead of diet. Ooh, I should put that on a shirt." He marked the three words down the front of his body with his palm. "Dance Don't Diet! T. M. Mambo-cise."

I nodded enthusiastically.

"Dieting is stupid. That fake doctor that everyone in Coral Shores is all of a sudden crazy about. They are just throwing their money away. Diet tea. Por fa-vor! Pft." He crossed his arms and cocked his hip to the side.

There was my opening. "Elliot believed in him."

"Don't get me started on Elliot. La estúpida. Who goes to a dentist for fertility treatment?"

"A dentist?"

"Oh, you didn't know? Mi'ja. Mario Fuentes is a dentist. A. Dentist. He couldn't get licensed to practice in the US. You know—all that Cuba–America politics stuff. So, he reinvented himself as a New Age herb doctor. But listen to this, chica, before he became Mr. Rainforest, he was a 'cosmetic surgeon.'" Jorge made air quotes. "He did butt implants, and lips, and you know. He killed Miz Fiyah. She went to him for boobs, and he pumped her full of—¿como se llama esa cosa?—that stuff they use in the bathroom between the tile." He snapped his fingers by his forehead, trying to make the word come.

"Caulking?"

"¡Sí, eso!"

"Ay mi madre. Why isn't he in jail?"

"Don't get me started! The other guy, Dr. Ramirez, took the blame. He said it was his special formula and that the people that work for him didn't know what was in it." Jorge rolled his eyes. "He was a real doctor. You know, the one with the license for the clinic. Pero like he was eighty and had lung cancer or something, and so he didn't even go to jail!" His hand clawed the air before making a fist. "He went to hospital prison and died a week later."

"Wait. So, did Fuentes know he was using bad stuff?"

"Claro. My friend suffered for a whole week before she died. She went to Fuentes the day after with a fever and chills and vomiting, and he said she had the flu. The *flu*. And then the day after that, the clinic, a little cement building insured for two million dollars, mysteriously had a fire."

"¿Que qué?"

"Hialeah especial, chica."

My gossip session with Jorge changed vibes as people trickled in for the next class, Karen's Crochet Circle. They began unfolding tables and chairs, arranging them into one large table. He greeted the incoming teacher and asked her to plug his Broadway Movement and Meditation.

As we left the room, I asked Jorge if Elliot had really said she was taking a break.

He leaned in close and whispered, "Not exactly. Pero, like, I saw her run out of the seminar with her hand over her mouth. I swear she was about to toss her cookies. So, I figured she was finally pregnant. And if she was, that she'd likely stop teaching because that's how she lost the last one. Like, right? So, like, she almost for sure was going to quit."

His logic was skewed, but he was giving me a goodbye hug in the lobby, and I couldn't grill him further. Before I retrieved Manny from the playroom, I took a second to admire Elliot's photograph again. "Wait. Did Jorge just say he saw Elliot the night she died?" I looked around to make sure no one had heard me talking to myself. Did Detective Pullman know that? Was Jorge questioned that night? A hairbrained theory formed in my mind. *Could Jorge have killed Elliot to set up Fuentes? He'd get Elliot's classes and justice for the death of his friend Fiyah. It'd be two for the price of one.* I wished I'd been quicker on my feet and thought to ask him more probing questions. I almost chased after him but thought better of it. The fitness center had a strict time limit on childcare, and my theory was loco.

Forced to walk by the spot Elliot died again, I said another prayer. As I did, I looked to the heavens and noticed the center's security cameras. An idea flashed into my head, and I convinced myself it was kosher. *The detective had, after all, asked for my help, right? I should gather some evidence for my crazy theory before embarrassing myself by telling it to Pullman.* I knocked on the administration office.

"Hi. Sorry to bother you," I said to the young person who opened the door. "I have a question about the fitness center's security cameras."

"Ma'am, I'm sorry if something has gone missing, but we advise everyone not to leave their personal belongings unattended."

They began to shut the door, but I stopped them with an extended hand.

"I should have introduced myself better. I'm assisting Detective Frank Pullman, and I'd like to review the security footage from the evening of Elliot Truman's death."

Their face drained of blood, and I could see I'd scared them numb. I didn't know if my great idea was that great after all. I had a feeling my wrist was going to get smashed to bits when the door slammed shut. But then that didn't happen. In a low voice, the staffer told me to wait a moment. While they went to get whoever they were going to get, I stepped into the office and closed the door behind me. They returned in a minute with someone who, I guessed, was a superior with a higher pay grade. The genial-looking man had a sunburned dome with a crew cut ring of white hair. He looked like he'd been a coach all his life.

"May I help you?"

"Yes, hello," I said, then repeated my line about assisting the police.

"They've already reviewed everything. What was your name again, Miss?"

"Miriam Quiñones," I said, and added, "Smith," because I could see I was getting nowhere with a Spanish-sounding name.

"Smith? Are you the girl that married Bobby?"

Internally I sighed. I hated using the Smith name, and I hated when people called my husband "Bobby." "Bob" wasn't much better. But you use what you've got and adapt.

"Yep, that's me." I plastered on the friendliest, perkiest face I could.

"I was Bobby's lacrosse coach." The man propped himself on the edge of a desk with one leg dangling off. "How's he doing? I heard he was back."

Lacrosse? Robert had never mentioned he'd played lacrosse. Honestly, I wasn't sure I even knew what the game was, but the thing that stuck in my craw was that there was clearly a lot about Robert that I didn't know.

"You all bought the place on Manatee?" He said it like a question.

I nodded that he was correct.

"So, you're a policewoman. I thought Bill said you're a Spanish teacher."

"Professor." My father-in-law had it almost right. "I'm not an officer. I'm assisting Detective Pullman." I felt my nose grow a yard with each syllable. No way was he going to believe a professor was helping the police investigate a crime. I needed something plausible. "As a translator."

"Huh, okay, right, Elliot died the night that Spanish guy was giving his seminar. Tragic. We're going to miss that girl. She was a doll."

Girl. Doll. Calling Human Resources. The Coral Shores Fitness Center needed an Equal Opportunity refresher class.

"Well, come on back, and I'll show them to you, but you know our video doesn't have sound. So, I don't know if you'll be able to translate much."

"No problem, I can read lips," I said.

He set me up with a nineteen-year-old techie named Becca, if her name tag was to be believed. The young woman had drawn cat ears over the Cs in her name, pupils in the letters, and a triangle nose and whiskers under them. Robert's old coach left us alone after a minute of hovering.

The security footage was stored in the cloud, and each camera had its own folder. I asked to see the feed that showed the hallway and bathroom door from that night. There was Elliot leaving the event room and hurrying to the bathroom. It looked like someone down the hall from her called her name, and she replied with a shake of her head before darting into the bathroom. The person's identity was not clear. They were too far from the camera, but they were about the shape and size of Jorge. They carried a duffle bag and a plastic grocery bag. After about three minutes, Elliot emerged. It looked like she was having trouble breathing. She took a few steps, clutched her stomach, and collapsed. Her thermos hit the floor and the contents flooded onto the linoleum. Her arms and legs twitched once, then she went still. I got piel de gallina watching it. I rubbed the goosebumps from my forearms but couldn't shake the reality that I was watching someone's life end. I made the sign of the cross and got a side-eye from the techie.

"Can you take it back an hour?" I asked.

The techie slid the time bar on the screen and took me to the moments when most of the audience was entering the room. I saw Alma and me. *Is that what I look like?*

"Can we go back a little further? I want to see when Elliot and the Fuentes people arrive. There." I pointed at the screen. "That's perfect."

On screen, Elliot Truman hugged Mario Fuentes and led him to the room. His lab coat–clad staff made several trips with boxes and a foldable rolling cart. Then Juliet Pimpkin, in sunglasses and carrying grocery bags, walked by the camera. *Another meal for the center's staff?* A few moments later, she came back into view and went into the seminar, hands free of bags. Soon after, attendees filled the room, and we were back to the footage we'd already reviewed. Elliot didn't leave the room until her bathroom visit. The theory that had drifted into my head that maybe Jorge had something to do with Elliot's death didn't have wings to fly.

I thanked Becca, the young staffer who had helped me, and went down the corridor to the childcare room. Prepared for a late charge, I put my hand on the handle but quickly withdrew it. There was a camera above the door. *Duh!* I hurried back to the office and knabbed the techie before her coffee break. She was not happy, but she did oblige me.

"Thank you. I will repay you a coffee next time I come. I promise," I said. "I need to see the daycare door camera for that night."

"I like the salted caramel mocha frap. Venti," Becca said.

The tech found the day and time quickly and played on her phone while I examined the video. I'd asked to go back to much earlier in the evening and hoped to see Jorge interact with Elliot. The camera's vantage was mostly on the childcare room's door, but a corner captured the end of the hallway where I'd seen the figure I thought could be Jorge. It was him. He passed through the area several times. Disappointingly, there was no sign of Elliot, but there was a surprise. Juliet Pimpkin and Jorge Trujillo having an intimate conversation.

Chapter
Twenty-Seven

The childcare attendant gave me a get-out-of jail-free card for my first tardy and hadn't charged me the late pickup fee. I added her to the IOU coffee and baked goods list. Maybe Juliet also owed the fitness center staff favors, thus the breakfast the other morning and the grocery bags of goodies the evening of the Fuentes talk. But I somehow doubted it. She was the type of person to keep the scales balanced in her favor at all times. She'd want people owing her, not the other way around. What had she and Jorge been discussing in the video? Had it been something like that? They didn't exactly run in the same social circles. Mambo-cise was too "urban" for Juliet. Did Jorge owe Juliet a favor?

"Let it go, Miriam. Stop trying to pin it on Jorge."

"¿Qué, Mami?" Manny asked from the back seat.

"Nada, mi amor. Tu mamá se volvió loca."

I did feel I was going a little cuckoo. I was no closer to getting Alma released from house arrest, and my list of suspects, motives, and means was more muddled than the mint for a mojito.

Manny unbuckled himself as soon as our car rolled to a stop under our royal poinciana tree. I pressed the unlock button, and he tried his best to open his own door. He was growing up so fast. Maybe it was good that I was going to be a stay-at-home mom for a while. I helped him get out of the car. He bolted into the house, singing a song about his police car toy that we hadn't been able to find that morning. Panic punched me in the gut. Why was the front door to my house open? Had we been robbed? Was the robber still in there? Did they have Manny? I ran inside with a plan to gouge the eyes out of whoever had their hands on my baby boy.

"There you are. I've been waiting."

My panic was replaced by annoyance. What was my mother-in-law doing sitting in my living room uninvited? *I have to change the locks!*

"Hello, Marjory. To what do I owe the pleasure?"

She smiled, and I could tell I hadn't masked my sarcasm very well.

"There is a puppet show at the library this afternoon, and I want to take the grandchildren." She twisted in her seat to speak to Manny, who was coming out of his room with a toy. "You want to see your cousins, Savanah and Reagan." She waved for him to come close to her. "Isn't that right?"

"Yes, Grandmother." He opened his arms and hugged her. "I see Vanna and Ray."

Marjory winced at my son's grammar. She looked me in the eye and said, "He needs to practice his English. Reagan and Savanah had an extensive vocabulary by his age. Multisyllabic words and complex sentences. I will have to take his education into hand since it is obviously too much for you to handle."

She had just crossed a line that had me wishing she was a robber so I could wrestle my son from her arms and beat her out of my house. *Ayúdame, Caridad por favor.* I sure was praying a lot for someone who hadn't been to a mass in over a year. The patron saint of Cubans answered my prayer with the Michelle Obama motto "When they go low, we go high." That needed to be my SOP—standard operating procedure—with my mother-in-law. Don't let her ruffle your feathers.

"A puppet show! That sounds perfect. Let me get him washed up and ready," I said. After Manny had gone to the bathroom and I'd changed him into a clean shirt, I got his push-bike out of the garage and sent them on their way. I wasn't keen on the idea of him spending the entire afternoon with her, but at least his cousins would be there too. Savanah had proved she was a kind kid. She'd look out for him. I decided to text Sally later and ask her how she was handling the afternoon with Grandmother Smith. *Granny Smith. Oh, she'd hate that name even though it fit her well. She was hard and acidic.*

"Go high, Miriam. Go high," I said as I jumped in the shower to rinse off the Mambo-cise sweat. The cool water refreshed my attitude. By the time I'd dried off and dressed, I had a plan for my suddenly free afternoon. Operation Free Alma needed an anthropological approach. To explore the hows and whys of Sunny's and Elliot's deaths, I should be looking at behavior, culture, and expression. The tools needed to do that were observation, listening, and research. All three were in my toolbox, but I hadn't put them to use methodically.

It was time to do some research.

With a plate of Maria cookies and a tumbler of café con leche by my side, I opened my laptop. A search for "Hialeah botched cosmetic surgery" produced ten pages of results. The images were grotesque, and I felt sorry for the horror those people must have suffered. Adding "caulking" refined the search and made the photographs that I thought couldn't get worse, worse. The top articles were from news outlets. *The Miami Herald* reported that Fuentes testified he'd been trained by the clinic's owner and had no knowledge of the dangerous materials in the proprietary body enhancer compound. Next, I clicked on a WSVN video of the protest outside the charred remains of the clinic. In Spanish and English, the gathered, mostly black and brown people, were shouting for justice. A mother cried angry tears for her beautiful daughter who was now disfigured. In the background, there were a few homemade signs. One of them had an orange and red flame with "We will never forget Fiyah" in black letters above it.

"Is that . . .?" I said and hit "Pause." I clicked the full-screen option and went back to the beginning. The person holding the sign was none other than The Mambo King himself, Jorge Trujillo.

I searched the videos from the other local news stations, hoping one of them had interviewed Jorge. None had, but it was positively him with the sign. Observing his body language, I'd say he was mad enough to torch the place.

My phone rang. I put the news video on mute and answered the call on speaker.

"Miriam," Delvis said. "I need you at the studio today to record a new outro."

"What's an outro?"

"Intro. Outro. The end part of your video segment. Can you come in? I promise it will only take a few minutes. It's audio only."

There went my afternoon of research.

"Sure. I can be there within the hour, is that okay?"

"Cool. Dale."

I did one more search before leaving the house. It was for Jorge Trujillo. If he'd ever been in trouble or arrested, it was well hidden. The only thing associated with his name was exercise and dance. It seems he'd been the king of flash mobs about ten years ago. He'd organized thirty men in heels, wigs, and prom dresses to dance to Lady Gaga's "Born This Way," among pulling off other stunts. I expected to find some reference to his DJing, especially if he was at Miami Music Week level, but nothing came up.

The song was an earworm that stuck with me on my drive to the UnMundo studios. My usual route was blocked by road construction, and the detour made a wide loop that got me turned around. I ended up near the airport on the south side of Hialeah. The area had a plethora of "Love Hotels" that rented rooms in hourly increments. Many of them were cheesy and themed. As a kid, I'd wanted to know what a Roman bath was and thought the idea of a heart-shaped tub was the coolest. When I hit my teen years, I understood what they actually were and was grossed out by the mere mention of them. But in a culture that lived in multigenerational households where private space for intimacy was next to impossible, the hotels made sense. I'm sure some of the patrons were having extramarital affairs, but a good portion of them were just regular working-class people trying to get their groove on away from familial eyes.

"Come on. Come on. Come on. Turn green already."

The stoplight was at a weird junction of five roads, and it was taking forever. I bided my time, imagining what the rooms of El León Dorado, the hotel a few cars ahead on the right, were like. The one-story building had a fountain supported by gold-painted lions with a larger lion in the center shooting water from its mouth. The creature had a tilted crown on its head that reminded me of the iconic Biggie Smalls King of New York photo.

"Finally."

Traffic started to move.

"Is that Roberto's car?" I turned the corner hastily and circled the block. A red Tesla with a paper license plate was parked at El León Dorado love motel.

"Miriam, you are in Miami. There is going to be more than one red Tesla in the city. Cálmate, niña."

The red light caught me again. I was stuck there and fixated on the Tesla. I pulled into the parking lot of the business next to the hotel and got out of my car. I had to know, or the thought of it would be like an earworm I couldn't get rid of.

I gasped when I looked in the back seat of the car. Manny's police car toy was on the seat. It was Roberto's Tesla. What was it doing there? What was *he* doing there? Was he having an affair? Was he there with Juliet?

Chill, Miriam. You don't know for sure for sure.

I went to the motel office, a freestanding, supersized toll booth–looking thing, and asked the man in the box if a brown-haired man

194

with a tall, thin blonde American had rented a room. He didn't look up from his word search book. I asked again, and he pointed to the rate chart taped to the window. I took two twenties from my wallet and passed them through the semicircular opening.

"Sí," he replied.

The man tucked the bills into the pocket of his striped short-sleeved shirt. It appeared forty dollars only bought a single word. I took out my phone and googled Juliet Pimpkin Coral Shores. Several images from gala events popped up. Enlarging the best of the bunch, I held it to the glass and asked, "¿Ella?" The man nodded and circled a diagonal word in his puzzle.

My Roberto was at a love hotel with his high school ex-girlfriend who was his second cousin and his mother's preferred mate for him and the daughter of his new boss. I could barely breathe.

I wish we'd never left New York!

Robert had become a different person. Was he having an early midlife crisis? There had to be an explanation. Maybe they were doing an environmental assessment on the property? Maybe the love motel was the next Pimpkin Development project?

I tapped on the motel office window. Mr. Wordsearch ignored me. With a voice close to a scream, I asked for the room number. The man closed the shutter on the aluminum speak-thru. If he wasn't going to give me the room number than I'd have to knock on every room in the place. Before I could get close to a motel room, the office door opened. A large Doberman pinscher leapt out, skidded to a stop in front of me, and growled. The beast kept growling as drool dripped from the corners of its mouth. It didn't stop threatening me until Mr. Wordsearch whistled. The dog galloped to its commander, wagging its stubby tail. I was given hand directions to turn around and leave the property.

I sat in my car for ten minutes, shaking. Almost being eaten by a guard dog was scary, but my unsettled nerves were mostly from rage. "Roberto, who have you become?" I whispered.

Chapter
Twenty-Eight

Delvis was ready for me when I arrived at UnMundo. She took
me to a second-floor sound booth that had black eggcrate foam
on the walls and smelled of piña colada air freshener.

"Wow, Delvis. You made me look increíble," I said after viewing
the edited segment. "I thought I'd rambled nonsense."

"Stop with the imposter syndrome already." Delvis patted me on
the back. "Your storytelling is what makes this different. It's what's
going to set us apart from the competition. This new show will help
us break through to the Latinx market."

I was confused by her words. I mean, of course, I knew the term
"Latinx." It usually referred to young people of either Latin American
or colonial Spanish Caribbean descent living in the USA. Latinx
aren't necessarily fluent in Spanish. They might have grown up hearing it from their parents and abuelos, but they didn't speak it with
confidence. It was the syndrome I was hoping to avoid with
Manuelito.

"What do you mean, 'new show'?"

"The idea that I've pitched to Ileana and the top brass is a You-
Tube channel sort of like the *Pero Like* content from a few years back."
Delvis combed her blue hair with her fingers. "You've seen it, right?"

"Yeah, yeah. But what does that mean for me? Will I have to do
two versions? One in English and one in Spanish?"

"No, not at all. And remember, this is like a pilot episode, so the concept will evolve. But the idea is basically Spanglish. You do *Cocina Caribeña*, the Spanish version for *La Tacita*, then, in post, we put in English subtitles and graphics for the *Caribbean Kitchen* YouTube version. We will record a different intro and outro for the Latinx audience. But you don't have to change the recipe or the cooking. Got me?"

I was quiet. More like I was overwhelmed. This job had been sold as a short-term gig, three months maternity, and then I was done. I hadn't signed up for a YouTube channel.

"What's wrong? Is it the money? If this takes off, your contract will have to be rewritten. So, don't worry, you'll get more money."

"No, it's not the money. I hadn't even thought about that."

"So, what is it?"

"I'm not a personality. Don't you want like a celebrity chef or an actor or somebody? I mean, I'm a mom with a PhD in food anthropology. I'm so not *Pero Like* cool."

"Seriously, you need to stop. Trust me. You are cool. All that cultural history and stuff you know is dope."

I think she has it wrong. She's the cool one with her tattoos and blue hair. I'm a boring mom in cargo capris and a floral peasant blouse. Is that the reason Roberto is cheating on me? Have I become boring and unattractive?

"Okay, so, first we need the Spanish outro, then we'll record the English stuff. Here, I've written this, but you can adlib a little. Put on these headphones and just speak into the mic when I give you the signal from behind the glass."

The outro was pretty basic. "This sancocho recipe is on our website. While you are there, tell us your favorite meal and why. Is it your abuelita's pastelón or your Titi's flan? See you next week." I got it in two takes. The English stuff took the better part of an hour. Delvis had me say the same lines over and over with directions to go faster, slower, more upbeat, more natural. Acting was Alma's thing, not mine. She'd tried out for the school play, not me.

Alma. I hadn't talked to her since yesterday. Pobrecita. People were driving past her house on the daily and seeing a police officer guarding her front door. That only added to the drug lord rumor. I hoped she wasn't going to lose her career because of a false anonymous tip. I was nowhere nearer to clearing her name. In reality, I was further away than when I'd started. Jorge had me sidetracked. Fuentes was the thing that connected the three illnesses. He should be my focus. In my gut, I felt that the diet powder had something to do with Sunny's death. There were two things I didn't understand. Okay, there was a laundry list of things I didn't understand, but one—who had called in the tip? And two, how had the diet powder packet with the trace of cocaine gotten in Alma's purse? Was the diet powder tainted? Elliot wasn't taking the diet powder. Or was she? Were all of Dr. Mario Fuentes's products tainted? Did he know he was selling bad herbs? Did he care? He'd "accidentally" killed somebody before. Miz Fiyah. There I was, again, back to Jorge.

"Miriam? Miriam. Miriam. Earth to Miriam."

"Huh?" I got out of my head and back into the present.

"We're done for today. Okay." Delvis was at the control panel. "I've got to finish here. You remember how to get back to the lobby, right?"

"Yeah, sure. No problem." Slinging my purse over my shoulder, I left the booth and found my way to the elevator. When the doors opened on the first floor, there was a poster of Ileana and the gossip guy. The image was an odd, forced perspective that made them look like giants in front of a tiny couch and coffee table. I wondered how she was doing. Was she okay after her fainting spell? I decided to ask her myself. After going down the wrong hallway, I found her office. The door was closed. If she was in a meeting, I didn't want to knock and interrupt her. So, I found her administrative assistant and asked if Ileana was free.

"Sorry. She's not here. She went home right after taping. No se sentía bien. I can leave her a message to call you."

She wasn't feeling well. My stomach spasmed. I hoped she wasn't going the way of Sunny or Elliot.

"Is she okay?" I asked.

"Un dolor de cabeza nada más." The administrator swatted the air and returned her gaze to her computer screen.

I hoped it was only a headache.

"¿Algo más?" she asked in that polite way that meant she needed to get back to her work.

I thanked her and left. Checking my watch, I saw it was after two. As if on cue, my stomach growled. I hadn't skipped lunch on purpose. There wasn't enough time to go by Yoli's for a full sit-down meal. Anyway, I had a sudden urge to crash the puppet show that started at three. The idea of Marjory handling three grandchildren for more than an hour made me nervous. So, I went through the Pollo Tropical drive-through and got a side order of fried yucca with cilantro garlic dipping sauce. Balancing the dip in the hand holding the steering wheel, I tried my best to get the fries to my mouth without dripping sauce on my clothes. I was successful until I hit the detour, and then the image of my husband in a heart-shaped bed with Juliet Pimpkin had me stuffing my face. I followed the detour correctly and didn't pass by the hotel. But it didn't matter. My mind was on a loop.

Robert is having an affair. My husband is cheating on me. Roberto is cheating on me. ¿Ay, mi madre, qué voy a ser? Robert is having an affair.

Parked at the library, I dialed Alma. It rang with no answer. It felt stupid, selfish, and inconsiderate to leave her an all-about-me message when she was dealing with her own stuff. Also worrying was the fact that she was incommunicado. She must be more depressed than I thought. She needed my support, not me dumping on her. I texted her to call me, with a kiss emoji and a heart.

It was my first time at the Coral Shores Library. The one-story building had a grand marine limestone entranceway with a bike rack to one side and a statue of a sailor in a storm to the other. The statue's green patina made it look like a wave from Biscayne Bay had splashed seagrass onto the man. I noticed Manny's push-bike was next to a pink tricycle with a Barbie logo. The thought of raising my son as a single parent brought tears to my eyes. I ducked into the bathroom and splashed my face with cool water. Drying my face with the rough paper towel, I heard a mom and her daughter come into the two-stall bathroom.

"Hurry up and wash your hands, Sophia."

"Pepper?" I asked as I turned, blotting my cheeks.

"Oh, hey, Miriam. You okay?" She pointed to my face.

"Just cooling off. Miami is so hot and humid. You'd think I'd be used to it, having grown up here, but I guess those years away spoiled me."

"I hear you. Sometimes I miss the Oklahoma weather. Not the tornadoes. I don't miss those. But I love a little snow in the winter and having all four seasons. I think Miami has only two. Hurricane season and tourist season. Both are hot and last six months."

I forced myself to laugh with Pepper. The sickening thoughts of Robert and Juliet having a tryst at a love motel were still on repeat in my mind. The images I'd conjured had faded some, but not the anxiety.

Pepper tore off a length of towel and gave it to her daughter.

"How are you doing?" I asked.

"Coping by cupping." She mimed drinking.

I held the door for her and Sophia.

"The funeral is Friday. I'm not ready for it. I still can't believe she's gone. You'll be there. Right? It's at St. Brigid's."

"Of course."

Pepper looked like she needed a hug, so I gave her one. When she squeezed me back, it felt good. I think I needed a hug, too.

"Where's Manny?" Pepper asked as we entered the children's room.

"He should be with my mother-in-law and Sally's girls."

I looked for my dark-headed son among the squirming sea of kids on the floor in front of the red puppet theater scene. He must have sensed I was looking at him because he sprang up and ran to me. Marjory, at a round table with other adults, noticed him leaving his spot. She waved at me, crossed her arms, and continued chatting with the lady beside her.

"Mami. Mami. Quiero libros." Manny took my hand and dragged me to the picture book section. He plucked several books from the "birds of a feather" display and shoved them into my hands before running back to his front-row seat.

I loved that he loved books. And it seemed like, despite it being a small community library, there was a nice selection. I added two A–Z books to the pile: *AlphaOops! The Day Z Went First* by Alethea Kontis and *Eating the Alphabet* by Lois Ehlert. The picture-book section was at kid level. So I got on my knees and spent a few minutes searching for titles in Spanish or with Hispanic themes. Sadly, I didn't find any. That was something I'd make sure changed.

The lights dimmed, and a fanfare of horns played. The puppet show was beginning. A woman in an apron-style dress with appliqued fairy-tale characters on the skirt sat in a wingback chair. I guessed that she was the children's librarian as there was a chorus of *Hello, Mrs. Greene!* from the kids, and when she shushed them, they instantly quieted. She opened an oversized book and announced the day's story: "There Was an Old Lady Who Swallowed a Fly." As she read, a pair of teens managed the puppets. It looked well rehearsed, and the children were transfixed by the animal carnage.

I took Manny's books to the front desk and told the staff person I was a new resident needing a library card. She asked to see my driver's license to verify I lived in the village.

"I haven't changed my license yet.," I said.

"Do you have a utility bill? Or a bank statement?" The woman was trying to be helpful.

"I'm sorry, I don't. Is there any other way to get a card?"

"You can purchase a nonresident card for a hundred dollars a year." She grimaced.

"That's a lot," I said. Manny was going to be so disappointed if we left the library without any books. "Can you hold these for me while I run home to find some type of ID?"

"Tina, put them on my card. She's my sister-in-law," Sally said.

I felt Sally's arm on my waist. She gave me a side hug. "Thank you," I said.

"Are you a Smith?" the staffer asked, and I nodded. "Well, why didn't you just say that? Here, fill this out, and I'll get you all set up." She passed me an index card–sized application.

I looked at Sally and opened my eyes wide in mock astonishment. She leaned into me and said. "I know. I know. The power of the Smith name."

With a few strokes and an infrared barcode beep, I had a Coral Shores library card. Manny's books were scanned, and yellow return-date cards were put in the pocket of each book. I asked Sally to walk with me to put the books in the car.

"Can I ask you a question?"

"Fire away," Sally replied.

"Robert stayed with you for a week or so before the house was ready. Right?"

"Yeah."

"Has he seemed strange to you?"

"Strange. How?"

"You know, different." I put Manny's stack of books in the back seat next to his booster and clicked the alarm on the car. "Like something is going on with him."

She didn't answer immediately.

"I feel like he's not the same Robert as when we were in New York," I added and stopped in front of the statue.

Sally fiddled with the diamond ring on her finger while she thought. "I guess he's seemed a little anxious and preoccupied the last few times he's come over to the house. I know Drew is working on some legal documents for him. Maybe that's got him stressed."

"Do you know what it's about?"

"Sorry, no. Maybe family stuff? I think I overheard them talking about a trust."

"What, like a trust account?"

"Yeah, the Smiths are loaded. And there's always been some secrecy as to how loaded. You signed the prenup."

"A prenuptial agreement?" My jaw went slack, and my brain went from zero to divorce.

"Oh, that's right. You eloped and then had the family ceremony later. That was smart. I wish I'd done that. Our wedding was a circus, with Marjory and my mother fighting for the center ring."

"So you think they've been talking about money? But Andrew's a criminal attorney, and Junior is the financial whiz. Right?" I was grasping at straws. I didn't want what was in my head to be true. Was Robert setting up a trust account for Manny because he was about to divorce me and marry Juliet?

"Yeah, but when it comes to the Smith men, there's always been this team mentality with the brothers. It's Senior and Junior versus Andrew and Robert."

I turned away from Sally and covered my eyes with my hand. I was fighting back tears. My voice was ragged as I asked, "So, something is going on?"

"Sweetie, are you crying?" Sally put her hands on my shoulders and pulled me into an embrace. "Stop worrying. I'm sure everything is okay."

"But Robert's changed. He's different." I broke away from her attempt to comfort me.

"Of course." Sally shifted to her back leg and put her hand on her hip. "Moving and a new job are stressful. Add to that that he's now only a few blocks away from his mother. Of course, he's acting different. This family will do that to you. Whatever has him stressed will pass. It will be okay."

"I don't know about that."

"It will be okay." Sally linked her arm with mine. "Come on. Let's get back in there and rescue the kids from Marjory. I hate the way Savannah talks after spending even a few hours with her. An afternoon with your grandmother should be tea parties and ice cream, not an eloquence class." Sally mimicked Marjory's voice. *"Enunciate. Do not slur your words. You are a Smith."* She switched back to her regular voice, "She's seven, for goodness sake."

I again had to duck into the bathroom to splash water on my face. It was becoming a thing with me. When I joined Sally in the children's room, the kids were finishing up their story-time craft. Reagan and Manny had a sticker worksheet where they'd stuck the various animals from the story in the belly of the old lady. Savanah and the older attendees had made mobiles out of construction paper animals. I snapped a few photos of the cousins.

And then it hit me.

What if this is the last time he gets to be with his cousins?

What if the divorce means we have to move to Punta Cana so my parents can help me with childcare?

Before I had to make a third trip to the library bathroom, I put on my sunglasses and hustled Manny to the car. Thankfully, the books kept him from noticing the tears running down my face as we drove home.

Chapter
Twenty-Nine

R obert did not make it home in time for dinner or his son's bedtime story. When Manny asked me to read his favorite book, *The Bossy Gallito*, a bilingual version of a Cuban folktale that Roberto and I usually read to him together, I almost lost it. The story about a wedding was too much for me to handle.

It was nine thirty when I heard the keys in the door. I'd already had three glasses of wine and read too many "How to know if your husband is cheating" articles on the internet.

"Babe, I'm home," Robert said. "Man, what a day."

He put his black leather messenger bag on the dining room table. I closed my laptop and pushed it away to prop my elbow on the counter as I pivoted toward him. His tie was loose, and his shirt was wrinkled, like he'd been rolling around in bed with someone.

"I'm starving," he said as he moved to kiss me. "Did you just smell me?" He made a face and sniffed his armpit. "I'm sorry. Do I stink? Probably. I was in the field all day."

"Really?" I poured myself the last of the bottle.

"Yeah." He went to the fridge and took the sweet ham and swiss cheese out. "Where's the bread?" He started opening cupboards. "Ah, there." Slicing the roll of egg bread, he slathered mayonnaise on it and built his sandwich. He took a big bite and wiped his mouth with the back of his hand. "Mmm."

I watched him eat. He'd smelled of metal and salt, like a man that had sweated. I didn't know if that was worse than smelling another woman's perfume on your husband. Did Juliet have a signature fragrance? Would that have been proof? Wasn't his car parked at the love hotel enough proof? And that he was planning a trust account for Manny? At least he was taking care of his son in the divorce.

"Babe, what's wrong?" He put the mayo and cold slices back in the fridge.

"You tell me."

"Babe, are you mad at me? I know I haven't been around to help you as much as I'd like, but it won't last forever. I'm working hard—"

"Uh-huh. In the field."

"Yeees. The site is way out west, practically in the Everglades, and with Miami traffic, I might as well stay there until it dies down." He untied his tie the rest of the way and let it hang.

"So, you were in the Everglades today?"

"Yep." He put his hand in his pockets and leaned his butt against the sink. "That's why I smell like I ran a marathon. Hot. Buggy. Swampy Everglades. It's kind of like the subway in summer but without the oddballs proselytizing conspiracy theories." He threw the last bite of sandwich into his mouth. Turning to rinse his hands in the sink, he cleaned a glass and took a drink of tap water.

"The Everglades. Is that what they're calling El León Dorado these days?"

"Lion, what? Babe, what are you talking about?" Robert dried his hands on the dishtowel.

"The love motel. I saw your car at the El León Dorado love motel today."

"What?! That's impossible."

"Not impossible. I saw it with my own two eyes. Manny's toy was in the back seat of your *new red Tesla*."

"Babe—"

"Don't 'babe' me. I saw it. And I know who you were with! Your ex-girlfriend."

"You are talking crazy."

At that point, the point where he called me crazy but didn't actually deny it, I stormed off and sequestered myself in the study. I was so mad I wanted to break things. My anger simmered down when I funneled it into organizing the library: textbooks, cookbooks, fiction, Caribbean history, island travel guides, two poetry books (José Martí and Julia de Burgos), and my reference encyclopedias. I had ones for edible flowers, vegetables, fruit trees, and of course, herbs. The latest addition to the collection, the herb book I had bought at the botanica, didn't fit in the shelf. Not because it was oversized but because I'd filled every available space. I slumped against the wall beneath the box seat on the floor and flipped through my new book. The illustrated plates were pretty enough to frame. As I'd already discovered, it wasn't an encyclopedia about cooking herbs, but it did have recipes. There were recipes for teas, salves, and poultices for everything from dysentery to malaria. The tea for cooling an elderly person's stomach, a.k.a. a digestion aid, had stachytarpheta jamaicaensis, called blue porterweed or snake weed in Florida. I ran my finger over the delicately drawn purple flower. There was a yard full of the plant on the way to the Tot Lot. It had a butterfly garden plaque and a bench under a lattice arch. A cloud of orange butterflies usually hovered over the plant. I had to hold Manny back from running into the yard to try and catch the mariposas.

I read about fertility potions and tonics for impotence, obviously not a problem for my cheating husband. Could I forgive his affair? Would marriage counseling help? Or was it too late? If he was already planning a trust for Manny, maybe his mind was made up. He clearly loved Juliet more than me. He was spending all his free time with her and was working for her father. Did Marjory know? She'd be elated—finally, a daughter-in-law with the proper pedigree. I fell asleep with the book in my lap and woke up with a crook in my neck.

"Ow," I said, massaging my neck. It was a little after seven AM, and the sun was up. I looked out the window to check if Robert's car was parked under the royal poinciana tree. It wasn't. I was surprised I hadn't heard him leave. Maybe he'd been quiet on purpose. It was clear he was good at sneaking around. If it hadn't been for that road construction, I wondered how many more weeks or months it would have taken to discover his infidelity.

I went to check on my son. He stirred slightly as I opened the door to his room but didn't wake. He'd wake up in a few minutes on his own. In the meantime, I took a hot shower and dressed in shorts and a tank top. Manny, rubbing his eyes, found me.

"Buenas días mi príncipe," I said. "¿Qué quieres para desayunar?"

"¡Panqueques!"

His joy was the light that would get me through the tough times. I could do this. I could be a single mom. It would be okay. Lifting him onto my hip, I tickled him with kisses and went to the kitchen to make pancakes.

Manny's police car was on the eating counter. Under it was a note.

Babe, I love you. I am not having an affair. It seems impossible that my car was at The Gold Lion, but I'll find out why. It wasn't me. I promise. Love, Your Roberto

My heart fluttered as I put the note in my pocket. *Caridad, please let my husband be telling me the truth.*

While I prepared the batter, I told Manny the story of the first time I'd eaten pancakes not made by his abuela. It was a school trip to Walt Disney World in Orlando, and the hotel had free breakfast. I loaded my plate with pancakes because the teacher had told us it would be a long day, and we needed to eat a big breakfast so we'd have lots of energy to ride the rides. When mangos were in season, we ate mangos with every meal, especially breakfast. For pancake syrup, my mom would caramelize sugar and butter, then sauté mangos in it. So, at the hotel, when I saw a bowl of dark yellow fruit in an orangish syrup, I thought it was mini mangos and spooned them on top of my pile of pancakes. I took a big forkful of pancake and immediately spat it out. They tasted weird. I told the teacher that there was something wrong with the mini mangos at the hotel. She laughed. There was nothing wrong with the peaches. I'd just never tasted peaches before. Manny laughed with me as I made a puckered face. I didn't have any ripe mangos, so I added little chunks of cream cheese and guava to the pancakes.

Manny got the first golden-brown disc out of the pan. I cut it into bite-size pieces, against his protest that he could do it himself, and gave him a glass of juice with his gummy vitamin. I made myself a café con leche and joined him once my pancakes were done. He pressed the siren button on his police car, and the wine I'd drunk the night before screamed in my head that it was too early for that kind of noise. I turned it off and took away his toy until he finished eating. My pounding head subsided slightly. I touched Robert's note in my pocket and hoped it was true. But honestly, how could it be? The red Tesla at the love hotel had a paper license plate and Manny's toy in the back seat. The little bit of happiness I'd mustered while making breakfast was gone, and I was lost as to what to do next. Alma would recommend a mani-pedi and lunch with a waterfront view, but that wasn't going to happen. She was still under house arrest, and I was no closer to freeing her.

After I'd cleaned Manny's sticky hands with a damp towel, I put the dishes in the sink and went to get my phone from the study. If I couldn't see Alma, at least I could talk to her. That was, if she took my call. The encyclopedia of herbs I'd fallen asleep with was on the floor next to my phone. I picked them both up, closed the book, and put it on the cushioned window seat. I had a voicemail from Delvis and noticed I'd put the phone on silent. Tapping the green phone icon, I saw I'd missed two other calls that morning. One was from Detective Pullman, and the other was from Alma. Neither had left a message.

Delvis's voicemail informed me that she needed me at the studio again. "Please drop by the studio at ten AM. We need you to record a tag line." She promised it would be quick.

I called Alma back, but there was no answer. A half second later, a text came in.

Detective en la casa con mas????

"More questions," I said aloud.

It couldn't be a coincidence that I had gotten calls from my BFF and Detective Pullman within a minute of each other, and now he was at her house. I hadn't spoken to him since Sunny's memorial, when he'd asked me about Jorge. I needed to tell him about Jorge's Fiyah connection to Fuentes. And my far-fetched idea that Jorge was framing Fuentes as revenge for Miz Fiyah's death. When I said it like that, it did sound far-fetched. Why would someone kill two innocent people as revenge for another innocent person's death? And also, how? There was still no proof that the two deaths were actually connected to Fuentes's teas. Maybe they were connected. I decided to drop by Fuentes's office after my visit to UnMundo. I'd only seen his storage space. Maybe I'd get an answer if I took a look around his office.

While Manny played in his room, I flattened and removed the last of the moving boxes, saving enough to build a fort later. Delvis had asked me to be at UnMundo at ten, and it was about time to leave when I heard the ding-dong-dwong. I needed to get that doorbell fixed. It was probably circa 1954, the original installed when the house was built.

"Caridad, por favor que no sea mi suegra." I said a prayer that it wasn't my mother-in-law. Although if it was, it was decent of her to ring the doorbell instead of using her key. I had to get the locks changed too.

It wasn't Marjory at the door, but someone just as anxiety triggering. Detective Frank Pullman.

"Hello, Detective."

"Hello, Ms. Quiñones. May I come in for a few moments?"

"Sure. But only a few. I have to leave for work soon." Work. It felt good to say that word.

"I'll only stay long enough for an espresso."

"Is that a hint?"

Frank Pullman grinned. "Cuban coffee is superior."

"Don't let your Colombian wife hear you say that. Come on. Flattery will get you everywhere."

I sat him at the dining room table and quickly made coffee. He was being awfully nice, and I hoped that meant good news for Alma.

"I hear you're my translator," he said.

I froze for a second. He didn't sound mad, but he didn't sound pleased either. How was I going to explain my stretching of the truth?

I laughed. "Oops?"

"Yes, 'oops.' Don't do it again."

"Okay. Got it." I sat down with our coffees.

He took a sip. "Hits the spot. Thanks. So, tell me what you know about Jorge Trujillo?"

"He's an exercise instructor at the Coral Shores Fitness Center who does drag on the side."

Pullman waved his hand for me to stop talking. "Come on, Veronica Mars, tell me what made you ask to see the video?"

I made the itsy bitsy spider movements with my fingers while I thought of what to say. "Fuentes is a dentist who pretended to be a cosmetic surgeon who Jorge's friend Miz Fiyah went to and got shot full of caulking that killed her, but Fuentes didn't go to jail. The old man did, but he died of cancer a week later. Oh, and there's news footage of Jorge at a protest in front of the burned-down clinic. Jorge says it was an insurance scheme to get rid of evidence and collect two million dollars. I think I might believe him because even though he was mad enough to burn the place down and he wanted justice for his friend, I don't think he has it in him to risk hurting anyone. That's what makes me doubt my theory that he killed Sunny and Elliot to point the finger at

211

Fuentes and avenge Miz Fiyah's death. Elliot was his competition, but I think they were friendly because he knew a lot about her infertility struggles, and that's why I lied so I could see the video. I wanted to see if he gave her a drink or a pill or something. He said he saw her the night she died. He saw her going to the bathroom to throw up because she was pregnant again. Was she?"

Pullman stared at me. "Okay. So, what did you see on the video?"

I couldn't believe that was his response to my diarrhea of the mouth. Did that mean what I'd hypothesized was right? "Um. The video. I saw Jorge ask Elliot something from down the hall, but he never got close to her. He was gone before she collapsed."

"Did you see him talk to anyone else?"

"More like argue."

"What do you think they were arguing about? What is their relationship? Are they associates? What do you know about Juliet Pimpkin?"

I knew that the name Juliet Pimpkin made me want to cry. But I wasn't going to tell the detective about my husband's affair.

"I don't know what they were arguing about. I don't think they're friends. She's Coral Shores elite, and in her mind, he's the help. So, yeah, I thought it was weird and unexpected."

"Tell me about her."

I rolled my head over my shoulders to loosen the tension that had built up just hearing her name repeated.

"You should ask someone that knows Coral Shores better than me."

"I thought she was close to your husband."

I clenched my jaw. What was Detective Pullman implying?

"Second cousins, right? She's family. You have to have heard something about her?" he asked.

How could the idea that my husband was sleeping with another woman be any more awful? The answer was that the woman was a cousin! So gross and wrong.

Pullman wasn't going to leave until he got what he came for, so I told him the little bit I knew about the Pimpkins. I did my best to get my facts right about the Weatherman Pimpkin business and their falling out.

"And she seems to be very involved with"—I wanted to scream *my husband*—"the Women's Club and golf and galas and all that Coral Shores society stuff."

"How is she connected to the good doctor?"

"Fuentes? Hmm," I said, and thought a moment. She was a patron of his. I'd seen her drink his youth tea at family dinner. Did she take any of his special brews? "I don't know how well she knows Fuentes, but she was talking to him at the event. They did seem like an odd pairing, but Juliet's obsessed with not aging. So, I just assumed she was a super fan of his teas. Are you saying there's something more to their relationship?"

"Is Ms. Pimpkin friendly with Alma Diaz?"

"Alma is friendly with everyone, but that doesn't make them friends. It's part of being in real estate. Everyone you meet could be your next sale. Or so Alma says."

"So, Ms. Diaz and Ms. Pimpkin have had business dealings?"

"I don't know. Ask Alma about that. But I can promise you they aren't good friends. Juliet doesn't even pronounce Alma's name right. She calls her *Al*-ma not *All*-ma. It's kind of offensive, don't you think? One time is a mistake, but every single time—that's passive-aggressive."

"Huh. Thanks for the coffee. I don't want to keep you any longer. You said you had to get to work. Call me if you hear anything." Pullman pushed his chair under the table and walked through the living room to the front door.

I followed, but he let himself out. I realized the detective had never answered my question. Was there a relationship between Fuentes and Juliet? Was she sleeping with him too? I didn't peg him as her type, but maybe her type was anything male with a pulse. Argh! My mind was going bad places.

"Mami," Manny said.

I felt a tug on my shorts. It was my son offering me a piece of play food. "Gracias." I pretended to eat the piece of wooden pepperoni and mushroom pizza. He was such a sweet boy. My heart hurt to think that Juliet Pimpkin, the woman who didn't like children, would be his stepmother.

Chapter Thirty

M anny ran down the corridor to the daycare center, pushed the door open with his whole body, and practically jumped into Rosario's arms. It was reassuring that he liked daycare, and it made me wonder if pre-K wasn't a bad idea. I waved to Rosario, gave her hand signals that I was going upstairs for five minutes, then scooted away to find Delvis.

"Cool. You're here. Again, sorry I made you come back. I promise this will be the last time this week."

"Did you do something different to your hair?" I asked.

She smoothed her fingers over the shaved sides. "You like the fade?"

"Looks great on you."

"Gracias." She looked down at the board. "So, listen. We need to get this tagline recorded. I've got a couple I want you to try. Let me know if you like one of these better than another. *The Caribbean Kitchen*—abuela approved." She changed the pitch of her voice. "Make your abuela proud. Learn to cook with *The Caribbean Kitchen*." She shifted tone again. "*The Caribbean Kitchen*, no judgment. Just good food."

"How about? *The Caribbean Kitchen*, where culture and cooking meet." I could tell Delvis wasn't impressed with my suggestions, but she let me record my version anyway. I tried all four taglines several times and was done in fifteen minutes.

"I'm going to debut the channel with the milkshake episode. I'll upload it later today. I'll link you as soon as the graphics department gets the new animated logo to me. Cool?"

"Cool," I replied.

"Ya tú sabes." Delvis grinned and did a dance grind. She was hyped on the project, and I hoped that was good news for me. I needed this job as a soon-to-be-divorced woman. What was I going to tell my mother? Mami had been so happy I was married and starting a family. And Papi would be so angry at Robert that he'd threaten to swim from the Dominican Republic to Miami to give him a piece of his mind.

All those thoughts swirled through my head as I turned the hallway corner and ran into Ileana.

"Ay, perdón," I said before realizing whose toes I'd smashed. "Oh, Ileana. I'm so sorry. I wasn't watching where I was going. I'm so happy to see you." I gave her a hug and kiss on the cheek. "I was worried you were victim number three."

Ileana looked at me like I was crazy. "¿Qué? ¿Qué, victima?"

"Well, after you drank the tea and fainted on the show and then you went home early the other day, I thought maybe you were going to be Dr. Fuentes's third causality."

She gave me another quizzical glare. "Niña, no sé de qué hablas."

We stepped aside so a gaffer could wheel her cart of lights and cords by us.

"You collapsed on set after drinking Dr. Fuentes's tea." I leaned in and whispered the next part into her ear, "I think he is poisoning people. Two women have died after drinking his products."

"No seas loca. Mario is not poisoning people. I did it to myself. I fainted because of the hot lights. Y porque estoy una idiota and was on a two-day fast. The camera adds ten pounds. Y mi'ja, being over fifty doesn't help." Ileana put her finger to her mouth and made the keep-it-quiet sign.

"You shouldn't do that to yourself. You look amazing."

"Gracias, niña, pero you'll find out in a couple of years. The camera is cruel. Pero anyway. Enough about me. I was on my way to see Delvis and preview your new show. I love her idea, no? We need to capture los millennials y los Gen Z."

I nodded along with Ileana. It wasn't as if I really had any say in the new show, and as long as Ileana and the network were happy, that meant I had a paycheck and could support myself as a single parent. My mind was stuck on one track. Divorce. My marriage was breaking up because my husband was having an affair. I felt my chest tighten.

"I know it's going to be un gran éxito. You are young and smart and funny. It's going to be amazing." Ileana patted my arm and proceeded on her journey to Delvis.

I appreciated the vote of confidence but was uncertain about her proclamation that it would be a grand success. Did millennials and Gen Zers want to cook sancocho? *Miriam, you are a millennial. Oh my, duh. I'm my target audience. Well, the older end of the demographic, but yeah. Sancocho rules.*

The elevator opened, and I extracted Manny from his playtime with a promise to stop by Tres Sillas for early lunch. Yoli and Beatriz were millennials too. I needed to do some research on what my audience wanted. I also needed a recipe for next week's show. Maybe my tía would be there. I'd love to see her. She'd been a great tía for fourteen years. We needed to catch up on all the memories we'd missed making. I wondered if she'd share a few recipes with me. I bet she had a ton of great food stories.

It was in between the breakfast and lunch rushes. Beatriz, Yoli, and Tía Elba were seated at the counter, enjoying a café and a break.

"Hola, Tía," I said.

Tía Elba swiveled her stool to the door. She looked the same as when I had worked there as a teen. Maybe a deeper shade of hair dye and a few more gold necklaces, but the same apron and thick-soled black shoes. It hit me when she smiled. I missed my Cuban family. It had been years since I'd seen my tía. She'd been like a second mom to me.

217

"Venga acá, sobrina." She opened her arms and motioned me to her.

She told me that, having finished prepping the day's special, tamales, she'd been about to leave when the Elegua statute in the kitchen toppled. If a person practices La Regla de Ocha, also known as Santería, Elegua, the orisha of doorways, will be honored in their home and business with a clay idol that looks a little like a potato with cowrie shell eyes and a nose. Tía was very serious about her religion. She had altars all over her house. So, if Elegua gave her a message, then that message was to be taken seriously. But being that Elegua is a childlike trickster who likes candy and playing pranks, she didn't know if what was coming was a trick or a treat. Adding to the potency of his statue shifting, Tía had made one of Elegua's favorite dishes as the day's special. She told me that her tamales must have called him and that he'd opened the door for me and Manny to come see her today.

I didn't believe that Elegua was responsible for our visit, but I was happy for whatever was the reason Tía had stayed a few extra minutes at the café. I loved seeing her, and her tamales story would be perfect for my next show. I asked her if she'd share her recipe with me. She was thrilled with the idea that her name would be on *La Tacita* next week.

"I am your number-one fan," Tía Elba said.

She was probably my only fan. I laughed to myself and thanked her for her support. "Gracias por tu apoyo, Tía. UnMundo is taking the segment and making it a video for their YouTube channel. They want to attract los jóvenes."

"Qué bueno. De young people don't know how to cook." Tía gave Yoli the side-eye.

"¡Mami! It's just that your cooking tastes better," Yoli said, hugging her mom from behind. "People come to the restaurant for your food. I couldn't do it without you. Y también Mami, you are only fifty-five. You're not ready for adult daycare."

There were adult daycare centers in every strip mall in Hialeah. It was an odd phenomenon.

"Those places are not so bad. They play dominoes. They dance. They go on field trips. Pero you are right, maybe when I'm setenta y cinco," Tía said. "Mejor que you give me some nietos so I can stay home and be an abuela." This time she gave Bette the side-eye.

I could feel a little tension about the subject of grandchildren. "Until then, do you mind watching Manuelito por un rato? I have to run an errand y mejor que he is not with me."

"Claro que sí." Tía smiled with delight.

And I couldn't ask for a better babysitter. He'd probably be wearing a gold chain with a St. Lazarus medallion and smelling of Royal Violets when I came to collect him. All of that was fine as long as he didn't turn into a Papi Chulo. I could just imagine my mother-in-law's reaction to Manny in sunglasses and an open-front shirt walking in with a swagger and saying, "Oye. Mami." There was a little Hialeah part of me that secretly wanted it to happen.

I told Tía I'd be back soon, but I was ignored. She and Manny were already engaged in lunch plans. She was going to make him whatever he wanted to eat. I almost warned her that that would not be a good idea based on experience. He might ask for cookie-jelly-bubblegum—flavored ice cream.

Driving to Dr. Mario Fuentes's office, I formulated a plan. I'd tell him I was having problems getting pregnant and wanted a fertility tea. Hopefully, that would lead to talking about Elliot, and maybe I could find a connection to Sunny. And finding the explanation for Sunny's death was the key to getting Alma out of trouble. Could Fuentes be the anonymous caller? But why? *Stop it, Miriam. Go, listen, and ask the right questions for the situation, not for the answers you want.*

I parked in front this time. As I approached the door, it opened. One of his staff in her lab coat uniform exited, waving dollar bills. She was going on a colada run and asked if Mario wanted anything else.

The answer was no. She held the door for me and called to the doctor that he had a client.

"Hola," I said as I stepped over the threshold. This side of his enterprise was more like what I had expected. There were photographs of Amazonian flora and a glass jar apothecary. The public area was small, with only a single chair and table beneath a framed image of a tree with pink foliage. In tribal-esque font, the tree was labeled "pau d'arco." Behind the counter, there was a wall of herb-filled jars. I noticed an essential oils vaporizer on the counter puffing out a scented mist.

"Bienvenida. Soy el Doctor Mario Fuentes. ¿Como puedo ayudarte?" Fuentes came from the back through a beaded curtain and to the counter.

"Gracias. Soy Miriam Quiñones." I shook his extended hand. "My friend told me you helped her when nothing else would work. My husband and I have been trying to have a second child, and we can't get pregnant. Can you help?"

"Sí, puedo ayudarte. Please come into my consultation suite." He opened the gate that blocked the break between the counters.

I followed him into a beige paneled room that had a drop ceiling and fluorescent lights. It felt clinical but dated. There was an examination table—the kind with a roll of paper on it—and a small sink with a single cabinet above it. There were two chairs, plastic with metal legs. We sat facing one another. I counted the linoleum titles between us, six, and waited for him to ask the first question. He crossed his leg, putting his ankle on his knee, and clasped his hands.

"So, you want to get pregnant?"

"Yes. We've been trying, but I am having trouble," I replied.

"No to worry. I have made many babies."

Eww. His word choice gave me the creeps. I remembered the story about the fertility doctor that had fathered a hundred kids. Women thought they were selecting a donor from a catalog. They thought they were choosing, by hair and eye color, height, and education, someone that would make a good match for their family genetics. But instead, they were getting the doctor. It took over a decade for the truth to come out, and in that time, all these half siblings were going to school and crossing paths without knowing it. It made me realize you never knew what you were getting. You had to trust that the doctor was honest and legitimate. Like poor Miz Fiyah, who thought she was getting a boob job, not a death certificate. Was the medical equipment in the room from the plastic surgery clinic? My mind had taken a side trip, and I'd tuned out what the doctor was saying. I refocused on his voice and listened to him boast of a ninety percent fertility rate.

"Most of the time, the problem is with the woman being too cold," he said.

"¿Frio?" I asked to clarify. Did he mean cold like a low body temperature? I remembered when we were getting pregnant with Manny, I had monitored my ovulation, and a slightly higher temperature was one of the signs of fertility. Or did he mean sexually frigid? That was such a chauvinistic stereotype of women. Latinidad was plagued by machismo, but I'd thought we'd made some strides toward equality and respect.

"Yes. The womb is too cold for the egg to develop." He made an oval shape with his hands.

Was that the womb or the egg? After all, he was a dentist and not a medical doctor. And if he thought it was okay to inject caulking into a person, he might actually think a human egg looked like a chicken egg.

"But first, before I can solve your problem, I need to do an exam."

My heart raced. There was no way I was letting that man give me a physical exam. No. Way. I loved Alma and wanted her free, but I was not getting undressed for a quack doctor. Relief washed over me when he took a penlight from his lab coat pocket and shined it in my eye. Then he looked in my ears, nose, and mouth. He looked at my fingernails and took my pulse. Lastly, he took my temperature via my ear with a digital thermometer.

"Yes. Yes. I know I can help you." He put his head out the door and called for his staff. "Daniela, tráeme la libreta de recetas."

The lady that had left for coffee came in and gave Fuentes a notepad. She had a Styrofoam cup with a stack of thimble-sized cups on the lid. It was the to-go version of a pot of espresso. She served the doctor and then offered me one and left. I drank the sweet, bitter coffee in one sip and threw my used cup into the trash can by Fuentes's chair.

After scribbling a few words on the notepad, he stopped mid-writing and looked at me. If we were in a cartoon panel, there would have been a lightbulb above his head.

"Have we met before?" he asked.

There was no point lying, and maybe this was my way into talking about Elliot and Sunny. "Sí, el otro día en UnMundo."

"Sí, sí, sí. Ahora recuerdo. You are from Coral Shores. Yes?" He pointed at me with his pen. "Daniela, ven acá."

"Yes. I went to your talk at the Fitness Center. It was very interesting until the end when you know—"

"Yes. Pobrecita." He Xed what he had written, crumpled the paper, and threw it away. Fuentes wrote something on a fresh sheet. He motioned to Daniela and whispered into her ear, then tore off the prescription pad's top page. "This tea will solve your problems. Daniela will explain it." Fuentes tucked the pad into his coat pocket before handing my script to his assistant. He left the exam room without a goodbye. A door closed somewhere down the hall.

Daniela smiled and asked me to come to the front with her, where she'd explain the regimen and collect the doctor's payment. While she handwrote an eight-by-ten, fill-in-the-blanks receipt, I asked her if the doctor had a lot of Coral Shores clients. She told me the first one was the thin lady. She was probably referring to Sunny Weatherman. And then came Mrs. Truman. But the blonde lady was bringing in a lot of American clients. Daniela passed the receipt to me over the counter along with a once-too-often-copied instruction sheet. The instructions were in Spanish and poorly translated English.

Boil water.

Pour hot water over the herbs.

Let steeple 10 minutes.

Strainer leafs from tea.

Drink 2–3 time a day.

I shuffled the instructions to under the receipt and looked at the price tag for the first time. Five *hundred* dollars! *Plus* a hundred and fifty dollars a week for the special tea. I thought I felt the ground shift. The palms of my hands got sweaty. My knees buckled. I clutched my purse tightly to my side. Where was I going to get six hundred and fifty dollars to pay for a quack doctor's consultation of my fake fertility problem? *Think quickly, Miriam.*

"Daniela," I said with doubt in my voice. The assistant nodded that I had her name correct. "¿Es posible que haya un descuento?"

My plea for a discount was met with pity, but I could tell she had some trepidation. She looked to the back of the office and moved our negotiations down the counter away from earshot.

"Tú dijiste que tú eres de Coral Shores. ¿Sí?"

"Sí."

"¿Conoces a la rubia, Juliet Pimpkin?"

I knew the blonde, and I hated that I knew her, but I smiled and acted like she was my best friend. Alma would forgive my lie for the sake of a discount if it got her charges dropped. So, Juliet Pimpkin was friends with Mario Fuentes? How had that happened? Had Juliet been so jealous of Sunny's youth that she stole her tea doctor from her? That sounded so juvenile, but also so Juliet. She had gone to the trouble of sending Pepper a bale of hay as a mean-girl prank. So, stealing from her young rival was not out of character. My initial gut reaction to her the first time I had met her at the Tot Lot was correct. She was a mean girl.

"Sí y también soy . . . era amiga de Elliot Truman." My conscience just could not stomach using my husband's girlfriend's name, so I offered Elliot's name instead.

"La pobre, que triste. No sé qué pasó con ella." Daniela took a beat to acknowledge the loss of a life but then shook her head and continued on with business. "Es mejor usar el descuento de Juliet." She crossed out the $500 and replaced it with $375.

I gave her the credit card that had Robert as the primary user. I told myself it was compensation for his adultery. Daniela gave me my credit card receipt and took a gallon-sized plastic bag from a drawer. Looking in a three-ring binder, she referenced a recipe and began scooping herbs from various glass jars. It did not look exact or scientific in any way. She didn't weigh anything. A scoop was not an exact measurement. I tried to see the recipe, but it was too far away. When Daniela stepped away from the binder to get a jar from the shelf on the other side of the room, I leaned over the counter and covertly took a photo of the page. I hoped I could read the words when I enlarged it later.

Daniela gave me the week's supply of tea and added that if it was too bitter for my taste, I could add honey or sugar. Thanking her, I left. When I got to my car, I turned around and went back to the shop. My emotional reaction to Juliet had made me lose focus. Yes, I'd wanted to ask about Juliet, but also I'd needed to probe about Sunny and Elliot. And then there was the question of Jorge. Opening the door, I saw Dr. Fuentes talking to Daniela. His hand gestures were wild, and her body language signaled she was being chastised. When the doctor realized my presence, he stopped talking, pivoted toward the door, and smiled like a used car salesman.

"Señora Quiñones, did you forget something?" Fuentes asked.

"Um, yes." I had to think of an excuse fast. Daniela was the one I'd wanted to talk to, not him. "I forgot mi mama saw you on *La Tacita* and wanted to try your weight loss drink."

Mario Fuentes's fake smile turned genuine. He complimented himself on his bestselling blend of herbs that harvested the Amazon's ancient powers and offered me a buy one, get one free deal.

"Daniela will help you." Fuentes put his hand on her back. "And don't forget the fertility tea doesn't work—"

I suspected as much.

He switched to Spanish. "—si no duermes con tu esposo."

His hand moved down Daniela's back. Her eyes opened wide like he'd given her a pat or goose on the butt. *Gross. Men are gross.* Even saying the word "sex" makes them horny. Poor Daniela, did she need the job that badly that she had to put up with his inappropriate sexual advances. But who was I to judge? Maybe she was sleeping with her boss. He wasn't unattractive if you could imagine his dark brown hair cut in a modern style and if he didn't open his mouth. What kind of dentist has crooked teeth?

Daniela made a yuck tongue as soon as he left us. The beaded curtain rattled and clanked, finally settling still. I didn't want to lose my chance to ask about Sunny and Elliot. Daniela clearly didn't like Fuentes all that much. Besides the tush tap, he'd been lecturing her about something when I'd walked in. I used that to my benefit.

"Sorry if giving me a discount got you in trouble," I said.

"No te preocupes." Daniela took me into confidence. "I don't like what's going on here. Voy a cambiar trabajos, pronto."

I was glad to hear she was changing jobs. Her not caring about her boss and job security was good for my mission. I asked her outright about Sunny. How long had she been a client? Had she and the doctor gotten along? Had he liked her?

As she wrote up the bill and took the payment, she told me Sunny had been his oldest client. He'd met her at a wellness retreat in Brazil, where he had gone to study with the shamans. She had been there to take ayahuasca, the psychedelic brew that induces a spiritual journey to awaken and heal the inner self. But Sunny got sick, and the shamans wouldn't let her take the strong medicinal in her fragile state. They didn't want a rich white American with malaria dying on their property. Mario went with her to the hospital as her translator since he was conversant in Portuguese and English. He stayed with her during her recovery and nursed her back to health with teas. Sunny credited Fuentes with saving her life and became his first and best client. She had given him the money to start his herbal business.

If Sunny was Mario's sugar mama, why would he want to kill her? Maybe her death really was related to cocaine. Maybe sobriety was too unbearable, and she relapsed. I really wanted to pin her death on Fuentes, or at least a bad batch of herbs that had poisoned her by accident. But it stood to reason, if she'd been poisoned, it should have come up in the tox screens. My line of questions about Sunny was a waste of time, and the minutes were ticking.

When Daniela gave me the bill for the diet tea, I used Robert's credit card again. She took a box of the diet drink from the display and then checked in several places for a second box but couldn't find another. She needed to go next door to restock.

"Ven conmigo," Daniela said, grabbing a set of keys.

I followed her to the expansion space, where she gave me my free box of diet drink from the display shelf. I thanked her and was about to ask her about Elliot when we heard the doctor yelling her name through the thin wall. She made an annoyed face and flipped him the finger. Then, in a further act of rebellion and spite, she took one of the reusable bags from the same stack I'd taken one a few days ago and began filling it with boxes of the powdered drink from the cardboard box with the Chinese lettering.

"Are you sure?" I asked her when she pushed the sack into my arms.

"Sí," she replied but warned me not to drink the diet drink with the fertility tea. The fertility tea was very strong. She'd warned Elliot to be careful too.

Another shout came from the office. There was no time to ask anything else. Daniela pushed me out the door, locked it, and then scurried into the main office, leaving me on the sidewalk, holding the bag.

Chapter
Thirty-One

Although Manny didn't smell of violet cologne when I picked him up from Tres Sillas, Tía Elba had Cuban-ized him. He had an azabache, the coral and jet protection amulet that most Cuban's wore as children, and two saints for his room.

"Los perros, Mami. Yo vi los perros," Manny said with his endless enthusiasm for life.

Tia had taken him to the botanica, where he got to pet San Lazaro's dogs. Since he had such an attraction to the saint syncretized with the Yoruba orisha Babalú-Ayé, she bought him a small saint and warned me to watch my son's health, as San Lazaro was the saint of the sick and the poor. She said his affinity could also mean that he was destined to become a healer or a doctor. I knew that Manny's obsession with the statue was all about the dogs, but I didn't want to hurt or insult my aunt. She lovingly scolded me for not having La Virgen de la Regla, the patron of motherhood and children, in his room to watch over him as he slept.

"Mi'ja, mejor you put her in your room," Tía said, putting the saint in my hands. She winked at me and patted my stomach.

The nine-inch statue had an intricately painted white and blue cape. It reminded me of the one that had been in my childhood room. I'd look at the silver crescent she stood on and wonder how she got to the moon. I'd look out my window to the night sky to see if I could see

227

her among the stars. Some versions of the saint held a baby like this one did, but my childhood one did not. I caressed the dark brown face of the baby, and sadness washed over me. Manny would be an only child like me. My marriage was over. There would be no more babies, no brother or sister.

"¿Qué pasa, niña?" Tía asked.

"Nada," I said, gulping back my tears. "Nothing. I'm just a little sad we have to go. I'm sorry I didn't get to spend more time contigo hoy, but I'm so happy Manny did. Promise me we will have dinner sometime soon."

"Claro." Tía kissed me and gave me a takeout box full of croquetas and tamales.

Tres Sillas was filling with hungry diners, so I blew Yoli a kiss as she headed into the kitchen to cook for the lunch rush. Beatriz gave me an over-the-counter hug and a kiss since her ventanita had a line. Her coffee was perfect, but her repeat customers also came for the flirting and ribbings that she gave them. I liked her and was very happy that my cousin had found someone to love. It would be nice to have them over to the house on a Sunday when the restaurant was closed.

Manny and I walked Tía to her car and said our goodbyes in the parking lot. I set Manny on the hood of the car and took a selfie of the three of us. I immediately sent it to my mom and wondered what the reaction would be. The fight that had broken up our family hadn't started with the sisters-in-law. It had been between my father and his brother. No one ever said what it was about, and as a kid, I hadn't dared to ask. Maybe she'd tell me now that I was an adult. Family secrets were like a root rot that slowly withered branches and eventually killed the tree. That was what had happened to the Quiñones tree. We'd lost my tío's branch.

Mami didn't reply to the image. Did that mean she hadn't seen it yet or that she was still holding a grudge? I let it go. There were more immediate matters to worry about than resolving a

228

twenty-year-old argument. Alma still wasn't free, and I'd learned next to nothing for my more than five-hundred-dollar expenditure. Daniela had given me the history behind Fuentes and Sunny's friendship. Either it was genuine, or else he was a leech. I'd put my money on the leech scenario. Actually, I had kind of put my money, or at least Robert's money, on it. She'd also told me that Juliet was his new money stream. She was bringing in the Coral Shores market. I'd learned nothing about Elliot. I still didn't have a strong motive for Sunny or Elliot's deaths. And no evidence that Juliet or Fuentes were the culprits.

"¿Y Jorge?"

"¿Qué, Mami?" Manny asked.

"Nada, mi príncipe," I replied.

Time had run out to ask about Jorge, and to be honest, I didn't think he was involved if the two deaths were connected. He had no tie to Sunny. Other than the Unitarian Universalist church.

"But that was years apart."

"¿Mami?"

Oh no, I was thinking out loud again.

"Mami. Mira Mami, Papi!" Manny bounced in his booster seat.

"¿Qué, mi amor?" I asked.

I'd done it again. I hadn't been paying attention to the detour and ended up taking the long way. Manny and I were at the stoplight by El León Dorado. A red Tesla had pulled into the hotel's driveway. My son had recognized his dad's flashy new car. I willed the light to turn and hoped I could see the passenger through four lanes of traffic as we drove by.

The light changed to green, and I gunned the Prius. I glanced to the left and saw Robert walking away from his car.

"Papi. Papi. Papi." Manny saw him too.

"Sí, mi príncipe, tu papá." It was his lying-straight-to-my-face father. I wished I could have taken a photograph as evidence. I would text it to Robert with a Pinocchio gif. My marriage was over. There was no coming back from this. I felt like such a fool. Had he been having affairs in New York City? Or was it just with Juliet? Did men like mean girls the way that women liked bad boys?

I opened Tía's takeout box and stuffed a croqueta into my mouth. By the time we'd gotten to Coral Shores, I'd eaten six. My fingers were greasy, and I had crumbs in the corners of my mouth. The travel-size wet wipes I kept in the car door pocket had dried out in the Florida heat. I pulled over and idled in front of someone's house. It took a full stretch and twist to reach into the back seat, but I wrestled my mom bag from the back seat floorboard and got a fresh napkin. The bag was Manny's diaper bag that I'd repurposed into an emergency everything bag. I had a box of wet wipes, a change of clothing for him, a few toys, and a stash of Maria cookies. Manny asked for one of the toys, a Little People polar bear.

"Oso blanco," Manny said, and gave the white bear a noisy kiss.

"Se llama un oso polar." I watched Manny move the bear through the air on an imaginary adventure. He was such pure joy I forgot all my worries for a moment.

When I came back to reality, I noticed we were near the church where they'd held Sunny's memorial, and decided to drive by it. Maybe I'd get lucky, and the chatty teacher would be there to answer all my questions about Sunny and Jorge. I could pretend to be inquiring about the school for Manny. The place where we'd parked for the memorial was full, so I parked along the side street. As Manny and I walked to the gate, I saw a person kneeling on the ground with empty flowerpots around her.

"Mrs. Weatherman?" I asked as we entered the courtyard.

The woman looked like a million dollars, even though she was sweating and in a floppy sun hat that would look ridiculous on most people.

"Yes." She turned toward my voice and sat on her bum. "Oh, you're Alma's friend. Remind me of your name."

"Miriam. Miriam Quiñones." I hesitated and almost added the Smith part since she was Coral Shores society, but didn't. I wouldn't be a Smith much longer.

"Miriam, nice to see you again. And who is this handsome young man?"

Manny became bashful and hid behind me. "This is my son, Manuel. We call him Manny." I spoke to him in Spanish and asked him to introduce himself. He poked his head out, smiled, and waved.

"He seems about ready for kindergarten. Are you here for the school?'

"He's not yet five, but yes. I'm looking at schools for next year."

"You know they have a half-day program for pre-K here that is excellent. It might be full, but I have a little influence with them and would be happy to talk to them for you." She crossed her legs and set down her trowel.

"Maybe. I hadn't thought about something for this year. Haven't they started already?"

"Yes, but just by a few weeks. Well, hello there, Flossie." The calico cat came from the greenery and headbutted Stormy. Manny, seeing the cat, lost his bashfulness and moved to sit with Stormy. "This is my friend Flossie. She's about to have babies."

I guessed I was wrong about the cat being well fed. That wasn't fat; it was pregnancy.

"Ven aquí, gato." Manny made gimme-gimme hands, trying to get the cat to come closer to him. Flossie, who was curled in Stormy's lap, purring, gave him a nonplussed stare.

"Puedes tocarla suavemente," Stormy said in Spanish with a decent accent. "You're surprised I speak Spanish?"

"A little, actually. French wouldn't have surprised me, but Spanish—sí, un poquito."

"Un poquito is about all I remember." Stormy laughed. "Lorenzo, my second husband, was from Buenos Aries. We'd spend July and August in Argentina to escape the Miami heat. It was cold and often rainy, but the architecture and the food." She made a chef's kiss.

Manny was sweetly petting Flossie. To a passerby, it might look like a grandparent in the garden with her grandchild. It struck me as sad that Stormy would not get to grandparent any of her own grandchildren. She would have made a fun abuela, I could tell. Having lost two children, Raine and Sunny, she was the opposite of an orphan.

I sat on the coral rock patio across from Stormy and asked, "Did Sunny go to Buenos Aires with you?"

"No. She was twenty by then. She visited a time or two, but she didn't like the cold weather. Her name fit her well. She loved the sunshine." Stormy looked away.

"I'm sorry. I can't imagine how much pain you must be in. I'm so sorry for your loss."

"Thank you, Miriam. I'm sorry you didn't get a chance to know my Sunny. She was kind and sweet. You might have become friends."

Stormy drew in a sharp breath, clenched her fist, and covered her mouth with it. The emotional shift disturbed the cat. Flossie moved from Stormy's lap to a patch of sun by the butterfly shrubs. Manny followed her, mesmerized by the furry being.

"Are you okay?" I asked. I mean, of course, she wasn't okay. Her daughter had passed away suddenly. But having witnessed two deaths recently, I didn't want there to be another one.

"I'm just so mad. Sunny was sober. She was clean. I had a hair strand test done. No drugs in the last twelve months! Then enough cocaine to explode her heart. It doesn't make sense. It just doesn't make sense. She wanted to beat the odds. She was clean."

I was glad Manny was entertained with his new feline fancy. Explaining drugs and cocaine to my son was a talk that would eventually have to happen, but, at four years old, that day was years off.

"So, wait—Sunny died of an overdose? Is that what the autopsy concluded?"

"That's what the first autopsy said. The second autopsy told the bigger picture. It was a heart attack caused by uncut coke. There was enough in her system to flatline an elephant, much less a one-hundred-pound recovering anorexic. The anorexia damaged her heart and her other organs. That's why sobriety was so important. And she was sober. That's what's killing me." Stormy took the trowel and stabbed it into the ground.

"What do her friends say? Have you asked them if something was bothering her recently? Have you asked Juliet?"

"Juliet? I hope she wasn't hanging around Juliet again. Was she? What makes you ask that?"

"I don't know. I've only been here a few weeks, but it seems like Juliet knows everybody. And they were both active in the Women's Club, I gathered. So . . ."

"The Women's Club. That was for her father," Stormy said as she stood and removed her gardening gloves.

"For Sunny's father? Isn't it for women only?"

"His great-grandmother founded the club in 1941, to aid the troops. They made bandages and knitted socks. He talked about her like she was Florence Nightingale. Well, Sunny desperately wanted to be redeemed and forgiven by him, and that's why she joined. For him. To finally have him see her as fitting his image of a perfect daughter. The Weathermans, like the Pimpkins—and sorry, sweetie, but your mother-in-law is a Pimpkin by blood"—Stormy gave me a conciliatory pat—"are stuck up, petty, greedy— well, I won't say the word because of little ears, but it starts with an "A" and ends with an "E." I hope Sunny wasn't seduced by Juliet again."

"Again? They were friends once?"

"When Sunny left here"—Stormy pointed toward the school— "we put her in Shores Prep. Her father hated this place, said it was for weak-willed snowflakes. Anyway, the school had a big–little program. Incoming sixth-graders would be paired with a high school senior. Sunny got Juliet as a big sister. My sweet, impressionable child got the queen bee of the school's in crowd. Her father thought it was wonderful. I've always suspected he engineered it. I wouldn't have put it past him to have paid someone off. He wanted the Pimpkins and the

Weathermans to be thick as thieves again. Well, that's a whole other story, but I can say Juliet is exactly like her grandfather: money hungry, cunning, and cutthroat. She had my little girl following her like a puppy. I could not wait for Juliet to graduate and leave the school. But it didn't end there. Juliet kept manipulating Sunny. She'd send her long emails with advice about who to date, how to dress, and who to be friends with. Even when Juliet wasn't there, I knew she was the puppet master. The house party, the one that oddly enough gave me my child back, thanks to Alma—that was Juliet's house. Channel seven reported it as spoiled rich kids breaking into a vacant waterfront mansion and throwing a wild party. I knew the truth, though. Juliet had planned the party and made the guest list. She'd even hired the DJ, the one that teaches salsa at the center. But I could never prove it. She charged admission and had a two-drink minimum! It was like a private club. I have no love lost for that woman. None whatsoever."

Stormy had poured her heart out to me about her daughter's rocky youth, and I could only think about myself. Juliet Pimpkin was an awful person who was stealing my husband from me. She was probably doing it just for fun. She was doing it because she could. It was a power trip for her.

"That's enough talk about the past." Stormy stepped to the bench and took a sip of water from an insulated bottle. "The future belongs to little ones like yours. Let's get you a tour of the school. Come with me." She bent at the waist and spoke directly to Manny. "Vamos, señorito."

Manny smiled and hopped up. He took her hand, and I followed them into the church. Stormy found Mrs. Lucy, the school director, and left us with her for a tour. We started with the pre-K, as it was about to let out for the day. The director informed me they had half days, nine to twelve, on Monday, Wednesday, and Friday; and full days, nine to two thirty on Tuesday and Thursday. As soon as we stepped into the classroom, Manny let go of my hand and joined the children. They were about to start their closing circle, and the teacher invited Manny to participate. The teacher read them a funny poem and then asked them each to tell her something good about their day. Several of the kids said snack. One said art. When Manny's turn came, he said cat, in English. He even called her by name. "I like Flossie cat."

"He's fitting in nicely. I think he's ready for school. I have space in our half-day program. Your son could start on Monday," Mrs. Lucy said.

"Well, let me speak to my husband about it, and I'll get back to you." She seemed satisfied with my reply, but it just reminded me that Robert and I were not actually talking. Was my marriage over? Could I afford to send Manny to private school? It was very nice and friendly. I liked that it was Montessori, and I'd noticed they had things labeled in English and Spanish: nose: nariz, blue: azul, bird: pajaro. He'd had no problem with staying in daycare at UnMundo, and he slipped right into today's closing circle like he was an enrolled student. He was ready for some type of structure and learning. I'd tell Robert my plan, but there would be no discussion. I'd made up my mind. Manny was starting preschool on Monday. "Actually, can I have the enrollment paperwork?"

"Of course. Let's go to Fellowship Hall and get you a cup of coffee to enjoy while you wait for me to prepare your school packet. Parents pick up their students from there, so that will be nice for you to see. Manny can stay with the class until then. Okay?"

"Sure."

The director called the assistant teacher to her and let her know to bring Manny to the hall with the other kids. We walked from the back of the campus to Fellowship Hall. The room looked about the same as it had for Sunny's memorial. But instead of trays of pastries, the table had a lost-and-found bin, a canned goods collection bin, and an aide with a clipboard.

"Gabriela?" I asked as I approached.

"¿Señora Quiñones?" she replied.

"What are you doing here?"

235

"What are you doing here?"

Our simultaneous questions overlapped.

"I started my practicum. I'll be here three days a week in the pre-K program. Today was my orientation. Are you thinking about Agape for Manuelito? Dime que sí."

"Maybe."

"That would be perfect. I'm trying to get Pepper to enroll Sophia."

"How is Pepper? I should call her. I know Elliot was her best friend. It has to be hard."

Gabriela nodded and made a face that gave the impression that things weren't good.

"Maybe mention school would be good for Sophia? The little girl doesn't need to be around all that crying and—" Gabriela raised her hand like she had a wine glass in it.

I sighed. "I'll call her today."

"Gracias. Oh, I've got to go." She fanned the clipboard. "I'm learning their dismissal protocol." Gabriela walked to the older woman at the door and gave her the sign-out sheet. It was the teacher I'd spoken to at the memorial. She glanced my way and waved.

"Here you go." Mrs. Lucy handed me a large mug with the Agape Montessori logo on it. "Cream and sugar are over there. I'll only be about ten minutes." She left the hall.

The coffee smelled rich, and instead of looking for a place to dump it, I added sugar and a touch of cream. It wasn't the usual weak American coffee for a change. Sipping the hot liquid, I watched as parents and caregivers came in, showed ID, and signed the paper on the clipboard. Gabriela would then run to the classroom to retrieve the student. After I'd watched this scene repeat itself a few times, I meandered to the wall of congregation photographs. Studying the one of Jorge at the Pride parade, I knew something about it was bugging me. I took a snap of it with my phone.

"Here we go," Mrs. Lucy said from behind me. She handed me a yellow folder. "Do you know Jorge?"

"Yes, actually. I take his Mambo-cise class."

"We adore him here at UU. Yep, not only am I the director of the school, but I'm a member of the church. Some weeks it feels like I never leave this place." She laughed joyously. There was no sardonic twinge to her. "Jorge leads our Rainbow Circle for young adult LGBTQ. And oh my goddesses, he did a drag queen fundraiser event for the church last year that was amazing. He donated a drag make-over. My husband won it. I have to show you the pictures. It was so much fun. We used it as our Yule card."

Mrs. Lucy scrolled through the photos on her phone. She shared the phone with me, and through its cracked surface guard, I saw a Black man in a short spiky wig. He had tons of contour makeup and bright red lipstick. He looked great even with the concealed beard stubble. When she showed me one of the full-length images, my mouth dropped at the glamour of a six-foot-tall man in a red satin evening gown and five-inch heels.

"I know! Look at this one. This was our holiday card."

Her husband had a garland of holly as a stole, and at his feet, in gothic font, was the text "Holly Berry Wishes You Happy Holidays!"

"Holly, Halle. I get it now. I love funny Christmas cards," I said.

She smiled at the image on her phone and then kissed it. "I have the best husband."

I wished I felt the same about Robert. I had until about a month ago. Before I could go down depression lane again, Manny came zooming toward us. Gabriela had brought him into the hall with the last student to be picked up.

"Mami, Mami. I want to stay school!" Manny said.

"¿Perdón? Yo no entiendo inglés." Of course, I understood his English, but I was the Spanish-speaking parent. Robert was the English speaker. We are a team. Were a team.

He repeated his desire to go to school in Spanish. And I told him we'd think about it, but I was glad he'd made friends and liked it. I'd always thought Manny would go to Catholic school like me. The same as my mother and her mother before her. But he didn't have to carry on the tradition if this place was where he fit best.

Mrs. Lucy leaned close to me. "I think he's ready for school. We'd love to have your family join the Agape family." She patted my back.

"Do we have to attend the church to go to the school?" I asked.

"No. We are independent from the church. Separation of church and state is practically a UU commandment. But you are more than welcome to try it out. Unitarian Universalist have a lot of ex-Catholics. And plenty of Jews too. One of our members, Rey Baumel, calls himself a Jew-nitarian." She laughed.

"How did you know I was Catholic?' Was she stereotyping me because I was Latina?

"Your Caridad del Cobre necklace." She pointed to my chest.

"Oh. I forget I have it on sometimes."

"And I noticed your son's azabache."

"That's not a Catholic thing. It's more cultural," I said. My tone was more defensive than I'd intended. So, I softened it with an earnest compliment. "The coffee was delicious. Best American coffee I've ever had." I passed her my empty mug.

"Thank you. It's Fair Trade coffee from Mexico. I love the chocolatey undertones, don't you? And please take the mug. All our Agape parents got mugs this year. Last year it was a steel water bottle."

I thanked her and told her I'd review the folder of information. It occurred to me I hadn't even asked what the tuition would be. Could I afford it on my part-time job? I doubted it, no matter how reasonable it was. Robert would have to pay for Manny's school. *I'd ask for that in the divorce settlement.* My brain was determined to go down worry lane. I started to fret about getting a lawyer.

"Adiós," Gabriela said.

"Adiós." I was glad to be pulled back into the now. We exchanged one-cheek goodbye kisses, and I promised her I'd call Pepper.

On the way to the car, Manny begged to pet Flossie one last time. The pregnant cat was rolling in a patch of herbs.

"Mint?" I asked.

"Catnip," Stormy replied. She'd removed her sun hat and had tidied up her planting debris. "Not only do cats love it, but it makes a great tea for humans. It's good for indigestion and inviting Aunt Flo to visit." She winked.

"How do you know that?" My mouth was quicker than my editor, and I fear I'd sounded a bit harsh. The woman's daughter had just died. I didn't want to be rude to her.

"I come from a long line of Irish kitchen witches." Stormy grinned and waved as we left.

Chapter
Thirty-Two

M anny nodded off with a croqueta in his hand. I scooped him up and deposited him in his bed. His day had been full of fun and new things. Mine had been full of I don't know what, but I needed to review it before he woke up from his power nap. I quickly made a fruit salad of papaya and mamey and poured a tumbler of water.

Sitting at the dining room table with a few sheets of blank paper, I wrote down all the stray bits of information I knew about Jorge, Sunny, Elliot, Juliet, and Fuentes. There were three important things I'd learned today. One was that Juliet and Fuentes were business buddies.

"I should have asked if Juliet was getting a referral fee," I mumbled. A piece of ripe mamey fell off the fork and plopped back into the bowl. My salad looked like an artist's gradation of orange from light peachy to autumn red.

Two was that Juliet had toyed with and manipulated Sunny since middle school. Three was Jorge was probably not connected to the deaths. Yet before I crossed out his name, I drew a big circle around it. Something was bugging me about Jorge. In the circle, I wrote *drag, Miz Fiyah, Elliot, Juliet hallway*, and *Fuentes protest*. And then I remembered something Stormy had said. The DJ at the house party was the salsa instructor. Had she meant Jorge? I wondered if that party had been what killed his DJ career. I needed to ask Alma for details. I added *DJ at Sunny's party* with a big question mark to my list.

My phone vibrated.

"Hello, Detective."

"Hello, Ms. Quiñones. Do you have anything new for me? Our last conversation was very helpful," Detective Pullman said.

Was he being sarcastic or sincere? It was hard to tell, and I didn't remember telling him anything significant during our last tête-à-tête only a handful of hours ago. I looked at the pages I'd just written.

"Okay, well, first off. Ileana Ruiz isn't Fuentes's next victim. Or at least I don't think so. She fainted because she'd been fasting for forty-eight hours, not because she drank his tea." I said.

"Yeah. Dehydration according to the EMTs."

"So you knew that." Disappointed, I looked at my sheet of paper. "Did you know that Fuentes gives a discount to Juliet's friends?" I heard a low and long "hmm" from Pullman. Maybe I finally knew something he didn't. So, I continued with my Fuentes intel. "Fuentes met Sunny at a spa in the Amazon rainforest several years ago. She gave him the seed money to start his tea company."

A new motive occurred to me. Could Fuentes have spiked Sunny's drink powders with cocaine to get rid of her? He knew she had health issues. Maybe he didn't want to pay her investment back?

"That's good to know, but did you learn anything new about Juliet Pimpkin?" Pullman asked.

Juliet, Juliet, Juliet sang in my head like the Brady Bunch's "Marcia, Marcia, Marcia."

I snapped the paper in annoyance and reviewed my scribbled notes. "Huh, well. How's this? Juliet was Sunny's middle school frenemy. According to Mrs. Weatherman, Juliet tormented and manipulated Sunny all through high school and beyond. Did you know that the house party house, the one that Alma was supposedly responsible for, was actually all Juliet? It was her house, and it was her party."

Again, there was a baritone hum from my phone. "What else? Do you know if Elliot, Sunny, or Juliet had hair extensions or maybe wore a wig?"

"Hair extensions? A wig? Why?"

"Just answer the question, Mrs. Quiñones."

"How would I know? I've only been here, like, two weeks! They weren't even my friends. I met Sunny once. And Elliot, like, twice or something!"

My outburst made a crater of silence that I filled with anxiety. Had I slammed the cell door on my BFF's chance of freedom?

"Miriam," Pullman said, and then paused. "Miriam. I'm going to tell you something in confidence. And you have to promise not to say anything about it to anyone else. If you do, I'll know it came from you. Got it?"

"Got it."

"We found synthetic hairs on both Sunny and Elliot. The synthetic hairs match, but we can't attribute them to anyone."

"What color are they?"

"Black."

"Long or short?"

"Short. Why?" Pullman asked.

"Hold on a second. I'm going to message you an image."

I sent Detective Pullman the snapshot I took of Jorge as Cha-Cha Minnelli in the Pride parade.

"What am I looking at?"

"Enlarge it. That's Jorge Trujillo in a short black wig."

Maybe Jorge was involved after all. My subconscious knew it, and that's why I'd been fixated on the photo of Jorge. I wanted to cross him off the list because of Miz Fiyah's tragedy. Just because I liked Jorge and hated Juliet didn't mean he was innocent, and she was guilty. Although, come to think of it, I would get some pleasure from seeing her put in jail. But how and when would Jorge in a wig have come into contact with Sunny and Elliot. The video from the Fitness

Center would have shown something. And I didn't remember Cha-Cha Minnelli being at the Women's Club lunch.

"Interesting," Pullman said. "You're going to Mrs. Truman's funeral tomorrow, aren't you?"

"Memorial or funeral?" I really needed to call Pepper. "They've released her body? So, that's means you have a cause of death?"

Pullman didn't reply.

He was taking forever, like a plantain ripening.

I cleared my throat.

"The medical examiner has released the body," Pullman said.

"And that means you have a cause of death. Right?"

"Go to the funeral, Veronica Mars. Listen. Watch. And since your fingers must not work, as I'm always the one who has to make the call, I'll phone you tomorrow for a report. Have a good day." Pullman ended the call.

Frank Pullman could drive a nun to cuss. I sure wanted to, but instead I checked that Manny was still asleep so I could call Pepper.

"Hey there, sweetie," Pepper answered the phone.

"Hi, Pepper. How're you doing?"

"I'm on my third giraffe of Santa Tropics San-guee-ah."

Ay, mi madre. She was going for the gold in day drinking.

"Pepper, are you alone?" I heard snoring. "Pepper!"

She snuffled awake. "Huh. Oh, hey there, sweetie."

"Pepper, is Gabriela home yet?"

"She's teaching at the grape school."

"The Agape school?"

"Yep, that one. They all leave me. All the good ones leave me. Like Elliot. Elliot is gone."

"Pepper, where is Sophia?" I hoped Pepper wasn't by the pool with her.

"She's with her daddy."

Gracias, Caridad for small miracles. I heard snoring again and a voice in the background.

"Hello?" The voice picked up the line.

"Gabriela?"

"Sí. ¿Señora Quiñones?"

"I'm so glad you're home. She shouldn't be by herself."

"Estoy de acuerdo," Gabriela agreed.

"Please don't let her drink anymore today. What time is the funeral tomorrow? And where? Does she have to give a speech?"

Gabriela gave me the time and location. Thankfully, Pepper didn't have to give a eulogy. I told her I'd be by at ten thirty tomorrow and to keep the liquor cabinet locked. No Irish coffees for breakfast. She agreed and promised to try her best to keep her employer sober.

Tia Elba must have tired him out because Manny crashed for longer than usual. I took advantage of the time and inventoried my pantry. Next week's dish for *Cocina Caribeña* was going to be tamales, and I knew for sure I'd need to run to the Latin grocery for corn, masa, and husks. Maybe I'd do two versions to show some of the variations around the islands.

My shopping list was done, and I wanted to test-run my tamales tonight while I had Tía's for comparison. It took about three minutes of turning the water off and on, flushing the toilet and opening and closing the hall bathroom door to stir Manny. After a little juice and finding his police car, we were ready to go. I didn't want to go back to Hialeah, so I did a search and found a Presidente market in North Bay Village. Caught by the drawbridge, I turned off the engine and narrated the parade of sailboats and cruisers that went through. The intercoastal waterway between the mainland and the barrier island could take you all the way from Miami to New Jersey. A pod of pelicans flew through the open bridge like they'd been waiting in line too. If I remembered correctly, there was a rescue organization, Pelican Harbor Seabird Station, nearby, and I wondered if they were former patients. Or maybe visiting a friend à la flyby.

"Pájaros." Manny pointed.

"Son pelicanos. Comen peces enteros." I threw my head back and pretended to gulp a whole fish down.

"Yo quiero comer pescado."

I laughed and told him I wasn't making fish for dinner, but maybe tomorrow I would. A notification beeped on my phone just as the safety arm lifted. I'd look at it later.

The grocery store was little and old, but jam-packed with everything a Latin kitchen might need. They even had a hot meal cafeteria. The black beans looked and smelled delicious, as did the lechon with mojo. I put two batons of Cuban bread in my cart and a bag of sweet cornbread from the in-store bakery. Double checking that I had everything on my list, I went through the produce section once more. Mangos were on special—four for five dollars. I added a bag of limes, some malanga, and a whole pineapple that would take a few days to ripen, and one guanábana. Mami had sent me a photo of the soursop tree on the property that they managed in the Dominican Republic. I think it had given me the hankering for them. I didn't remember Manny ever having tried the white-fleshed fruit that smelled like pineapple but tasted like a cross between a strawberry and a citrusy apple. So, I decided to get a few more just in case he loved them as much as I did. A twenty-something in a bathing suit reached for the same rough-skinned green fruit as me.

"Disculpa," I said.

"Take it," the young woman said and offered me the fruit in her hand. "I'm actually looking for the papaya. Oh, wow, are you—" She curved her index finger and put it above her lip like a mustache.

"Who?" I replied.

"Que cool," she said, then smiled, lifted her phone, and began typing something into her phone.

In the checkout line, Manny "helped" unload the cart onto the conveyer belt. My phone beeped, and hoping it was Alma, I checked it quickly. It was Delvis. Her message was the emoji with the stars in its eyes and something about being tagged. The earlier notification was from her too. I didn't unlock my phone to read it because the cashier was giving me the stink eye. It wasn't until I got home and put away the groceries that I read it.

The link was to *The Caribbean Kitchen* YouTube station. The Spanglish version of the papaya smoothie segment was up. I called Manny over, and we watched it together. Delvis had gone with the "Abuela Approved" tagline. The animated graphic at the start of it was a cartoon version of me with a milk mustache. It was visually similar to Facebook's avatar stickers, a big head with a small body. I wouldn't have chosen it for myself, the milk mustache part, but it seems to have gotten me a fan. The bikini-clad woman's papaya search and the finger mustache made sense now.

Manny wanted to watch it again and again. He also wanted a papaya shake. I tickled him and told him it was time to build a fort. With him happy in his cardboard fortress, I began my test cook of Tía Elba's tamales. Opening the package of dried corn husks, I put them in a big bowl of hot water to soften. I had to modify her restaurant-sized forty-person recipe to a dinner portion. Ileana had told me *La Tacita*'s audience was mostly moms and abuelas. But the *Caribbean Kitchen* target was millennials and Gen Z, so I decided to use canned corn instead of fresh. The bell peppers, onions, bacon, cumin, and garlic smelled delicious on its own. To the sauté, I added the pork chunks. And while it cooked, I blended the canned corn and cornmeal into a thick porridge. As I poured a half can of tomato sauce into the pan, the phone rang. After five seconds of silence, it rang again. The caller tried a third time.

"Leave a message!" I yelled. Abandoning the stove at that moment meant something would burn. The phone would have to stay on the dining room table. The voicemail beep sounded.

"Good."

Guessing who it was made me anxious. I turned off the eyes and moved the pans to cool as soon as I could. The persistent caller was Robert. Did I want to listen to his message? Would he divorce

246

me in a voicemail like all those sad stories of breakups via text message? But what if it was about Alma? Maybe his brother was at the courthouse clearing her? I listened to his message with my fingers crossed.

Babe, don't cook tonight. I'm taking you to dinner. I have to tell you something.

I ruined half of the husks, wrapping my tamales in a rage. Robert was going to divorce me over dinner. I felt it in my bones. He wanted to do it in public so that I wouldn't make a scene. I'd never made a scene, but I told myself I'd start if he thought he was going to get away with cheating on me unscathed. Was he taking me to the French restaurant on the boulevard? Did he think just because it was in Coral Shores and there would be people there that knew him that I would hide the waterworks and my broken heart?

After I'd made and saved the tamales, I left the cleanup for later. I joined Manny in his cardboard fort. My brain was playing a matinee of breakup scenarios when the front door opened.

"Babe? The house smells delicious. I guess you didn't get my message. Babe? Manny? Where is everybody?"

Manny couldn't hold it any longer. He burst out of the fort like a quarterback through a banner, exposing my hiding place in the process. The cardboard structure toppled.

I lifted my head but didn't uncross my arms. Robert held a bouquet of flowers and, from my vantage point on the floor, looked like a too-handsome-to-be-real rom-com star.

"Babe, you okay?" Robert extended his hand to help me up.

I refused it. "I got your message." Getting on my knees, I stood. Robert passed the bouquet of yellow, orange, white, and red Gerber daisy flowers to me.

Not so gently placing them on the kitchen counter, I found a vase, filled it with water, and stuck the flowers, wrapped and all, into the vase.

"Are you mad?"

Was I mad? Of course, I was mad! Men were clueless. They thought pretty flowers could heal all wounds.

"I don't know if I can go out tonight. I have a job that I need to keep." I put the meat skillet in the sink and began to scrub it.

"Yeah, I saw the video. I'm so proud of you," Robert said. "You have your own cartoon logo and everything. That's pretty cool. Manny, do you like cartoon mommy?"

Shutting the faucet off and drying my hands, I turned to him. Manny sat on the counter with Robert's protective arm around him like a castle wall. The intro to the papaya milkshake Spanglish demo was playing. I heard my voice from the tinny speakers say, "Abuela Approved." Manny giggled and asked his father to play it again.

"Come on, babe, get changed. I've got reservations at a place you are going to love."

"Where?"

"It's a surprise. Come on—go change."

I stared at him with my arm akimbo and my hip cocked to one side.

Robert met my stare and upped it a pout. "Give me a chance. I can explain everything. I *will* explain everything."

I guessed he wasn't that dense after all.

"Fine. Where are we going?"

"The flag place, La Band-era, I think it's called."

"Ban-dare-ah." I corrected his pronunciation to be petty.

"The place with the two-story Puerto Rican flag mural."

"La Placita?" I asked.

"Yeah, that's it." Robert was sliding his son down his back, through his legs, and then flipping him in the air to repeat the process. Manny was in hysterics, loving the physical play.

The restaurant was only a few years old. It certainly hadn't been around when I'd lived in Miami, but Mami had told me about it. One of her favorite telenovela stars, Julian Gil, was a partner in it. I was more interested in the other owner, the five-time James

Beard–nominated chef Jose Mendin. Robert was not forgiven, but I wasn't going to pass up the opportunity to eat mofongo. I freshened myself with a spritz of lime and coconut body spray, then slipped into a simple dress. Robert exchanged his long-sleeved shirt and tie for a beige linen guayabera. With his black work pants, he looked a little like a waiter at a Cuban restaurant.

In the Tesla on the way to drop Manny at Andrew and Sally's, I almost told Robert to turn around and take me home. Being in his car reminded me of Juliet and the love motel. But I knew I'd have to coparent with him, no matter what happened. It was better to rip the Band-Aid off quickly. This dinner needed to happen. If a divorce was in my future, I needed to face it head-on.

Robert asked me to stay in the car so as not to prolong the hand-off of Manny. We had a reservation to keep. I watched Manny scoot by Andrew and run into the arms of his cousins like he was coming home from a tour of duty. The trio's giggles and squeals broadcasted all the way to the curb.

Andrew waved and shouted. "Don't worry. He's going to be fine."

I stuck my arm out the window and gave a thumbs-up. Manny wasn't what I was worried about.

Robert and his brother hugged, bro style, with slaps on the back and fist bumps. Then Andrew handed him a thick envelope from his back pocket.

Divorce papers?

"Great. The whole family is in on it."

"Did you say something, babe?" Robert asked as he got in the car.

"No, mi amor, nada." I lied. Everything was wrong. Everything!

Robert put the envelope in the visor and threw the car into reverse. The law firm's address peeked out from its storage. It might as well have been a neon sign. I couldn't stop glancing at it the whole drive.

Because of La Placita's location in the MiMo District, parking was strictly valet. Robert surrendered the car with a smile and a "gracias, hermano." If he was speaking Spanish, then he was chill and confident. I noticed he didn't take the envelope from the visor. Maybe it wasn't a divorce dinner. I exhaled a breath I didn't know I had been holding. Our table was a domino table with cup holders in the corners, trays for the tiles, and a nostalgic scene under clear epoxy in the playing area.

"You like it?" Robert asked with his arm around my waist.

"It's wild. I love it."

He squeezed me and kissed my head. "I thought so. I asked for it special. I know how much you enjoyed playing dominos with our neighbors."

"Y mi papá."

"Oh, you played with your dad a lot?"

"He'd let me be his partner sometimes at family barbecues."

"I hope your parents can come for a visit soon. Maybe for Christmas?"

The tension in my chest and shoulders lessened. Making family plans for our future was not the conversation I'd thought we were going to be having. "I don't know. Holidays are the busiest time of year for vacation rentals. Maybe after the new year?"

"We could always go to them," Robert said.

"Could we? I'd love that." I took the menu the waiter offered.

"Pick some dates. As long as I'm not starting or finishing a big project, I can take off for a long weekend."

The waiter asked for our drink and appetizer order. We both ordered Medalla, the iconic Puerto Rican beer. I was disappointed it was canned and not bottled, but figured the bottles might not be available for import, as I'd never seen them stateside. From the cuchifritos menu, we got sorullitos and alcapurrias. Robert told the waiter we'd order our main course after we got our appetizers.

"So, are you serious about going to Punta Cana to see my family?"

"Yes. It's important that Manny knows his abuelos. And honestly, I'd like to get to know them better too. Video calls are great, but in person is better. Plus, I can't taste your mom's flan over the phone. Maybe hers is better than yours." He shot me a devilish grin.

There was the charm that had slayed me and made me fall for him. I matched his smirk and told him. "Mami's is the original, but mine is better. Hers is too sweet."

"Should I tell her that? She needs to know."

"Don't you dare!" I threatened to throw a domino at him.

We'd just started a round when our drinks and fried food arrived. The crab fritters were glistening direct from the oil. The sweet cornmeal sticks were the perfect golden color. I couldn't resist them and had my mouth full when the waiter asked for our order. I flicked my hand at Robert for him to order first. He chose the pastelón de asado for his main course. And because I had my mouth full of cuchifritos, he guessed, correctly, that I'd want the mofongo. I nodded enthusiastically.

The music was good, and the decor was laid back and fun. We drank, ate, and played without much talk. Before long, I blocked the game. Robert needed to play a six, but I had them all.

"¡Toma!" I said, laying down my tile for the kill. "I win!"

"I think I desire a do-over. Wasn't that the practice round? You have much more experience than I do with this game." Robert laughed.

Our beers were finished, so I flagged the waiter for two more. Nothing but garnish was left on our appetizer plates. Robert had liked the crab fritters and asked if I'd ever made them before.

"Not ones of crab. I've made the meat versions."

"This crab one is damn good." He found the last crumb of the crispy yucca exterior and savored it.

"These were good, but they will never compare to the first alcapurrias I ever had. Straight from the fryer at a food stall on the beach, they are so good. We were on a family vacation to visit Mami's prima, Sandra. She'd recently married a Puerto Rican guy and moved to Luquillo, a popular beach town on the Atlantic side of the island. I was twelve that summer, old enough to be unsupervised and still kid enough to play and have fun with my younger cousins. I remember I climbed a coconut tree. The trunk was curved from the wind. I thought I was so cool with a machete in one hand and a coconut in the other."

"I want that for Manny. I think we should have another kid," Robert said.

I stared at him, speechless. For a few moments, I'd forgotten that he was cheating on me. Did he think a baby was going to solve our problems? There was no way I was going to have a child to save our marriage. That never worked, and I was about to say as much when our entrees were delivered. I took a swig of the fresh Medalla the waiter had brought and waited for him to leave us.

"Tú estás loco."

"Why are you calling me crazy, babe? We've talked about having a sibling for Manny." Robert cut into his layered beef and plantain dish.

"You're"—I lowered my voice—"having an affair." I pointed at him with my fork. Okay, more like I stabbed the air in his direction.

"About that," Robert said. "I want to tell you the truth about Juliet."

"I'm listening."

He set his utensils down and pulled out his phone. He scrolled and found what he wanted, then passed the phone to me.

"She borrowed my car that day. I wasn't with her. I was twenty miles away in a pickup truck with the surveyor."

"This doesn't prove anything." I looked at the image of Juliet in my husband's car. She was parking at El León Dorado.

"Go to the next one."

I swiped left to a shot of a video screen. The glare and distortion made details difficult to read. It was Juliet with a man whose shape didn't match Robert's.

"Who's she with? That could be you in disguise." I said.

Robert gave me an incredulous look. "Keep going, there are three more photos. Enlarge it and see the time stamp at the bottom." He took another bite of his dinner.

"Fuentes? Fuentes! What is she doing there with him? Eww. Gross. That doesn't make sense. She can afford a suite at the Fontainebleau. What is she doing at a love motel in Hialeah?"

"So, you see, I'm not having an affair." He reached across the table and put his hand over mine.

I yanked my hand away. "Fine. So, you weren't with her on that day. What about all the golf dates and late nights at the club? I know you dated her in high school. Also, you never bought me flowers in New York. Now you've done it twice within, like, a week. Something is up with you, Robert William Smith. No me digas que no."

"Yes, I dated her for a hot minute in high school. But hormones are to blame for that."

"Eww. So, you did sleep with her."

"Once. And then everyone started teasing us about being kissing cousins, and I got grossed out that I was sleeping with my mother and . . ." Robert closed his eyes and shook his head. He was erasing the incestuous image like his brain was an old-timey Etch A Sketch.

"But you liked her then, and you like her now."

"No." He exhaled sharply. "Listen, babe. Juliet is a mean, petty, conniving, heartless ghoul."

"A ghoul?"

"Yeah, a ghoul like a ghost that feeds on death and disaster."

I rolled my eyes. "I know what a ghoul is. I do have a PhD after all." I took a small bite of my dinner. It was cold. "If you know she's terrible, then why are you working for her father and hanging out with her. All. The. Time." I took another fork full of the smashed plantains. There was still warmth at the core of the mound. So, I dug into the middle of the heavily seasoned mash. It was one of my favorite Puerto Rican dishes, and I'd hate to miss trying it from a James

Beard chef. There were variations of it in the Dominican Republic, where it was called mangú, and in Cuba, fufú. I ate a bit, then pushed the almost full plate away.

"Okay. Truth is, I hadn't planned on ever talking to her. I'd actually forgotten all about her, but then my mother engineered our crossing paths."

"I always knew your mom hated me. I'm not from the right family. And I'm not blonde or white enough for her."

"Babe, stop. Mom's a piece of work, but she doesn't hate you."

"Uh-huh." I drank a sip of beer and replaced the can in the holder. I squeezed the aluminum a few times, making it click like the dice bubble in a Sorry game. "Go on."

"So anyway, I found out Pimpkin Development was about to buy one of the last if not *the* last tract of pine rocklands in South Florida— it's basically a prehistoric limestone forest. There are, like, eleven animals and over a dozen plants that are on the threatened list. This is a shrinking habitat that cannot be replaced once it's gone."

My Roberto was so sexy when he talked environmentalism, I couldn't help but like him. Caridad, I hoped he was telling me the truth. I loved him, and I loved the family we'd made together.

"Look, you and I both knew the Department of Environmental Resources job was not for me. So, I talked to Senior and my brothers. Senior is giving me my stock inheritance now. Andrew is going to be my silent partner and my legal advisor. Anyway, I've convinced Paul—he's reasonable; it's Juliet's grandfather that's a jerk— I convinced Paul that it's better for his bottom line to donate the property as a conservation land trust. It will also be good for the company's image. Paul asked me not to say anything to Juliet because she might make a stink and stop the deal. I'd forgotten how petty she can be, and manipulative. To keep it all from going sour, I had to pretend like Juliet and I were friends. But we are not, trust me. She is awful."

"But you told me I'd like her and should be her friend."

254

"That was before she showed her true colors."

"What do you mean?"

"I don't want to start a catfight."

"Excuse me! That's sexist."

"You're right. Let me put it this way: she said some not nice things about you to me."

"Like what?" I pounded my fist on the table.

"It doesn't matter. I don't want to waste my breath on her. Let me tell you about the trust. I—well, Drew—has started the ball rolling to form the nonprofit organization to manage the land trust. I'll be on the board of directors, but I'll keep working as an environmental engineer, just not for Pimpkin. It's been agreed, just not advertised, that after the westside condo project, I'm leaving Pimpkin Development to start my own consulting firm. See, babe? I'm not having an affair. I've been too busy. I'm doing this for us."

"And the environment."

"Yes, and the Florida Atala."

"The what?"

"It's a black butterfly with blue spots and a red abdomen. I was trying to be funny."

"You're cute," I said.

"So, do you forgive me?"

"I'm getting there. I might need dessert to think on it." I batted my eyelashes at him.

"Flan?"

"Tembleque for me."

"The tembleque is excellent," a voice said.

We were so immersed in conversation that neither of us had noticed the man in chef whites standing beside our table.

"Raul told me"—he motioned to the waiter—"you hadn't touched your mofongo. Is there something wrong with?"

I couldn't believe the chef had left the kitchen for me. I was so embarrassed. That was not how I wanted to meet him.

"Chef Mendin, there is nothing wrong with your food. It's delicious. I'm sorry I was talking so much, I let it get cold. Mi culpa. Not your fault."

"Phew." He made a motion like he was wiping sweat from his brow. "So, abuela approved?"

"Claro que sí," I replied.

The chef put his finger over his top lip and winked. "Good. Enjoy the tembleque."

"I will. Gracias," I said to him as he departed.

"What was that about? The little mustache thing and the wink?"

"While you've been busy *not* having an affair"—I blew him a kiss—"I've been busy making a fool of myself on YouTube. My producer, Delvis—" I paused, realizing that I'd used "my producer'" in a sentence. Wow. My life had changed. "My producer, Delvis," I began again, "launched the Spanglish version of the cooking segment. And the animated logo— you saw it—has gone viral."

I showed Robert the number of hits on the segment. He read some of the nice comments out loud. It was embarrassing, and I begged him to stop, which he did after I threatened to eat his flan.

On our way to get Manny, Robert showed me the envelope he'd tucked in the visor. It was the draft of the land trust, not divorce papers.

"Roberto, I have to confess. I thought these were divorce papers, and you were taking me to a restaurant where you knew I wouldn't make a scene when you told me."

"No wonder you've been acting weird. What gave you that idea?"

"You mean other than seeing your car at a love motel?"

"Babe! That wasn't me!"

"Shh. I know that now." I put my hand on his thigh and then stroked the back of his neck. "But I didn't when Sally mentioned you were talking to Drew about a trust. I jumped to conclusions and thought you were making a trust for Manny because you were divorcing me to be with Juliet."

A stoplight caught us, and he leaned over and kissed me. "I would never replace you with that ghoul. Never. I love you."

"I love you too."

The car behind us honked. Miami was just as horn-y as New York City.

Chapter Thirty-Three

I woke up with Robert spooning me. The last few weeks it had felt like we were roommates, not a couple. But the dry spell was broken. I rolled to face him.

"Wake up, sleepyhead. You're going to be late for work," I said.

"I don't want to leave this bed. I've missed us."

"Me too. But you have to go save the blue butterflies for your son's generation."

We kissed deeply before getting out of bed. I slipped into a nightshirt and went to check on Manny. He was still asleep. Sally reported that the cousins had played dress-up and restaurant most of the evening, with a ten-minute frenzy on the in-ground trampoline.

I made a simple breakfast of papaya and banana with a queso de campo slice and a wedge of Cuban bread. Robert and I ate at the dining room table, with our knees touching, like we were teenagers on a date.

"What do you have planned for today?" he asked.

"I have to go to Elliot Truman's funeral at ten thirty. Then I'm going to take some tamales to Alma."

"How's she doing? Drew is trying his best to get her freed. Says the evidence is laughable. But the judge is being a dick." Robert put up his hands. "His words, not mine."

"Does Drew know why? Does the judge not like Cubans? Or women? Or Realtors?" I took our plates to the sink.

"The judge is a Cuban woman, so I'm guessing not, but Miami is a pretty vicious real estate market. She might have a vendetta against Realtors."

"Not even funny."

"I know. Sorry. So, this funeral is it at St. Brigid's?"

"Yes. Why?"

"Why don't you take a look at the school while you're there?" Robert stood and began gathering his things to go to work.

"About that . . ." I sauntered to him and walked my fingers up his tie. "What if Manny started half days at Agape Montessori next week? It's three days a week, and they encourage bilingualism, and I know one of the aides. She's very good."

"Shh." He put his finger on my lips. "You don't have to convince me. I trust you, babe. I love the idea. Sign him up."

"But what about the tuition?" I hadn't looked at the application packet, but I was sure it wasn't cheap.

"We'll figure it out. Plus, you're a big TV star now." Robert grinned. "I'm going to be a kept house husband walking around in designer boxer shorts with a martini. Lounging under the mango tree by the pool. Right?"

"Ha ha ha. I don't think so. You'll have to choose between the Grey Goose and the Versace. I don't think I make enough for both. And we don't have a mango tree or a pool. Go to work, loverboy." I kissed him, then lovingly pushed him toward the door.

Last night's sleeplessness called for more coffee. As I waited for the espresso to drip, I found myself blushing at the memory of why we hadn't slept much. I took my large mug of sweet café con leche to the study and sat in the window seat. I had a few hours before the funeral, and Elliot's death was bothering me. How does a yoga teacher in good health, from all appearances, drop dead? Detective Pullman had been evasive about the cause of death. What did he know, and why wasn't he sharing it?

I felt emboldened to ask him and went to get my phone, which I found in my purse with a zero charge on the battery. I took the charger and plugged it into the wall socket. The study desperately needed a reading chair and side table to put a drink on. It also needed a chair for the built-in desk that I had cluttered with files and other non-book things. One of the items on the desk was the bag from my last visit to Fuentes. I took out the boxes of weight-loss powder, stacked them into a pyramid, and then examined the gallon bag of fertility tea. I held it to the sunlight. A pair of walkers crossed into view and looked my way. I waved before realizing I didn't have any bottoms on.

"Great. I wonder how long that will take to get to my mother-in-law. Your son's wife is an exhibitionist!" I shook my head and sighed.

I dropped to the floor and checked the battery percentage. Not enough juice to even turn on.

"What's in this stuff? Could any of it kill you by accident?" I moved the dried herbs with my thumbs, crumbling some of them into powder. The quantity was meant for a week. What if it was like malanga, poisonous in one form, but not another? Or what if the herb wasn't harmful in small quantities, but it was in large amounts? Fuentes's assistant had warned me, and Elliot too, that the fertility tea was strong and shouldn't be mixed with the diet drink.

My phone beeped to life. I had messages. Delvis's had tons of emojis and exclamation marks. She was happy we had sixty-seven thousand shares and three thousand five hundred followers. There was also a link to the second Spanglish video. I guessed she had published it to coincide with today's *La Tacita* broadcast. There was a text from Mami. She was happy I'd reconnected with Tía Elba, but said maybe don't mention it to Papi.

I went to the recent calls and clicked on Pullman's number.

"Good morning, Ms. Mars," Pullman said.

"I think I'm more of a Jessica Fletcher." I hoped my joking with him would bode well and loosen his tongue.

"What do you need, Jessica? We weren't scheduled to talk until after the funeral."

"Yeah, about that. What was the official cause of death?"

"There were several."

"What do you mean? Doesn't there have to be one clear-cut cause to release the body? I mean, her death was suspicious, right? You *are* still looking for a culprit, right?"

"Why does this matter to you? Mrs. Truman's death has nothing to do with your friend Alma."

"I care because healthy thirty-year-olds don't just drop dead. There has to be a connection between Elliot, Sunny, and Fuentes."

"Hold your horses there, Mrs. Fletcher. I know you want to pin this on Fuentes so you can get your Ms. Diaz off the hook, but I have news for you. Elliot Truman was not as healthy as she looked."

"What do you mean, 'not healthy'? Ay, mi madre, did she have cancer? Did they find a tumor when they did the autopsy? Oh my goodness, was it in her brain?"

Frank Pullman exhaled. After a beat, he replied, "Elliot Truman had undiagnosed liver disease. Alpha-1 antitrypsin deficiency. It's hereditary, and since she was adopted, she probably didn't know she had it. So, that was the underlying cause of death."

"Underlying? What does that even mean? What was the overlying cause? I mean main cause."

"Mrs. Truman died from asphyxiation. She choked on her own vomit. My question is how and why. If she was a frat boy, that might make sense, but a fit nondrinker? Nah. I don't like it."

"So you think there still might be a connection to Fuentes."

"I didn't say that. Goodbye, Mrs. Fletcher. We will speak after the funeral. Please pay attention to Jorge Trujillo and Juliet Pimpkin. Thank you."

Click.

"Well, that was interesting." I uncrossed my legs and knocked my mug onto the herb encyclopedia. "Ay, ay, ay." I poured the river of coffee back into the mug and rushed to the kitchen to dry the book. Thankfully, I'd drunk most of the coffee. I patted the page that had taken the spill. It was the illustrated plate of ruta graveolens, common rue, ruda in Spanish. The weedy-looking plant had yellow flowers that reminded me of crepe paper.

Rue was one of the herbs in the apothecary jars at Fuentes's. Daniela had put a big scoop of it in the bag. What did I know about rue? Nothing. I went to the index and found that ruda had several entries. There were a few recipes for gastrointestinal issues like bloating and gas and three cures for infertility. One of which called for fresh goat milk as a base.

I took the mostly dry book and placed it in a spot of sun on the window seat next to the bag of dried herbs. The brown and green-gray leaves all looked similar to one another. I held the bag close to the picture to see if I could distinguish the exact herbs in the tea mix. Doubt seeped into my head.

"That could be dried rue. Maybe?"

I did an image search for dried rue and determined it probably was what was in the tea. Then it occurred to me that I'd taken a photo of the recipe. I nearly ripped the charge cord from the wall as I brought the phone closer to my eyes. At max zoom, there were words, but they were blurry. In the edit menu, I heightened the contrast and sharpened the pixels.

"Ruda!"

The fertility tea recipe definitely had ruta graveolens in it. The question was, was it poisonous if not prepared properly? The images of the dried herb from my search had all been packaged. Reviewing them, they all said "external use only." I melted onto the floor and went down an internet research rabbit hole. Rue was mostly used as a compress for inflammation. Several sites warned that it should not be consumed because it might cause liver damage. I went back to the encyclopedia and read the Cuban ethnopharmacological history of the herb. The bitter herb was used for intestinal parasites, as it caused the gut to spasm. That was the same reason it was used to invite Aunt Flo when she was late. Stormy had mentioned something similar about catnip.

"Ay, mi madre," I mumbled.

Rue was not a fertility herb. It was the opposite. It was supposed to be used sparingly and on occasion, not taken daily or, like in Elliot's case, two to three times a day. That would explain Elliot's dizziness, accelerated liver decline, and why she had clutched her stomach before falling to the floor at the Fitness Center. I kept reading about the side effects of rue poisoning. Shortness of breath. I'd have to check the video again, but I was sure she was gasping for air. Skin blisters. Elliot didn't have them. Oh, but that's if the oils touched the skin. Vomiting. Elliot didn't have morning sickness. She had rue poisoning.

"¿Mami? ¿Dónde estás?"

"Aquí, mi príncipe, aquí."

I crawled on my hands and knees to the doorway so Manny could see me. He rubbed his eyes, then smiled. I was tackled and smothered with kisses.

"Te vas a jugar con Sophia hoy. Tenemos que comer y vestir rapidito."

I'd stretched the truth. The funeral was still two hours away. There was plenty of time. But I wanted to run by the Fitness Center before going to Pepper's house. I needed to see the video again.

While Manny ate his oatmeal O's and sliced banana, I dressed. My functional wardrobe of metropolitan black was proving sadly useful. When Alma was cleared of charges, we'd go shopping. I wanted Miami colors and tropical patterns and lightweight fabrics. She'd be thrilled to be my stylist. Caridad, I missed her.

The Starbucks drive-through was five cars long. As much of a hurry as I was in, it would have been longer to get Manny in and out of the car seat. So, I waited patiently and tried to remember "Kitty's" coffee preference. But her name wasn't Kitty. *Becca*. Her name was Becca, and she liked cats and salted caramel mocha frappes. I ordered the drink and asked if they had sweets with cats on them.

"We have cake pops decorated with whiskers," said the disembodied voice.

"Perfect. I'll take two."

I paid for the order, secured the drink in the car's cup holder, and then passed Manny one of the cake pops.

"Flossie!" Manny peeped.

I was surprised he'd remembered the calico cat's name. Maybe his love of dogs was waning. He'd be seeing the cat three times a week pretty soon.

Becca was at the registrar window when we walked into the Fitness Center. She was answering questions about the open gymnastics session for kids.

"Yes, of course, it's supervised," Becca said.

"Excuse me," I said to the lady fretting about the specter of broken limbs and concussions.

She gave me an I-was-here-first look.

"I'm just dropping this off for Becca, the best Fitness Center employee." I placed the drink and treat on the counter and mouthed I'd be back in a second.

As I rounded the corner to take Manny to the childcare room, the administrator's office door opened. Jorge, with his back holding the door open, was speaking to someone about room capacity. Dressed in bicycle shorts and a Mambo-cise muscle tee, I guessed he was skipping the funeral.

"Hola, guapo," I said. While I didn't usually call people handsome in place of their proper name, in that instant, I knew flattery would set me off on the right foot.

"Miriam!" Jorge kissed me on the cheek. "¿Y quién es este?" he asked, pointing to my son.

"Mi hijo, Manuel."

Jorge bent at the knees and exchanged greetings with Manny like he was a favorite goofy tío. The kindness and caring Jorge showed to my son did not mesh with the idea that he might be a calculated killer. I'd marked him off my suspect list until Pullman had mentioned the synthetic hairs that matched. How had they gotten on both Sunny and Elliot?

264

"Jorge, can I ask you a question about Elliot?" I'd switched to English for the sake of little ears.

"Mira, I know we were rivals, sort of, but I loved that girl. I'll be at the funeral, don't worry. Just have to teach a class, then I'll quick-change y voilà." He made a magician's flourish.

"Good. But that's not it."

"Apúrate, mujer, I have to teach." He began walking.

I took Manny by the hand and followed. "Did you ever loan Elliot or Sunny your Cha-Cha Minnelli wig?"

"¿Que qué?"

"The short spiky black wig?"

Jorge had one foot in the classroom. "No, but I did lend it to that 'beach' Juliet, and she ruined it. Why I ever trusted her after everything that happened five years ago, I don't know."

Manny tugged at me. "¿Playa?"

"No, mi amor, no vamos a ir a la playa." My mother-in-law had nothing to worry about. Manny's bilingual skills were fine. He'd translate "beach" to "playa" with no problem. We'd been to the beach the first weekend we'd arrived, but not since. Manny had enjoyed the sandcastle Roberto had built for him and delighted in smashing it with his fists. But the beach Jorge had referred to didn't have sand and was spelled with an "I" and a "T."

Jorge was already cheerleading to his students, telling them to warm-up and stretch. I'd have to catch him at the church if I had any more questions. My phone beeped that it was one hour until the funeral. I needed to get to Pepper's in case she'd started the day with mimosas or bloody marys. The overprotective mom was still grilling Becca on the center's safety standards when Manny and I passed the registrar window. I waved to her sympathetically. Truth be told, I was okay with not watching the video footage again. Seeing Elliot gasping for air and dying once had been one time too many.

I arrived at Pepper's a little early. Thankfully, she was sober as a nun on Good Friday. Gabriela had conveniently cleaned the bar and wine cooler, then misplaced all the bottles and the key. I was pretty sure the liquor would magically appear after the funeral. Pepper was quiet on the drive to St. Brigid's Church. I didn't know if it was mourning or a hangover. We'd left the kids in Gabriela's care since her practicum at Agape didn't start until Monday. She was happy to hear that I'd decided to enroll Manny in the Montessori, and put in another pitch to Pepper that Sophia should attend. Pepper had shrugged in a "sure, why not?" way.

"Pepper, do you remember Elliot ever mentioning having problems with her liver?" I asked as we walked to the domed church.

"Jaundice has to do with the liver, right?"

"Yes. Did she have jaundice?"

"Yeah, and I thought it was weird because in my mind only babies got jaundice. She wasn't yellow or anything, but she did start taking vitamin D and getting more sun. Why?"

"Just curious because I think I overheard the detective say the underlying cause of her death was hereditary liver disease." I was stretching the truth. *Overheard.* I had to twist his arm to get him to tell me anything.

"Oh my." Pepper broke into tears. "She never knew, did she? Because . . . because . . . because she was adopted. And if she had . . . had her own baby, she'd have passed it on to . . . to . . . to the baby."

I pulled Pepper onto a cement bench surrounded by palms and attempted to calm her down. Her jagged breaths quieted down to deep intakes of air, and eventually the waterworks stopped. I'd made sure we arrived early. So there was plenty of time.

"Come on, let's find our seats. Do you want to sit with Elliot's family up front?" I asked.

"I probably should, right? Maybe behind her parents."

"I think that sounds like a good idea."

Elliot's parents were in their sixties but looked like they were forty-eight at most. Money bought youth, I guessed. The sanctuary was large, and attendees were beginning to arrive in numbers. After giving my condolences to the parents and Elliot's husband, I left Pepper in the second row and told her we'd meet up after the service.

"Aren't you going to sit with me?" Pepper asked.

"I should probably find my mother-in-law and sit with her."

"Marjory. Really?"

"I know, I know, but I have to do my penance." I smiled weakly.

It wasn't a bad idea. A painful one, but not bad. I'd bet money that Marjory would sit with her preferred partner for her son, Juliet Pimpkin. She was one of the two people Pullman had told me to watch. I still didn't know what to watch for, but I knew I'd enjoy having the upper hand for once. Robert loved me, not Juliet. *Sorry, not sorry, Marjory. Sorry, not sorry, Juliet.*

Three teenagers in plaid St. Brigid's uniforms stood in the right, center, and left aisles, distributing programs and prayer cards. The Latina teen handed me mine and then did a double take. She made a finger mustache. I nodded an affirmative to the question I read in her eyes.

"Puedo?" She took a phone from her skirt pocket. "For mi abuela."

I told her I'd be happy to take a photograph with her but that we should step outside to be respectful to the family. In the vestibule, we took a standard shot and then one with finger mustaches. The young woman told me her Colombian grandmother watched *La Tacita* every morning and had made her watch the Spanglish video. The teen complimented me on being funny. My show's tag line was true. I was abuela approved. Only two episodes, and I already had fans. I asked her to send me the photo via AirDrop so I could share it with my producer.

My show. My producer. Fifteen seconds of fame was going to my head. My mother-in-law walked by at that moment and shot an arrow into my elation. I plummeted back to earth.

"Miriam. Come here this instant," she said.

"Good morning, Marjory." I hugged my teen fan and thanked her for being awesome. The teen went back to her post and I turned

267

on my best fake joy to woo my mother-in-law. "I'm so glad I ran into you. I was hoping we could sit together."

"I said, come here." Marjory crooked her finger and beckoned me to her like the Hansel and Gretel witch.

"Yes?" I stood beside her and mustered a tight smile.

"What is this nonsense? Did Bobby approve it? Does he know what you're doing? "

"Marjory, I'm not sure what you're talking about. Could you give me a hint?"

"I'll give you a hint. Co-seen-a."

That might have been the second time in five years that I'd heard Marjory Smith attempt to speak Spanish. The first was when she had met my parents at our marriage ceremony. Then she'd said 'O-la, oon p-la-ser.' And just like then, she looked like she'd eaten a Sour Patch Kid.

"I caught my housekeeper watching TV in the den this morning. And lo and behold, guess who was on the screen cooking a peasant stew like some common immigrant?"

Wow. Marjory was really letting her xenophobia flag fly today. I could take Michelle Obama's high road, or I could cuss her out in Spanish. Naturally, I wanted to do the latter, but for the sake of my Roberto and my son, I went with the former.

"Oh. I'm so glad you got to see my show. My producer tells me we are in two million US homes. I can't wait to tell her it's two million and one." I froze my face in a smile and waited for her reaction.

"Humph. I expected it would come to this. I warned Bobby not to marry the help. A cook. My grandson has a house cook for a mother. You've neglected your maternal duties to chase the spotlight on some two-bit network." Marjory reddened with each word.

"Thank you for your concern, Marjory. I assure you Manny is fine. I won't hold your monolingualism against you. How could you possibly know that UnMundo is in a hundred and twenty-two countries? Definitely not two-bit."

I'd never pushed back at my mother-in-law. It felt liberating, and I wanted another round. My arsenal of ten-dollar words was at the ready. The socioeconomic legacy of colonialism in the Caribbean was in that pot of peasant stew, and I'd be more than happy to educate her on it. Unfortunately, she was saved from my lecture by Juliet Pimpkin.

"Marjory, there you are, darling," Juliet said.

My mother-in-law literally tsked me before slithering to Juliet's side. She didn't even say goodbye. She let Juliet, in full snark, do that for her.

"Goodbye, Miriam." Juliet fluttered her fingers and took my mother-in-law into the sanctuary. Her tone had me mentally throwing brass candlesticks at the back of her head as she walked away.

"Hola, chica. I told you I'd make it on time." Jorge was beside me.

"Wow. And you look great." I said. "Do you want to sit together?"

"Sí, vamos. Let's sit behind that 'beach' and gossip about her. I have chisme."

Pullman would be happy. I was sitting with the two people he'd wanted me to watch. In the few minutes of chat time we had before the service music started, I learned that Jorge had lent his wig to Juliet and that she had washed it and flattened the spikey bits. Their argument in the hallway video was about the wig. Jorge wanted reparations. It had been their second argument. The first one had been in the administrator's office, and Elliot had witnessed it. Jorge had taken the wig from the bag, flipped out, and thrown it at Juliet. Elliot had picked it up from the floor and put it back in the plastic bag. That explained how the hair had gotten on her.

"My trademark look is ruined!" Jorge said.

He'd aired his complaint loud enough that there was no way she couldn't have heard him. Juliet didn't flinch or acknowledge him.

Jorge then told me about the infamous house party. It had been the second party he'd DJed for her. And even though Juliet wasn't at the party, she was the reason he was there. The police raid that happened had put an end to his career as DJ Broadway Sprinkles. His student visa had expired and being in the vicinity of illegal activity flagged him with the authorities. He had to return to his home country for almost a year. He blamed Sunny and her wild friends for derailing his dreams. His shot at stardom had been the following week at Miami Music Week, and he'd had to give up his spot on E11EVEN's lineup to catch a plane home to Honduras. He said he angry-cried the entire two-hour bus ride from the airport to his mother's house in Tela. The two-dollar-an-hour dishwasher job he was lucky to get at a beach tourist trap was so depressing he had thought about drowning himself in the Caribbean Sea. But the job eventually allowed him to return to Miami. The company that owned the tourist trap also owned the Coral Shores Country Club and dozens of other mid-level resorts. Jorge was able to finesse a transfer work visa.

A well-dressed, sunglasses-indoors type stopped at the end of the pew and whispered into Juliet's ear. Juliet sighed, rummaged in her purse, and passed the trust fund baby a packet. It looked like one of Fuentes's diet drink powders, but the packet was black, not green. Her action reminded me of something that I couldn't quite pinpoint. I zoned out of the funeral, trying to recall why but couldn't figure it out. Jorge's visa struggles also had me pondering. *Had he been mad enough to seek revenge on Sunny? Should I move him to number one on my suspect list?* Pullman was certainly interested in him. And Jorge had connections to the country club. Maybe he was one of the waiters the day Sunny was killed? I had more work to do.

Chapter Thirty-Four

Pepper didn't want to attend the interment. She said the guilt was too much to handle. I had no idea what guilt she thought she had. It wasn't like she'd had a crystal ball. No one had known Elliot had the disease. In his eulogy, Elliot's husband asked that friends donate to gene research and the Alpha-1 Foundation. I watched Pepper donate two thousand dollars from her phone before we got out of the parking lot.

"I need a drink," Pepper said.

When we got to her house, all the liquor and wine had returned. I knew Gabriela couldn't keep it hidden forever, but I worried about my new friend. If Pepper's drinking habit kept its pace, she'd have a liver problem too.

"Cosmos?"

"Pepper, I can't stay. I have to deliver something to Alma."

She pouted.

"Another time. And I'll call you tomorrow. We can have lunch or something. I'll cook. Have you ever had pastelón? Puerto Rican lasagna?"

She shook her head and began preparing a cocktail.

"It's delicious. I'll make it for you."

"Pastelón, right? I've heard of it. Layers of sweet platanos with ground beef," Gabriela said, entering the room with the kids.

"I'll make one tonight and bring it over tomorrow. Heat it and eat it. Okay?"

"Okay." Pepper sniffled.

We hugged, and I told Gabriela in Spanish not to leave Sophia alone with Pepper if she drank more than one cosmopolitan. She assured me she wouldn't and that Mike would be home early from work to relieve her of childcare and Pepper-sitting.

At home, I made Manny's lunch, then brought his Duplo building blocks into the living room so I could watch him while I reported to Pullman. I told him my theory about the rue poisoning and what I'd learned about the wig.

"I don't think Elliot was poisoned intentionally, but I do think it might happen again. The tea recipes aren't exact. It's just one scoop of this, one scoop of that. Fuentes doesn't take much of a medical history from his patients, much less order any blood tests. It's neglectful. It's malpractice, really. Can an herbalist be sued for malpractice? Can he be arrested for being a con man? Elliot's death is kind of his fault. I mean, her liver disease was exacerbated by the rue, right? She did die from choking on her vomit, which was directly caused by his wrongful prescribing of a toxic herb. That's manslaughter, right? Detective?"

"I'm listening, Veronica. I'll mention the herb thing to the medical examiner. Tell me about the wig again," Pullman said.

I told him about Cha-Cha Minelli and Holly Berry.

"Juliet ruined his trademark look, and they fought about it the night Elliot died. I don't think Jorge had anything to do with the deaths. The hair got on Elliot when she picked up the wig, probably."

"That explains Elliot, but not Sunny. Okay, good work, Ms. Mars."

"You're going to keep calling me Veronica Mars, aren't you?"

"Yep." Pullman chuckled.

"I guess I'm going to have to watch the series." I laughed. "So what's next? What's my next assignment?"

"Your next assignment is to stay away from my investigation. I'll let you know if I need any more of your help. Goodbye, Ms. Mars."

"But what about Alma? My friend isn't in the clear."

"Your friend is going to be fine. Don't worry."

"Can I see her?"

There was a long silence.

"Can I see her?" I asked again.

"Yes. On one condition. She has to stay in her house. Do you understand me? In her house."

"Okay. I got it. We won't set foot in her yard."

"I'm serious."

"Me too. Thank you." I put the phone down and did a happy dance while I wrapped some tamales in tin foil and set out for Alma's house before Detective Pullman changed his mind.

My proclamation to Manny that he was going to see his favorite primo-cia proved to be false. Gordan wasn't on Alma's front step. He wasn't anywhere. There was no police car in the drive. Alma answered my knock and squeezed me tightly.

"Where's your guard?" I asked.

"No sé. Don't care."

"What's changed? Aren't you still under house arrest?"

"Yeah, but I guess they can't spare the police. So, now I get random check-ins. And I can work from home! Come meet my assistant." Alma pulled me to the dining room, where two laptops, a laser printer, and stacks of flyers had taken over the table's surface.

"Meet, Ana, short for Anastasia. Ana, this is my best friend, Miriam."

Ana stood and shook my hand. She was an attractive woman with straight blonde hair and long, blunt-cut bangs.

"Can I make you some coffee?" Ana asked.

"No, it's okay. You two keep working. I've brought lunch. It will take about ten minutes to heat. Venga, Manny," I said, encouraging my son to follow me.

"Él puede quedarse con nosotros," Ana said. "If you don't mind. He reminds me of my little nephew that I miss so much.

"¿Hablas Español?" I hoped my shock didn't come out in my tone. I knew there were blonde and light-eyed Cubans, but she was blonde-blonde and tall.

"She's Russian-Cuban," Alma explained. "And she's helping me expand into the Russian market in Sunny Isle. I couldn't do it without her. She's even teaching me a few phrases."

"You can't always judge a book by its cover. I should have checked my assumptions at the door. Sorry."

"Don't worry about it. Sometimes I let people gossip in Spanish before revealing my language skills." Ana laughed. "That's how I get all the tea. But I know you're Alma's best friend, and that would have been mean."

"Gracias. Tamales in fifteen." I left the dining room and went to the kitchen. "Alma, where is your steamer?"

She answered from afar. "It's the bamboo basket kind. Under the counter."

"Found it." I checked that the basket fit tightly over the pot on the stove. Filling the pot with a few inches of hot water, I set it to boil, then placed the tamales on wax paper in the steamer. While I waited for our lunch to heat, I surveyed Alma's kitchen offerings to make a side salad. She had a bag of watercress and half of a Florida avocado. With the tomato I saw on the counter and a little olive oil, lime, and salt, I had the ingredients for a perfect salad.

As I was plating, Ana walked in and offered to make drinks. She'd obviously been in Alma's kitchen before, because she went directly to the cupboard with the glasses and brought out four.

"Does your son drink from a regular glass or a sippy? I don't think she has a sippy cup."

"As long as you move your files and laptops from the table, he can use a small juice glass," I offered.

"Okay. How about this one?" She traded a tall glass for a vintage-looking orange juice glass with a worn state of Florida map on it. The kind of map that tourist diners used as placemats. The ones with cartoonish alligators, flamingos, and 1960s swimmers.

"Perfect," I replied.

I heard Alma talking to Manny. He'd asked if her computer had Mikey Mouse. Soon, Mikey's high-pitched voice was jabbering.

Ana set the drinks on the counter. "Will we need knives, forks, and spoons?"

"No, only forks."

Ana opened a drawer and took out four forks.

"Ana," I whispered, "do you think this is going to hurt Alma's business? You know, the arrest and the cocaine rumors."

"Yes, it already has. But she'll bounce back. Everyone knows who the real cocaine queen in Coral Shores is." She took a plate and a glass to the dining room.

I followed with the same. What did she mean "the real cocaine queen"? I couldn't exactly ask for clarification in front of Alma and Manny. I waited patiently as she moved all the paperwork to one end of the table and put down cloth placemats and paper napkins from a sideboard. When we got back in the kitchen, I stopped her before we made our last run.

"Who? I'm new to Coral Shores. Who's the queen?"

She leaned into me. "Juliet Pimpkin. She always has coke. She'll even give you a free sample. Or so I've heard."

"Juliet? Really?"

"Mm-hmm. She's always bugging me to introduce her to my Russian friends that party. They have yachts. I hate them." She laughed.

"¿De verdad? Juliet."

"Sí. She was bothering me about it the day Alma got arrested. I was in the kitchen, putting cookies in the oven, you know, for that baked smell. It sells houses. I learned that from Alma. Anyway, I was there getting ready for the open house when she comes in and starts asking me if I can get her invited to Timati's video wrap party."

"Who is she?"

"He. He's a Russian rapper."

"Oye. Where's my tamale?" Alma called.

"Coming," I replied, with Manny's avocado and tomatoes-only plate in my hand.

"We'd better get in there. Alma turns evil when she's hangry." Ana took the remaining plate and glass from the counter.

Questions floated around my head throughout lunch. Had the anonymous tipster confused Alma with Juliet? Was Juliet a dealer? Dealers didn't give stuff away for free. Maybe it was her way of garnering favor, like breakfast for the Fitness Center. It was her bargaining chip. Was Juliet Sunny's dealer? Was she the one who had given Sunny the lethal dose?

Manny's battery ran out soon after lunch, and his grumpiness meant it was time to go home for a nap. The opportunity to ask Ana more about Juliet didn't present itself, so I got her phone number to contact her later. Manny almost fell asleep on the quick ride home, but thankfully he was lucid enough to walk himself into the house and directly to his bed.

"Pobrecito," I said as I closed the door to his room.

I heard keys in the door and braced myself for my mother-in-law.

"Babe, I'm home."

"Shh. Manny's just gone down for a nap." I put my arms around him, and we kissed. "What are you doing home so early?"

"It's Friday. I took off early so I could spend the weekend with my sexy wife and my perfect son," Robert said.

"Sexy, huh?"

"Sexy, rwah." He kissed my neck, creating shivers that tingled my body. "Let's go to the bedroom. Manny usually sleeps for an hour, right?" Robert wiggled his left eyebrow and led me to our bed.

Ana's revelation distracted me from my gorgeous and loving husband. As we slipped under the covers, I asked him, "What does Juliet do for a living?"

"Babe, I don't wanna talk about her anymore. I swear the only person I'm having sex with is you." Robert pulled me closer to him.

"I know. I know. Last time I'll mention her name, just tell me what business she's in, like what is her job at Pimpkin Development."

"She doesn't work for her dad. She works for her grandfather. Pimpkin Global. It's an import-export business to Asia."

"Okay, but what do they im—"

Robert covered my mouth with his and kissed me long and hard. Pretty soon, Juliet left my mind completely as Roberto proved how much he'd missed me.

Chapter
Thirty-Five

After I'd made the pastelón I'd promised for Pepper, we had a movie and pizza night. Robert chose the Disney movie *Cars*. Manny was in love with the talking vehicles. And of course, Sheriff, the police car character, was his favorite. It was nice. It felt like a christening of the house. I'd mentioned to Robert that maybe Friday night movie and a pizza should be our new Coral Shores tradition.

In la media de la noche, I heard my phone ring. At first, I'd thought it was in my dream because it sounded so faint, but then I opened my eyes. I was in bed, and my phone was in the kitchen. When I got to it, of course, it stopped ringing.

Missed call. Alma.

Why would Alma be calling me at 2:38 AM?

The phone rang again. I clicked the green answer circle.

"Is everything okay?" I asked, and moved to the study so I could close the door for quiet.

"Sorry for calling so early."

"Try late. Chica, it is still night. What's wrong?"

"Mira, I couldn't sleep, right. We lost the sale that Ana and I were working on. It was the third one this week. I feel like I'm cursed."

"Amiga, it's going to turn around. I prom—"

"Let me finish. So, like I couldn't sleep, right? And I was feeling cursed, right? Then I remembered the despojo you gave me. So, there I am in la ducha, splashing the stinky water over me, when it hits me. I'd already given the detective the diet powder."

"¿Qué?"

"Listen to me. The diet powder they confiscated from my purse. The one with the traces of cocaine was not mine. It had to have been planted. ¿Me estás escuchando? Are you hearing what I'm saying? I'd given the detective the diet powder the first time I met him right after Sunny's death. It was in a *green* package. The diet powder they took from my purse when they searched my house was a *black* package. I don't know where it came from, but it was not in my purse when I started the day. You know why I know that? Because I'd changed bags that morning to match my outfit. I don't know how I forgot that. I wish I'd used the despojo the first day you gave it to me. I feel so estúpida. How could I forget that I'd already given him the drink mix? How could I have forgotten I'd changed bags? Estúpida. Estúpida. Estúpida."

"Cálmate. You aren't stupid. Stress scrambles your brain. Hold on," I said and spun on my heels. What color were the diet powders Daniela had given me? "I'm putting you on speakerphone. Don't talk loud. Okay?"

"Sí, sí, sí."

In the study, I looked at the pyramid of tea boxes. She'd given me two boxes—my buy one, get one free—from the display. Then she'd gotten mad at Fuentes yelling for her, and she'd tossed in a few boxes from the large cardboard box. The packaging looked the same until I began inspecting it.

"These aren't the same."

"What isn't the same?" Alma asked in a whisper.

"The boxes of diet drink aren't the same. Two boxes have a green top, and the others have a black top." I opened each box. The packets inside matched the color of the top.

"Okay, so? Old stock. New stock. They changed the packaging. Why does it matter?"

"Shh."

"I wasn't being loud."

"No—shh, I'm thinking. Something is right there out of my reach. You know like a word on the tip of your tongue."

"You need a despojo. I bet there's a twenty-four-hour botanica."

"Shh." I held a green box and a black box in each hand. I rattled the black box and closed my eyes to replay Daniela taking it out of the cardboard shipping box. "The Chinese letters."

"Miriam, put me on video so I can see what you are seeing."

"No, no, shh. I'm almost there." I minimized the call and went to my camera roll. I'd taken a pictures and video of the storage room when I'd snuck in there. Zooming into the image, the letters on the box were a little fuzzy, but I thought I could make out two English letters. "I'm sending you a photo. Tell me if you can read what I read." I cropped the image and sent it.

"Mi'ja no soy china. I can't read Chinese."

"At the bottom. Do you see a "P" and a "G"?"

"Yeah. I mean, the photo is a little unclear, but that could be PG. So?"

"Ay, mi madre, it's all making sense now."

"What is making sense? Miriam, what are you *talking about?*"

"Shh!" I took her off speaker. "Alma, be quiet. Listen to me. Think. Do you remember seeing Juliet at the luncheon?"

"Is this about Robert and his affair?"

"Alma, Robert is not having an affair with Juliet or anyone else. Think. Was Juliet at the luncheon?"

"Hold on, let me walk through it in my mind." A beat later, she told me she didn't remember seeing Juliet at any of the tables. She'd gone to each table to saludar everyone and show her face. "Why?"

"Well, Juliet said, at the park later that day that she'd been at the luncheon. She was kind of crass about Sunny's death, as I remember."

"That sounds like her. I don't know why people like her so much. She's rude and snobby. Who cares if your family founded the town? Big whoop."

"Stop. Okay. So now tell me, did you see a lady with black hair?"

"There were a few. But like someone I didn't know?"

"Exactly."

"Hmm. Okay, so like there was a woman with short black hair wearing sunglasses that came in late and left early. She kind of sat toward the back."

"Did she talk to Sunny? Give her something?" I asked.

"I don't remember. Why? What does it mean?"

"Make coffee. I'm coming to your house."

I left a note for Robert and slipped out of the house with the bag of teas. Alma had café con leche and vatrushka, a Russian cheese Danish–type baked bun ready when I got there.

"This is good," I said.

"I agree. I love them. That's why Ana brought me a dozen of them yesterday. She gets them from a Russian bakery in Sunny Isles."

"Ana told me something yesterday that I thought was odd."

"Okay. What?"

"She said that Juliet always has coke."

"Probably. I mean she likes to act like a prim and proper society matron, but she was a party planner in her twenties, I think. Like rent out a night club and fly in a mid-list celeb kind of parties. Invite only–type deals."

I licked a crumb from my lips and moved my empty mug. The caffeine and sugar were working. The clues were finally connecting in my brain.

"Alma, I think I know who set you up, and I think I know who killed Sunny, but I don't quite know why yet. Maybe you can help me figure it out. Yeah?"

"Yeah! So, you definitely think Sunny was murdered?"

"Yep. And I think Juliet killed her."

"Wow. Okay. Why?" Alma put her feet on the corner of my chair.

And I put mine on hers. "Juliet has been bullying and coercing Sunny since middle school. She's manipulated her and used her like a toy. That house party with all the cocaine that you were blamed for, that house belonged to Juliet, right."

Alma nodded.

"Okay, so, I think Juliet planned the party. I think it was her cocaine, and she let you and Sunny take the fall. And now I think she's at it again in a way, but on a bigger scale."

"You're making it sound like Juliet is some drug lord."

"Exactly. So, listen to this. Juliet works for her grandfather, right? His company is called Pimpkin Global. They import from Asia. Specifically, China. I think Juliet got involved with Fuentes that way. Aren't all his teas from China?"

"Are you saying Juliet and Fuentes are importing cocaine from China?"

"No, but now that you say it—" I swatted her feet from my chair, stood, and reached over the table to grab the bag of drink mixes I'd gotten from Daniela. I dumped the contents and looked at each box. "Made in China. Look." I pointed to the tiny letters on the box. I then opened a green-topped box and a black-topped box. "Do you know what cocaine looks like? Like, can you identify it?"

"It's a white powder. I've never done it. You know that."

I could tell that memories of her brother were torturing her. It was painful and I hated bringing up his death for her, but we had to get to the truth. I tore open a green packet and a black packet, pouring each of the crystalized powders into little ant hills. "Do they look the same?"

"No."

"Does that one look like cocaine?" I pointed to the anthill from the black packet.

Alma put her nose close to the table.

"What are you doing? Stop!"

"Chill, chica. I'm not snorting the stuff. Coke has a certain smell. It smells sweet."

"Well, that doesn't help because the diet mix has sucralose and monk fruit in it."

282

"Yes, but coke also smells a little like gasoline."

"Gross! Why would anyone want to snort that stuff? How do you know it smells like gas?"

"I had to take a drug prevention training to be a volunteer. You know, after my brother died," Alma said. "This one could be cocaine." She pointed to the off-white powder that had come from the black packet.

"Are you sure?"

"Miriam, I'm not a professional, but yeah, if your guess is right, then this is probably coke."

"Ay, mi madre! I had boxes of coke sitting within reach of my baby boy. Ay, mi madre! We have to get rid of this stuff. Get dressed. We are going to return this to Fuentes's office, and then we are calling Detective Pullman."

"Are you crazy? I'm not supposed to leave the house, and now you want me to break into someone's store? Loca, I love you, but I have to say no."

"Well, we can't keep it at your house! It will make you look guilty!"

"Good point. But why can't you go by yourself?"

"I need a lookout. You can stay in the car and text me if you see anybody coming."

"Okay. I guess I can do that, but we have to get back before sunrise. Someone will probably be around to check on me in the morning." Alma started for her bedroom to change clothes.

"Do you have any gloves?"

I put on Alma's yellow dishwashing gloves and wiped down the diet drink boxes. I'd have to find a place far from Alma's house to throw away the opened packet. I carefully swept the cocaine into a glass of water and watched it dissolve before pouring it down the drain. I flushed the sink with more water, not wanting to leave any trace of the drug.

"Alma!"

"No grites, I'm right here." Alma was dressed in black sweatpants, a long-sleeved black turtleneck, black sneakers, and a black hat.

"Is that a beret?"

"Yes, I bought it in Paris. I think it looks stylish."

I stared at my friend. She was dressed appropriately for a break-in. Okay, minus the silly hat. And there I was with neon-yellow hands. "It's not a fashion show. But never mind, I think I know how Sunny died. I think Juliet was at the luncheon in disguise. She was wearing Jorge's wig, and she gave Sunny a packet of the black mix. I remember the water turned slightly pink when she mixed the powder into it. Just like it did when I did it now. Sunny thought she was drinking her diet drink. She didn't know she was taking coke. And with her weak heart, it was deadly. I think Juliet wanted her play toy back. I think she wanted Sunny hooked on coke again. Sunny was sober. Stormy had a hair strand test done. Sunny hadn't touched a drug in months—years."

"Pobrecita, Sunny. She was doing so good," Alma said.

"Juliet took it a step too far. I don't think she wanted to kill Sunny, but she did want her hooked again so she could manipulate her. And then when she died, she needed to pin it on you so her drug business wouldn't be exposed."

"You should call the detective."

"I will."

"Miriam, like, call him now. This is serious."

"I will as soon as we put this junk back in Fuentes's storage space. Come on. We will be back in less than an hour."

"¡Miriam, estás loca! Call the detective."

"Alma, we need to put this junk back where it came from. Look what they did to you with a trace of coke—a trace! You do not want this stuff in your house. I don't want it to have any connection to you or me."

"But what if we get caught? Or stopped on the way there?"

"It's three thirty in the morning. We won't get caught."

Chapter
Thirty-Six

Hialeah was well lit but mostly deserted that early in the morning. Neon and illuminated signs advertised pawn shops, cake makers, Cuban pizza, and a car wash. I pulled my car to the side of the building, like I had last time, and turned the engine off.

"What about security cameras?" Alma asked.

"I'll check before I walk behind the building." I put on the hoodie Alma had demanded I wear. It was black except for the bright pink letters across the shoulders. I turned it inside out.

"Does he have an alarm?"

"I don't think so." I had one foot on the pavement about to get out of the car. "Chica, stop with the questions. Let me do this fast, and then we can get out of here fast. Text me if you see anything."

"How are you going to get inside? Do you have a key?"

She had me there. I hadn't thought about that. The last time I'd "broken in," the door had been unlocked.

"No. But maybe I'll get lucky. Worst-case scenario, I'll throw it in the dumpster. Better the drugs be in Fuentes's garbage than in yours. Okay, I'm going. Keep an eye out."

Alma nodded, biting her lips while making the sign of the cross. I checked for cameras and didn't see any. Most of the backdoors had a cast of light that didn't reach the wall that defined the property's limits. I tied the handles of the bag into a knot and held it close to my chest. I covered the bag with the hoodie and tucked my yellow-gloved hands in my armpits. As I got close to Fuentes's doors, I remembered the roaches in the dumpster. A shiver went up my spine. I gave the dumpster a wide berth, kept my head down, and checked the door-knob to the storage space.

Locked.

I checked Fuentes's office space door.

Locked.

The bathroom window was still cracked for air circulation. But the jalousie's metal frame touched the iron security bars, and there was no way I could slip through there unless I shrank to the size of a toddler. I contemplated throwing the boxes of tea through the win-dow and into the bathroom and was about to do it when I heard a noise.

Was that a rat? Fuentes had said there were ratones in the dump-ster. But the noise sounded like it had come from inside. I put my ear to the opening. There was definitely someone or something in there. I ran to the dumpster and threw the cocaine drink boxes in it like a basketball from the free-throw line.

A thought crossed my mind: maybe Juliet and Fuentes were inside. Maybe I could catch them red-handed. I felt my pockets for my phone and pulled it out with some difficulty, thanks to the dish-washing gloves. I had a text from Alma.

Car just pulled into the lot. Hurry!

I tried to unlock my phone, but the screen didn't read my rubber-clad fingers. Using my teeth, I freed my right hand and wiped the sweatiness away on the hoodie.

I texted back, *What kind of car?*

Alma replied, *IDK but now there is another car. Come back!*

Two cars. It had to be Fuentes and Juliet. It wasn't like they could move a major shipment of cocaine in broad daylight. I had them with their hand in the apothecary jar if I could record them. I put my phone on video, snaked my hand into the bathroom, and held it there in hopes of getting a damning conversation between the two. Noises like boxes being lifted and shifted continued, but I heard no voices. Suddenly, there were footsteps in the corridor. I yanked my arm back and dashed behind the dumpster.

The glint of red eyes met me. Not one rat but a whole family of ratones scattered, abandoning their feast. I held my breath, not only because of the stench but from nerves. Keeping watch of the door from the gap between the open lid and the dumpster, I saw the doorknob turn. I put my camera lens up with anticipation. *Please, please, please be Juliet Pimpkin.* I held my eyes shut for a nanosecond, to say a prayer, and when I opened them, I was stunned. Detective Frank Pullman was walking, looking directly into my camera.

"Ms. Mars, you can come out from behind the dumpster."

I stopped filming and lowered the phone.

"Miriam Quiñones, please come out."

I stood as still as a monument, a monument to stupidity. I'd been caught, but I didn't want to admit it.

"Ms. Quiñones, I know that you are behind the dumpster. I know it is not a rat this time. Please just come out. I can't be wasting my time out here." Pullman crossed his arms over a bulletproof vest.

I stepped into view and smiled, hoping for some good grace and luck.

"Nice glove. Going for the Michael Jackson look?"

"Huh?"

Pullman pointed to my one gloved hand.

"What are you doing here?" Pullman didn't wait for me to answer. "Did you think you were going to catch the bad guys yourself? Really? Such a Veronica! Come on, let's get you someplace safe."

"Safe? What's going on? Why are you here?"

"This is a raid. We've already arrested Mario Fuentes at his house. He's on his way downtown to booking."

"For drugs?" I asked.

Detective Pullman had me by the elbow like I might make a run for the border.

"Yes, for drugs. Although he swears he knows nothing about it. He even gave us the keys to this place. He's saying the black label boxes were a misprint and that Ms. Pimpkin agreed to take them off his hands at a discount."

"Oh, and about Juliet—"

"Yes, I know she's the one that set up your friend."

I stopped walking.

"Wait. How did you figure that out?" I asked.

"Remember when you told me that Juliet pronounced your friend's name with an "al" instead of an "all"? Well, the anonymous tipster said it that same way. It took a few days, but the voice recognition folks confirmed it. Juliet made the call. It's her voice, muffled by a cloth."

"Okay." Relief washed over me. My best friend was cleared. "But how did you know I was here?"

Pullman motioned with a cock of his head for me to follow him. We turned the corner, and I saw Officer Gordon Smith in plainclothes, with his butt on the hood of my car, talking to Alma.

"I've had Officer Smith watching the house. I knew you'd do something stupid, and I had to protect Ms. Diaz," Pullman said.

"Sorry, cousin. I couldn't tell you," Gordon said. "Ms. Diaz, I'm real sorry." He moved his hands to his hips.

Alma's eyes were wide, like a cat cornered. "Are you arresting us?"

"No! Well, at least I don't think so. Boss?"

Pullman looked from Alma to me and back again. "No, but I should."

Alma and I exhaled in unison.

"Officer Smith. Please escort these ladies to their homes." Pullman turned to go back to the evidence search.

"But what about Juliet. You are going to arrest her, right?" I asked.

"Yes. I'm just waiting on the judge's signature. It should be any minute now. As soon as the judge has had her coffee." Pullman chuckled.

"Yeah, Judge Alvarez does *not* like being woken up before dawn," Gordon said. "I did that once, and I almost lost my head." He laughed.

"Can we watch her getting arrested?"

"No, Ms. Quiñones, definitely not. N-O. *No!* Take them home, Officer Smith." Pullman walked away, shaking his head and talking to himself.

Gordon told us to get in our car and follow him. Not only was he in plainclothes, but he was also in a plain car, a dark blue four-door with a big scratch on the hood. I was happy yet frustrated. Alma's name would be cleared, and her business would rebound. But my frustration was from wanting to see the look on Juliet's face when she got cuffed. A mile from Coral Shores village limits, three police cars with their lights on, but no sirens, passed us.

"Alma, where is Juliet's house?"

"Miriam! Didn't you hear what the detective said?"

"I know, I know, I know. But I mean, what if we had to pass by her house on the way to your house. I swear we wouldn't stop. Just drive by, you know."

"Miriam. You are going to get us in trouble. And I just got out of trouble!"

"Porfa," I pleaded. "The woman borrowed my husband's car without his permission. She let me and everyone else think she was having an affair with my husband. And my mother-in-law loves her. I need, *need*, to see her get arrested. Por favor!"

"Fine. It's kind of on our way. It's the big house on the corner of Queen Angel and Ocean Concourse. The house with the huge Chinese temple dogs."

When the light turned green, I let Gordon get several car lengths ahead of us before I made my move. I knew he'd do a U-ie and find us quickly, but all I needed was a minute and some luck. The cop cars had turned off their sirens, but the blue flashers were still going. In the predawn light, it looked like a disco. I idled the car across from the action and rolled the windows down. In my review mirror, I saw Gordon pull up behind us and get out of his car. Juliet Pimpkin, in a silk robe with a sleep mask still on her forehead, came out of the house. Her hands were behind her back, and officers were on either side of her.

"Call my lawyer. This is nonsense!" Juliet screamed.

An officer came around her, carrying an evidence bag full of diet drink packets.

"I buy that from Dr. Mario Fuentes. If there's anything in there, I know nothing about it." Juliet shied from her escort's grip. The officer on the other side gripped her arm tighter. "*Ow!* Police brutality!"

Alma and I laughed as Juliet was led down her house's grand steps to a waiting police car.

"What are you looking at?" She was talking to us. "They're the ones that you should be arresting. Call ICE. They're probably illegals. Check their papers. They're Spanish. They're all involved with drugs. You should be looking at *them*, not me."

My jaw dropped. "Did she really just say that?"

"Wow. I think she did," Alma replied.

Gordon slapped his hand on the roof of the car and leaned into the window. "Show's over. Come on. Let's get you both home before Detective Pullman sees you out here."

"Thanks, Gordon," I said.

"I never liked her much anyway. She always made fun of my garage band in high school. She called it a garbage band. I don't know what Aunt Marjory sees in her."

Gordon tailed us home, never letting more than a few feet come between our bumper and his. I got into the house before Robert woke, and crumpled up the note I'd left him. Better he did not know that his wife had been part of a search, seizure, and arrest in the middle of the night. When he finally roused, I had coffee and breakfast ready. I wondered to myself how long it would take for the news to reach my mother-in-law's ears. A little part of me wanted to be there when she found out, but I knew I'd used up all my lucky charms not getting arrested myself.

Chapter
Thirty-Seven

I t had been almost two months since Juliet Pimpkin's arrest. Manny was loving preschool, and the Spanglish version of *Cocina Caribeña* was getting national attention. I was scheduled to be interviewed by Maria Hinojosa for Latino USA on National Public Radio. We would be talking about the show but also about the importance of food culture in the diaspora. My dreams were coming true, kind of. I wasn't working in academia, but NPR was close enough to an academic star by my name. Remezcla ran a piece about the YouTube channel that caused Delvis to pop a bottle of champagne. Life was good. Even my mother-in-law had been staying out of my hair. Manny and I would occasionally come home to an expensive toy in the living room, but there had been no micro-aggressions or slights to my Spanish. Leopards don't change their spots. I knew Marjory hadn't done the work to correct her prejudices, but I was enjoying my peace and quiet while I had it.

"Babe, where's the ketchup?" Robert opened the French doors and yelled across the dining room and living room.

"Mi amor, everything is out there. We're almost done. I'll be there in a second," I told him.

"Here you go," the locksmith said, passing me a new set of keys.

"And you promise these are the only set in existence?" I asked.

"Lo prometo."

"I'm so glad Bette has a sister that's a locksmith." I smiled at the woman. "You are staying for the barbecue, aren't you?"

Omarosa squinched her face up like she didn't want to intrude on a family gathering and made an excuse that she had work.

"Porfa. It's Sunday. Bette told me you don't work weekends. Come on. Let's eat. Leave your tools there and come meet everyone."

Omarosa and I joined the others on the newly finished patio. Roberto had convinced me that we had the money to do it. And actually, my renegotiated UnMundo salary covered most of it. The outside kitchen had a built-in grill with a sink and a chiller. The gorgeous teak table that sat sixteen had arrived yesterday in time for our overdue housewarming party. I introduced Omarosa to Detective Pullman and his wife Claudia, then to Pepper and her husband. Of course, she knew Tía Elba and Tío José via Yoli and Bette, who were also there. Sally and Andrew waved to her from the far end of the table. The last to be introduced were Alma and Gordon. I noticed an instant attraction between Omarosa and Gordon and was happy that the only seat not taken was next to him. I, for once, was not the chef. Robert was at the grill, and the smell of chorizos and burgers filled the backyard air. It was still hot in Miami, but the pergola had a fan and a mister that made the late autumn day perfect.

Alma had noticed the spark between Gordon and Omarosa too. She was talking him up to her in Spanish. She made his part in the whole arrest scenario much more elaborate and braver than it had been. That was until Detective Pullman cleared his throat.

"Alma, maybe I forgot to tell you. Detective Pullman's Spanish is very good," I said.

"Oops." Alma laughed. "Well, then why don't you finish the story."

"Do you think that would be wise, counselor?" Pullman said to Andrew.

"You are correct, Detective. The case has not gone to court yet. It's best not to jeopardize it," Andrew confirmed.

"You law types always stick together. I still don't understand how Alma was under house arrest but not under house arrest," I asked.

Pullman and Andrew exchanged looks to determine who would speak. It was Andrew. He told us that Pullman had figured out Juliet was the tipster and that Alma was being set up. So, in order to keep Juliet from knowing she'd been identified, they'd asked the judge to slow-walk her release.

"It was really for Alma's safety too. If Juliet had gone to that extreme to seek revenge, who knows what she was capable of?" Andrew said.

"What do you mean 'revenge'?" Alma asked.

Again, a look passed between law enforcement and lawyer. "It looks like Juliet's bullying of Sunny was more about a family grudge than anything else. And that's all I'm going to say." Andrew took a sip of his beer.

"This is the first I've heard of this. What?" I said.

Robert placed a plate of steaming burgers and sausage on the table. "Weatherman Financial advised all their clients to divest from Pimpkin Global. And then Sunny's grandfather sold his personal shares in the company as well. That's what caused the split between the families. Weatherman almost bankrupted Pimpkin Global. Pimpkin wanted Senior to sue, but he refused. He said it was too messy. Plus, he'd only just made partner. My father doesn't like messy cases. Okay, that's enough Coral Shores gossip. What's that word you use? Chisme. No more chisme; it's time to eat."

Sally's kids, Sophia, and Manny were playing in Manny's new cottage. I snapped a few pictures of them before I called them to the kids' table. My son was very proud of his outdoor playhouse and had begged to sleep in it the moment Robert had gotten it assembled. Robert had almost given in, and told me he'd sleep al fresco to watch him. Thankfully, it rained that night, and Manny forgot about his wish by the next day.

Our South Florida home and life were coming together nicely. I looked around the table at all the old and new faces and thanked La

294

Caridad for the blessings of family and friends. The only people that were missing were my parents. I wished they were there. On impulse, I stepped away from the table and video-called them. My father answered, and by the time my mother joined him on screen, I'd decided to throw caution to the wind. I showed them our new patio and made a point to zoom in on my tíos and prima Yoli. Papi smiled, to my surprise, and asked to speak to his brother. Listening to them reminisce in Spanish, it seemed that my tío had long ago forgiven his brother for not loaning him the money to expand the restaurant. But the two stubborn brothers had just never gotten around to saying I'm sorry to each other. My tíos made plans to visit my parents in the Dominican Republic after Christmas. I could hardly believe my ears. An almost twenty-year fight repaired with a single video call. I wished it had been that easy for the Pimpkins and the Weathermans. Maybe then Sunny would still be alive.

"What's for dessert?" Gordon asked.

"Well, I'm glad you asked that, cousin. I ordered a very special mango flan. Can you come help me with it?" Robert got up from his chair.

"Don't worry, Gordon, I can help him. You stay and talk to Omarosa," I said.

"Miriam, you are not the chef or the server today. Let Gordo give me a hand. Sit down and have another glass of your friend's sangria," Robert said and winked at Pepper.

Pepper passed the carafe of her Saint Tropez sangria to me, and we toasted Elliot. Gordon and my husband took their time returning. I worried they had dropped the flan or some such, but then I saw them coming around the side of the house. Gordon was carrying a shovel, and Robert had a potted tree.

"What is that?" I asked.

"Well, the topping for the flan might take a little longer than I'd planned. The nursery told me this tree should fruit in about two years." Robert smiled.

"Is that a mango tree?" I clapped. Several of our guests laughed at my delight.

"Yep. Where do you want us to plant it?"

I looked around the backyard and pointed to the corner where Manny's playhouse was. "There! It will be perfect there. I can see it from the kitchen window, and if we ever build that pool, it will make a nice shady corner. Oh, Robert, I love it! Thank you." I gave him a hug and kiss that nearly caused him to topple.

"Babe, you deserve it. You're the best mom a kid could ask for and the best wife I could have ever hoped for," Robert, said then whispered for my ears only, "and the sexiest, too."

"Okay, that's enough, lovebirds." Alma got up from her chair and went to the chiller. She removed a large, boxed dessert from the little refrigerator. "This might not be an abuela-approved recipe, but it is still a flan and delicious."

"Does anyone want coffee with dessert?" I asked.

Detective Pullman and his wife raised their hands, as did my relatives. Tía followed me into the house to help with the coffee.

"Gracias por venir," I said. "I'm so glad to have my family back. I missed you and Tío and Yoli more than I realized."

"Mi'ja, I'm the one that should be sorry. I should have talked sense into José a long time ago. ¿Dónde están las tazas?" Tía Elba asked.

I pointed to the cabinet where she'd find the espresso cups. But she was too short to reach them on the middle shelf. As I helped get them down, she put them on a bamboo serving tray.

"Familia is all we have in life. We must stick together. Especially now." Tía patted my abdomen. "I'm glad you did what I told you."

"Huh?"

"La santa Yemaya has blessed your family. Don't forget to give her a clean glass of water every day and every once in a while a piece of watermelon or pescado or coconut."

"Okay, Tía." I knew my tía took her orisha worship very seriously, and I could manage the glass of water but I didn't think I was up to cooking for a statue. I poured the espresso into the little porcelain cups. Tía insisted that she carry the tray since she had more serving experience than me. As I held the French door open for her, Tía's cryptic message hit me like a wave at the beach when you weren't paying attention to the surf.

Tia thinks I'm pregnant.

No. No way. I couldn't be. But, actually . . .

I started to count the days since my last period.

Ding-dong-dwong.

"I have to get that doorbell fixed." I closed the door to the backyard and went to see who was at the front door. I hoped it wasn't Marjory. We intentionally had not invited her.

"Miriam. I'm so glad I have the right house."

"Mrs. Weatherman," I said, surprised to see her on my front step. "Please come in."

"No, no, dear. I don't want to inconvenience you. You clearly have a house full at the moment."

"Yes, a belated housewarming. Please join us. We've just served the flan."

"Thank you, darling, but I'm only here to drop off a gift for Manny, if that's alright."

"Of course, I'll get him—one second."

Stormy smiled and told me she'd get the gift from her car while I went to get Manny.

On hearing the word "regalo," Manny abandoned his playmates and ran through the house to the front door. Stormy Weatherman held a wicker basket with a blanket over it. As she lowered it to Manny's eye level, I heard a faint noise coming from the basket. I don't know what I had been expecting, but I certainly wasn't expecting the gift to be alive.

"Mew. Mew-mew."

Stormy pulled the blanket back, and there was a tiny ball of multicolored fluff looking at us.

"Flossie's kittens are ready for their new homes. This is the only one of the five that looks like her."

"Gatito. For me?" Manny asked Stormy.

She looked at me for a yes or a no, but there was not much I could do at that point. My son already had the kitten in his arms.

"What are you going to name her?" Stormy asked him.

"Camo!" Manny replied.

"¿Que?" I didn't know where that odd name had come from.

"Camo. Como Primo-see-a's pantalones," Manny said.

I laughed. "Camo like camouflage," I explained to Stormy. "His favorite relative, my husband's cousin Gordon, is wearing camouflage pants today."

Mrs. Weatherman chuckled. "That's not a bad name. I think it fits her perfectly. Her patches do look a bit like a camo design."

Stormy set the basket inside the door and told Manny to treat the kitten kindly. "Kittens are babies that need lots of sleep. So be gentle with her and let her get plenty of naps." She touched the basket that was obviously meant to be a pet bed and not a laundry hamper. "I'll come by later in the week and take Camo to the vet for her vaccines. If that's alright?"

"That would be great because I have to admit I know nothing about cats," I said.

"Darling. They're just like children. Treat them with love, provide them with food, water, and shelter, and they will be fine." Stormy adjusted her long string of beads, blew us a kiss, and left.

"Hey, babe, who was at the door? Are you coming back to the party?" Robert asked from the dining room.

"Yep, be right there," I replied.

"Is that a cat?" Robert left the French door ajar and came to my side.

"Meet the newest member of the family. Her name is Camo. Mrs. Weatherman gave her to Manny."

Robert sat on the floor next to his son. "I love cats."

"Really? I didn't know that," I said.

"Mom would never let me have one, but I loved them. This is so cool. A cat named Camo." Robert ruffled his son's hair and kissed him on the top of the head.

The day had been full of surprises. Not only did we have a mango tree, but we had a new member of our family. Actually, maybe two new members. I put my hands on my belly.

Recipes

Batida de fruta bomba/Papaya Smoothie

In Cuba and in the Cuban diaspora, we call papaya fruta bomba. Why? Well, let me put it to you this way: papaya is crude slang for part of the female anatomy. So, when you are in Miami at a ventanita or lunch counter, order it as a batida de fruta bomba.

Ingredients

½ a ripe papaya, cubed (about 2 c.)
ice (6–8 cubes)
1 lime (for zesting and juice)
4 T. of condensed milk
¼ c. of water
5 mint leaves

Remove the seeds from the papaya. Cut the fruit into chunks, discarding the thick skin. Use half the fruit now, and freeze the other half for later use.

Into the blender put the ice, fruit, water, and condensed milk. Julienne the mint, and zest the lime; then squeeze half the lime into the mixture. Blend until smooth.

Saint-Tropez Sangria

Pepper Halstead makes this cheap sangria to thumb her nose at the Coral Shores elites. She orders her Boone's Farm by the case, as it reminds her of her teenage years in Oklahoma. If you can't find Boone's Farm at your local gas station, convenience store, or corner bodega, Barefoot Wines Fruitscato works just as well.

Ingredients

1 bottle Boone's Farm Apple Blossom or Barefoot Fruitscato Apple
12 oz can Sprite
1 Granny Smith apple
1 white peach
1 nectarine
10 green grapes

Clean and cut fruit into appropriate sizes. Mix wine and fruit in a pitcher. Chill in refrigerator for an hour. Before serving, add the Sprite, stir, and serve.

* For a lighter version, replace Sprite with a lime or peach seltzer.

Picadillo de Pavo

Picadillo is an easy and satisfying weekday dinner. In my Cuban American and Puerto Rican house, I call it Latin Sloppy Joe. This recipe is mine, as a working parent who doesn't have hours to prep and cook. It is also a little healthier than the traditional beef version, as I am not a big fan of red meat. (I probably eat it only two or three times a year.)

Prep time: 5 minutes
Cooking time: appox. 30 mins.

Prep your ingredients for the picadillo. Start your rice, then start your picadillo. They should both be done within minutes of each other.

Serve the picadillo over the rice, with a side of platanos maduros (a.k.a. amarillos) or an avocado salad.

Ingredients

1 lb ground turkey
olive oil
½ a large, sweet onion or 1 Spanish (yellow) onion
1 jar of sofrito
salt to taste
½ T. adobo
1 tsp. cumin or to taste
3 cloves of garlic
12–15 green olives

Drizzle oil into pan and sweat the thinly sliced onion and crushed garlic. Add meat and powdered spices. When browned and separated, add the jar of sofrito. Use a little water or vino seco to get the remainder of the sofrito from the jar (shake and pour slurry into pan). Add olives and let simmer until rice is done. Some people also add raisins. (I am "team olives," but I don't hate the sweetness the raisins add. I just pick them out before eating my dinner.)

Rice is the traditional side to accompany the picadillo, but mashed potatoes work too. This is how I learned to make the perfect rice: Rinse your rice. The extra starch on the rice is what makes it sticky and clumpy. Follow the ratio (usual 1 part rice to 2 parts water) and add a generous drizzle of olive oil and 3–4 cloves of garlic. Salt to taste.

Every Cuban, Dominican, and Puerto Rican household probably has a rice cooker, if not two: one large for parties and one small for family dinner. They are essential and make rice perfectly each time. Growing up in Miami, rice cookers were called Hitachis because that was the brand that made them. Now there are dozens of brands and a variety of colors. I think I've seen a pink Hello Kitty one. But mine, growing up, was a buttery almond color.

Fricasé de pollo/Chicken Fricassee (Cuban style)

This stew's French influences most likely came from colonist and planta-tion owners fleeing the Haitian revolution to eastern Cuba between 1791 and the early 1800s. Enslaved Africans led by Toussaint Louverture won independence and the right to self-governance. If you don't know this part of history, I encourage you to read up on it or watch Haitian Revolu-tions: Crash Course World History #30 *on YouTube.*

Prep time: 1 hour
Cooking time: 1 hour

Ingredients

8–10 chicken thighs and legs (with bone but skinless)
½–¾ c. bottled sour orange mojo
1 sour orange
olive oil
2 Spanish (yellow) onions
2 bell peppers
flour for dusting
3 medium-large potatoes or 6 small potatoes (golden or red)
½ c. vino seco/white cooking wine
15 oz. can of tomato sauce
1 T. of tomato paste
1 packet sazón or 1 T. Sazón Tropical red
3–5 cloves of garlic minced or pressed
12 green olives

½–1 T. cumin
½–1 T. oregano
1–2 bay leaves
salt & pepper taste

Marinade chicken with mojo, minced garlic, sliced onions, and sliced bell peppers. (I like to use the red, yellow, or orange ones; they tend to have a milder and sweeter flavor than the green bell peppers.) Squeeze the juice from the sour orange on top and place in fridge for 1 hour.

Remove chicken from marinade, reserving marinade for later use. Pat chicken dry and dust with flour. In a Dutch oven or large pot, drizzle olive oil and cook chicken until golden. After the thighs and legs are seared, add the marinade, and sweat the onions and peppers until soft, about 10 minutes.

Pour the can of tomato sauce plus the spoonful of paste into the pot. Add dry spices, olives, and wine. Stir and cook for 5 minutes.

Peel and chop potatoes, adding them to the pot. At this point, if you do not have enough liquid to submerge the potatoes completely, add a little water. Cover and cook on low–medium heat until potatoes are soft, about 30–40 mins. Serve over white rice.

Acknowledgments

M y path to publishing was a long journey with a world record sprint at the last leg.

Thank you to everyone that kept me on the path when it sometimes felt too steep:

The Florida Chapter of Mystery Writers of America
My SleuthFest family
The generous Sisters in Crime community
RMC—*Twenty years of friendship*
Michael L. Joy—*Your "Are you writing?" nagging worked.*

Thank you to everyone that helped me believe in myself during the sprint:

The Crime Writers of Color community—*I could not have done this without your support.*
Kellye Garrett, Mystery Maven—*I treasure every text, tea, and truth we've shared.*
Gigi Pandian—*You told me to "go for it" and not shy away from the subjects that mattered to me.*
Richie Narvaez, El Maestro—*My bio, short stories, and synopsis are always better after your critiques.*
Sarah Nicolas—*Bouchercon serendipity.*

Acknowledgments

Saritza Hernandez—*With you, I don't have to explain who I am and why I am—I get to just be. Representation matters. Mi gente.*

Faith Black Ross—*You remembered my Latinx Miami story. I'm going to frame that email.*

Cheerleaders: Sarah Cannon, Devon Greyson, & Mia P. Manansala.

My local squad: Bezel, Elizabeth, Maria, & Roxane.

Read an excerpt from

CALYPSO, CORPSES, AND COOKING

the next

CARIBBEAN KITCHEN MYSTERY

by RAQUEL V. REYES

available soon in hardcover from
Crooked Lane Books

CROOKED
LANE

NEW YORK

Chapter One

Halloween was a week away, and we didn't have a single decoration up. The living room was littered with shopping bags, extension cords, four-foot-tall plastic jack-o'-lanterns, and one handsome Frankenstein.

"Babe, we're going to need a ladder and a staple gun," Frankenstein said.

"Can you borrow one from a neighbor?" I asked as I squeezed my foot into a shoe that had fit perfectly a few weeks ago but was now tight. My costume, like my husband's, was a modification of something I already had. I'd taken a white apron and smeared it with beet juice. In red marker, I'd written *Chef Vampira* on a paper toque, the tall hat fancy chefs wore. I was not a trained chef, but I had reached local stardom with my cooking shows, *Cocina Caribeña* and *Abuela Approved*.

"Do I look undead enough? Do I need more white makeup?" I asked.

"No, but I need more spirit gum. This bolt keeps falling off." Robert held the plastic hexagon out to me. For his costume, he'd taken one of his old, heavy New York suits and cut it to make him look like he was too tall and brawny for it. The cuffs were cut into a jagged hem, and the jacket's back seam was unstitched halfway. He'd used a hair product I'd found at the store called Moco de Gorila, gorilla snot, to slick his dark-brown hair into a hard shell. Gross name, but boy, did the stuff work. The green makeup and plastic bolts were from a kit. I knew he wouldn't need the wool suit in Miami, but it still pained me a little to see it in shreds.

We'd moved to a three-bedroom, two-bath house with a yard in Coral Shores, a village within Miami, from a tiny NYC apartment about three months ago. That was partially the reason there were no lawn decorations up. I'd had to buy them since we'd never had a yard or storage space for them before. The other reason was that it had been a whirlwind since I'd set foot back in my hometown of Miami. My best friend, Alma, had pushed me into an unexpected job that I now loved. It wasn't the food anthropology professorship I'd studied years for, but something slightly adjacent to it, at least. I did try to squeeze historical facts and tidbits about cultural crossroads into the show whenever possible. The show filmed once a week, and episode lucky thirteen was set to tape Monday. I planned to make joumou, Haiti's much-loved pumpkin soup, as a nod to the Halloween theme.

In addition to our new house and my new job, I'd gotten our son Manny settled into preschool. We'd bought real, grown-up, quality furniture and had a cement patio poured. Oh, and I'd helped solve a murder.

"Mami. ¿Dónde está Camo?" Manny asked.

"No sé, mi príncipe," I replied.

"Little man, I heard some rustling over there." Robert pointed to a pile of bags.

Manny, who had been in his police officer costume since he had sprung out of bed that morning, excited for the Fall Festival, called for his calico kitten. The festival put on by Agape Montessori, his new school, was a much-loved village event open to the public. Or so I was told when the school's director talked me into having a booth. UnMundo, the Spanish language network that I worked for, had agreed to sponsor the booth and provide three hundred treat bags for the kids. Robert had also volunteered to staff a stall. His was sponsored by his environmental engineering consultant firm and was about the endangered Florida Atala butterfly. His educational non-candy giveaway goodies—a butterfly eraser and a pencil set plus butterfly temporary tattoos—were sitting on the dining room table neatly packaged in recycled paper bags, a project that had taken the two of us most of the night.

"Ponte las pilas," I said, looking at the time. Even though Robert didn't speak Spanish, he'd picked up a good bit of it being married to me and knew the phrase meant to get energized. "We need to get going, or we'll be late. I'm sure there's setup to do before the gates open at ten."

"Mami. ¿Puedo llevar a Camo con nosotros?" Manny asked. He was cradling the young kitten on its back, and the multicolored fluff ball had a paw on his cheek. I snapped a picture with my phone. Super sweet. The two were in love with each other. That was another surprise the whirlwind of the last three months had blown into our lives. We hadn't planned on having a pet, but Stormy Weatherman, the mother of the lady whose murder I'd solved, had shown up at our doorstep with the kitten last week. Manny had named the cat Camo, an odd name despite the cat's camouflage-like patterning. My son's favorite relative, Officer Gordon Smith, is to blame. The day Stormy came by, we were having a housewarming party to inaugurate our new patio, and Gordon happened to be wearing camo cargos. Gordon was also the reason for Manny's costume choice.

"No, mi amor," I answered. No, he could not take his pet to the fair. I encouraged him to put the kitten in his room and motioned for Robert to get the boxes of treat bags.

"Okay, got the first load." Robert walked toward the door. "Don't you have something on the stove?" he asked, glancing back to the kitchen.

"Huh?"

"That big pot of water. Did you start cooking something this morning?"

I didn't know what he was talking about, so I went to check. The cassava I'd peeled and left to soak in the large cast aluminum pot was on the eye. "Oh. No, that's not on. It's just soaking." I dumped the milky water into the sink and refilled it. I loved the root vegetable, but it took planning to prepare. It required a day—two was better—to leach the toxins from the tubers to make it safe to eat.

"Okay, let's go. Everybody ready?"

"What about my nuts?" The other bolt on the side of his neck was hanging loose.

"Fix it in the car," I replied, and handed him the tube of spirit gum.

Parking was already full at the Coral Shores Unitarian Universalist Congregation. Manny's school, housed on the church grounds, had gone full haunted-house vibe. Overnight the place had been decorated with bats, pumpkins, and a twelve-foot-tall blow-up black cat with an arched back. There was a photo-op pumpkin patch in the courtyard. It had hay bales with faux autumn leaves scattered on them. Because Florida. Can you imagine palm fronds turning all shades of red, orange, and yellow, then falling to the ground? No gracias. Miami already had frozen iguanas falling from trees whenever there was a cold snap. The courtyard also had several painted plywood panels with ovals to stick a face in. There was a scarecrow family, a farmer with a pig wearing a witch's hat, and a dancing skeleton that looked like it had been copied from a vintage Grateful Dead T-shirt. The parents had gotten an email with images and details about what to expect. The festival didn't have an admission fee, but tickets had to be purchased for some activities. The tickets collected at each station would be converted to dollar donations to local charities. The pumpkin patch proceeds went to Urban Oasis Project, according to the email. I'd forgotten which other organizations would be benefiting.

"Go around back." The shout came from a woman with the stars and solar system on her dress.

"Mrs. Lucy!" Manny yelled from his booster seat. He waved and grinned with glee.

"What a perfect costume for the school's director. Love it!" I said as I turned the corner to drive to the back of the property. Agape Montessori was run independently from the church, but they had a symbiotic relationship.

"Ms. Frizzle is Mrs. Lucy? She looks so different," Robert remarked.

"Wigs and costumes have that effect. I wonder if her husband will be in drag. He is guapísima in drag," I said.

"What?" Robert gave me a quizzical look. He wasn't narrow-minded, just more middle of the road than me despite my conservative Catholic upbringing.

"Their Christmas card—sorry, their Yule card—was Sam Evans. You know Mrs. Lucy is married to CSUUC's choir director, right? Anyway, the card was Sam in a red dress and makeup. He was Holly Berry. Get it?" I laughed and then looked in the rearview mirror to back my Prius into the tight space between two other Priuses. Unitarian Universalists, I'd learned, were fans of the environment and social justice and LGBTQ rights. To say they were progressive and liberal was an understatement. The back field where the volunteers were to park had a double row of electric and hybrid cars. As we walked through them to find our stations, I noticed all the cars, except mine, had collages of stickers: *One Human Family*, *COEXIST* spelled with symbols, the walking fish, *My Other Car is a Broom*, *Love Your Mother* with an image of Earth.

"Miriam, I'm so glad to see you," Stormy Weatherman greeted me. She was dressed head to pointy toe in green with herbs and talismans hanging from her skirt's belt.

"Let me guess. You're an Irish kitchen witch," I said.

"You are correct." She bent at the waist to address Manny. "And how is our feline friend Camo doing?"

"I love her!" Manny replied. His ease with English had blossomed in the nine weeks he'd been in school. I'd been hesitant to put him in preschool but had to face the fact that he was no longer my little baby. The three-day-a-week program had been great for both of us. I had time to research and cook for the show, and he was making friends and learning to read.

"Excelente," Stormy said. She liked to practice the Spanish she'd acquired from her Argentinian husband, a second marriage, with us.

"Stormy, this tall green monster is my husband, Robert," I said, placing my hand on his bicep.

"Hello, Mrs. Weatherman. It's been a while. How are you doing? I was sorry to hear about Sunny. My deepest condolences." Robert took her hand in his, tilted his head, closed his eyes slowly, and nodded like he was saying a silent prayer.

"Thank you." Stormy sniffled and withdrew her hand. She shook away the emotion that was building.

I couldn't imagine the unbearable grief of losing both of her children in such tragic ways. Rayne, her firstborn, had taken her own life as a teenager. And this past August, Sunny had been killed by Juliet Pimpkin's maliciousness. Sunny was only thirty. She had been in recovery from a cocaine addiction and doing really well until Juliet came back into her life. *If you look up mean girl in the dictionary, you'll find a picture of Juliet Pimpkin.*

It was impressive that Stormy wasn't buried under a blanket crying all day. People dealt with grief in different ways, I guessed. She'd chosen to immerse herself in projects for the school, like a memorial garden in honor of Sunny, who had attended Agape for elementary school.

My arm was yanked board stiff. Manny had sprinted forward a few steps and strained my grip on his hand. His best friend and classmate, Sophia, was with her mom, Pepper, setting up a bean bag toss game.

"¿Puedo?" Manny pleaded.

"Sí, pero te tienes que quedar con ellos, okay?" I instructed my son.

"Okay, Mami," Manny said as he ran to his friend.

Pepper waved to me and gave me a thumbs-up. After the kids had hugged each other, Sophia twirled to show off her Disney princess costume. It was the yellow one. Belle.

"Give us our marching orders," I said to Stormy.

She consulted her clipboard. "You"—she pointed to me—"are toward the front on this side. Booth three. And you, Robert, are across the aisle in booth twelve."

"Perfect. Let me find my space, and then I'll get the stuff from the car," Robert said, looking at me. He then shifted his gaze to Stormy. "It was good to see. I hope we can mend some of our families' history."

"Yes. You must come to dinner. And stop by the house anytime to see how Camo is growing." I kissed Stormy on the cheek as we departed.

"I forget sometimes that you know everyone. Founding family and all," I said to Robert.

"It's a blessing and a curse, to be honest." Robert gave me a side hug. "I'm sorry you got dragged into it. But hopefully, that will all be over soon. Juliet's court date is coming up. Let's hope she gets the book thrown at her. I still can't wrap my head around it. Drug smuggling!"

"Shh! Lower your voice. There are children and parents all around."

Juliet had *accidentally* given Sunny a diet drink powder that was actually cocaine to hook Sunny back on the drug. The woman had manipulated and played with Sunny throughout her teens and early twenties. Thank goodness Juliet was sitting in jail, partly because of my sleuthing, and couldn't hurt anyone else.

Mean girl, smuggler, *accidental* murderess Juliet was also my husband's third cousin, whom he'd dated briefly in high school, and her father was a business associate of Robert's. It was messy, to say the least.

"Delvis!" I shouted at the blue-haired woman leaving booth three. "I need to catch her." I patted my husband on the back and left him at his booth.

Delvis's blue hair was not a Halloween costume, nor was she a senior citizen. Delvis was the producer and director of my YouTube cooking show, *Abuela Approved*.

"Ooo, Chef Vampira, I like it," Delvis said. "The bloody apron is a nice touch."

"I have fangs too." I took the teeth from my apron pocket and popped them into my mouth.

"Let me take a shot for our Instagram. Here"—she handed me one of the treat bags—"make sure the logo shows."

I bared my fangs as I held the sealed swag bag with UnMundo's globe logo. "What's in here?"

"Caramelos from Dulces Cubanos, a Hialeah candymaker Ileana likes." Delvis leaned in and whispered conspiratorially, "I think she's dating the owner."

I didn't need to know about our boss's love life, but I was happy to hear that the host of UnMundo's morning show supported a local business. The little swag bags were heavy.

"What else is in here?" I said, and gingerly loosened the sticker that held the bag shut. "Yum. I love ajonjolí. Ooo, and dulce de leche, de coco, de maní." The candies might be foreign to the majority of white American kids in the village, but I had grown up on them. Hialeah, a Spanish-speaking municipality, was a few miles from Coral Shores but a world apart. Both were part of metropolitan Miami. The hard sesame candy was my favorite, with the peanut brittle coming in a strong second. "Did you make a few bags nut-free?"

"Yeah. The ones with the *Abuela Approved* sticker are caramel only. I added some Chupa Chups and a mini UnMundo fútbol to make up for there being less candies." Delvis pointed to a box of bags under the table.

I opened one and inspected it—three caramels, two lollipops, and a foam soccer ball. "Cool. I don't know how many trick-or-treaters will have nut allergies, but we don't want to leave them out of the fun."

"I know, that's the worst. When I was a kid, un viejo in our neighborhood would give out boxes of raisins and pennies." Delvis made a face. "No kid likes pasas over chocolate."

"Note to self: raisins are a no-no. How about chocolate-covered raisins? Chica, I'm so behind in my Halloween prep the stores will be out of candy by the time I get around to buying ours." I slid into the booth and set my purse on the folding chair.

Delvis laughed. "Doubtful, but you might have to pay a premium. Okay, I've got to go. You good?"

"I'm good. Hey, thanks for bringing this stuff. I'll return the tablecloth and banner on Monday."

"Cool. See you at taping." Delvis waved her tattooed arm at me and left.

"From the network?" Robert asked as he approached my booth.

I nodded and began lining the goody bags into rows.

"Babe, can you help me? I have a screw loose." He pointed to his neck and passed me the glue. "It keeps coming off."

"Come around." I motioned for him to come into the booth and sit.

He held my purse in his lap, knowing I, like most Cuban women, had a superstition about putting my purse on the floor. Setting it on the floor was a sign of disrespect to your money. It would walk away, and you'd be poor.

"Stay still." I peeled the old glue off and painted on a new layer. Holding the plastic bolt to my husband's neck until the glue dried, I scanned the promenade. There was a pumpkin-decorating booth with a pyramid of baby pumpkins. Next to that was a prize wheel with stuffed narwhals, sparkly puzzles, and coloring books stacked around it. Then there was Robert's butterfly booth. "Who's that lady? I think she's looking for you."

Robert swiveled his head to see what I was talking about. "Oh no. Hide me."

I moved to block the line of sight. "Who is it? You never hide from people."

"That's Lois Pimpkin, Juliet's mother." Robert sighed.

"What is she doing here? And why is she looking for you? Do you think she wants to stir up trouble? You had nothing to do with Juliet being caught."

"It doesn't matter. Lois thinks her daughter can do no wrong and that she couldn't possibly be the mastermind of a multimillion-dollar smuggling operation. She swears it's a case of mistaken identity." Robert made air quotes and shook his head.

"Stop moving your head." I added glue to the other prosthetic for good measure. "Well, what does Paul Pimpkin say about it? I mean, you kind of work for him. That's got to be awkward."

"Paul is embarrassed. He's actually thinking about changing Pimpkin Development to something without the family's name in it to distance himself from her and Pimpkin Global. But you know, Samford *is* paying for his granddaughter's lawyers. I mean, he kind of has to, since Pimpkin Global doesn't look good in all of it. Juliet used PG's shipping containers. Best-case scenario is she gets a light sentence."

"Stay still. This stuff needs to dry." I stole a glance at Lois. She was still pacing in front of Robert's empty booth like a madwoman.

"Paul knows she's guilty. But his wife is next-level delusional about their daughter's criminal tendencies. Lois blames everyone but her precious Juliet. Paul and Samford are barely talking, from what I've heard. And Lois isn't making the family dynamic any better with her conspiracy theories about Colombian cartels. Samford has always disliked his daughter-in-law and wishes she'd just shut up. He's hired some serious guns."

322

I looked across the promenade. "Well, the coast is clear for now. She's gone, and you no longer have a screw loose." I smiled and tried to kiss him, but my vampire teeth got in the way. I took them out, narrowed my eyes, and grinned. "You can't get away from me that easily."

"Trust me, I don't want to get away. I'm a willing victim to your vampire charm."

Robert pulled me to his lap, and we kissed. Just as his hand slid onto my rear, someone in our proximity cleared their throat.

"This is a G-rated event."

We broke our embrace and turned toward the voice.

"Hi, Pepper. Everything okay? Where are the kids?" I asked.

"That's what I came to tell you. The gates are about to open, and I have to run the cornhole game. So Gabriela has the kids. I hope that's okay," said Pepper, referring to her live-in nanny. She was dressed as a farmer in overalls, a checkered shirt, and a ratty straw hat.

"Of course. Thanks for telling us."

"I'll find them and give her some money for tickets," Robert said.

"Don't worry, Frankie sweetie. I gave her forty dollars." Pepper's Oklahoma accent was coming on strong, which happened when she drank. I hoped her tumbler had coffee in it and not Kahlúa. Maybe it was for effect, to add authenticity to her costume. Pepper's best friend, Elliot, had died suddenly, and instead of going to grief therapy, she was self-medicating on bad days. For a little while, Elliot's death had been thought suspicious and maybe linked to Sunny's, but it turned out she had died from a rare liver disorder exacerbated by bad herbal medicine from that quack doctor Fuentes. Sadly, I hadn't figured out she was taking too high a dose of rue until after the fact.

Pepper dug into her bib pocket and pulled out a red ticket. "Here's my ticket." She waved it at us. "Come on, on with the show. You two are like a Hallmark romance movie. Two star-crossed monsters, the undead and the once-dead, find love at the county fair."

Robert and I laughed. I popped my fangs back in and made like I was going to bite Robert's neck.

"Maybe this Hallmark romance is actually a murder mystery," Pepper said, rubbing her hands together.

"Don't jinx me," I batted back to her.